Syreen has found allies for her cause, but she still has to defeat her enemy's forces. She finds allies in places she'd never expected, learns about her true origin, and about a millennia-old enemy.

In addition to all the mess she yet has to clean up, she now has to worry about a force so terrible even her ancestors had fled from. But it will be her destiny to pick up the fight.

Time Of Withering
Copyright © 2023 Valerie J. Long
ISBN: 978-1-4874-3900-2
Cover art by Martine Jardin

Published by eXtasy Books Inc

Look for us online at:
www.eXtasybooks.com

TIME OF WITHERING
THE FORGOTTEN PEOPLE 5

BY

VALERIE J. LONG

DEDICATION

In fond memory of Diana Rigg.

PART ONE—EDUCATION

CHAPTER ONE

W elcome, *our daughter. Welcome, Syreen Starborn.*
This single line of a song sung by stars distant and close echoed in Syreen's mind.

Does that mean what I think it means?

— Your heart knows the truth. —

Assiduous's usually reassuring mental presence didn't help her now.

It's unthinkable. How could it be? Look at me — I'm a person of flesh and blood, not a tiny piece of burning gas.

— Your body is just that, flesh and blood. Your mind is not. Your achievements cannot be explained by mere mortal existence. No Navigator of our People ever mended the fabric of space. No Navigator of our People ever performed hyperflight. By the way, we cannot stay on the hyperplane forever. —

She sighed. *You're right. I've got more immediate problems to tend to. Not the least of which is our passenger.*

— Should I assimilate him to unburden you? —

No. We have to assimilate his knowledge first.

— A wise decision. I did not think of that. —

Syreen smiled. *Let's have a rest and make plans now.*

She chose a solitary star without planets in the near vicinity, only a few dozen light years away, and let her living ship drop from hyperspace there. While *Assiduous* recharged, she could deal with their passenger — or better, their prisoner, the former *master* of Associated Planets and its heart, Nysa.

When she resurfaced from deep integration with her ship, she first checked the feel in her limbs. Her broken bones —

1

result of the master's not-so-tender treatment — were set and healed, along with the bruises and other minor inconveniences.

She felt his mental assault starting before she even raised one leg to climb out of her pilot chair, still located in the middle of *Assiduous's* huge hangar.

Stop that.

She walked over to the chair *Assiduous* had grown out of the hangar floor for him. Only her previous mental command held him there. *Does it? I ordered him to stop that before.*

You will not use your mental powers again, unless I tell you so. You will stay in that chair for now.

"I've had enough of your abuse." She stepped before him and focused on his eyes. "Aboard my ship, you will behave as is becoming for a guest."

He cocked his head and smirked. "Dream your dream, insolent girl. You can't keep your guard up forever, and in due time, you'll beg for mercy. I will crush your mind and body, and when I'm done with you, I'll make sure no one will ever dare to cross me again."

His chair's armrests wrapped around his wrists. Shackles grew from the floor and around his ankles. A spear-like shape shot from the same floor and stopped only a hair-width before his throat.

Assiduous's voice boomed all over the hangar. *"You will not hurt my pilot, nor threaten to do so. I can keep my guard up forever, and you can't hide from me."*

– *Not even mentally.* –

The master flinched. The spearpoint yielded just enough to prevent injury.

Syreen couldn't entirely hide her own surprise.

You can communicate with him mentally?

– *I can. However, I cannot command him.* –

The master laughed. "You can't win. There's no place you can go. My fleet will crush your pathetic opposition. There

will be no world welcoming you."
      She felt her anger rising.
      Tell me everything.

CHAPTER TWO

Syreen paced up and down *Assiduous's* bridge. *This is too big for me alone.*

The familiar surroundings, with her pilot chair back where it belonged, offered little comfort.

— *You are not alone.* —

"No, you're right. We're in this together — sorry."

— *No need to feel sorry. You're my Navigator. What else could I do but aid you every way I can?* —

"But we can't win this one. I expected that taking their master out of the equation would make them surrender. From what he told us, we can't hope for that." She shrugged. "I really thought he was the driving force behind all their misbehavior. I was wrong — he found willing aides in Nysa's government and in the Associated Planets Navy's admiralty. They're happy with their newfound power and their big toys and won't even consider changing their ways."

— *I would not call a dreadnaught a toy, but I understand.* —

"Which means I gambled too high, and now all the guild worlds will suffer for my cockiness."

— *Unless we can do something about it.* —

Syreen laughed bitterly. "Aside from the nine dreadnaughts engaging us, there were at least sixteen more docked around their military base Nysa Four when we left. Once they've heated up their engines, our odds are naught." She frowned. "Sorry for that pun. And I didn't mention the other battle groups yet."

— *I agree that the numerous AP battle groups spread around this*

4

galactic sector pose a serious problem for our mission. Knowing what we can do together, Nysa is a solvable task, though. –

"You call twenty-five dreadnaughts *solvable?*"

– Indeed. My assessment is based on five aspects. One, as you were already denied surrender, we need not waste time with another request or announcement, but can initiate corrective action immediately. Correct? –

She considered whether another request would help – from what the former master had told, near to nothing. "Agreed."

– Two, we'll be going in at full speed, not as a sitting duck. Three, we can drop from hyperspace, deal out, and reenter the hyper plane before they can return fire. –

Syreen found herself grinning mischievously. "Go on."

– Four, you could still dodge a chance shot coming our way. –

"Of course."

– Five, if we act now, we probably can still catch the docked dreadnaughts with their pants down, as you occasionally put it. Probably together with some of their docked battle groups. –

"That will cause a lot of collateral damage."

– True, but this is a price they have to pay for their insolence, for threatening other worlds, and last but not least for violating all three edicts. We must enforce the edicts. –

"You've got a point." She leaned against the chair, absently stroked the large phallus-like shaft inside and recalled the foundation for her actions.

Edict Number One proscribes deliberate damage to the fabric of space. Edict Number Two proscribes deliberate destruction, sterilization or rendering uninhabitable of worlds, especially, but not limited to, kinetic strikes, large-scale application of nuclear or biological weapons, and systematic destruction of geological stability. Edict Number Three proscribes deliberate interference with the genetic code of intelligent beings.

Syreen felt an icy grip around her heart. "On Crown, I promised the guild that I can enforce that embargo against the

AP. I must not hesitate to do what's necessary, even if it may cost the life of many brave men together with the many not-so-brave men."

— *I know you don't like it.* —

"But that's what being an enforcer is about. I know. Okay, tell me when you're charged, and then let's go."

— *I am ready for battle.* —

"In that case—can you bring our prisoner up here and put up some screens so that he may witness his mischief failing?" She started mounting her seat.

— *I will do so.* —

She felt up her crotch until she sensed a little wetness, then impaled herself on Assiduous's big cock in the center of her seat. The second plug penetrated her anus, followed by the stings in her thighs. When she leaned back and felt the last stings in her neck, a seat with manacles and shackles floated into the room and came to a rest in front of her.

"What's this show about?" the master asked. "A tribunal?"

"Just watch the plot," she said. "See how an enforcer can spoil your plans."

CHAPTER THREE

Syreen entered deep integration with her living ship. This way, they could share their thoughts and senses. This way, she could make them react to threats that approached them faster than light.

Their flight back to Nysa took only a moment. They resurfaced close to Nysa Four and above the planet's north pole. A single thought released three strikes with their concussion pulser — three orbital bases with twelve docked dreadnaughts and a score of smaller warships were beaten to shreds by the strong gravitational shocks. Another strike did the same to three more bases on the other side of the planet.

This was the easy part.

The nine active dreadnaughts with their wake of battle cruisers and destroyers were heading system-outward. If Syreen didn't stop them, they'd jump into systems supporting the embargo to perform *educative measures,* that was, to destroy civil orbital stations there.

Not on our watch.

Assiduous launched three gauge boson torpedoes.

"Our dreadnaughts will shoot you to pieces," the master shouted. "You can't win!"

The torpedoes reached their target areas. The gauge bosons instructed protons, neutrons and electrons within range to un-exist. As all matter consisted of atoms, and atoms consisted of protons, neutrons and electrons, no matter remained.

The dreadnaughts with their escorting ships were no more.

Syreen emerged from deep integration and smiled at her

passenger. "We won."

"That's an instrument failure. They'll return fire any moment."

"You're too smart to lie to yourself. There won't be return fire."

"But — the instruments don't even show survival pods. It must be a misreading."

"There are no survival pods. A gauge torpedo completely eliminates matter. You'd have a hard time proving there's ever been something."

"But that's . . ."

"That's why you can't win. Note that a single torpedo could eliminate a moon — or a large enough chunk of a planet to make it burst apart."

For the first time since she'd met him, he seemed speechless, and perhaps even a little bit intimidated.

Heck, I feel horrified myself. And I'm not done yet. She shrugged. "Excuse me. There are people I want to talk to."

She reentered deep integration and steered *Assiduous* toward Nysa Three.

CHAPTER FOUR

Syreen left hyperspace at a safe distance to the planet—safe to dodge possible shots, but close enough to have a conversation with the local authorities—and slowed down. She emerged from deep integration again.

The news from Nysa Four would reach Nysa Three within the centicycle. She added her own message.

"Nysa harbor authorities, this is Navigator Syreen aboard the living ship *Assiduous*. Last time I called, I requested your surrender. My patience is exhausted. I eliminated most of your navy, and now I ultimately request your unconditional surrender. Pass my request on to your government. Your failure to comply will require me to eliminate the root source of violations of all three edicts—that is, to eliminate Nysa Three and Nysa Four."

She noticed a group of three light cruisers leaving orbit around Nysa Three and approaching her on an interception course. They started to spread out, probably to get a better firing solution.

Her EMP shot fried their wirings.

"*Assiduous, this is Nysa harbor authorities. I've forwarded your message to our Navy headquarters, who will surely instruct you to kiss their ass and prepare your last will.*"

Three of Nysa Three's orbital stations launched missiles.

Disarm them.

— Okay. —

Syreen took it as a good sign that he didn't even complain.

Crunchy snacks for you.

– Okay! –

"Nysa harbor authorities, this is *Assiduous.* The next orbital station to launch missiles will be eliminated as a legitimate military target. There will be no further warnings."

They didn't launch missiles. Instead, the closest station fired at her with a powerful laser.

Syreen barely dodged it and answered with another EMP shot. *This is annoying.*

– They're not taking us seriously. –

Oh, in a way, they do. Otherwise they wouldn't shoot us.

– You got a point there. –

Assiduous's sensors picked up the signature of a battle cruiser with three light cruisers coming around the planet.

"Assiduous, *this is Commodore Hardincourt,* APS Rubicon. *Cut your engines, discharge your guns, and prepare to accept a boarding party. Failure to comply will force me to open fire.*"

She sighed. *Bonehead.*

"Commodore Hardincourt, this is Navigator Syreen. You seem to misinterpret the current distribution of power in this system. I already eliminated twenty-five dreadnaughts with their battle groups and I can assure you I'm easily able to eliminate your ships as well."

"Navigator – what do you want from us?"

At least he doesn't start shooting. Intrude into their computers and make sure he can't.

– Will do. –

"Commodore, I'm here to deliver the guild ruling on the embargo and to reestablish the edicts. Are you ready to receive my data and talk for your nation?"

"If that's what's needed to stop this madness, I'll do the talking, yes."

"In that case, I'm willing to offer you safe conduct for a visit to my ship. You may bring along any number of unarmed advisors that fit into one shuttle."

"I herewith accept this invitation. Await our arrival within a

cycle."

She smiled at the master. "Finally, there's one officer who's able to use his brains."

Her passenger frowned and shook his arms. "How long will you keep me tied up like this?"

"As long as required. We might have to dodge another shot any time." *And I can't allow you to attack me right then.*

CHAPTER FIVE

There was no sudden surprise. No other AP ship appeared with blazing guns, no station fired at the living ship — and no one tried to call them, although there was a lot of message traffic all over the system.

They probably found out what we did.

— They know. It's all over their news and messages. —

You're listening?

— I'm analyzing them. We must be prepared for whatever they're coming up with. Should there be any order regarding us, you should be the first to know. —

Oh, they'd hate to learn you can do that.

— I won't tell them. —

Syreen smiled.

"I'm hungry," the master complained.

"We'll dine later. Excuse me for now." Syreen watched the approaching shuttle. It slipped through their hangar door, tickling her crotch, and sat down on the hangar floor.

Would you please remove His Snootiness to another room?

— Of course. —

The chair with the protesting master moved toward a wall opening and disappeared behind.

Three people left the shuttle. One wore the stripes of a commodore. That had to be Hardincourt. He had brought a Lieutenant and an Ensign along.

"Hello?" the commodore said.

"Welcome aboard, Commodore," she said over the intercom. "Please follow the light, and don't be surprised by the force field elevator."

The three officers followed the light and uttered surprised gasps when the force field lifted them up. The light guided them along the corridor to the bridge. Again, there were some "Ohs" when they entered the bridge. They tried in vain to take their gazes off the nude Syreen in her seat.

"Welcome, Commodore Hardincourt," Syreen said. "Please have a seat."

Three seats rose from the floor. Again, the officers' faces showed surprise.

"Variable furniture? Convenient." The commodore waved at his company. "May I introduce? Lieutenant Moreton, my Intelligence officer, and Ensign Forsythe, Communications."

"Welcome aboard, gentlemen. I am Navigator Syreen of the people you call Forgotten People, and all this around you" — she waved one arm — "is the living ship *Assiduous*, Enforcer of the Forgotten People."

"*Welcome aboard,*" boomed all around them. "*May I offer refreshments? I can offer you forwine, but also an excellent biribona juice from Banjo.*"

"Banjo?" Hardincourt echoed. "I think I remember such a world, but not its location."

"It's in the Crown sector." Syreen smiled. "On the other side of the *chasm*. There's no trade between our sectors, which will probably not change for the next megacycles."

"Crown sector — then this juice must be really old. Well preserved?"

"It's less than a kilocycle old. I brought it from my recent visit to Banjo."

"But you said it's behind the *chasm*."

"Commodore, the conclusion is easy — indeed I did cross the chasm, something no ordinary spaceship can do. I brought plenty of proof. First of all, a guild message vault, the integrity of which already has been confirmed by the guild on this side of the chasm. For a practical person, the allies I brought along might be even more tangible and convincing—Crown destroyers and the Finney Fianna."

He frowned and glanced at his company for help, but the two junior officers appeared just as clueless.

Syreen shook her head. "Please, let's not get ahead of ourselves. *Assiduous* asked about refreshments."

"I will sample that juice. I assume it's not intoxicating?"

"Of course not," Assiduous replied. "It is neither intoxicating nor toxic."

"Well, then . . ." Hardincourt looked around again. The lieutenant and the ensign nodded. "Three juices, thank you. What did you call it?"

"You're welcome. It's called biribona juice."

The three officers watched small tables with filled glasses grow from the floor.

"You're not joining us?"

Syreen held up a glass that had appeared out of her chair. "Of course I am. Cheers."

This is neither the time nor the place to drink to the Duke's health and remind them of my connection.

Three "Cheers" answered, they drank, and then the commodore put the glass down and a serious face up. "Let's get to business. You claim to have eliminated twenty-five of our dreadnaughts with their battle groups."

Syreen nodded. "I did. I wrecked sixteen dreadnaughts that were still docked to orbital stations around Nysa Four, together with most of the ships docked to the same stations, and then I eliminated the nine dreadnaughts that were accelerating toward the exit points together with their battle groups."

"Can you prove the latter?"

"Assiduous duly recorded the events. I cannot provide remnants, though—the elimination was complete. There are no obstacles to interstellar traffic left."

"That's hard to believe."

"But that's what a gauge torpedo does. The ships are no longer there and there was no jump shock. You will find more evidence in your own navy recordings. Ships having returned from Klondike witnessed the effects of gauge torpedoes, too."

Hardincourt nodded. "Lieutenant Moreton, you may check that issue later. The recordings will be classified, but the recent events should justify a temporary clearance for you."

"Yes, sir."

The commodore focused on Syreen again. "Would you tell me why you did it? Many people have died today."

"Believe me, I feel very sad about what I had to do, but I had little choice. I could not allow these ships to leave Nysa and do what they were ordered to do. *Assiduous,* please replay our prisoner's testimony regarding the order of the tencycle."

The master's voice echoed across the bridge. *"Admirals, Commodores, Captains, your orders as confirmed and approved by the Nysa government are as follows – visit the star systems on your respective lists and perform punitive action as follows. One, eliminate each and any guild presence, be it in orbit or on the surface as mentioned in your intelligence report, together with any orbital station or metropolitan area harboring them. Two, eliminate each and any armed space forces, especially each and any warship identifying as Crown Navy or Finney Navy. Three, eliminate each and any trader who followed this petty embargo – that is, every trader who rejected cargo from or to the Association. Perform inspections at your own discretion, and make sure everyone got the point – nobody crosses the AP."*

Syreen focused on Hardincourt. "You're a commodore yourself, so you might have listened to the same order – you might already have a list of worlds to perform *punitive action* upon, and you know as well as I do that these orders command you to perform attacks without prior declaration of war – which is piracy by your own regulations. You know the penalties for piracy – and yet, during my first visit, I offered your fleet and government a chance to surrender."

She sensed his dismay about his own government's and admiralty's orders.

He shook his head. "Pardon me, but I must ask for clarification. You only learned about these orders after your request for surrender. Why did you come here originally? You mentioned something about a guild ruling on the embargo and about edicts."

Syreen nodded. "You are here to talk. You shall get answers. Do we have enough time before your crew gets nervous?"

"Ensign Forsythe will advise us in time, should we have to call my crew." He waved at the nodding junior officer.

So they do have a deadline but won't tell us. Fine with me.

"Okay. In that case, I will show you the evidence as presented to the Crown guild tribunal. *Assiduous,* please replay."

CHAPTER SIX

A fter the end of the replay, Syreen found her guests silent, but quite appalled inside.

"Well," the Commodore said. "Well — after what I've just seen, primarily the data recorded by our own ships, I have no doubt on the tribunal ruling — but you already told us of the embargo anyway."

"So you understand now why I am here?"

He nodded and glanced at his crew. "Yes, I understand. I understand your rationale. I also understand your duties toward the guild —"

"I fear you don't," Syreen interrupted him. "Indeed, I promised the guild tribunal on Crown to follow up on embargo violations, so that they don't appear like toothless tigers. But that's not the core of my motivation. Do you know the principles the guild is based on?"

"Sorry, no. I never cared much about the guild."

"Their foundation is a simplified version of the three edicts — the edicts my people put down as engravings on a barren planet. Edict Number One proscribes deliberate damage of the fabric of space, or destruction of living stars. Edict Number Two proscribes deliberate destruction, sterilization or rendering uninhabitable of worlds, especially, but not limited to, kinetic strikes, large-scale application of nuclear or biological weapons, and systematic destruction of geological stability. Edict Number Three proscribes deliberate interference with the genetic code of intelligent beings."

"Yes, those were mentioned in the recording."

Syreen nodded. "Yes. These edicts — the edicts of my own people — are the core of my mission and my duties, and I must not fail to implement them at all costs."

"Okay — but that's basically the same, isn't it?"

She sensed his doubts and remained silent.

Hardincourt leaned forward. "If it's not the same, what's the difference? You're following your orders, be they ratified by a tribunal or put down in engravings, right?"

"That's not the point. The question is what I'm required to do in order to enforce the edicts."

"And what are you required to do?"

"If your people won't follow reason, my duty is to put down engravings on another barren planet. Your planet, Commodore Hardincourt."

This statement made him pause, but not for long.

"And you think we'd let you start your orbital strikes without defending us? Even your impressive ship couldn't withstand our concentrated fire."

Syreen shook her head. "You might be right on the latter, but I wouldn't start orbital strikes. I would turn Nysa into a supernova that would scorch all planets in this system. And before you have to ask — yes, I currently command the means to do so. You passed them on your way in — the egg-shaped containers lining our hangar."

Three faces stared at her. She sensed the horror in them all.

"The tencycle I'd have to implement these ultimate measures would be a sad tencycle. I'm as horrified by this prospect as you are. But I'm also appalled by people who won't hesitate to throw rocks at innocent planets, who won't hesitate to wipe out peaceful civil orbital stations, who are so fouled up in their deepest roots that they're unable to return to reasonable, civilized behavior. I have to put an end to that."

"How can you even bear that thought?" Hardincourt asked with a voice full of sorrow.

18

"Actually, I can't. But neither can I give in to grief and despair until my mission is done. Tell me, Commodore, to me you appear as an honest officer — how can you bear what your nation asks of you?"

The commodore closed his eyes. "I can't, either. But do you know what happens to officers who won't do as they're told?"

"I assume the penalty is as ugly as everything else."

"Right on point. You've met Cortez, I guess. He was my first commanding officer. He was sentenced to death for high treason — death by slow strangulation because of his failure at Klondike. I don't know how he failed — that's classified — but I know he was a good officer, and I also know he would follow even strange orders."

"He did. I shot his ship, so he could no longer fight me. Afterward, we had an interesting talk about orders of illegitimate sources."

Lieutenant Moreton flinched. "Illegitimate sources?"

"Yes. Your former master — I still don't know him by name — seemingly failed to inform the AP of his origin. He is no human, but a male of my people, of the Forgotten People."

The lieutenant and the commodore looked at each other.

"I told you there was something odd about him," Moreton said.

"And I told you to keep your thoughts to yourself," Hardincourt shot back. "Such statements in the wrong place could get you killed."

He turned back to Syreen. "Sorry, Navigator."

"Don't worry about me. *Assiduous,* this won't be in any official recording, okay?"

"*Okay.*"

A thought made her chair rise, so that she almost stood. "Now, Commodore Hardincourt, it's your turn. Tell me why you're here — aside from buying time and gathering first-hand intel. Is there anything you can offer me now?"

"Offer you?" He seemed puzzled.

"In exchange for not eliminating Nysa Three and Nysa Four with every living soul on it. The situation here must be resolved before I leave, but leave I must—soon, so that I can prevent at least some *punitive action.*"

The commodore lowered his head. "No, I fear I can't offer you anything."

"Not even returning to your ship and talking to your superiors?"

"Oh—I can do that, but I don't expect any positive outcome."

"In that case, tell me one thing, if you may—what would be needed to convince your government that I'm serious, that I'm able and ready to act?"

He shook his head. A tear ran down his cheek. "Nothing. I fear they're unwilling to listen to reason."

There must be another way.

"What do I have to do to talk to your government in person? Could you arrange a meeting?"

Hardincourt wiped the tear away. "Aboard this ship? Not within our lifetime. It's one thing to risk a flag officer if you don't trust the offered safe conduct, but a member of the government? They'd fear blackmail."

Syreen sighed. "Yes, of course. I'd use that single member as blackmail to get—what? Instead of killing everyone. Highly logical."

"We're beyond logic," Lieutenant Moreton chimed in. "Ensign Forsythe, would you please return to the shuttle?" He nodded to Syreen. "If you permit. I'd like to discuss classified information with the commodore and you alone."

"Of course. Follow the lights. *Assiduous,* would you please guide our guest?"

They watched the junior officer leave.

Syreen nodded at the lieutenant. "Sorry that I must correct you in one regard—*Assiduous* will take part in our discussion."

"Oh. I forgot—of course."

"Now what is it you want to discuss?"

Moreton hesitated and glanced at Hardincourt. The commodore gestured him to continue.

"Okay—well, it's about our government's reasoning. I received a classified message that until this moment not even my commanding officer knew about, and of course, by even mentioning it, I've put my neck into the noose."

The commodore shook his head. "They won't learn from me."

"Nor from us." Syreen made her chair turn toward Moreton.

The lieutenant licked his lip. "Okay. Uh—it's about your ship, and the message came about the same time as the one about the punitive action. Our superiors pointed out that some intel about the existence of an ancient super weapon is highly alarming. According to our government, every effort should be made to ensure this super weapon cannot get into the wrong hands—that is, other than ours—so that it can't be deployed against us."

Moreton shrugged. "There were no instructions on how to achieve that, but there were commentaries by our intelligence leaders advising us to be very cautious in our reports. Between the lines, the advice said that our superiors might be overly nervous with regard to the current situation because they know they made some terrible mistakes. They might even be mentally unstable. I think we all know which mistakes this most likely refers to. So, to be ultimately honest—I don't think that talking to our current government would help you at all."

Syreen gently probed his emotions. "So what other course of action would you like to propose? You didn't tell me your state secrets without reason."

"Please understand—this isn't easy for me. I regard myself

as a loyal member of the AP Navy. As such, I have to comply with my orders. But I'm also loyal to my people—as an officer of our Navy, it is my utmost duty to protect them against each and every enemy without hesitation—even if that enemy comes from within. What you told us—an illegal alien at the head of our Navy, possibly using his position to mislead our government, violations of the edicts—smells of treason." He glanced at his commodore.

Hardincourt nodded. "Go on, lad."

Moreton briefly closed his eyes and brushed his cheeks with both hands. "This situation requires bold action. I propose you talk to our senior counterintelligence officers. You know, most government-loyal flag officers were deployed on missions. Some of those left behind may be willing to listen to reason, like we are now."

Syreen felt his sincerity and his unrest. He was convinced they'd listen to her but wasn't sure of the outcome.

She could have asked what they could do to resolve the situation but didn't voice it.

"Okay—where do I find them?"

Moreton stared at her. "You'd go there?"

— No! —

Relax, pal. I won't go anywhere close to the master's chimeras. "No. In the current situation, I won't leave my ship. I need to know where I can call them."

"I'd otherwise recommend you should talk to Admiral Derfflinger, head of NCI—sorry, Navy Counterintelligence— on Nysa Four. But if you call her there, everyone will know about it."

She showed him her predator smile, and he flinched. "Nobody will know."

Let's hack their communications.

CHAPTER SEVEN

Syreen smiled at her guests again. "We're in, and you better stay out of the picture for now."

An image of an older woman with admiral's stars on her uniform shoulder boards, sitting at a clean desk, appeared before them. She was focusing on a tab in her hand.

"It would be impolite to just watch. *Assiduous*, please."

A chime sounded. The admiral looked up and waved. *"Hadn't I made clear I don't want to be disturbed?"*

"My apologies, Admiral Derfflinger." Syreen nodded. "I am Navigator Syreen, commandant of the living ship *Assiduous,* and enforcer of the edicts. I'm calling you to discuss potential approaches to a solution that will not require me to turn Nysa into a supernova."

The admiral sat up straight. *"You can't — wait, what? A supernova? Are you mad?"*

"I'm not the one who started throwing rocks at innocent planets, Admiral. I'm not the one who sent out a fleet to shoot civil orbital stations. Tell me, Admiral Derfflinger, how can we end this madness?"

Admiral Derfflinger sighed. *"That's not something to debate over an open channel. By the way, how did you get past my orderly?"*

"Admiral, this is an encrypted communication not even your orderly knows about. In order to establish privacy, I took the liberty to allow *Assiduous* to intrude your comm system and tunnel us through to you."

"You mean, you hacked us?" The AP officer appeared quite

calm.

Syreen showed her a friendly smile. "We did. *Assiduous* calls your systems *primitive*—they're easy to deal with. I'd prefer to call them *basic*—they're working according to their specs, and that's okay. But I didn't call you to discuss computers."

"No. You mentioned the edicts — I assume to refer to the embargo established by the guild?"

"Yes, Admiral Derfflinger. I traveled across the chasm to the Crown system to get a guild ruling on the multiple violations of edicts I observed and recorded. May I assume that you had a chance to review the actions of Admiral Santiago at Klondike?"

She watched the intel officer nod. So far, she was playing along astonishingly well. Syreen didn't have to read the woman's feelings to know she was very curious, which probably wasn't a bad trait in an Admiral leading the counterintelligence department.

"Good. I also assume you know the wording of the edicts in the guild codex. Do you also know where the guild got these edicts from?"

"Not exactly. I've heard they found it somewhere."

"They found a single building made of crystalline carbon on an otherwise barren planet. The engravings showed the original wording of the edicts—the wordings my people put there."

"Your people — you mean the Duchy?"

"I'm not talking of mankind, Admiral. I am a member of a much older race. You call us the Forgotten People, but I'm here to remind your people that we're still here and that our edicts are still valid."

The older woman leaned back and swallowed. It was clear to see that she needed a moment to digest that message.

"And now you're here playing hide and seek with our fleet."

"With what's left of your fleet, yes. Too many brave

commanders didn't recognize that their case was lost. Your fleet has too many Santiagos and too few Cortez."

"There are still a few Santiagos around, as you call them. Nine battle groups with their dreadnaughts may be too many even for your formidable ship. They should reach Nysa Three any time now."

"It's my sad duty to inform you that those battle groups will no longer pose a threat to anyone. I eliminated them."

The admiral glanced at her tab. *"Eliminated? I received no such messages."*

"You couldn't. There's no one left to send a message. Admiral Derfflinger, you surely saw the reports about the kinetic strike at Klondike, and about the ugly projectile."

"I did. Why are you mentioning that now?"

"What happened to the rock, according to your data?"

"The records say it vanished — like jumping into hyperspace, only without the aftershock. There was no trace of it."

"And Santiago's flagship?"

"Gone without trace — I tried to convince the admiralty to send a ship for investigation. A waste of time, they said, and referred me to the already available data. I couldn't convince anyone to collect samples of the space region."

"It would have been wasted effort. There's nothing left to sample. That's what a boson gauge torpedo does — eliminate matter."

Admiral Derfflinger's face froze. *"You say you killed them all. For now, I have to accept your word for it. And next, you will kill the rest of our people?"*

"I'd rather avoid that. You know the orders your ships were sent out with — kill any civil orbital stations that followed the edict, or embargo, as you called it. Tell me, Admiral — what does it take to bring your government back to reason? Because if they don't, I'll have to resort to ultimate measures."

"Why do you ask me? Ask them."

"I already asked for their unconditional surrender. Your

government didn't bother to answer, despite the aforesaid consequences. I've heard you might have insights on why they're acting like this."

"You may have misheard something. I'm not in a position to judge my superiors' motives."

"Admiral Derfflinger, I've called you and no one else because you're exactly in such a position — but I haven't told you everything yet. *Assiduous,* please transmit a picture of our prisoner."

The officer looked at her tab. *"Yes, I already assumed you captured our supreme commander. That doesn't change anything."*

"I must inform you that your supreme commander is no human. He is a member of my people, and he is able to issue strong mental commands to your people — like I can." Syreen saw understanding growing in Derfflinger and nodded. "Doesn't that confirm suspicions you already had?"

"No, it doesn't. Nothing you say suffices as confirmation, sorry. But I'm willing to admit that it does support *my suspicions. It seems I'm not giving away a state secret by telling you this."*

They both smirked at each other.

"Now, if you could provide further supportive evidence, I'd take that into account, too."

Syreen began to like the officer. "Like, for example, video footage of him boasting about his mental powers?"

The admiral's eyes widened. *"That would be something I'd consider as confirmation."*

Send it, all of it. From the moment he set a foot inside you.
— Done. —

Syreen had to wait until Admiral Derfflinger had watched and digested the scenes.

"How could you bear that? It's horrific."

She pushed her own feelings aside. "You must know, Admiral — I thought I knew what to expect, but it's been much worse. It would have been much easier to just wipe out the

Nysa system. There's only one reason I ventured on this painful mission — because I thought that by capturing him I would end all this trouble, that Nysa would return to sanity, that I wouldn't have to annihilate warships and kill brave soldiers. You know what I got instead — Nysa sends its fleet out to slaughter, carnage, massacre. That's what makes my suffering truly horrific — that I endured it in vain. Please tell me I'm wrong."

Derfflinger made a sad face. *"Sorry, I can't. I can only agree with you — Nysa indeed sent its fleet out. You suffered in vain, because whatever I could do now, it's too late to stop those ships that already jumped. My apologies."*

Even without her extra senses, Syreen could see the sincerity in Derfflinger's face. "Your honesty soothes my pain. So you do accept my evidence?"

"It all adds up. Yes, I do. I believe you, I accept your evidence, and I accept your claims." She tapped her pad. *"I never thought I'd ever see this day, but it's my duty to declare our government infiltrated and misled, and thus to invoke chapter thirteen."*

The lieutenant on *Assiduous's* bridge gasped.

"This is Admiral Derfflinger, Nysa counterintelligence. The code for your sealed orders is twenty-one, seventy-three, nineteen. Loyal Nysa officers, according to chapter thirteen, section one, you're required to discard all orders containing contradictions to our rules of engagement and regard them as invalid in their entirety. Lay down your arms and return to your home bases. Should you encounter armed resistance, try to request a truce. Should your request be denied, surrender. Should your superiors appear to discard this order, you are required to relieve them from duty, if necessary by force and personal sacrifice. This is Admiral Derfflinger, Nysa counterintelligence. I am fully aware of the consequences and will submit myself to a tribunal of neutral judges once the current situation is resolved, according to chapter thirteen, section two. Computer, distribute by emergency drone relay and courier, where necessary."

"What's chapter thirteen?" Hardincourt asked aloud.

Moreton glanced at Syreen. "Put simply, chapter thirteen contains the rules and regulations under which a military coup may take place. The actual wording is way more complicated. Every captain's order contains straightforward and basic instructions on what to do and what to avoid, which can only be accessed with the code just transmitted — and for most officers, this will be the first time in their career that they hear of chapter thirteen, as its existence isn't advertised for obvious reasons."

The Navigator nodded an acknowledgement at the Lieutenant and then focused on the admiral's curious face. "I am sorry, Ma'am, that I didn't disclose the presence of two AP Navy officers to you until now. I didn't want to be the one ending their career the Cortez way, if you understand. With me are Commodore Hardincourt and his intelligence officer, Lieutenant Moreton, both aboard under safe conduct. They were the first ones willing to talk to me."

"*So I assume Lieutenant Moreton directed you to me. That is laudable, brave — and very foolish for a green officer.*"

Syreen shook her head. "It was a most foolish — if not to say desperate — action for me to call you. I didn't really expect to convince you, but I had to try anyway."

Admiral Derfflinger made an attempt to smile. "*Time will tell who's the biggest fool. Invoking chapter thirteen was always unanimously regarded as foolish by our instructors and among fellow officers. But I felt the same — I had to try, and now we'll see how that turns out. Too late for too many, I fear.*"

"My ship is much faster than any in your fleet. If you're willing to go one step further and advise me of their destinations, I might be able to intercept some of them."

"*You might reach one system.*"

"I might reach a dozen systems tencycles before the first drone. I could relay your message and move on."

"*A dozen systems?*" The admiral took a deep breath. "*Well, if you are ready to leave us to our internal problems for now — if you*" *trust us not to revert to our old ways as soon as you're gone – I will disclose our deployment plans to you."*

"I will have to trust you there, as you trust me. There's been too much distrust lately."

"Thank you. I'm aware of the obligation you place on us – should you find us in a disagreeable situation upon your return, you will probably not seek further debate."

"Too true. In any case, my duties here aren't finished yet. I'll need to witness your change."

"Agreed – there's much left to talk about. Later. Right now, I will provide you with assistance for the next part of your mission. Commodore Hardincourt, Lieutenant Moreton, you will not return to your ship. You and your crew aboard Assiduous *will join Navigator Syreen. You will bear witness that I made my decisions in my right mind, without pressure, and as I saw my duty. I must apologize for the hardships this will mean to you, but we may not waste even a centicycle now."*

"Yes, ma'am," both officers agreed in unison.

"Agreed. Admiral, I'll leave you to your duties now." Syreen disconnected the line and turned to Hardincourt. "How much time do you need to contact your ship?"

"Give me just a centicycle and an open line to call them. Lieutenant, would you please tell Ensign Forsythe?"

CHAPTER EIGHT

Syreen examined Admiral Derfflinger's data on the AP fleet deployment together with *Assiduous*. For units deployed from Nysa, they knew the time of departure and the first destination, but not their individual jump solutions. They had to guess. For those units that received or would receive their new order by drone, they knew the drone schedules.

As a result, there were a few systems where the master's last order had already arrived and probably been executed, where she would be too late. In other systems, the order was new and would soon be acted upon. In most systems, the order or a newly deployed fleet unit was yet to arrive.

There was no point in arriving too late, except for retaliation, but that had no priority. They had to focus on the systems she could save — the second group, then the last.

She briefly closed her eyes and sketched a route that would touch most of the affected systems.

"How bad is it?" Hardincourt asked. "Can we save a few?"

She put her solution on a display and watched the commodore examine it.

Her own sad smile was mirrored in his worried face. "Many, but not all. No matter how fast we travel, I can't be everywhere at the same time."

"My ships are nowhere near as fast as yours, but if you consider sending out my *Rubicon* and my light cruisers, you could reach four more systems. You may trust my officers — they will be glad to follow their newest orders."

Four more systems — she closed her eyes again and did the

30

math. "I'll provide you with jump solutions for seven-sigma jump sequences. Tell your pilots we're expecting them to make that miracle work."

"*Seven* sigma?" He glanced at the screen that appeared before him. His eyes widened. "By all ghosts in space!"

He swallowed. "*Rubicon*, Lieutenant Gordon, this is Commodore Hardincourt aboard *Assiduous*. Be prepared to receive four jump solutions for our fleet and execute immediately. You're going to save some lives."

"*This is* APS Rubicon. *Acknowledged and received, Commodore. Wait, what's this —* seven *sigma?*"

"Move your ass, Gordon."

"*Yessir.*"

Syreen watched the four ships accelerate hard and noticed the lieutenant and the ensign enter her bridge. "Okay, folks, let's move, too. Take your seats."

Ready to go, pal?

— Yes, my pilot. —

Okay.

She entered deep integration. *No more holding back. Show me what you can do.*

The living ship turned away from Nysa and dashed forward. A few centicycles later, they entered hyperflight, and she could divert a part of her attention to her passengers.

"How long until we reach the jump point?" Hardincourt asked.

"We already entered hyperspace, and we'll reach our first destination within the next halfcycle."

"What, we already jumped?"

"Hyperflight, Commodore. I'm not jumping, I'm flying. I can stay on the hyperplane and do turns around obstacles. I don't need to stop and recheck my course."

He glanced at Moreton. "I still haven't fully grasped how far we're outclassed."

The intelligence officer nodded. "I'm still amazed how much we're allowed to learn about it."

"You're right," Syreen said. "I would have preferred not to disclose our abilities to you. But saving lives takes precedence over any precautions, and I wouldn't want to lock you away. I want your full, unreserved cooperation. I feel that my trust in you will be the best way to gain your trust in me. Am I right?"

Moreton made a sour face. "An honest answer to an honest question—maybe I will learn to trust you, but it's still my duty to report all I learn to my superiors, and I doubt it will gain *their* trust. Admiral Derfflinger's, maybe."

"Fair. However, right now I don't need their trust. I need your trust only, and your cooperation, in order to clean up the mess your superiors made. I'll have to deal with them later, and I will, of that you can be sure."

The lieutenant smiled. "That much I've already learned about you. No empty promises."

Hardincourt waved a hand. "How do you plan to stop our ships?"

"Well, once we drop from hyperspace, I'll transmit Admiral Derfflinger's chapter thirteen message. Thereafter, there are two possible courses of action. The preferred one is—they follow their new orders or at least refrain from violence and start talking. The other would be—they try to continue their punitive action, and I will stop them by any means necessary."

"You expect them to listen?" The commodore radiated doubt.

"I expect them to comply with their orders. But I'm prepared to find a few officers who don't—either because they like violence or because they're mentally controlled. It will be their subordinates' duty to relieve them from command, right?"

"True, but . . ." Hardincourt shook his head. "Not many of our officers would dare to make that step."

Syreen leaned forward. "I know. But if they don't comply with their new orders, they'll fail their duty toward their crew and their nation — and I still have to stop them."

"You don't like it." He folded his hands. "I understand. That's why you need our trust so dearly — because you will have to kill some of our people."

"I will have to kill some rogues — and a lot of brave crewmen along with them, yes."

Commodore Hardincourt focused on her with a stern face. "This is war, and it's a dirty war. You will stop it, whatever it takes, right?"

She nodded.

"Good. Don't hesitate to do what's necessary. Don't let remorse stop you. Wrap your heart in ice and be a soldier."

Syreen nodded again. "That's what I plan to do."

CHAPTER NINE

Syreen waved a mental goodbye to the stars' songs before they dropped from hyperflight. *Assiduous's* sensors picked up what she already knew—an AP battle group with one battle cruiser, one light cruiser and three destroyers had arrived not long before her and was heading system-inward.

"Welcome to Vigo." She smiled at her passengers. "Please excuse me for now."

One mental command released the message with Derfflinger's chapter thirteen order. Another activated her radio. "Vigo harbor authorities, this is Navigator Syreen aboard the living ship *Assiduous*, currently on a mission to enforce the guild edict on the Associated Planets, and right now acting as courier for a high priority message to the AP ships in your system. Should you require any kind of assistance with regard to their presence, please let me know."

Lieutenant Moreton leaned forward. "They will need at least a quartercycle to read and digest their orders, I'd say. And that it was relayed by a living ship."

Commodore Hardincourt laughed and shook his head. "They'll have to digest the fact that it's hardly a cycle old but originates from Nysa anyway. But if they're worth a credit, they'll react to the presence of another warship in this system first."

Ensign Forsythe—meanwhile in his own seat on her bridge—scratched his chin. "I'd say if their radio and sensors will compete for the skipper's attention, sensors will win. However, I can't guess who among them will overcome his surprise first."

Moreton chuckled. "In any case, the slower one will get a proper talking-to."

While her guests made fun of their own surprise, Syreen received first reactions.

The five AP ships had cut their deceleration. That way, they would pass Vigo Orbital too fast to dock, but kept the option of running away — or so they thought. Syreen couldn't blame them. They hadn't observed *Assiduous* in action yet.

They're good. Only two centicyles later, the destroyers began to spread out, while the battle cruiser moved between *Assiduous* and the light cruiser. That way, the bigger ship could shield the light cruiser in a fight, while the destroyers could either try to escape or get in her back.

"*This is* APS Ravenheart, *Commodore Ogilvy speaking. Navigator Syreen, I confirm receipt of chapter thirteen order. Will you grant us permission to return to our homebase?*"

"Commodore Ogilvy, granted. That's the sole purpose of my visit here. By the way, you were quick reading your new orders."

"*Navigator, I just skimmed enough of them to find out what this is all about. I will thoroughly read them on my way home, trying to find an explanation of what happened during the last kilocycles. Moreover, they'll have to keep my mind off that image on our screens. A living ship, by all ghosts in space!*"

Syreen watched Ogilvy's ships turn toward an exit point on convergent vectors. "I have a good feeling with this one."

"You may," Hardincourt agreed. "He's a hardliner, but he's reliable. If he says he's returning, he will."

"Thank you. Excuse me for another moment, and we're on our way again."

Radio. "Vigo harbor authorities, this is Navigator Syreen aboard the living ship *Assiduous*. My apologies for having disturbed your quietude. The edicts have been reestablished. For now, I must depart."

She sank into deep integration with her partner. Another moment later, they reentered hyperflight.

CHAPTER TEN

Syreen glanced at the Commodore. "Yes?"

Hardincourt started upon the sudden address. "Uh."

"You wanted to ask something?"

He sat upright. "Yes. Where are we going next—if I may ask?"

"Oh, sure you may. Sorry. I put up that display for you—I thought it would tell you all, but of course it doesn't."

Now the officer smiled. "No. I'm the one to apologize, but I don't know star maps by heart. I can tell you're navigating fine, but our destination—" He broke off and shook his head.

"It's the Kamika system. We're here to intercept *APS Champion* with its battle group."

"The *Champion*?" He glanced at the Lieutenant. "Isn't that Margold's ship?"

Moreton nodded. "I think so, yes. I wonder why they sent him—he's not the one I'd expect on such a mission. But, well, I didn't foresee Ogilvy going out to shoot civilians either."

Hardincourt sighed. "Me neither. But after Cortez's sentence—well."

They frowned at each other.

Syreen could sense their dismay. "So you'd say he should be willing to listen to reason?"

"Yes. Yes, he should. Perhaps I should talk to him?"

"Of course." She frowned. "If he's willing to talk. However, the first announcement is my responsibility."

"Sure."

When *Assiduous* emerged from hyperspace, Syreen let out a sigh. They had arrived in time to stop the AP battle group. She triggered Derfflinger's chapter thirteen message, followed by her announcement to the Kamika harbor authorities. Now they had to wait.

Assiduous picked up traces of a brief message exchange between the command ship and the three light cruisers, then between the light cruisers alone.

Next, the smaller ships split up and cut their engines. The battle cruiser accelerated forward.

"What's that madman doing?" Hardincourt stared at the plot.

"He's trying to complete the mission." Syreen sighed. "Excuse me."

She entered deep integration with her partner. *Lessons time.*
— *I feel sorry we have to do this.* —
Thank you, mate.
— *Watch this.* —
APS Champion had just launched a full missile volley at Kamika Orbital. She felt amusement rather than anger.
A madman's deed indeed. Hack your snack.
— *Okay.* —
While a small part of the living ship's mind dealt with the missile target computers, they accelerated toward the battle cruiser. She felt a growing tingle in her crotch.

Their EMP pulse cut the AP ship's engines together with all other aggregates.
I should have asked first — is there any way we can change the ship's trajectory now?
— *Just a little gravity pull. Where do you want it to go?* —
A safe distance away from planet and orbital. I don't want any incidents while I'm aboard.
— *You can't go aboard. It's a hostile ship.* —
It's a ship with a certain familiar hostile presence. Remember the master's puppets?

— Yuck. Yes, I do. —

One of them is aboard. I will go and take him. Put incoming calls off until I'm back. Oh, I will need a uniform now — white, no decorations.

— Yes, my Navigator. —

When she climbed out of her chair, Hardincourt seemed to notice her nudity for the first time. "Oh — you are, well — "

"Undressed. I know." She fetched a plain white uniform from a new opening in the floor. "I'm about to fix that. Would the three of you like to accompany me aboard *APS Champion?* I'd like to show you something, and I have to borrow your shuttle."

"I'm very curious." Hardincourt rose, followed by his crewmates. "But is it wise for you to enter a hostile ship that hasn't surrendered yet?"

She smiled her predator smile — without her fangs, of course. "I assure you I can handle the few crew members who could come our way. Most will be happy to get into their survival gear."

"What did you do?"

"I grilled their electricity. Engines, weapons, computer, radio, lighting, life support. That ship is dead metal now, but the crew is still alive, and their emergency oxyboxes will do. It's a convenient weapon to avoid unnecessary casualties." She guessed his question before he could voice it. "Sadly, it doesn't work fast enough against multiple dreadnaughts. When I'm facing strong opposition, I have to resort to other means."

She fetched one boot and put her foot in. There had been a time she had flown barefoot, but the task before her required proper appearance.

After finishing the second foot, she picked up a beret and waved toward the exit. "After you, gentlemen."

APS Champion couldn't offer any assistance, but Syreen

found no flaw in Ensign Forsythe's docking maneuver.

"Well done," Hardincourt confirmed her assessment.

She rose. "Sorry. There should be no doubt that I'm not using you as a living shield. From here, I must go first."

The commodore nodded and waved at the door. "I understand. Please."

Syreen passed through the airlock and pulled herself forward along the handrails.

Champion's corridors were only dimly lit by phosphorescent stripes along what had been floor and ceiling — of course, the artificial gravity was gone, too.

The AP officers had no trouble following her, while the ensign had to stay behind again. No one crossed their path — most of the crew had probably already reached the emergency pods.

"How do you find your way aboard an AP battle cruiser?" the lieutenant asked.

"I'm a Navigator." Her smile was probably lost in the dimness. "I can follow the evil smell. Oh — and my previous special ops assignment to the battle cruiser *APS Oppression* might help, too. I've seen the layout in bright light before."

"The *Oppression* was lost on Wagaki," Moreton said. "Broken emitters, the records say. How could you get an assignment on that ship? It must've been quite a while ago."

"Special ops, as I said — of course not AP special ops, but the Duchy's."

"Who sent you on such a mission? I'd call it suicidal, only you're still alive, obviously."

"The Duchy Fleet Commander in Charge assigned me, and I couldn't object — it was me myself, back then."

"You?"

"One day, I'll tell you the whole story. For now, we should focus on what's behind that lock." She pointed forward.

"The bridge — and?" Moreton pulled himself forward.

"You need a code to get in."

"No, I don't." Without power, no computer would answer to a code. Spaceships needed backup mechanisms. She opened a concealed panel, felt for a lever and started cranking it.

First, the airtight seals were retracted, then the door started moving. Syreen winked at the officers. "Come, but stay behind me."

The battle cruiser's bridge was comparably well lit — secondary lighting had kicked in after the EMP strike. Most stations were deserted. Three people were buckled to their seats at command, navigation and weapons. One man in a filthy lieutenant's uniform was hovering above them.

He turned his head toward the door. "You!" An evil smile crept onto his face when he spotted her company. "Grab her!"

Syreen could sense his mental orders. She waited until Hardincourt and Moreton started reaching out for her, horror raging in their minds, but unable to resist. Only then did she issue her own command. *Disregard his order — you will follow no mental command but mine.*

She focused on the abomination. *Come to me.*

"Noo, you can't take a searcher! Impossible!" With its yell, the creature exposed its fangs, and Syreen heard two gasps behind her.

"I've heard that line before. Yes, I can take a searcher — my powers by far exceed yours and your master's. Come to me."

Come. Don't fight.

She cast an apologetic glance at her company. "I'm sorry. There are only two ways to incapacitate a searcher — either by burning it to ashes or by draining it. I fear I can't spare you the gory part."

"What do you mean?" Hardincourt asked.

She had already gotten hold of the creature, pulled its throat to her lips, and sunk her own fangs into its arteries.

Once she let go of the dried carcass, she felt her powers

restored.

"What was that?" Hardincourt asked.

"A searcher. A violation of the third edict—a creature created by your former master. You could feel its mental powers until I shielded you from it, right?"

"Yes. That was horrible. But—uh, you . . ."

"The People can have fangs, too. That's something I couldn't easily adapt to, but it's a necessity for us. Don't be worried, I don't usually bite my company. My point is— you've witnessed the searcher's powers, right?"

"Yes."

"Okay. So perhaps you may speak in defense of the *Champion's* crew. I will relieve their minds now."

Your mind is free now.

Champion's commandant shook his head and glanced around, finally focusing on Syreen. "Status report? Uh—what happened? And—who are you and what are you doing on my bridge?"

"Navigator Syreen, of the living ship *Assiduous*, Sir. I'm here to accept your surrender—once you've had the chance to read your latest orders. Commodore Hardincourt came along to brief you on the situation."

"Reactors and engines are still dead, Sir. The ship's running on emergency power. Zero maneuverability, Sir." The lieutenant at the helm waved at his crewmate.

"Weapons are dead, Sir. Zero readings, zero targeting."

"Thank you." Commodore Margold didn't take his gaze from Syreen, but pointed at Hardincourt and Moreton. "Why should I surrender to a one-woman boarding team? You're clearly outnumbered."

She smiled. "These gentlemen, unlike you, follow their orders, which do not encompass opposing me. Again, I'm offering you a chance to review your updated orders, but don't test my patience. I just relieved you of a mind-controlling abomination, so you may claim innocence—unless you do something unwise now."

"You better understand that you're the one in a very unfavorable situation now," Hardincourt added. "Give me a chance to explain the situation, please."

"Are you trying to lecture me?" Margold glared at Hardincourt. "You're not my superior."

"No, but Admiral Derfflinger is, and I've witnessed you disobeying her lawful orders."

"Which orders?"

Hardincourt frowned. "The same orders that your light cruisers received and obeyed. You know that ignoring an order that you could have read is no better than discarding it. Commodore, I really, really recommend you check your log for those orders now — the orange-box log, of course."

Margold muttered something but checked his board anyway. "What the — sorry, scratch that. Indeed, there's been an incoming message, priority orders, I don't remember having seen that. Content — chapter thirteen — by all ghosts in space!"

He held up a tab, checked it, and pocketed it again. "Dead. Now I'd really like to listen to that message, but — well. Okay, Commodore Hardincourt, you've got me there. What can I do now?"

Hardincourt pulled himself forward. "May I offer you my personal pad to replay Admiral Derfflinger's message, and also to review my copy of the secret orders?"

Champion's commandant appeared shaken now. "Yes, of course, gladly, but what's this all about?"

"Mind control," Syreen chimed in. "You've been controlled by that greasy lieutenant." She pointed at the dead body. "If you focus on it, you should be able to recall some of it. The same kind of mind control, only on a larger scale, had been applied to your government, too. That's why Admiral Derfflinger invoked chapter thirteen."

Back on *Assiduous,* Syreen watched her plot. Two tugs from Kamika Orbital were now heading toward *APS Champion.* Two light cruisers had already docked to collect most of *Champion's* crew to take them home. The battle cruiser would remain behind with a skeleton crew.

"What will Kamika do with it?"

"Probably just put it in parking orbit," Hardincourt said. "After all, you stopped the missiles in time, so no one was hurt. Now they know the embargo won't last forever, and once the situation returns to normal, they'll want to trade with us again. So there's no need to anger the AP. I'd say the local guild will recommend something along that line." He barely suppressed a yawn. "Where are we going next?"

"Wapiti, then Chlongoorong. Follow the lighting to find a room to rest — I'll call you in case we encounter a difficult situation, okay?"

"Yes, okay. I'd better take a brief nap now. You're coming along, guys?"

Moreton and Forsythe followed him.

Syreen focused on her next flight.

— They haven't been very helpful so far. —

They're nice. And I'd like to have them around anyway. Just in case.

— As livestock? —

No need to tell them, but yes.

— I didn't expect that. —

Syreen hadn't known what a mental grin of her partner felt like, but now the smile seemed to reach all across her body. She had to grin, too.

CHAPTER ELEVEN

Syreen checked the arrangement of ships in the Brannock system and frowned. *Call our guests, please.*

The AP had sent not one, but three battle groups with one battle cruiser, three light cruisers and three destroyers each to Brannock, obviously prepared for firm resistance, and all heading toward Brannock Four with the system's main military base.

From her previous visit with her corvette *Raydancer,* she remembered Brannock's defenses consisting of four heavy cruisers, three stingship bases with their score of stingships, and some custom vessels.

One of Brannock's heavy cruisers was already heavily damaged and trying to get away from the battleground. The other three were approaching the AP fleet on interception courses from their different positions. Three stingship wings had started from their bases and were heading toward the enemy, too.

No way they'll stop that fleet, even though the AP hasn't deployed stingships yet. Poor bastards.

Admiral Derfflinger's orders were under way. Even before the message could arrive, the AP launched its first volleys of missiles against Brannock's orbital stations—against all of them, including the civil orbitals around Brannock Two and Three.

"Brannock system control, this is the living ship *Assiduous,* Navigator Syreen speaking. I'm recording hostile AP activity in your system. As enforcer of the edicts, it is my duty to

45

incapacitate any AP units not complying with their most recent orders to cease fire. Whether you accept my assistance or not, I will do what's necessary — please instruct your target computers to regard me as ally, not enemy."

Now get those missiles, please.

— They're using active scramblers. I can't get through. —

Smart. Seems someone studied battle recordings and drew conclusions. Okay, we're going in.

Syreen entered deep integration. Together, they dashed through hyperspace to come between missiles and targets. Their concussion pulser turned the missiles into dust.

She had to dodge the first pulse laser shots next. Two battle groups were targeting her with admirable precision, while the third would soon engage the local defenders, with no doubt about the only possible outcome.

A sequence of hyperspace skips carried her close to each of the AP battle cruisers. Sparks launched from *Assiduous's* legs fried their electrical equipment and turned the powerful battleships into metal coffins.

Ouch.

The light cruisers wouldn't give up, and a few shots grazed her body — *Assiduous's* body. Worse, some had also severely damaged another Brannock heavy cruiser — and the third battle group's destroyers were shooting rescue pods now.

The tingling in her crotch grew, and her next concussion pulser shots smashed that battle group's ships hard, turning their steel bodies into bizarre, twisted wreckage.

She directed her attention back on the first two battle groups' survivors. The light cruisers and destroyers had cut their acceleration and discharged their weapon systems. Two of the light cruisers were cautiously approaching their lead ships.

"*Assiduous*, this is AP light cruiser *Ferret*, Captain Harris speaking. I herewith confirm receipt of the chapter thirteen order. As acting commandant of the nineteenth expeditionary force, I've ordered all vessels to stand down and restrict themselves to search-and-rescue activities. I will enter negotiations with the Brannock authorities regarding our capitulation as soon as possible. I'm placing my crews at your mercy, sir."

She kept her answer short. "Granted, Captain Harris."

We will feed now, and thereby clean the system of all that debris.

Only now could she focus on Hardincourt, who had arrived on her bridge during the battle. The officer was staring at the plot, at the symbols of destroyed or incapacitated ships. She sensed his emotional uproar.

"Are you wondering if you're still on the right side of this conflict?" she asked straight away.

"I'm wondering if there is a right side in this conflict." He turned to her, made a few steps toward her chair, and placed one hand on her bare shoulder. "The Brannock people, perhaps. I've been here once. They're decent people. They didn't deserve this attack."

"Agreed," she said and smiled at him. "I've been here before, too. Good people."

"Yes." He stared down. "Unlike my people. It's hard to learn that the same nice fellows you've been sharing your drink with are shooting rescue pods and civil orbital stations without hesitation. It's also hard to see our ships wiped from space like gnats—to recognize the power in the hands of one solitary woman, not kept in check by any other power." He squeezed her shoulder. "Sorry. And then, it's hard to admit that all the checks in place didn't keep our own navy from doing the unspeakable, while at the same time you're offering them more mercy than they deserve. In your place, given your means, I'd have wiped them out."

"Like gnats. Whatever that is."

Hardincourt's glance fell at her face. "You don't know gnats? Tiny, scurrying insects?"

"I'm a spacer. Perhaps one day I'll go dirtside and spot one. But I get your meaning. Would you mind briefing Captain

Harris on what this is all about? Meanwhile, I'll try to comfort the local authorities."

Who were already calling for her.

"*Assiduous, this is Brannock defense control, Lieutenant Marat speaking. Can you provide additional credentials? Which star nation does your ship belong to, and what made you travel to Brannock?*"

"Lieutenant Marat, you may check your records on my previous visit. Back then, Captain Richard McArthur of the Brannock Marine Infantry interviewed me as Duchy Fleet Commander in Charge Syreen, no surname, commanding the Duchy corvette *Raydancer,* on an exploration mission, traveling from Kyris through Brannock to Silver Seven."

"*Let me check that — heck, you're that sharpshooter!*"

"I am." She smiled. She'd heard stories about *that Brannock jockey* all across the sector.

"*And now this. Sorry, but I have to ask again — which star nation does your ship belong to? The Duchy? And what made you travel to Brannock?*"

"Lieutenant Marat, no, *Assiduous* is no part of Duchy fleet. My living ship belongs to my people only, the so-called Forgotten People. Our duty is to enforce the edicts, and I chose Brannock as one of the systems where I might arrive in time to deliver new orders from the AP admiralty to their own ships — or to stop them from doing the worst. Which I did."

"*So you're Duchy Fleet Commander in Charge, but you command a ship that's not Duchy fleet?*"

"It's complicated, Lieutenant."

"*Well, it certainly is above my pay grade. However, I'm instructed to relay our government's most sincere gratitude for your assistance just in time.*"

Yes, and those instructions just arrived together with their most sincere best wishes for my further journey and that it may happen soonest. This time, Syreen suppressed her grin. "I'm currently cleaning up some of the debris I caused, but we'll be on our way soon. There may be a few more systems requiring similar assistance. Please forward my greetings to your government, to your fleet, to Captain McArthur, and to your local guild office."

And once you're fed, mate, we'll travel on.

Chapter Twelve

Syreen emerged from deep integration and smiled at Hardincourt. "You've got questions on your mind, Commodore?"

The AP officer sighed. "Yes. I've been thinking about the future. What comes next, once you've stopped all our bullies and sent them home? Will you raise the embargo?"

She gave him a long, stern glance. "The embargo will be raised once compliance with the edicts has been reestablished. There must be two positive votes about that—the guild's, and mine. That's part of my agreement with the guild board on Crown. Now you may ask what's needed for that positive vote. Let's start with the guild. I won't cross the chasm again just for that vote. We expect a guild board to be reestablished for this sector, and quite obviously it can no longer be located on Nysa."

"I see."

She smiled and shrugged. "There are surely guild procedures for it, but I don't know them all. What I know is that the guild will need a trigger to start their procedures, and that's a formal public announcement from the AP government saying they will comply with the edicts."

"That sounds too easy." Hardincourt shook his head. "I know, they are my people, but letting us get away scot-free . . ."

"Their procedures will include a thorough check on the announcement's credibility, which means it will have to be accompanied by appropriate measures."

"Which are?"

She shrugged again. "That's their business. I can tell you about my own requirements."

"Oh. You didn't mention that to Admiral Derfflinger."

"As you may remember, we were in a kind of hurry to leave. I haven't made up my mind over this topic entirely. Perhaps you can help me compile a list of reasonable demands."

Hardincourt glanced at his silently watching subordinates. "You want me to provide you with the means to strangle our navy?"

Syreen arranged her seat to let her sit upright. That way, her crotch disappeared from immediate sight. "I wouldn't put it that way. You should know — after I claimed the AP corvette *Raydancer* for my mission, I studied your regulations. There already are paragraphs regarding violations of the second edict — it's forbidden. However, that didn't prevent Admiral Santiago from violating it. So I'd say the disciplinary action against such violations must be changed, and officers and superiors not trying to prevent such violations must suffer severe consequences, too. In turn, this kind of preventive action may never be treated as mutiny or desertion. Those superiors subsequently punishing officers who did their duty and tried to prevent violations must suffer the same consequences. What do you think?"

"So far, that sounds sensible to me. What kind of consequences do you have in mind?"

Syreen sensed how the Commodore relaxed. Obviously, he had expected worse, and worse he would get. "To me, this is a crime far more severe than piracy, and the sanctions should reflect that. So spacing the culprits without suit would be the most merciful sentence."

Her statement made all three men swallow hard.

"However, your government and admiralty may convince

me otherwise, should the overall package appear satisfactory. You know, there are two other edicts to consider, the least obvious of which may be the first one."

"Which is?" Ensign Forsythe asked.

Syreen turned to him. "Edict Number One proscribes the deliberate damage of the fabric of space, like actions that could create a rift, or the destruction of living stars."

"I wouldn't even know how to do that," Forsythe admitted.

She nodded. "The pitiful current situation reflects that universal lack of knowledge. Have you heard of the *rift* between Chengdu and Nizwa, or of the *chasm*?"

"Yes—a part of space that is difficult to navigate or not navigable at all."

"And has it always been like this?"

"As far as my instructors say, no—but it's been like this for generations."

Moreton leaned forward.

Syreen waved at him. "Yes, Lieutenant?"

"The situation in the rift has noticeably deteriorated over the last megacycle—with decreasing traffic due to pirate activity. Would that mean that reduced traffic causes such damage?"

"Your observation is correct, but you swapped cause and effect. The sad truth is that poor hyperjumps cause such damage. You might compare that with mending your uniform. If you apply a needle, you reach the desirable result. If you try to use a knife for sewing . . ."

The commodore stared at her. "What exactly are you telling us?"

"What I'm telling you is that six-sigma is the needle and four-sigma is the knife, and a number of five-sigma jumps will cause the same damage as a four-sigma jump. So, one of my demands will be a strict best-jump policy for all AP space traffic. Negligent navigation will be sanctioned. Negligent skippers — navy as well as merchants — will be banned from space travel. All jump calculations will be recorded and subject to inspection upon arrival. You may add some leeway for junior officers still learning the ropes and for emergency jumps, but I need to see a basic ruling on this."

Now Hardincourt chuckled. "Oh, that will cause a stir among my fellow skippers. I know many of them are all too glad that they can delegate jump calculations to their staff, and they will approve almost anything above three sigma. You can imagine what that means for their educational efforts."

She took a deep breath. "I don't have to imagine, I've seen it. I've observed a young ensign finishing his calculation without ever calling up the trims."

She watched Forsythe.

The ensign blushed. "Like on my second trip. My first pilot never showed me the trims, and when I did my first calculation for Captain Gregory, I got a thorough dressing-down."

Hardincourt grinned. Then he faced the Navigator. "I see what you mean. Now that you've told us of the true consequences, I think a change in the respective regulations should be easy to negotiate."

She didn't correct him on the topic of negotiating. "Which leads me to another request. The AP has other regulations that are not properly implemented. From now on, I require every in-flight inspection to be recorded. Every inspection crew must prove beyond doubt that there hasn't been any misconduct with regard to female merchant crew members, including those called ship cats. Officers will be made fully responsible for any lack of disciplinary leadership."

Hardincourt frowned. "I can imagine what you are referring to, but what exactly does your last sentence mean?"

"You should know that I've traveled as ship cat or junior

crew member in the past, and that my covert mission also included observations of onboard AP activities. I've seen and personally experienced AP crew attempting rape, I've witnessed male AP crew blackmailing and sexually harassing female AP crew members, and I've witnessed AP officers regarding such behavior as acceptable, if not welcome venting, instead of a lack of discipline. It is obvious to me that the current disciplinary measures are insufficient — so any officer unable to enforce the regulations must be removed from duty, and the sentence must match his subordinates' crime. And for me, rape is an act of piracy, no less."

The commodore had shrunk back over the ferocity of her statement, now he paled. "You mean . . ."

"I mean that any skipper had better accompany the inspection crew until he can be sure they behave. Any more such venting of sexual stress will result in venting of the culprits including their skipper — and should too many skippers fail their duty, their admiralty may enjoy a trip to space without suit, too." She mentally forced him to keep his gaze at her. "Before you object, consider the victims' situation. They've always been fair game."

"I still think that's too hard on the officers. You can never be sure."

"If they're not sure, they can join the boarding party. Moreover, that's why I mentioned recording. The very moment the boarding party switches their equipment off, the skipper must go in with some marine infantry. Do you think the next inspection party will try the same?"

Syreen could sense understanding growing in him.

He nodded. "I understand what you're getting at. However, the way we're interpreting our regulations, there's usually a second chance."

She nodded. "Just make sure everyone understands that the second chance is the last chance. As I said — I'm asking your help to make my requests sound reasonable. The crucial point is — the trouble starts with misconduct. Ultimately, letting misconduct remain unpunished makes people believe they can get away with everything — including violations of edicts."

"The basics of discipline and leadership," Hardincourt said with a sad face. "Yes, I understand, and it's a shame you had to tell me."

CHAPTER THIRTEEN

It couldn't always be easy. Syreen observed the plot—the AP battle cruiser *Obliteration* was already docked to Cuarenta Orbital. Three AP destroyers and one light cruiser were watching the main jump points.

Unlike the Canticle system, the orbital was still intact. *I must be grateful for small favors.*

As in the systems before, Admiral Derfflinger's message went out first, followed by her own announcement to the local authorities.

At Canticle, the AP forces had surrendered and submitted themselves to local justice. She had a bad feeling that it wouldn't be as easy here.

Nor could it be like Danos—half of her Crown destroyers with their Fianna support had already fought and defeated the two AP battle groups sent there. She had merely delivered her message and traveled on.

Cuarenta Orbital remained silent. Instead, she soon received a call from the battle cruiser.

"*Assiduous, this is* APS Obliteration, *Lieutenant Hassleton speaking. Cut your engines and surrender to a boarding party of* APS Badger, *which will soon approach you. Your failure to comply will result in punitive action against Cuarenta Orbital's crew.*"

She was still contemplating her reply when the next call arrived. "*Lieutenant Hassleton, this is* APS Badger, *Captain Carmichael speaking. We will do no such thing. We will comply with Admiral Derfflinger's orders, as you should, too. Your threat of punitive action against Cuarenta Orbital has been recorded and will be used at your court-martial for sure.* Assiduous, *please record our surrender."*

The destroyers quickly sent similar messages.

That settles it.

"Captain Carmichael, this is *Assiduous,* Navigator Syreen speaking. I appreciate your compliance with your updated orders, and I would appreciate even more your assistance in setting *Obliteration's* crew back on track. Would you mind joining me at Cuarenta Orbital?"

Next, she called her guests. "Commodore Hardincourt, would you please join me at your shuttle? I'll have to deal with *Obliteration's* boarding party myself."

When she sensed the battle cruiser's guns heating up and its targeting lasers touching her skin, she jumped closer and triggered her EMP cannon.

Take care, partner. I won't be away for long.

— I will be with you. —

Syreen sensed only a slight tremble when the AP shuttle docked.

Ensign Forsythe completed the docking sequence and nodded. "We've arrived."

Hardincourt nodded and unbuckled his belt.

Syreen smiled. "Very smooth. Thank you, Ensign."

The AP junior officer blushed, but smiled, too.

Two guards were already waiting behind the airlock, their tasers pointing at Syreen's chest.

Relax. I'm here to help. Cooperate. She smiled at them. "We're here to help you get rid of some AP bullies. Where are they?"

They both lowered their guns. One pointed down the only corridor. "This way. At the guild, level seven, red section."

"Thank you. Keep an eye on our shuttle, please." She marched forward, followed by the three AP officers.

There was a familiar foul touch among the emotions of hate, fear and confusion on the station. *I knew it.*

Three men in AP uniform were already waiting at the next intersection. The youngest wore captain's stripes, the other two carried the chevrons of senior petty officers, shock batons, and seasoned faces.

Syreen sensed curiosity toward her and her company. She stopped, saluted and waited for the return salute.

"Captain Carmichael, I assume? I'm Navigator Syreen. These gentlemen are Commodore Hardincourt, Lieutenant Moreton, Ensign Forsythe."

Carmichael nodded and introduced Senior Chief Petty Officer Gordon and Chief Petty Officer Cocker.

"How do you envisage our approach?" he then asked. "I've brought some help, just in case."

She smiled at the senior noncoms. "I'm sure they know how to stop a brawl. I assume Commodore Cossner and his team are holding the guild people hostage, so I will have to walk in and release them. Once I'm done with that, you may persuade your comrades to reason."

"You don't want to go in there alone!"

"Yes, I do." She gazed at Hardincourt. "There's another searcher ahead. You know what that means."

The commodore nodded, then faced Carmichael. "Yes. She has to go alone. That creature is capable of mind control — and that's what happened to Cossner."

All three *Badger* crew members radiated shock.

She patted Hardincourt's shoulder. "Tell him. Meanwhile, I'll clean up that mess. Follow me in five."

Syreen passed the guild entrance with caution, but as her senses had already told her, no one was trying to ambush her in the entrance hall.

Only two guards in their familiar ornate guild robes were lying on the floor, staring at her with dead eyes in a pale face, their throats covered in blood.

She swallowed hard. *Two more on your bill, Master.*

A panicking mental cry made her accelerate toward the main guild hall. She dashed through the door, spotted two older men in guild robes in a corner, four young women in waitress-style garments, one of them pale and lifeless lying on the floor, and finally five men in AP uniforms, one of them just leaning forward with bared fangs to the throat of a trembling waitress.

Freeze all. Close your eyes.

She focused on the searcher. *You will come to me.*

The creature had no choice but to follow her command, but it fought hard against her control. So she had no choice but to eliminate it—again by sucking it dry.

Once its limp body dropped to the floor, she released her mental control over the other people.

While they tried to figure out what had changed, she pulled the waitress into a firm hug. *Calm down. You're safe now.*

Commodore Cossner spoke up first. "Who are you, and what are you doing here? Guards, arrest her."

She smiled at the three men who now raised their shock batons. "One step further, guys, and you will be spaced without suits." Next, she focused on the officer. "Commodore Cossner, you'd better come up with a very good explanation of what happened to the poor lady down there, and how such treatment of hostages or prisoners, whatever, can be justified by AP regulations. I am Navigator Syreen, and I'm here to make sure you follow your own laws. You're already charged with invading a foreign star nation without advance declaration of war, and now I find you on a murder crime scene."

Cossner grimaced. "You'd better consider the current distribution of power here."

Her senses picked up approaching people, and she waved at the door. "That's what I do."

With six more AP people entering the room, Cossner radiated triumph for a moment, but only until he recognized Commodore Hardincourt and Captain Carmichael and watched the petty officers taking his men's shock batons away.

Carmichael did not salute his superior. Instead, he walked up to the battle group leader. "Sorry, Sir, but it is my duty to arrest you for dishonoring your navy and your nation."

"What?" But Cossner found confirmation in the other AP officers' faces.

Hardincourt shook his head and pointed at the dead searcher. "We all know what your orders were, and that those orders weren't sound. You could have known, too, if not for that abomination. You'd better play nice now."

Syreen turned her attention away from them and approached the two guild representatives, the waitress still firmly wrapped in her hug.

"Gentlemen, I must apologize for having arrived late. I am Navigator Syreen, enforcer of the edicts. May I assume you've received and read the embargo ruling?"

One of them nodded and waved at the other. "This is Guild Secretary Amos Cortos from Cinquanta, our neighbor system. I am Guild Secretary José Canedas. It is my pleasant duty to bid you welcome at Cuarenta, Navigator Syreen. You arrived almost in time to prevent the worst. Too late for poor Anita, but that's clearly not your fault. The AP will have to answer for her death."

Cortos bowed. "Welcome, Navigator. Indeed, if there's anyone to blame, it is us, the guild. We failed to act against the growing number of misdoings performed by the AP until it was too late, and we must be grateful for everything you did — from bringing the guild back on track with that perfectly manufactured *Crown* guild ruling, up to your intervention today."

Syreen frowned. "What do you mean by *manufactured Crown guild ruling?*"

Cortos winked at her. "We were discussing that topic. The message is sound and unaltered — but Crown is on the far side of the chasm, and the chasm is impassable, so the ruling must have been forged, right?"

She gave him her most stern look. "Did you just accuse me of forging a guild ruling?"

The secretary shrank back. "I—I didn't mean to imply . . ."

"But you just did. I can assure you the message is genuine. Moreover, you wouldn't assume I forged the Crown destroyers and their crews or the Finney Fianna—both of which I brought along when I indeed crossed the chasm. Which I did twice, on my way to Crown, and on my way back, each time with a complete guild vault."

Canedas shook his head. "I told you, Amos, that there must be more to it. But how, Navigator, could you cross a part of space that's deemed impassable by the greatest experts all over this sector?"

She sensed genuine curiosity, so she didn't count his question as another attack.

"Your experts can only judge within their experience. It's true, the chasm is indeed impassable—for your technology. But they have no clue what a living ship of the Forgotten People with its Navigator can do. They couldn't know what even my ship yet had to learn—that I'm capable of repairing hyperspace. Otherwise, I wouldn't have been able to go across either."

They both stared at her.

Syreen nodded affirmatively. "Don't let my looks deceive you. I am no human. I'm a member of the Forgotten People. Megacycles ago, my people engraved the original edicts in that carbon building on that barren planet where later the peace negotiations after the guild wars took place."

She gave them a moment to let her words sink in. "One day in the near future, I'll be willing to discuss all this with the guild—with you, with Guild Secretary Alexios Spyritis of Danos, with Guild Secretary Jacomo of Kyris, with Guild

Secretary Orville of Nizwa, and any other secretary interested in the further proceedings — after all, it will be your joint duty to establish a new guild tribunal and rule on the embargo. Now, however, it is my most urgent duty to continue my journey to the next system and help them get rid of further AP forces. I'm sure you understand that well."

CHAPTER FOURTEEN

Syreen pulled herself up and swung her legs out of the chair. She flexed her toes, her ankles, her knees, before she cautiously placed her feet down. For a moment, standing on her own legs felt awkward, but that feeling faded.

We've been together a bit too long, partner.

— You deemed it necessary. —

I know. I wasn't trying to blame you, I was just pointing out the obvious. Sixteen more systems, and no more trouble. The message drones were there first. Moreover, the affected nations seem to have understood that they need their own defenses. It was worth the strain. What are our guests doing?

— The AP officers are asleep. The master demands your visit, as always. —

I wasn't aware of that.

— You were busy. The priorities were clear. —

Indeed. Well — it seems I can no longer evade that confrontation. Announce my visit.

She spotted her uniform, neatly draped over a chair. She frowned. *I didn't put it there.*

— Hardincourt did. —

For a moment, she considered whether to put it on. Then she shook her head. For a meeting with the master, she didn't need armor.

Upon entering the master's room, Syreen noticed a movement from the corner of her eye and stepped aside.

The master dashed past her and turned around.

Stay there. She smiled at him. "I should appreciate your tenacity, but I pity your inability to learn and obey. Should I show you what I learned from Paolo about instructions?"

"I'll get you!"

"That was neither a yes nor a no. May I kindly ask you to answer my question?"

He spat on her feet.

She watched the wet spot. "You should not shed your bodily waste without order. Part of your first rule, remember? And your second rule—failing to follow the rules will subject you to punishment. So, what should I do with you now? A flogging?"

"I can imagine you'd enjoy that, bitch."

"Oh, I wouldn't waste my time watching. But I won't do that unto you. You may spend some thought on my reasons." Syreen shook her head. "Perhaps, one day, we can have a serious talk. Until you're ready for that, there's no point in calling for me."

She turned for the door.

"Hey!" he called after her.

Syreen glanced over her shoulder.

"You wouldn't leave me standing here forever, would you?"

She gave him her kindest smile. Of course her mental command fixed him in place. "Would I? Well, let's find out."

Before the door closed behind her, she heard his gasp.

I'll have to talk with some guild people now. Or no, I should visit Derfflinger first and return Hardincourt home. Or have a dinner and then a nap . . .

Syreen, back in her uniform, had just reached the entrance to *Assiduous's* mess when the expected call came.

— *The master seems to be ready to talk now.* —

Is he?

— *He said he'd play nice.* —

Well, okay. If he doesn't behave, you may eat his foot. You can tell him I told you so. But you can also tell him that I'll give him advance credit and allow him to join us for dinner. She focused her mind on the master. *Released.*

– *Us?* –

You may invite the AP officers. And make the mess look posh.

– *Posh, huh?* –

When Syreen entered, a large round table was set with a Duchy-red-and-green tablecloth, golden cutlery, golden chandeliers and crystal goblets. The chairs looked like they'd been ornately carved from wood and upholstered with silk. The tapestry showed motifs of her past — *Assiduous* in Silver Seven's cave, her Appalahoo sauroid team, the Gattaca touchdown, the space battle at Klondike.

– *Posh enough?* –

"Extraordinary. You outdid yourself. Now, where are our guests?"

– *Approaching through different corridors. I made sure they won't meet before they're here.* –

Excellent.

Commodore Hardincourt entered first and paused in midstep. Lieutenant Moreton and Ensign Forsythe squeezed past him, only to stop open-mouthed for a brief moment.

Hardincourt smiled at her. "It seems we've got something to celebrate — the end of our rescue mission?"

"Indeed. You're going home." She waved at the table. "Anywhere you like."

The lieutenant was eyeing the table. "Laid for five?"

"Yes. I've invited my prisoner to join us." She sensed his presence and waved at the door. "Here he is."

They all turned and recognized their former master, who raised an eyebrow. "Oh — I didn't expect company, and surely not subordinates."

The commodore shook his head. "Sorry, Sir, but you're not

our superior anymore. Current rules, as governed by chapter thirteen, section one, suspend your command."

You must obey me.

His mental command came as a surprise — but Hardincourt only smiled. "I could read that clear, but it seems it doesn't compel me. But it adds to the evidence against you."

Syreen had to smile as well. Her own mental order was still in effect — they would follow no mental command but her own, and this was the only order she'd given them. She turned to her prisoner. "You promised to behave. Now — please quit playing your games and sit down. By the way, by what name should we address you? *Master* seems rather inappropriate."

He briefly closed his eyes. "A long time ago, I called myself Peysoon."

"Thank you, Peysoon." She introduced the officers, waited for them to spread around the table, and chose the last free chair.

The men waited until she sat at the table, then took their seats.

Oh, okay. Time to recall my Duchy education. No more informal, merchant-style table manners. As highest-ranking officer, it's my duty to determine the pace of the meal and the topics of conversation.

"Feel free to order drinks to your liking. I will have for-wine." A mug rose out of the table before her. She waited for her guests to place their orders, then she lifted her mug. "Duke's health."

They echoed her toast.

After she set her mug down, she looked around. "Let us not spoil this dinner with the most recent events. Just to sum up — the chapter thirteen order has reached the AP battle groups, so we have reached a truce for now. Once we've returned to Nysa, we can talk about an overall armistice and about the process toward lifting the embargo." She nodded at Hardincourt. "We've discussed some prerequisites, and we'll surely need to delve into that. Right here and now, there's nothing we can do about the situation."

"I beg to differ," Hardincourt said. "Agreed — there's no urgent need for action, but what I'd really like to do is to better understand the reasons for the past events. If you allow — Mr. Peysoon, would you like to explain?"

She sensed momentary puzzlement in him, followed by relaxed amusement. "Just Peysoon. The *mister* sounds too much like *master*. Well — the short or the long version?"

"Why not both?" the commodore asked. "What's the short version?"

Peysoon nodded. "The short of it is — my mission was to find a relic to gain control over an ancient artifact at all costs. The ancient artifact, as you might have guessed, was a living ship like this — " He waved around.

Syreen felt a tingle in the back of her mind. *Not now, partner.*

"And the relic turned out to be this woman." He nodded again, this time at her.

Hardincourt leaned back. "And how did you get into this mission?"

"Very good question, Commodore. The short answer wouldn't satisfy you, though, so I'd better touch on that subject in the long story."

"Okay." Syreen tapped the table and gazed around. "I'm really eager to hear that story, but as I assume it will take some time, I propose we should have dinner first — if that's okay for you. After dessert, it'll be your stage, Peysoon."

She sensed agreement — and, to her surprise, felt his strong urge to tell his story.

CHAPTER FIFTEEN—THE MASTER'S STORY

I don't know when and where I was born. I remember I've been told that I was found in a quiet corner on Kendar Orbital. I wasn't told who found me there, and it doesn't matter. I was brought to the nursery down on the planet.

If you don't know Kendar — it's a private-run penal mining colony. They don't have many women there, mostly for the management's entertainment, and so they don't have many children there, but the few who are born there are stuck there. Even if you could afford a passage out — and they're doing everything to make sure you can't — there's no passenger line going there. I guess you know what merchants think about taking passengers along, yes?

Thus I was raised to become a good miner. Good miners are those who work hard, spend all their earnings, and don't talk back. Of course, as a young child, there was no money to spend and no talking back to anyone, only work — mostly runner and servant work, and once you grow up a bit, stress relief.

Yes, I'm talking of child abuse, and you don't want to hear the details. What it boils down to is — I've learned the hard way how this universe ticks. Either you have power and apply it, or you're run over.

So once I found out that I have my own powers, I started to use them — subtly, of course. I already knew very well what happened to those who played their cards at the wrong time.

Perhaps I should explain that, too—it appeared to me that, if I couldn't avoid the attention of older men at all, I should find a protector. Better to have one exclusive sugar daddy instead of many. I usually picked one of the stronger bullies, but not the ugliest or most brutal—but that relationship never lasted long. Those bullies inevitably would overstep a border one day—in order to stay at the top of the pecking order, they had to peck, and if they pecked too hard, team performance would suffer.

The company couldn't let that stand—anyone who impaired performance received instructions, thorough enough that he'd never misbehave again. And I lost my sugar daddy.

So I knew not to use my powers in any noticeable way. It wasn't advisable to gain attention, and it wasn't advisable to aspire to a place high in the pecking order, because that would draw attention. I kept my profile low and used my powers only to gain minor favors and keep myself out of the worst trouble. But I trained them.

I grew up and became useful for mining. Sometimes a drill gets stuck, and you need to exchange parts—not always in easy reach. Small hands, a slender body, can reach where the big guys can't. Otherwise, you need runners to carry spare parts, refreshments, whatever. Or you encounter a cavity, and someone should have a look. Not only is the access often too narrow, but also that's where you send the most expendable one in—me.

I knew better than to become physically strong—again, that would have attracted attention and drawn me into the pecking game. Instead, I became quite good at tunnel crawling.

The bright side of those dark caverns is—you can spend quite some time there without having to explain yourself, and Kendar has a lot of caverns. Some are even interconnected.

Well, to keep it short—one day I ventured into a new part

of the caverns, quite deep under the surface. I felt strangely attracted by a bulky shape down there. It didn't look like rock—at least not like the other rock around.

You can already guess what it was—a living ship, very much like this one, only kind of dried out, running low on resources.

When I touched its surface, I felt a kind of tingle under my palm. I couldn't enter, but I got a response, right in my head. Not in words, rather in symbols or ideas. The gist of it was— I would need a kind of key or token from its creators, a kind of *relic*.

Moreover, I sensed a flavor of urgency. And that's where my mission started. I just had to get away from Kendar.

As I explained before, it isn't easy for a miner to get away from Kendar. But I had learned a lot about my home. Processed ores—only the truly rare and valuable stuff, of course—are shipped out regularly. Management lackeys are coming and going. They're shipping entertainers in, pretty women, you understand? Sometimes they take them along when they leave—if those women prove to be useful and don't make mistakes. Mistakes like refusing service or getting pregnant.

Occasionally, I had a chance to talk to such a woman—one of those who had made a mistake, of course, because others wouldn't come down to the surface. My mental skills made them talk openly, made them give away secrets they should have kept to themselves. They weren't punished, though, because I couldn't allow anybody to learn about me or what they told me.

Some of them were quite nice to a young boy, actually, and were willing to teach me other things. What they didn't teach me, what I found out myself, was how sweet they tasted— and how much that boosted my powers.

Then I found the ship, and I knew it was time to employ

my powers in a different way. I knew that a few of the managers weren't attracted to women. So one day I gave one of the ore shuttle pilots an eye. He wasn't interested, but I had already planted an idea into his head—he'd tell a certain manager about that young lad.

It worked, I was invited to come up with the next shuttle, and so I met my ticket to Nysa. Yeah, I'll spare you the details. When his time to leave came, he took me along.

Nysa wasn't kind to me either. Personal toys like me weren't kept in high regard. Rich people had their easy ways to get fresh meat. Oh, such was generally frowned upon by most of Nysa's society, but their moral standards don't apply to those with the real power. I wasn't surprised, I already had learned my lessons well. I used my powers mainly to remain useful, and to be recommended around—to attach my strings and to expand my reach.

Now and then I met members of the government or the admiralty. I planted ideas into them—to increase their wealth by tighter checks on trade, by inspections to distant parts of the Association, preferably accompanied by a reasonable display of power, by tapping into new resources—that is, exploring unclaimed systems—and exploiting existing ones.

Maintaining a large fleet is expensive. But it seemed to be a price worth paying, because it fortified existing power structures, too. It was a job driver, and it created the right kind of loyalty in the new recruits.

The crucial point, however, was to spread out and search for that *relic* I needed—the one that *my* ship needed and still needs.

You know what came next. Intelligence reported about a researcher following a similar thread—remainders of a ship like the one I had found. Together with other hints, everything seemed to indicate the Duchy.

I decided to take things into my own hands. I assumed

supreme command and assigned the right man to the task. Ravenport had a reputation. I only had to instruct him to go in strong, and that was what he did.

Believe one thing — I hadn't instructed him to shoot civil orbital stations without warning. I won't try to fool you — had I known, I might not have stopped him, but I didn't demand it. What I ultimately demanded was to find that *relic*, provided one existed there, and bring it back to me.

My approach failed, and meanwhile I know why — well, almost. Today, after your last visit, after I sensed your determination, I recognized my previous approach was doomed to fail. You asked me to consider why you didn't retaliate — you surely had any reason to do so. I had to understand that you don't need it — you're strong without such means. And if I want to rely on your strength, I must follow your lead.

If there's any chance left to complete my mission, I had to tell you all — most of all, about my discovery, about the ship.

So here I am. Condemn me if you must, but please, complete my mission. Help that other ship, whatever it takes.

CHAPTER SIXTEEN

Syreen couldn't fail to notice the similarities in Peysoon's story. The foundling, the discovery of superhuman powers, even the first contact with a living ship. He had been played, just like her, but he hadn't been played nice. His sudden turn from foe to friend should have made her wary, but she trusted her senses and her senses told her that he was earnest.

– *It is imperative to find that ship.* –

Hush, partner. I agree, and we'll go there. But we need to do things in the right order. We can't afford to mess this up.

"What do you make of that?" Hardincourt asked. "He's a storyteller, ain't he?"

"He told the truth," Syreen said absently. "Only the truth, and only the prettier parts of it." She turned to Peysoon. "I can't excuse what you did, or what you made others do, but I understand how you got there. I feel sorry for what those men did to you. Most of all, I feel sorry that you had no chance to meet your parent."

Peysoon stared at her in disbelief. "What do you know about my parents?"

"Parent, Peysoon. Singular. One parent, just like me. I wasn't born of a human woman. I was born – or created – by a star, and so were you. I am Syreen Starborn, and my parent is the Duchess – the Duchy's central star. Your parent must be Kendar." She watched the AP officers gaping at her. "These are strange times."

"Are you mad?" Peysoon asked.

"Read me." Syreen spread her arms. "Use your mental

73

powers and tell us—do I lie?"

He briefly closed his eyes. When he looked at her again, she sensed a growing understanding in him.

"She tells the truth." He shook his head, then gazed around. "Although I can't fathom how such a genesis can happen, it happened like she said. We were created by stars." He focused on her again. "Syreen, shouldn't Cuarenta be able to tell us more?"

"Yes, why not?" She smiled at him. *Listen with me.*

Next, she closed her eyes and reached out to the local star. *Sing to me.*

Still so sad. Syreen sighed. *We must not linger here for too long.*

"I agree," Peysoon said aloud.

"Agree with what?" Lieutenant Moreton asked.

"We have to leave." Peysoon pointed at her. "I agree with her. There's no time to waste."

The lieutenant shook his head. "Why? What did you learn?"

"I learned how powerful a mind of our people can be—powerful enough to sow life—and yet so helpless against the threats that the universe has in for us."

"What threats? But—how does it work? The genesis, I mean."

The former master grinned. "You put your mind to it, and it *is*. There are no words to explain it."

"And the threats?" Hardincourt repeated Moreton's first question.

Peysoon shrugged. "We yet have to learn about their true nature. But consider how severe a threat must be to cause a star to meddle with the laws of nature and create a sentient lifeform."

The commodore raised his eyebrows. "You say that's against the laws of nature? Your existence?"

Syreen nodded and rose. "Our existence, yes. That's the

gist of what Cuarenta sang to us. But don't ask for details —
stars don't communicate by words, but through their songs,
and those leave a lot to interpretation, at least most of the
time." She walked to the door and stopped there. "I will now
take us to Nysa. If you like, have another drink on my bill
while you're ironing out the kinks in your new regulations."

Chuckles followed her out until the door closed.

Now, partner, let's see how fast we can really go.

— You think it's wise to spend all our power? —

*You were the one telling me it's imperative to help that other ship.
But don't worry, I will not deplete our power. I want to try a new
method.*

CHAPTER SEVENTEEN

Syreen opened her mind to the music around her. There was so much more the stars could tell her!

She reclined in her chair, accepted the pricks, and entered deep integration.

Listen with me, partner. Can you feel it?

— My Navigator! —

Can you feel it?

— Indeed I can. —

That's how we'll do it from now on. Smooth.

Together they entered hyperflight. Reaching out with all their senses, they felt their way forward.

— You're showing me a world beyond my wildest imaginations. It's almost as if the stars were pulling us forward. How is that possible? —

Harmony is the key. Become a part of the melody, and you can basically be everywhere.

— How did you find out? —

I listened to what Cuarenta told Peysoon and me. To be honest, I wouldn't have found out without him — by pulling him into the song, I got a first glimpse of it, subconsciously, so to speak.

— Indeed. How else could we have known? —

Now that we know, I'm wondering. How could we not? It's all about harmony. After all, harmony is what allows us to integrate.

— That's true, and yet . . . Why wasn't I told by my creators? —

Maybe they didn't know in that time? When you were — born? Hatched? What is it?

— That's another fact I don't know. I do not remember the moment of my own creation. One moment, I wasn't, and the next

moment, I was. A complete living ship, self-aware, with a yet small but completely operational body. –

So you became conscious after your body was complete.

– Yes, I already concluded that much. – Assiduous paused briefly. *– I became conscious with a complete body of knowledge, or what I deemed complete back then. –*

Perhaps you got all they could give you back then.

– Of course. But how could they have failed to know? –

Ah, that's the riddle, isn't it? Perhaps we . . . evolved beyond their own capabilities. That's what life is about, isn't it? Evolution.

– That's a valid hypothesis. –

But no more. Unless we find a way to travel back in time and ask them, we can't be sure.

– How will we achieve that? –

What?

– Traveling back in time. You just mentioned it. –

Oh. Sorry, that was meant as a joke. My instructors occasionally mocked me with it – that I'd better have a spare skirmisher in my pocket if I wasn't able to travel back in time and fix my mistakes.

– How can you put a skirmisher into a pocket? –

Syreen chuckled. *Just spread the pocket wide and push it in. It helps if the pocket is lubed.*

– But – oh. –

Their minds echoed with his roaring laughter. For the first time since their departure, she had to focus on keeping their course, but not for long.

Here, that's Nysa.

– Already there. Remarkable. –

They left the hyperplane and emerged from deep integration.

"Nysa harbor authorities, this is Navigator Syreen aboard the living ship *Assiduous,* returning from our mission for Admiral Derfflinger, who I'd like to meet in person as soon as it suits her."

She didn't wait for their reply. Instead, she climbed out of her chair.

That's the downside of fast hyperflights. We're more often separated than together.

— *We're not separated. You are inside me.* —

You know what I mean.

— *You mean the chair. Do we really need it?* —

Syreen shook her head. *For the drip feed, certainly. For deep integration I'd better be in a safe position. For talking, definitely not. Otherwise I'm not sure. And I'm not sure if I want to be without.*

Syreen entered the mess again. Four men interrupted their talk, rose, and stared at her.

The commodore harrumphed. "Navigator, didn't you forget something?"

She paused and followed the four men's gaze down her — nude — body. "Oh."

I forgot.

— *Sorry. I forgot, too. Coming.* —

A chair with her uniform grew from the floor. She took the jacket and slipped inside. Next she pulled up her pants, and then she closed the jacket's zipper. Finally she added her boots.

"Sorry, gentlemen. Old habits."

Hardincourt smiled. "Coming from someone as young as you, that sounds odd. Now — did you postpone departure? We were just discussing your first point — the second edict."

She sensed Peysoon strangely attracted toward her — not sexually, but intellectually — but she couldn't quite recognize it.

"Sorry, guys, but we've just arrived in the Nysa system."

Lieutenant Moreton checked his pad. "But it's been less than a halfcycle!"

"Yes." She spread her arms. "I've found a way to improve hyperflight. Now please, sit down. I've requested a meeting with Admiral Derfflinger, and I don't expect a reply anytime soon. We should have plenty of time."

"Improve hyperflight? But how?" Moreton asked.

"Let's say I called up the hidden trims, okay? With regard to hyperflight, I'm still learning the basics."

Ensign Forsythe smiled, remembering their previous conversation on trims.

The commodore clapped his hands and sat down. "Okay, guys, let's get back to business. The second edict."

Chapter Eighteen

When the expected call came, Syreen felt relieved. For what felt like cycles, the debate had run in circles. She wouldn't get any well-prepared regulation proposals out of these men — that wasn't their kind of business.

"Excuse me." She left them to their discussion of inspection strategies and returned to her bridge.

Put them through.

The female voice sounded excited. "*Assiduous, this is Ensign Rigg, Admiral Derfflinger's personal assistant. I'm calling to schedule the personal meeting with the Admiral that you requested.*"

Syreen smiled. "Ensign Rigg, this is Navigator Syreen aboard *Assiduous*. Thank you very much for calling."

"*Navigator Syreen, would you accept an invitation to Nysa Four? Admiral Derfflinger instructed me to tell you that she took all possible measures to ensure your safety. She also said you probably know best that in the current situation there can't be a hundred percent guarantee.*"

"I understand her very well, Ensign. Tell me — what do you think of the situation on Nysa Four?"

"*What do you mean? I don't understand your question.*"

"Oh, I'm sure you do. I'm sure you were involved in coordinating safety measures. You've been going around, talking with people — probably with people your Admiral won't meet. You surely have your own insight on the current overall situation. Please, share it with me. I won't bite your head off if it turns out incomplete or wrong, I promise."

"*Well . . . I don't know . . .*"

"You're not telling me state secrets, Ensign. We're preparing my visit, remember? I should know where to be diplomatic — not touch sore spots and all."

"*Oh — yes, if you put it that way — well, the chapter thirteen call came as a surprise to many of us, including me, but it was a kind of relief, too. Many of us had felt uncomfortable with the recent developments, especially with the way they treated Admiral Cortez — I assume you've heard about him?*"

"Indeed. Not nice."

"*No, it wasn't.*"

"You witnessed it?"

"*In person. We weren't allowed to look away, so I tried to stare straight through the scene — but that was near impossible. In any case, from that moment on I knew something was very wrong. I wasn't the only one. So there is that. On the other hand, your last battle cost us many good friends — friends who would have felt the same relief, had they been given the chance. Many people are not happy about that, and some say we should demand compensation — or even seek punishment. That's indeed a sore spot, as you call it. But there's also a lot of curiosity — people want to know what's going on, what's coming next, what will happen to the Association.*"

Syreen waited, but the ensign seemed to be finished. "Thank you, Ensign Rigg. Your assessment gives me a clue about what to expect. I'll gladly accept your invitation. Just tell me when and where. I assume Commodore Hardincourt and his team may accompany me? I'm taking their shuttle anyway."

"*That will be okay. The admiral would like to meet you as soon as possible. How much time do you need to make orbit? A tencycle?*"

"Less than a cycle, Ensign. I'm commanding a swift and fast ship."

"*A cycle? That's impossi — oh, of course. Sorry, I forgot. Anything I've been taught is useless with regard to a living ship. Okay — one cycle. We'll be ready.*"

Syreen was looking forward to her meeting with Admiral Derfflinger—and with Ensign Rigg.

Ensign Forsythe's touchdown inside the hangar building on Nysa Four's surface was gentle, and he didn't need long to report a safe tiedown.

Commodore Hardincourt touched her shoulder gently. "After you, Navigator."

She gazed through the open hatch. One older woman with admiral stripes and one young woman—well, about her own age—were flanked by six female marine soldiers on either side. The armored marines were facing away from the center path, their weapons ready.

Syreen paused a moment, but no call to attention came—it seemed to be a sensible move to keep the marines' attention directed at potential threats, not at formalities. She smiled. "Permission to come ashore, Admiral?"

Derfflinger nodded. "Permission granted, Navigator Syreen. Welcome to Nysa. I mean it."

Syreen sensed honesty and stepped forward. "I know."

She waited until Commodore Hardincourt, Lieutenant Moreton and Ensign Forsythe had left the shuttle, too, before walking up to the admiral and saluting smartly.

Admiral Derfflinger smirked when she returned the salute. "Your drill instructor would have been proud."

Syreen made a stern face. "There is harmony in precision."

"Harmony?" The admiral pointed at a rear door. "Interesting concept. Would you come along?"

"Sure."

Derfflinger waited until six marines had taken the lead, and then followed.

"You are cautious." Syreen reached out with her senses. To her own relief, she didn't find the mental emanations of another searcher.

"I should be." The admiral gazed around. "Let me put it

like this—a few people were quite happy with the situation as it was. They were probably profiting in many ways. While I won't blame anyone for welcoming quick promotions, there were opportunities for bribery, blackmail, and abuse of power, and not just with regard to the rules of engagement."

"How far would these people go to preserve their profits?"

"Any length. That's why I'm cautious—and that's why I chose female guards. They can only win from change."

"I see." Syreen sensed a hint of grief. "You were affected, too?"

"Luckily, no, or almost not. The usual hardships any officer candidate suffers, someone peeking into the showers and such, but nothing serious—I couldn't always protect my comrades, though."

"That bad?"

"Once you peel away the shiny skin, there's rot everywhere. *If you want a promotion, spread your legs now.* Where kindly requested sexual favors are the least you'd have to worry about. Some of the senior officers prefer, let's say, darker flavors of erotic."

Syreen felt anger rising behind her.

"I had no clue," Hardincourt said. "That's—that's outrageous. How can such misdemeanor remain unpunished?"

Derfflinger shook her head. "Because the victims were told to keep their mouths shut unless they preferred guard work at the mines—and you may guess what kind of guard work we're talking about. You can't imagine what stories came up during the last tencycle alone."

The Navigator glanced at Ensign Rigg.

The young woman shrugged. "It could have been worse."

Syreen sensed the lie but didn't dig deeper. Perhaps that wound had healed, and if not, she might make it worse.

Instead, she detected a new wave of hatred from ahead—multiple sources, determined and excited. They seemed to be hiding in a side corridor at the next junction.

"Ambush ahead," she snapped.

The marines stopped, crouched and leveled their guns. The admiral moved to cover Syreen. The Navigator let it happen.

Their turf, their call. She watched the marine soldiers advance toward the next corner. *Unless they try something nasty.*

They tried something nasty—a hand appeared, holding a small, tube-like item, and about to toss it. Before the attacker could release his grip, a precise shot from one of the marines hit home. The impact reversed the direction of hand and tube.

When the grenade exploded, most of its deadly content affected the side corridor. The few pieces of shrapnel ricocheting their way couldn't penetrate the marines' armor.

"Advance!" one of the marines shouted, and the six soldiers dashed forward.

There was no fighting. They just had to arrest three severely injured and stunned surviving attackers and collect a further five dead bodies.

A centicycle later, a marine sergeant stepped up before them and saluted to the admiral and then to Syreen.

"Admiral, Navigator—the current situation is cleared. May I propose that we leave soon? If this ambush was meant to delay us, we shouldn't waste time."

Derfflinger nodded. "I concur, Master Sergeant Rosner. Navigator?"

Syreen smiled. "This is sound advice. May I say that I admired your precise shot, Master Sergeant?"

The marine mirrored her smile. "Your praise is welcome. May I say that I'm infinitely grateful for your warning? How did you notice the ambush?"

"You may. I sensed their presence."

"A kind of premonition, eh?"

"I think you could call it so."

The sergeant nodded. "Okay. Let's move."

CHAPTER NINETEEN

When the small group reached a heavily armed door, Syreen sensed relief in their escort, and in the admiral, too.

"We've made it," Derfflinger said and held her palm against a sensor on the wall. The door opened with a hiss. "In one piece, and no further surprises. I'm glad."

"Would you have expected stronger opposition?" Syreen asked.

The admiral hesitated and glanced past her. "Lieutenant Moreton, what's your assessment?"

"My assessment? Oh—Admiral—well . . ." The junior officer fought for his composure.

"Come on. I want your professional assessment. I will add mine, but I want you to be unbiased, that's why you are first. So?"

Syreen gave him an encouraging and calming mental nudge. She was curious herself what he would say.

"Okay." Moreton licked his lips. "The ambush wasn't entirely unexpected. We had to assume opposition, even armed opposition once chapter thirteen was invoked. Partially from factions supporting the former government at any cost, partially from factions misjudging the current situation or simply being confused. The ambush had to be planned on short notice, the opposing forces had to be deployed on even shorter notice. With regard to all this, they seemed to be well prepared and sufficiently strong in numbers." He frowned. "There are three—no, four—basic options. One—they were incredibly lucky to guess or pick the right place. Two—your destination and choice of route was easily calculable, which would not match your reputation. Three—the opposition was able to muster enough teams to cover most of our possible routes, which would mean at least one or two teams should have followed us. Four—someone talked."

Derfflinger nodded. "Smart. Like your decision to send the Navigator to me. Yes, I came to the same conclusion. We must have a leak."

"And it was no one from our team." The lieutenant waved around. "They were all surprised by the ambush."

"You found time to watch them?" The admiral chuckled.

"Of course. I couldn't risk breaking the marines' formation, so I had to stand back."

"You are a wise man," Master Sergeant Rosner commented, struggling to hide her impatience. "And wouldn't it be a wise move to get inside now?"

"No, of course not." Moreton pointed at the door. "If we were sold out, the perfect place for a trap would be right there—where we're trying to seek cover, where we're entitled to feel safe, after surviving an ambush devised as a distraction." He turned to Derfflinger. "Admiral, unless you know the traitor and remember what you told him or her and what not, we have to assume this place is compromised, too."

The marine sergeant stared at him—for a moment, then she nodded. "Okay. In that case, we should pick a new location that's on no one's bill. Ideas, anyone?"

Syreen could sense their minds racing. One of the marine soldiers seemed to be too shy to speak up, though. The Navigator glanced at the marine's name tag. "Corporal Monner, what's on your mind?"

The addressed marine snapped to attention. "Sir, yes, Sir. I was considering the old briefing room."

"Which old briefing room?" Rosner asked.

Monner didn't even turn her head. "Our drill sergeant occasionally took us to an old, abandoned briefing room to show us some special tricks. No recording equipment, poor ventilation, poor lighting—and no chance visitors."

Rosner glanced at the admiral and received a nod. "Okay, Corporal, lead the way. Assume hostile territory ahead."

"Sir, yes, Sir!" From one moment to the next, she dropped from her ramrod posture to an attentive guarding stance, leveled her rifle and advanced to the tip of their formation.

Rosner followed at her elbow, then the next four marines fell in line.

Derfflinger smiled at Syreen. "I'm amazed how you managed to pick just the right soldier."

"It's basically the same as picking the recruit who's up to mischief. You can read it in one's face." *And that's not even a lie.*

"You've been dealing with recruits?"

"Of course. As one of the Duchy's best pilots, I was supposed to offer advice."

"I wonder what became of them."

For a moment, Syreen recalled some of their faces. "They were blown into space by your dreadnaughts' missiles."

"I'm sorry . . . such are the worst facets of war, aren't they?"

Syreen stopped and faced the admiral. "There was no declaration of war. No warning for the civilians on our space stations."

"But—surely the commanding officer had sent an announcement . . ."

"Admiral Cornelius Ravenport did not announce his intentions, nor did any of his subordinates correct his misstep. They just came to kill. It was another of those atrocities that ultimately led to the violations of the second edict—a deep-rooted foulness in your Navy. Keep that in mind when we discuss proper disciplinary action."

"Ravenport. Okay, but he's not typical —"

"Don't fool yourself," Syreen snapped. "He was promoted to admiral. Thus, his conduct, personality, and performance matched the AP Navy's standards. The same applies to Santiago. They're genuine products of your system, and as admirals, they are beacons that stand out and represent your navy. I'd accept a mistaken promotion for a lieutenant, perhaps even for a captain, but definitely not for a flag officer." She pointed forward and continued to follow the marines. "However, I do recognize that the AP also managed to promote many decent officers to flag rank."

"Most of our officers are decent men and women," Derfflinger objected.

"Yes, they are. And yet, many of those decent men and women sailed out with your fleet to perform punitive action against civilian targets." Syreen decided against mentioning inspections at this moment. *No need to rub it all in.*

The admiral remained silent, radiating embarrassment.

"However, I found many of them ready to follow your chapter thirteen order," the Navigator added. "They were misdirected — too easily."

"I'm glad you see it that way."

"Don't get me wrong. I'm here to guide you to harmony, not to retaliate."

"Harmony. You mentioned that before."

Syreen nodded. They continued their walk in silence.

CHAPTER TWENTY

In Syreen's eyes, the old briefing room lived up to its repu-tation—the description was spot on. No technical equip-ment, stuffy air, dim lighting, fading colors, specks on floor and walls, dusty corners. The neatly aligned tables and chairs with their polished surfaces formed a stark contrast.

Someone had clear priorities. Pragmatic.

After a quick but thorough inspection, Rosner and Monner left the room to organize their forces outside.

Ensign Rigg gave Ensign Forsythe a nudge, and they began to rearrange two tables and six chairs into boardroom style.

Rigg then invited the admiral to one end of the table and the Navigator to the other and took the chair to the right of her superior. Commodore Hardincourt ended up at Syreen's right, Lieutenant Moreton at her left, so that Forsythe faced Rigg.

"I think we can skip formal introductions," Derfflinger be-gan. "Navigator Syreen, thank you for accepting our invita-tion—which has already been proven quite dangerous, and we owe you for your guidance through our troubled waters."

Syreen smiled. "Nicely put."

"Let me say—we were glad to see you return unharmed, but we didn't expect you so soon—you didn't reach many worlds, then?"

"We did. Let me provide you with a summary of our round trip, and Commodore Hardincourt, Lieutenant Moreton and Ensign Forsythe can add their insights on the overall situation out there. Perhaps you can brief us on the current status in the

Nysa system, and thereafter I'd like to recap the events that ultimately led to the embargo." Syreen glanced around. "From that common ground, we can sketch the changes needed toward raising the embargo."

The admiral shook her head. "Now? Do you think we're the right people to make such decisions—even if we had the authority, which we haven't?"

"That's what I came for, yes." Syreen gestured around. "To discuss the rules that have to be added to your regulations and shape their wording. After that, you'll find the right people to ratify the amendments and submit them to the guild. Yes, I'm sure we have the right people—from junior to flag officer, male and female. If you like, call one of the enlisted marines in."

"That would actually be a good idea," Hardincourt said. "I'd recommend Corporal Monner, for two reasons. Firstly, she'll feel comfortable in this room, and secondly, she already dared to speak up once. Overall, she might be less reluctant to share her insights with us."

"I agree." Derfflinger glanced right. "Ensign Rigg, would you please ask Master Sergeant Rosner if she can spare Corporal Monner, and then ask the corporal if she'd like to join us. You may explain our reasoning to them, and that we'd really like to have representatives from all rank categories helping to shape our future."

"Yes, sir." The young officer quickly left.

Syreen rose next and fetched another chair to place it to her left. "I don't really need a table."

Shortly later, the ensign returned with the corporal. Monner was radiating a mix of awe and pride, but she managed to maintain her professional attitude when she sat down between Syreen and Moreton.

"Thank you for joining us." Syreen gave her an encouraging smile and another gentle mental nudge to help her calm down. "Now, let me start with a quick debrief of my trip. We started at Vigo . . ."

Chapter Twenty-One

Syreen nodded toward Ensign Forsythe, the last of her guests to bear witness to their round-trip. "Thank you for your insights, too."

"Thank you all." Admiral Derfflinger gazed around the table. "Those were most remarkable insights indeed. Of course, those officers not complying with my orders worry me, but I'm relieved that so many of those who sailed out recognized their fault and willingly returned to reason. That's certainly something to build on." She tapped the table. "I must apologize — this would be an opportunity for a toast. We took care of drinks in the original place, but not here."

"Of course." The Navigator smiled. "In that case, we should move on to the next topic, shouldn't we?"

"Sure." Derfflinger took a deep breath. "The current situation here on Nysa. It's difficult. Obviously, the government wasn't happy about my invocation of chapter thirteen. They immediately issued a warrant and requested my arrest. So far, they've played more or less by the rules. But they also ordered the navy to ignore my order and make this infamous coup fail — their words, not mine."

"You're not arrested, that much is clear." This time, Syreen didn't smile.

"No. Aside from what we were talking about before — misconduct, Cortez's execution, and the cases of corruption — most officers were appalled by the *punitive action* order. You probably eliminated those who'd have complied with it by taking out the dreadnaughts. As a result, the majority of commissioned officers will follow chapter thirteen and will stand back until the current crisis is resolved. They might feel forced to act against me should I fail to follow procedures, but so far, no one can complain in that regard."

"There were a few boneheads," Ensign Rigg chimed in. "Calling in, yelling, cursing, name-calling, you can imagine."

"Sorry you got all the heat." The admiral shook her head.

Rigg shrugged. "Well—yes, I did, but the heat was meant for you, so I could bear it personally. I applied the rules from the de-escalation courses and accepted their rants, thanked them for calling, and apologized for you being offline so that I couldn't put them through. However, I also dealt with them formally and forwarded the recordings to personnel."

Hardincourt laughed out loud. "Oh, that will teach them!" He turned to Syreen. "We've discussed conduct before, with regard to your requests—it still makes a difference whether you dress down a junior officer or an admiral. Insults against a flag officer are a major offense."

Syreen frowned. "Yes, I think we'll come to that later." She turned to the admiral again. "Go on."

Derfflinger shook her head. "That's basically the situation. We don't have much intel yet. Due to the chapter thirteen issue, I'm kind of out of the loop. My officers support that act, and in that way, they still support me. However, they insist on being neutral, and I told them I support that, too. Should I be found guilty of treason or such, the department must remain operational."

"And as her assistant, I'm out, too," Rigg added.

"What about you, Corporal Monner?" Syreen asked.

The marine sat up straight. "Me?"

"What's the talk of the day in the barracks?" Syreen grinned. "There's always a hot topic, and these days, I'd expect we're high up on that list."

"Oh, sure, that's true." The corporal eased, even without another supportive nudge. "Our officers gave us a summary of what chapter thirteen is about, and the sergeant said it's more important than ever to stick to the rules. But it's hard now—there are orders to be followed and orders to be ignored, and how are we supposed to know which is which? Use your guts, the Master Sergeant said. If the orders sound fishy, discard them. If they sound sensible, follow them. And once you commit to a course of action, stick with it. Well, there's a lot of talk about it, and the gist of it is—past events were very fishy. Chapter thirteen—what we were told about it—sounds very sensible in comparison. The overall consent is to maintain order and let the process go on." She gazed at Syreen. "I'd say we—female enlisted—are really eager to see change with regard to male conduct, and maybe that separates us. The guys see their opportunities fading, so they might be easier to misguide. I think it was a smart move to employ only female marines for this meeting."

"It was." Syreen nodded. "Any other insights?"

"Yes. I think nobody mentioned it before—what people know and what they say about you. Perhaps some of our leaders—the bad ones—made a mistake there, or some of the good guys tricked them, but everyone knows that you let Cortez go after what the AP did at Klondike. So, aside from the worst boneheads, most people understand that you're not our enemy, at least not personally. You're fighting us if you have to, and you're fighting hard, but because you're outnumbered, not out of cruelty. That's what people say."

Syreen felt touched. "Thank you, Corporal Monner."

"I second that," Ensign Rigg said. "People trust you. You say you'll raise the embargo once we return to the rules, and people believe that. They say you'll be fair."

"I will."

"Harmony." Admiral Derfflinger smiled. "Now I understand what you mean when you talk about it—you're creating harmony. Even within our ranks, even when you're not here."

Chapter Twenty-Two

Syreen gazed around the table. She saw curiosity and worries and still well-controlled impatience. *Yes, I feel the same.*

She nodded. "Okay, let's come to my requirements. Note — these are just *my* requirements. Once these are met, I will recommend lifting the embargo to the guild. The yet-to-be-established guild tribunal may raise their own concerns. I will not overrule them."

Admiral Derfflinger returned her nod. "I understand."

"Good. Another formal point — we, my people, must be able to do our duties as enforcers of the edicts. To that end, we need free travel within the Association."

Derfflinger and Hardincourt looked at each other. When the admiral nodded, the commodore spoke up. "You could say we already granted you free travel before, when we asked you to recall some of our units. Consider that one settled."

"Great. Now — I've mentioned my basic requirements to Commodore Hardincourt before. He and his officers had a chance to discuss them. I will nevertheless list them again — after I quoted the edicts, which are not subject to negotiation. Ready?"

No one objected.

The Navigator began. "Edict Number One — proscribes deliberate damage of the fabric of space, like actions that could create a rift, or destruction of living stars. Edict Number Two — proscribes deliberate destruction, sterilization or rendering uninhabitable of worlds, especially, but not limited to, kinetic strikes, large-scale application of nuclear or biological weapons, and systematic destruction of geological stability. Edict Number Three — proscribes deliberate interference with the genetic code of intelligent beings." She checked her audience and found them waiting. "Okay — the third edict is about experiments like Gattaca. You may check that one later. Violations of the second edict were what brought us together here and now."

"And such actions are already illegal," the admiral said.

"But that didn't stop Santiago," Hardincourt objected.

"No." Derfflinger sighed and focused on the Navigator. "But what do you expect from us then?"

Syreen didn't evade her gaze. "For an Enforcer like *Assiduous* — my ship — the solution is easy. The sanctions match the crime. Ultimately, a star nation failing the edicts will be erased."

"Erased?" Rigg exclaimed. "But — how?"

"I think I mentioned it before. We command the means to turn your star into a supernova."

The ensign gasped.

Syreen nodded. "Yes. The result would be nothing but slag. No survivor. And no, I'm not asking you to put such measures into your regulations. But I believe this kind of crime requires capital punishment for the culprit and all active supporters. And, as I already told Hardincourt, those who punish a brave officer opposing such a crime must be held accountable, too."

She focused on Ensign Rigg. "Consider a situation — you and your captain on the bridge. Your captain is about to violate an edict and you stop him. The penalty for mutiny is severe, but charging you with mutiny would be wrong, as it would support the violation. Such a thing must not happen. Your regulations should protect the good officers, not the bullies. Should protect you, in this case."

The Commodore leaned forward. "Moreton, Forsythe and

I found some suitable passages in our regulations that just need a little stricter wording. Those paragraphs about retaliation against whistleblowers and such — we should make clear that protection of the edicts comes before written orders, and before the line of command."

Admiral Derfflinger nodded. "That might cause our legal staff some headaches, but I totally agree with the rationale. I'd say, consider this issue settled."

This time, Syreen put on a stern face. "I will consider this issue settled once Cortez's executioner has been dealt with." She gave them a moment to recognize that she meant it. "However, with regard to the regulation changes, I agree."

The admiral smiled and nodded. "You've got me there. Of course, certain recent events have to be reevaluated. You may be sure Cortez's trial and sentence are top of the list. However, these legal procedures will require diligence and patience."

"Oh, okay. Of course, that's an important argument — I'll regard this case as independent of the embargo issue, okay?"

"I'm glad you agree." Derfflinger took a deep breath. "Shall we go on to the next point?"

"Sure." Syreen winked at the commodore. "Let's get to the hard one."

Hardincourt smiled. "You won't like it."

"I'm curious."

But the admiral seemed to be relaxed for the moment.

Syreen knew that could change soon, depending on how she played her part. "The hard one is about the first edict."

"But we never failed that!" Derfflinger shook her head. "We don't even know how to damage the fabric of space."

"Correct. You don't know how, so you could never deliberately violate the edict. Nevertheless, you're damaging it, ultimately creating regions like the rift — or the chasm."

"The *chasm?*"

"Yes. It's man-made, the result of too many too reckless low-quality jumps." Syreen leaned forward. "Let me explain. Consider you'd need to mend a seam of your uniform. What kind of tool would you use?"

"Mend a seam—you mean, like a recruit? With needle and thread?"

"Exactly. Now consider the same recruit using a knife."

"No, that wouldn't do any good."

"Correct—it would do more damage. So, what if I told you that a six-sigma jump is like a needle and a four-sigma is like a knife?"

"If it were so, I'd agree that a knife-jump is a bad idea."

"It is so. That's one of the things I can't prove easily, though. Your instruments can't record the difference." Syreen noticed a signal. "Yes, Commodore?"

"Beg your pardon, Navigator, I must object. I've had a little time to think about this topic, and now I'd say our instruments can indeed record the difference. Firstly, our instruments not only tell us how good a jump should be, but also how good it really was once we did it, and we can tell the difference between the sigma levels very well. Secondly, we know that lower levels cause strain on the emitters as well as drain our capacitors. We know for sure that we're indeed fighting some kind of resistance, and that we're forcing our way through."

Syreen watched the admiral.

Derfflinger had raised an eyebrow. "Go on, Commodore."

Hardincourt smiled. "Thirdly, we record the entry shocks of other ships' jumps. Again, lower sigma levels cause more powerful shocks, so that's another indication of force applied—in space, where we shouldn't meet resistance at all. I'd say, perhaps we can't prove the damage itself, but we must conclude that there's something we're applying our force against."

The admiral cocked her head. "I never thought of it this way, but okay, it adds credit to the Navigator's claim." She turned to Syreen. "Don't get me wrong — I accept your authority on this topic, but we must consider how to explain your requests to our future superiors."

"Thank you, Admiral." Syreen turned to Hardincourt. "Commodore, thank you, too. That's brilliant."

Hardincourt shrugged. "The least I could do."

Admiral Derfflinger folded her hands. "So I assume you want us to do six-sigma jumps only?"

"Where possible, yes." Syreen put on her stern face again. "You, the Navy, are the professionals. Discipline is your dominant trait, negligence isn't acceptable. Why should poor navigation be acceptable? I expect experienced navigators to do the best possible jumps. Instead of forcing a way through between obstacles, they should jump around them. I'll gladly provide examples, like for the Eiffel-Colossus-Nysa route. I expect junior navigators to learn about the trims and apply what they learned. I do not demand punishments for mistakes or emergencies, but I expect due diligence." She smiled. "In return, you save on maintenance."

For a moment, they all stared at her — and then burst out in roaring laughter.

Once the admiral had recollected herself, still with a tear in her eye, she spread her arms wide. "Are you sure you're in the right profession? You'd probably be a prolific merchant."

Syreen nodded. "I've been told the same by several merchants before. As you're in the intelligence business, you're probably aware of the circumstances that resulted in my second and third nomination as star angel."

Derfflinger glanced at Ensign Rigg, then at Hardincourt. Both made a puzzled face and shrugged.

"No. You are a star angel?" She frowned. "Wait — you said, *third* nomination?"

"I did. You didn't know?"

"To my shame I have to admit that I didn't—well, I've heard about a star angel—the first in generations—and that our offices were supposed to report any news about her, but I didn't make the connection. Let me put it like this—it was quite far down my watchlist."

"So you never heard about a school of haulers crossing the rift?"

"I did. That was an extraordinary event, as the rift and the region around was infamous for its pirate infestation."

"Indeed. I had to shoot a few pirates. Let me give you a brief on the whole story." She glanced around and found no disapproval. "I had just captured a frigate and rescued a flock of entertainers from Gattaca—yes, Ensign Rigg?"

"That was you, too? The one who blew up Gattaca Orbital?"

"No. That was Major Baker. I was supposed to be blown up with it, but I got away in time. Baker also was the one who left the girls to their fate on the Gattaca surface and then took the only shuttle—which forced me to go down with a frigate to get them out."

"With a frigate?" Moreton asked.

"Yes. Gammon class frigate *Bumblebee,* formerly AP Navy, now Duchy Fleet. I took her down in one piece, collected the girls and merchant crew I had arrived with, and left. However, now I had a lot of hungry mouths to feed. So I decided to offer escort services to merchants on Corfu, and, with the aid of my staff captain—former merchant skipper—I scheduled a route for them that optimized their profit and brought me closer to my final destination—Klondike."

"Ah—the battle." Derfflinger nodded. "But you didn't fight that battle with the frigate."

"No—I rejoined with my living ship there. But before, I fought some pirates with that frigate—including a team that had already captured the haulers *Athabasca* and *Veronica's Smile,* held their crews captive, and shot at me from their cargo bays."

Her audience had stopped breathing.

"I shot the gun and bridge of *Athabasca,* the gun of *Veronica's Smile,* and then I boarded *Veronica's Smile* and caught the pirates." The memory made her frown. "I returned possession to the original owners. By providing their jump solutions, we could even take *Athabasca* along—the damaged bridge could be repaired on Harmony. *Veronica's* captain issued the third registration there."

"Harmony again—how appropriate." Admiral Derfflinger nodded. "Another occasion where you restored harmony, and what could be a better place than a planet of the same name?"

She frowned when she noticed Syreen's grim face.

"That place doesn't deserve its name," the Navigator said. "It's the worst cesspit I ever visited."

When she started reporting her observations, she found her audience clenching their fists and teeth.

"One day I'll go there and clean up," she finished.

"Take me along," Corporal Monner said. "Sorry, Admiral—now that I've heard that story, I can't sit on my butt and ignore it."

"No, you can't," Derfflinger replied with a trembling voice. "I can't even say it's not our business. It must be made someone's business. Just not here, not now, not until we did what we came here for."

The marine corporal took a deep breath. "No, okay, but . . ."

Syreen placed one hand on her shoulder. "I already made it my business. Once I'm ready to go there, I'll return and ask for volunteers, and I hope your supreme command will then grant you a leave."

"Count me in," Monner said.

"Me too," Derfflinger said.

"Me too," Rigg said.

"If guys may come—" Moreton began.

"Sorry, no." The admiral smiled. "Thank you for volunteering, but this must be a ladies-only operation. The victims won't trust a man, no matter how honest his intentions are."

Hardincourt raised a hand. "We can provide fleet cover. Agreed—they shouldn't see men, but you still need all the support you can get."

Derfflinger nodded slowly. "Valid point. Okay, agreed."

She focused on Syreen. "Back to our agenda. Number one—strict rulings on violations of the edicts. Number two—strict best-effort jump quality. Which are the next?"

The Navigator smiled. "You might like this one. Strict enforcement of good conduct with regard to female crew members, whether navy or merchant, including those called ship cats. No excuses—anyone abusing a female crew member of an inspected merchant will be spaced without suit, together with his skipper."

That caused Derfflinger and Rigg to raise their eyebrows.

"Together with his skipper?" the admiral asked.

"Yes, together with his skipper. Because the skipper failed to make clear what conduct he expects of his crew, and failed to enforce it. I mean it. And in case there's a disagreement on what happened, the inspection crew has to prove their innocence, so they'd better provide untampered-with recordings of their inspection."

"That's harsh."

"You've neglected your rules of conduct for too long. Now it's time for a firm hand to reestablish them. What I'm requesting is a strict no-nonsense ruling. No leeway, no second chances. This is different from the hyperjump topic, because every man already knows what's right and what's wrong. So they're told once, and if they still think it's a game, they pay the price. As I said — together with their superiors." She leaned forward. "There will be only one way to be sure — the skippers must join their inspection teams until everyone understands they're serious. You may hammer out the details as you deem fit, but if you don't punish misconduct, I'll do it myself."

Admiral Derfflinger nodded slowly, and then closed her eyes for a moment. "Well, yes." Her gaze wandered from Rigg to Monner to Syreen. "Personally, I sympathize with your request. Professionally, I have to admit our failures and accept the responsibility you're putting in our hands. Yes, there's urgent need for change. I just can't see a way to implement it properly."

"Nor can I," Hardincourt shrugged.

"You don't have an inspector general?" Syreen asked.

"What's that?" Forsythe asked.

Lieutenant Moreton leaned forward. "I think I've heard that term before. Do you have an inspector general at the Duchy?"

Syreen shook her head. "No more. He was blasted away by your fleet together with our orbital." She laughed bitterly. "It doesn't matter. There's no one left to inspect anyway."

The Lieutenant lowered his gaze. "I'm sorry. I forgot."

"I won't forget." She waved her hand and focused on Derfflinger. "We're not here to mourn the past, we're here to shape the future. I will provide you with the respective sections of the Duchy's Books. Use what you like."

"That's very generous of you. Are you authorized to release that information?"

"Of course I am." Syreen smiled. "I'm still their Fleet Commander in Charge. In my eyes, rules for maintaining good conduct aren't confidential, moreover, providing you with the best procedures for good conduct is for everyone's benefit."

The admiral smiled back. "Wise. So we've got almost all we need."

"Almost?"

"Almost. We still need an editor to iron out the kinks in the new regulations, and then a new government to ratify them."

"I'm sure you'll do that. Meanwhile, I'll find you a guild tribunal." She turned to Hardincourt. "Commodore, may I borrow your shuttle once again?"

He nodded. "Keep it as long as you need it."

CHAPTER TWENTY-THREE

Syreen slowly lowered herself into her pilot seat. She barely felt the pricks in legs and neck while enjoying the sweet reunion with *Assiduous's* main connector.

— You feel satisfied. —

I feel successful. We made another step toward harmony.

— We need another step toward finding that ship. —

I didn't forget. I can no longer postpone returning home, though. I have a responsibility to the people who raised me.

— I agree. You must get rid of that burden. —

She sighed. *Yes.*

— You brought the shuttle with you. It is a useful tool. If we keep it, should I improve it? —

I'm not sure what that means, but yes, please do so. We can't repair Raydancer, *can we?*

— No. The little ship was very helpful, but it's too severely damaged. However, I didn't assimilate it yet as you seem to have some affection for it. —

It might deserve a place in a museum — for people to remember these events.

— You seem to be tired. —

I am very tired. The conversation was nice and constructive, but they were reluctant to let me go.

— I could have helped you to escape. —

No, no, it wasn't about forcing me to stay. Hugs and wishes and everything — it was an emotional and rather lengthy goodbye.

— I'll never understand these illogical peculiarities of livestock behavior. —

Syreen chuckled. *Nor will I. What about our guest?*

— He's sleeping. —

Lucky one. I could use a nap, too.

— You could take a nap while I'm recharging. Before we do another high speed trip, I should replenish my resources, too. —

Oh. Okay, let's find a strong sun and do that first.

Part Two—Experience

CHAPTER TWENTY-FOUR

Syreen felt refreshed and relieved. She stretched her limbs and yawned. Her gaze fell on a golden ceiling.

I can't remember going to my bedroom.

— You didn't. I moved you here. —

Oh. Thank you.

She felt a gentle song fading from her mind. The lone star was listed as *Relay Forty-seven* in the AP star catalogue. Its true name resonated through its song.

If Peysoon is awake now, ask him if he'd like to join me for breakfast.

There was a brief pause. *— He will be delighted to meet you in the mess. —*

Fine. I'll be there in five.

After a quick visit to the shower, she felt ready to meet the challenges the universe might have in store for her. A short walk led her to the mess.

Her prisoner or guest looked up upon her arrival. His smile widened. "What a beautiful way to brighten my day. Good morning, my dear lady Navigator." He rose and bowed, but didn't take his gaze off her.

Oh. Only now did she realize she hadn't bothered to fetch her uniform. *Well, he'd better get used to it.* She smiled and curtsied. "Good morning, my most welcome guest."

He raised both eyebrows. "Thank you."

She sensed his confusion and curiosity. More important was what she didn't sense—malice and mischief were gone. "Peysoon."

"Yes?"

"I have no time for holding grudges. History will judge the past. I will shape the future. What will you do?"

"I . . . uh." He spread his arms. "I don't know what this means, but . . . I . . . yes." He went to attention and saluted. "I'm in. Lead me, and I will follow."

She casually returned the salute — after all, she was still naked. "No."

"No?" There was a taste of disappointment in his mind.

"No. If you want to join my cause, you'll have to do more than follow. I need team spirit."

And here I surprised you again. She smiled.

"Oh." A smile crept into his gaze, then onto his lips. "I fear I'm not used to that team issue, but I can do spirit. I'll try my best."

"That's all I can ask for." She sensed something else. "Yes?"

Peysoon stood straight. "You're accepting me readily — shouldn't you have some reservations, for what I did in the past, even to you personally?"

Syreen nodded. "You're right, I should, and I do have reservations. I haven't forgotten or forgiven what you did to me and others. But I'm over it, and, as I said before, I'm willing to leave it behind and look forward. You won't remind me of the past, in words or deeds, and I won't bring it up, either. From today, I'll judge you for what you are now. Deal?" She held out her hand.

He hesitated, then accepted the offer and shook her hand. "Deal."

A moment later, he let go and cocked his head. "That wasn't what you came for."

"No. Actually, I came for breakfast."

"Yes. Indeed, that was what *Assiduous* mentioned."

"And I wanted to talk with you about our plans."

"*Our* plans?"

"Yes. You had a mission. That other ship. It's *our* mission now, and we should discuss how we approach it once I'm relieved of my other duties."

"Other duties?"

CHAPTER TWENTY-FIVE

Syreen watched the slender frigate gently setting down on *Assiduous's* hangar floor. Deep bruises on its surface betrayed the impression of careful handling.

A while later, a familiar face with a wide smile appeared at the outer hatch. "Permission to come aboard, Fleet Commander?"

"Permission granted, Yusef."

The pilot ignored the steps and jumped down, took a few steps and hugged her. "Good to see you in one piece."

She returned the hug. "I could say the same. You didn't go easy on *Bumblebee,* did you?"

He released the hug but held her hands. "Well, you know how it is — one AP battle group commander wasn't really willing to listen to reason, so we had to do something about it."

"That's why I left half of the Crown ships with you."

"Yesss — but, you know, you also told them you expected some distractions. So I told them I'd be fine with a couple of Fianna stingships, and, well, the three of us together did quite fine."

"Did fine? One frigate and two stingships against a battle cruiser?"

"Ah, but they didn't know that we were so few. We did a few intrasystem jumps and made them believe there were multiple units coming for them."

"Yet still comparably small units."

"*Bumblebee* is still a small vessel, yes. But *Assiduous* and Haiki added some improvements on our return trip from

Crown. Improvements to power, to precision, to speed — and to firepower. It's more like a Fumigator now. So what the AP believed they were seeing were half a dozen ships of unknown class with the firepower of a heavy cruiser, too fast and too small to hit. After a few instructive scratches, they were eager to strike sails."

Mo appeared behind Yusef. "Yusef was making miracles happen and scaring the shit out of them. When the AP commander called, you could see the fear in his eyes and hear it in his voice."

Syreen gave him a hug, too. "What happened to them?"

"Oh, we sent them home. We were confident you'd solved the situation there by the time they arrived." Mo gave her a nudge and waved to the back of the hangar. "You finally got yourself a shuttle, eh? Borrowed?"

"An AP gift."

"Really? Part of the deal?"

"I'll tell you later. What about our girls?"

Mo frowned. "Somewhat bored. Kyris Orbital has become a rather dull place after you put the local muscle in their place. They won't let us go dirtside, so we're kind of stuck here. Not that I'd complain, okay?" He smiled again. "We had a lot of excitement before, so I can appreciate dull for a while."

"But it's time to move on." Syreen pointed at the shuttle. "I'll pay my visit to Lord Hakon and to Jacomo, and then I'll go home."

"Home?" Yusef asked.

"The Duchy. The closest to a home I ever had. It's time to return there." She smiled at them. "Where's Haiki?"

"Fixing things, I guess." Mo's face mirrored her smile. "He might have missed our arrival here. Yusef's piloting is way too smooth."

"Okay. I'll find him. Make yourself comfortable."

Chapter Twenty-Six

W hile approaching Kyris Orbital's shuttle dock, Syreen's thoughts kept returning to her old crew. When she had first met them, they had been shipping frozen entertainers to their doom. Now they were one of the finest crews she had ever met in manners, skills, and professional attitude. Of course, Haiki wouldn't have left his repairs unfinished even for a minute to welcome her. Only after he had reapplied the last seal did he hug her firmly.

Oh yes, fine men they've become. Men I can be proud to work with.

— Men you can be proud to have led on the right track. —

Oh, you're still with me, partner.

— Of course. You will not roam this station alone. —

There are no more chimeras aboard. We would sense them.

— Together, we would. That's why I'm with you. —

Syreen let it stand.

When the shuttle was docked, she rose and checked her uniform, once again in Duchy green, with a burgundy beret. She found no reason for even the most critical drill sergeant to complain.

Her senses told her of an unusually high number of people waiting for her in the docking area. Many of them felt familiar.

The outer hatch opened.

People had formed two double lines—Duchy marines to her left, Kyris guards to her right. Two men and a woman were waiting at the far end. She recognized Guild Secretary

113

Jacomo in the center and Lord Hakon at his right side, but not the woman at the end of the Kyris lines.

A sudden whistle caught her by surprise, then the stomping of marines' and guards' feet when they went to attention in perfect synchronicity, followed by a loud "Ooray!" that made the walls vibrate.

So we're formal today, huh?

Syreen placed her heels together, left hand to her left leg, right hand to her beret, chin up, and froze. She allowed the tension in her audience to accumulate for a while, then she took her right hand down, nodded at the column leaders on both sides, and marched forward.

Jacomo smiled and nodded. "Welcome back to Kyris, Navigator Syreen." He glanced to his right. "Of course, you know your ambassador, Lord Hakon." The secretary turned left and gestured at the woman. "May I introduce to you the most honorable Minister of Foreign Affairs, Her Royal Highness Antaria Vod Merodion of Kyris."

Syreen didn't need his brief wink to recognize this as extremely unusual for Kyris. Whether it was the woman's suntanned complexion or the subconscious unease that she showed in her brief glances to bulkheads or roof—she was clearly no spacer. Syreen was still considering what to say when Her Royal Highness went on her knee.

"We are infinitely honored by the presence of a Navigator of the People. We can only apologize for not having welcomed you during your previous visits, which is due to our failure of leaving instructions on how to advise us about it."

The Navigator shook her head and held out her hands. "Please rise, Your Highness. Show me your respect by meeting me on eye level, so I can show you mine."

The Kyris aristocrat rose with a smile and took the offered hands. "Thank you, Navigator. We are just starting to recognize your dedication to—to . . ."

"Harmony."

"Harmony—oh yes, what a marvelous way to describe you. It truly matches your reputation as a threefold star angel." The royal minister insinuated a bow, then straightened herself and raised her voice. "May Our voice be made heard all around Kyris. The members of the parliament unanimously agreed to Our proposal as follows. This is our decision—from today, the most honorable Navigator Syreen of the People, together with her companion, the most honorable Enforcer of the Edicts *Assiduous,* shall be irrevocably granted unrestricted access to planetary Kyris, whenever and wherever they like."

Multiple gasps and wheezes from the audience around followed.

Syreen sensed shock in most of the Kyris natives and utter surprise in Lord Hakon and the secretary. She felt a bit shaken herself. From her previous visits she knew the attitude of the Kyris people toward strangers—they strongly disliked any visitors to the surface. All contacts, for trade or diplomacy, were handled on Kyris Orbital, unless someone like the AP ignored the rules and simply bullied their way to the surface. So this was probably the most generous gift Kyris could offer her.

She bowed. "I'm feeling truly honored. *Assiduous* and I will diligently consider the necessity before intruding on you."

"No."

The firmness of this single word made her flinch. Should she have politely declined the offer?

"No." The Kyris woman squeezed her hands. "No, Navigator—it was meant as I said it. You are welcome to Kyris any time. For leisure, recreation, to enjoy the solitude of our mountains and seas, or to mingle among our people. Do not burden yourself with considerations—just come. As a friend."

Syreen took a deep breath. Then she slightly shook their hands. "As a friend. In that case, Your Highness, please just call me Syreen, without fancy titles."

Realization dawned on the aristocratic face. "Syreen. My name is—I am Antaria."

"Antaria." Syreen opened her mind to Kyris's song, just to enjoy the moment. The star cheered upon her touch, and subconsciously she opened her mind even further.

Antaria's eyes widened, then filled with tears.

Syreen managed to catch her new friend before Antaria could collapse on the floor. Thus summoned back to local reality, her connection to Kyris's song faded into the background.

She looked around. The people around her had wet faces, too.

Lord Hakon was the first to speak up. "That was truly overwhelming, young lady, but what was it?"

"Kyris. The star's song. I must apologize, I didn't notice what I was doing."

"Never apologize for such beauty." The ambassador assisted her in getting Antaria back on her feet.

Antaria grabbed Syreen by her shoulder. "I knew it was a good idea to invite you—I couldn't know how good." She turned to the guards. "There cannot be an iota of doubt—who are we to tell the stars where to shine? You may spread the word of what you just were blessed to share. The Navigator and Kyris, they are one tune, and we're not the ones who direct their song."

She faced the Navigator again. "But how do you do it?"

"I don't know. It came to me naturally. But I'm no longer surprised. I can sing to the stars because they're my origin."

"I don't understand. What do you mean?"

"I wasn't born of a woman. My parents are the stars. They created me, my body, my mind. That's what they told me."

CHAPTER TWENTY-SEVEN

The awkward silence that had followed Syreen's last confession had somehow cut her visit on Kyris Orbital short. Her conferences with the harbor master, with the guild, and with the Kyris ambassador were cancelled.

Instead, Lord Hakon and Guild Secretary Jacomo were now returning with her to *Assiduous*. They had asked her for a passage to the Duchy, which she had happily granted. Her girls — she couldn't think of them in other terms — had joined them in the back of the shuttle.

The two Fianna pilots were coming along in their own stingships.

Antaria had turned Syreen's invitation down. While being honored by the offer alone, the noblewoman felt too uneasy in open space and had preferred to return to the surface.

"Splendid," Stephan commented and pointed at *Assiduous's* approaching shape before them. He and Herman were sitting at her side in the shuttle cockpit.

Syreen glanced through the shuttle window and silently agreed with the soldier. She usually ignored the windows — her instruments told her everything she needed to know about her surroundings. This time, she had to agree with Stephan. Her partner indeed looked great with his golden skin.

"You don't get to see him from outside often, do you?" Stephan asked.

"No, indeed not." She smiled. "I've spent most of my time

inside him lately."

"Does it feel like coming home?" Stephan pointed outside again, where *Assiduous's* hangar door—still looking like a crotch—now grew. "I mean, returning to the ship."

"Yes. Both." Syreen adjusted trajectory and speed. "*Assiduous* has become a home for me. But returning to the Duchy feels like returning home, too."

"So you're returning home in your home." Stephan grinned, but frowned once he spotted her grim face.

"Yes. It's time to set a few things straight."

"Oh. You're expecting trouble?"

She clenched a fist. "*I* am the trouble."

Stephan hadn't dared to address his superior again. Once their shuttle safely rested in *Assiduous's* hangar, he ushered their passengers out with Herman's aid.

"Any problems?" Lord Hakon asked.

"Bad mood." Stephan pointed at a doorway. "This way, if I remember right. The Duchy is a sore spot for her. We'd better leave her alone for now."

"A pity. I wanted to ask her a few questions on this hyperflight. Well, perhaps we can have a talk later. After all, the trip will take a few tencycles, won't it?"

"I wouldn't bet on that, but you can ask *Assiduous.*"

They passed the doorway. When Stephan looked back, he saw Syreen rising toward an opening in the hangar ceiling, probably on her way to the bridge.

"I assume we'll leave within the next quartercycle." He waved forward again. "Find a seat in the mess. I'll join you in five."

Syreen appreciated Stephan's silence, and that he had guided their passengers away from her. She was in no mood for talking.

Her partner couldn't fail to notice her unrest. — *I sense discord.* —

"I'm not happy about what I have to do next. Nor do I expect it to be easy." She banged her fist against a wall. "It could get messy."

— *In which way?* —

"I have to be prepared for hostage situations." With her fist held up before her face, she entered the bridge. "Which must not stop me from doing what's necessary."

— *Of course not.* —

With a sigh, she unzipped her jacket, then tossed it to one side. She sat down on the edge of her pilot chair and removed boots and pants. Last went her beret, and then she joined her partner again. *Ah!*

The Navigator opened her mind and listened.

Here's Kyris, there's one unnamed yet familiar pivot system, then Carix Alpha, finally the Duchy. My path is clear. There's no point in postponing the inevitable. Let's go.

"Kyris port authority, this is *Assiduous*, Navigator Syreen. Thank you for your hospitality. I'm looking forward to my next visit. Goodbye for now."

She didn't wait for the answer. They were already facing system-outward and the space ahead was clear.

A single thought sent them dashing forward. A few centicycles later, they entered hyperflight.

The short flight left her little time to contemplate her next moves. Soon she felt her mother's presence, singing a warm welcome.

The song also told of small objects orbiting the main planet or guarding the usual entry points for ships using hyperjumps.

Time for business. Exit.

CHAPTER TWENTY-EIGHT

After leaving hyperspace, Syreen transmitted Admiral Derfflinger's chapter thirteen order, immediately followed by her own message.

"To all AP Navy units in the Duchy, including ground forces, this is Enforcer *Assiduous,* commanded by Navigator Syreen. By order of your own superiors, you are required to lay down your arms. Moreover, in my second role as Duchy Fleet Commander in Charge, I request your immediate and unconditional surrender within the next halfcycle. You will have time to revisit your orders and negotiate the procedures for reparations and repatriation thereafter."

The first answer came quickly. *"Navigator, this is APS Illustrious, Captain Walker speaking. You're not in the position to make any demands. I have to advise you that any hostile action on your behalf may result in repercussions against the local populace. You are required to decelerate, discharge your weapon systems, and accept a boarding party to arrest you."*

Bonehead. She frowned. "Captain Walker, your announcement regarding repercussions against civilians has been recorded and will be used as evidence for another violation of the AP rules of engagement in your court-martial. Be assured that I am well able to eliminate each and any AP unit attempting hostile action — and that any act of terrorism against civilians may void my agreement with the AP admiralty."

There was a brief pause before a new, female voice spoke up.

"Navigator, this is APS Illustrious, First Lieutenant Sasaki

speaking. Captain Walker has just been relieved from duty. Admiral Ravenport has been advised of the new situation. He will contact you as soon as possible. Please bear with us, should we fail to meet your deadline by a few centicycles."

"First Lieutenant Sasaki, I will consider my actions carefully in the light of what you just told me. Just don't test my patience."

Fifteen centicycles later, a shuttle rose from the surface toward *Illustrious*. The dreadnaught transmitted copies of the chapter thirteen order and the conversation so far, which *Assiduous* had no trouble intercepting.

Syreen estimated the time the shuttle would need to reach the dreadnaught and then the time the admiral would need from the shuttle hangar to the bridge, then called the dreadnaught again.

"First Lieutenant Sasaki, I will extend my deadline by another cycle. Tell your admiral he needn't run."

"Navigator, thank you for your understanding."

Yes, this is way above your pay grade. I wouldn't want to place my bet regarding my home world's fate on a junior officer's decision either.

She kept her watch during the next cycle and left her passengers to themselves. Ravenport sent out messages to his fleet to maintain their position and keep their weapons cold. This was a smarter move than she'd have expected from him.

Finally, his call came.

"Navigator Syreen, this is APS Illustrious, *Admiral Cornelius Ravenport speaking. Please accept my sincere apologies for our previous communication. As First Lieutenant Sasaki already told you, Captain Walker is under arrest. I want to thank you for your understanding and for extending your deadline."*

"Admiral Ravenport, you're welcome. This is a much too serious topic to place on the shoulders of a junior officer, no matter how competent and diligent she is."

"Indeed it is. Neither First Lieutenant Sasaki nor Captain Walker had access to the intelligence reports concerning you, yet this time, wisdom didn't come with seniority. You are the one who wiped out our fleets at Klondike, correct?"

"Correct."

"You're also the pirate killer. You cannot be blackmailed, no matter the consequences. Our strategic situation is indefensible — we have already lost. Out of responsibility for my crew, I have no choice but to comply with your request. Please accept our unconditional surrender. What will you do with us now?"

Wow, that was quick.

— And wise. —

Indeed.

"Admiral Ravenport, I herewith accept your surrender. Here are my orders for you and your crews. Number one — you will leave your fifteen cruisers and one dreadnaught behind as reparations, equipped and armed, where the dreadnaught will serve as temporary Duchy orbital station. You will leave skeleton crews behind, which will be relieved by Duchy fleet personnel as soon as possible. Two dreadnaughts may return home with your crews as soon as your preparations are completed."

"I understand."

"Two, about your ground forces — they will remain in their quarters until their conduct has been reviewed by local authorities. Major offenders will receive their court-martial here, all others will be sent home as well. I will make sure there's transportation available for them."

"I understand."

"Three — Captain Walker will face a court-martial in the Duchy."

"I understand. I would have preferred to thoroughly dress him down myself, though."

"You may have a chance to do that anyway. Four — Admiral Ravenport, you will face court here, too, for your attack on primarily civil targets without advance declaration of war. That was a very unwise move."

"I understand. It must appear so to you. My orders were to eliminate any possibility of escape for anyone. I couldn't give up the element of surprise. I still cannot tell you everything, but I'm ready to face the consequences."

"You failed in this regard, though. You couldn't secure the relic you had come for—"

"And one corvette with two prisoners and one Duchy officer escaped, yes. How do you know about the relic? Did you find it, and if you did, how could you take it along in your skirmisher?"

"I learned about it from the admiral whose dreadnaught I blew up. He was checking his orders again before issuing mine, and I peeked over his shoulder, so to speak."

"Oh. That was a daring move – to ask for orders from an enemy officer. I still can't imagine how you could do that."

"Back then, it was a miracle to me, too. Let me put it like this—it is a special talent of my people to be very convincing."

"That was a topic in the reports, too. You claimed to be non-human?"

"That's true. My people are the so-called *Forgotten People*, the people who once built living ships—ships like the one I'm commanding now. To activate and control a living ship you need that relic—a female pilot of the People. I am the *relic*."

The admiral remained silent for a while.

"So we could have spent generations searching and never found it. Instead, the relic *left the scene on her own – with a quite spectacular exit. Pardon me, but this is bitter news indeed. What a twisted joke of fate. So much blood on my hands for nothing."* He sighed. *"May I ask one minor favor from you? After my court-martial, can we just talk? I want to understand what happened."*

"Granted, Admiral. Gladly."

"Thank you. I will explain our decisions to my crews now. We will advise you in advance about ship and shuttle movements."

CHAPTER TWENTY-NINE

Syreen took several deep breaths. *Keep an eye on them for me, partner.*

— *I don't have eyes, but I understand. I will take the watch.* —

She checked for her passengers' locations. They had gathered in the mess and were enjoying a forwine.

The Navigator climbed out of her seat, retrieved her Duchy uniform from the floor, beret, jacket with decorations, pants, boots, and put them on.

"Presentable, partner?"

— *Flawless, as always.* —

"Thanks."

She left the bridge, took an elevator down and entered the mess. A mental nudge made Stephan and Herman forget about saluting — it would have been appropriate, but it would also have spoiled the mood for all others in the room.

She waved a greeting at Lord Hakon and Jacomo, smiled at Haiki and Yusef, and arrived at the table of her army crew. "Stephan, Herman, please gear up for a formal visit to the Duke."

Stephan sat up straight. "The Duke? Us?"

"You are the Duchy soldiers escorting the Fleet Commander in Charge on her mission to liberate the Duchy from hostile forces. We're going right to the Duke's palace. This is your mission."

Her message took a moment to sink in. Then Stephan rose, went to attention and saluted. "Yes, Sir. This is our mission."

"Thank you. At the hangar in a halfcycle, okay?" She

turned to Yusef. "Yusef, would you lend me *Bumblebee* to travel down? I'd like *Assiduous* to remain in orbit—so as not to trigger fancy ideas in our AP friends."

Yusef rose with a smile. "I'll fly you down, so you have a little time to rest. I assure you, I'm able to handle atmospheric flight. Will you take Hakon and Jacomo along? They both said that after living on canned heat for many tencycles, they'd appreciate any chance to breathe natural air."

"What a strange way to see it." Syreen winked and grinned. "Of course. Lord Hakon, Secretary Jacomo, would you like to join us in a halfcycle?"

Syreen was the last to arrive at *Bumblebee's* airlock. She could have discerned from her company's mental signatures, but of course, *Assiduous* had told her when they were ready.

She avoided discussions with the men by assuming the co-pilot's seat, and she avoided discussions with Yusef by leaving her board deactivated. "Ready when you are."

"Okay." He went through a short checklist before activating *Bumblebee's* drive.

The Navigator closed her eyes and listened. Her mother's song, *Assiduous's* reassuring presence, *Bumblebee's* hum, their passengers' excitement.

Yusef hadn't over promised. She barely noticed the moment they passed the hangar door. There wasn't much more to feel about his trip down until he set them down on the palace apron as gently as the touch of a feather.

The screens showed seven guards in AP uniform. One of them made a few steps forward.

Syreen rose from her seat. "They're waiting for us."

Yusef nodded. "Just tell me if you want me to grill them."

The Navigator shuddered. Frigate lasers against guards would cause quite a mess. "No, I don't sense hostility. Relax."

Syreen found Stephan and Herman already waiting at the

airlock in full battle rattle — most of it AP equipment taken from *Bumblebee's* storage, but with Duchy badges replacing the original AP insignia. Hakon and Jacomo were watching.

She nodded at them. "A little more patience, please — first we clear the way, release the Duke, and then we can schedule your appointments."

Lord Hakon nodded back. "Of course. Good luck."

Syreen turned to her soldiers. "Let me go first."

Herman grinned. "We'll have your back."

They entered the airlock. Once the outer hatch opened, Syreen jumped out. She made three steps forward and waited for Stephan and Herman to follow.

The sole AP guard came forward and saluted briskly. "Navigator Syreen, I presume? I'm Master Sergeant Holm, at your service, Sir. Admiral Ravenport instructed me and my team to assist you until you've established your own ground team."

Which probably is the last order he issued before his court-martial.

She returned the salute. "Thank you, Sergeant. Would you please guide me to the Duke?"

"Yes, of course, Sir. Please." He waved toward the entrance. "We've kept a skeleton guard on duty for protection. Most of our staff has been recalled to the barracks until further notice."

"Thank you." Syreen felt relief — she had expected complications with regard to the occupation troops.

"You're welcome, Sir."

Together, they started toward the door. Stephan and Herman followed.

She glanced at Holm. "You were briefed about the current situation?"

"The admiral only told us that our mission is terminated, that our navy detachment formally surrendered to you, that we should return to our barracks — exceptions applying — and that we'd get a comprehensive debriefing later tonight. Next, he assigned me to this post. He said I should take a few level-headed men along."

"I'm glad for that."

"If I may ask, Sir—you're not angry at us?"

"No, Sergeant. I'm no longer angry. I came here to reestablish harmony."

"Harmony, Sir? Well, that sounds good." They had passed the entrance to the palace and were now crossing a marble floor to a huge open stairway. Holm pointed up and left. "This way to the Duke's quarters, please."

Syreen couldn't remember when she had last seen stairs, but she had no trouble negotiating them. "Has the Duke already been advised about the new situation?"

"Not exactly, Sir. The admiral said that I should leave the formal announcement to you. He only knows that he should expect important news."

"Oh."

"I think it's a wise move, Sir. I wouldn't be able to answer his questions anyway."

She took a deep breath. "That's true."

They were now walking the marble floor toward a large, two-wing door with floral ornaments in green, silver, and burgundy, nicely matching her own uniform colors. A solitary man with gray temples, green coat, burgundy trousers and a silver aiguillette watched their approach. Syreen recognized the face of the Lord Chamberlain William Northstonefirth the Fifth, First Advisor to the Duke.

She sensed respect and discomfort in her guide and stopped. "Thank you, Sergeant. I will find my way from here. You may return to your post for now."

"Yes, Sir. Thank you, Sir." He turned and left.

Syreen nodded at Stephan and Herman, then turned toward the door and covered the remaining distance with brisk steps.

She felt the advisor's scrutinizing glance and at the same time his curiosity. Four legs before the door she stopped and saluted. "Duchy Fleet Commander in Charge Syreen Starborn with an urgent confidential report to the Duke, Lord Chamberlain, Sir."

Lord Northstonefirth raised his eyebrows. "Welcome, Commander. May I ask about the report content?"

She took her hand down. "My lord, you may ask, and I'll gladly include you, but I must insist that the Duke will be the first to hear my words."

"And a fleet commander should make this assessment?"

Syreen didn't avoid his glare. "No, but the Fleet Commander in Charge, the first in command, should and did."

For a moment she considered a mental nudge. Then she saw realization dawn in him.

"You are not a prisoner of war."

She nodded. "I am what's left of Fleet, and I am free to act."

"Then you must see the Duke at once." He knocked, then waved at an ornament, and the heavy doors opened.

The advisor entered, followed by Syreen, Stephan, and Herman. The latter two earned a critical glance from the Lord Chamberlain, but no objection.

The duke turned to them from a window at the far end of the room. He looked much older than she remembered, most likely due to the worry lines that had dug deep into his features.

The advisor bowed. "Your Grace, a messenger of utmost importance."

The duke nodded. "Who is it, Lord Chamberlain?"

"The Duchy Fleet Commander in Charge, Syreen Starborn, with two escorts."

The two soldiers went to attention, and Syreen saluted.

"Come and sit." The duke returned her salute, made a few

slow steps toward a green-and-silver chaise longue, and sat down.

Syreen signaled the two soldiers to remain at ease and took a chair facing her ruler.

The old man managed well to hide the grief from his face, but he couldn't hide his mind. "Now, what is your important message, young lady?"

"Your Grace, I came to report you are again the Duchy's rightful and undisputed ruler. The aggressor declared his unconditional surrender to Fleet. The Duchy is free."

She sensed his disbelief and went on explaining, "On the day of the invasion, Fleet fought bravely. Two enemy dreadnaughts were destroyed. In the resulting confusion, one Fleet pilot was able to escape with a captured enemy corvette, to gather intelligence, to find allies, to defeat the Association, and finally return to her ruler. It took a lot more time than expected, but today, we are here."

"I find that hard to believe, brave young lady, but you are here, and as I see, with a Duchy escort under arms."

She rose and waved the two men forward.

Stephan and Herman took one step and saluted.

She pointed at them in sequence. "Private First Class Stephan Smith, Private First Class Herman Doeken, Duchy Army. During my escape, I managed to free these former AP prisoners. They supported our cause in every possible way, and they can bear witness to what I said."

The duke rose to return their salute. When he sat down again, he leaned forward to her. "Bear with an old and worried man. Tell me straightforwardly how you could achieve this impossible victory against a fleet still three dreadnaughts strong."

Syreen allowed herself a grin. "The latter was the easiest feat. I carried a message from the Nysa admiralty commanding their surrender. Which I got after defeating the

Association in their home system. Which again was only possible after I convinced the merchants' guild to put the Association under edict."

"Impossible." The advisor stood at her side. "The guild tribunal on Nysa would never issue such an edict."

"That's what I was told, too." She nodded at the Lord Chamberlain. "The edict was issued by the guild tribunal on Crown." She raised one finger. "Which is on the far side of a space region called the *chasm*, impassable for all conventional spaceships. I had help." She rose. "Let me introduce to you — Navigator Syreen of the Forgotten People, pilot of the living ship *Assiduous.*" She bowed and opened her mind.

Mother, sing to us.

CHAPTER THIRTY

Syreen kept her introduction short. Her audience was over-whelmed anyway. All men had a telltale wetness in the corners of their eyes.

The duke spoke up first. "Did I truly hear the song of our Duchess?"

She smiled. "You did, Your Grace."

"What does it mean?"

"It means harmony. I'm in tune with the stars. And that's because I was born from the Duchess. I am no human, but one of the Forgotten People, only in human shape."

The advisor bowed. "Your Grace, we're touching a sensitive subject there, not suited for the general audience."

Syreen looked back and waved at Stephan and Herman. "Your Grace, my lord, these two men shared all my secrets from the beginning. They were with me when we discovered my living ship, and they went with me to Crown and back. I'm putting my life in their hands. If there's any secret with regard to my people, they will protect it."

The duke gazed at his advisor. "Can We make such a decision, William?"

Lord Northstonefirth nodded. "Yes, Your Grace, I think you and your Fleet Commander together can indeed make such a decision, and with the recommendation of a member of the Forgotten People, who could object?"

The duke smiled. "Well. Gentlemen, you are now keepers of state secrets." He waved at his advisor. "We will postpone the formalities for now—surely this day will bring up much

131

more to catch up on."

Then he turned to Syreen. "You should know, Ancient One, that the Duchy is a very old nation. Our history reaches back to the time when the first settlers reached this sector. Much about that distant past is lost, but there are a few bits of information that persisted. Every skirmisher pilot knows about our psyjuice and how it is applied, and few experts know its recipe. What we didn't tell you is that its origin can be traced back to some people that the original settlers — my ancestors — met. Those people are nowadays called the Forgotten People."

Herman wheezed.

The duke folded his hands. "You see, Ancient One, that your people aren't entirely forgotten. They are more than just old lore to us, they are part of our history. We owe your people, and now that you returned to relieve us from severe distress, we owe you even more. We are at your service."

Syreen took a long, deep breath. "Thank you, Your Grace. May I ask you one favor — please don't call me Ancient One. It makes me feel like I'm your great-grandmother. In this role, I would be called Navigator." She briefly closed her eyes. "By the way, did you know that Giorgos Tarakis the Seventy-Third of Danos claims a similar kind of obligation toward my ancestors?"

The duke raised his eyebrows and glanced at his advisor. "William?"

The lord chamberlain shrugged. "This must've been lost across the ages. Of course, now that we learned about it, we should establish communications."

"Of course. Navigator, what else can We do for you?"

She tapped her knee. "Your Grace — for now, please let me just be your Fleet Commander in Charge. I think we should make plans for reestablishing proper order in the Duchy — release our people from prison, establish courts to deal with war crimes by the aggressors, organize our protection and all."

The duke nodded. "Of course. We hope that one day you will tell Us the whole story. But We should indeed turn Our attention to the most immediate issues now. Would you please assist Us?"

"Your Grace, Fleet is at your command."

"But there's little left of Fleet."

She opened her arms. "I didn't come empty-handed, Your Grace. I brought reinforcements."

"The little ship you escaped with? Well, that's a start."

"No, sorry. The corvette I captured is damaged beyond repair. But—firstly, I captured the AP frigate *Bumblebee* and hired some crew. They are really good and ready to serve us. Secondly, I currently command eleven Crown destroyers and eighteen Finney stingships. They are our allies and will eventually return home, but for now, they are helpful. Two stingships arrived with me, the other units will follow within the next hectocycle."

"That will certainly help, Your Grace." The advisor took out his tab and started making notes. "At least we can send messengers to our ambassadors in the neighborhood and ask for assistance and some urgent shipments."

"Merchants will be reluctant to travel here, I fear." The duke shook his head. "We're not considered safe."

"I made friends with some merchants." Syreen smiled when she remembered their friendly faces. "I'm sure many will come when I call them."

"Not merchants, no." The advisor frowned. "Friendship doesn't pay."

Herman stepped forward and waved at Syreen. "But they will follow the call of a triple star angel."

Syreen nodded. "Indeed they will. Some even promised me to fly any route I would ask for."

"I'm trying to imagine the events that led to such a

promise." The duke folded his hands.

"In two cases, I saved them from the hands of pirates and reestablished rightful ownership of their haulers. On one occasion, I had to rebuild their star library and repair their emitters. In any case, the Crown units can serve as escorts, which will relieve their fears." She held up three fingers. "Thirdly. The Association will leave their fifteen cruisers behind as reparations. An AP skeleton crew will keep them ready until we can provide our own crews."

Again, the advisor frowned. "That will be difficult. We lost almost all of Fleet."

"All in space, yes. We should call in all who were on shore leave, and I would propose to reactivate all retired officers who are willing and able to serve."

The duke nodded and gazed at his advisor. "Isn't that part of our emergency plans anyway?"

"Not to that extent, Your Grace, but we cannot afford to be picky. We will need every hand to get Fleet organized, and much of that will be office work anyway. I can't even imagine the logistics nightmare without an orbital station."

Syreen grinned. "Oh, but I got you one."

"An orbital station?"

"For now, one of the AP dreadnaughts will have to serve as orbital station. We will have to ask engineers about how to attach merchant docks, but there will be hangars with shuttles and other smaller vessels, there will be communications, and there will be heavy ordnance."

For the first time, the duke laughed out loud. "Lady, I don't know if I should call you wicked or brilliant!" He wiped a tear off his cheek and shook his head. "We should apologize. For just a moment, We forgot . . ."

"Both," Syreen interrupted him. "Wicked and brilliant, and I won't accept an apology for quoting facts."

His grace chuckled, shedding another tear. "Oh, indeed."

Then he made a serious face again. "We will invoke the is-lander protocol."

The advisor nodded. "I would have recommended that, too, Your Grace." He then turned to Syreen. "The islander protocol is one of our contingency plans for times of distress. It relies on distributed authority, in case communication is limited — or in case the centralized operations are limited. Lo-cal marshals and sheriffs will act independently until we can return to normal. Some will probably have assumed that role already."

She nodded. "That sounds good. Before we go into detail, there's one more point. I've brought two visitors with me."

The Lord Chamberlain looked alarmed. "Visitors? Who are they?"

"One is our ambassador on Kyris, Lord Hakon."

"Oh, that's good." The duke smiled. "He's a good thinker. We should invite him to this council. Who is the other one?"

"Guild Secretary Jacomo from Kyris. He wants to reestab-lish our communication with the guild. He was a good advi-sor to me — the one who directed me toward Crown."

This time, the Lord Chamberlain smiled, too. "You're a woman full of miracles. Your Grace, I would propose we move this meeting to a council room and invite a few more friends in. We only need to organize their transportation."

Syreen nodded. "If you don't mind, the AP sergeant who came inside with me, Master Sergeant Holm, was ordered to assist me. I'm sure he can organize transportation."

CHAPTER THIRTY-ONE

After fifteen tencycles of workshops, briefings, consultations, negotiations, court sessions, her talk with Admiral Ravenport, and too few and way too short sleep breaks, Syreen felt entitled to feel exhausted. Rest wasn't on her schedule, though.

The palace entrance hall was bustling with comm techs, vid reporters, assistants of ceremonies, palace guards, Very Important Persons and Very Importunate Persons, and some familiar and nervous faces.

She walked up between Stephan and Herman and patted their shoulders. "Come on, smile. This is not your execution."

Herman chuckled. "No. It's only an opportunity to cause infinite embarrassment."

"You won't cause embarrassment." Syreen squeezed his shoulder gently, so as not to make a crinkle in his new dress uniform. "Forget about the formalities. Be yourself and enjoy it."

"Easier said than done. They said this is the first such ceremony in seventy-three generations. Oops—here we go."

The two soldiers were called forward.

"Until later." Syreen gave them a nudge before letting their shoulders go. Then she glanced at a mirror to check her own appearance again, the green dress uniform with golden lining and all her decorations and the burgundy beret. She would be next.

Until then, she would listen to her mother. She closed her eyes and opened her mind.

A nearby cough called Syreen back to attention. She focused on its source.

"Fleet Commander Syreen, please." The young orderly pointed at the main doors.

"Of course." She refrained from checking the mirror again.

When she passed through the doors, the sudden bright sunlight made her squint. She managed to reach her marking on the elevated dais without stumbling, though, and gazed forward across the crowd assembled on the palace apron.

In the front, she recognized the freshly awarded and promoted lance corporals Herman and Stephan, and next to them her merchant hires Mo, Yusef, and Haiki, now wearing Duchy Navy uniforms, too, and with fresh decorations. Some Crown and Finney faces stuck out of the crowd behind them, and at one side she spotted Drake and Crow. Far behind, her corvette *Raydancer* pointed skyward from an improvised little pedestal. The sight gave her a stab of pain — the tough little ship would never fly again.

She had no time to examine the audience further. She turned to her ruler, who was sitting on an impressive throne on the other side of the dais, went to attention, and saluted firmly.

A herald in Duchy green with a long ceremonial rod stepped forward. "Listen, our dear citizens. I will tell you about our history."

He paused and glanced around.

"During the founding of our Duchy, there were severe dangers and hardships to overcome, and there were brave and gallant warriors fighting and sometimes dying for their people. Back in these old times, the founding council, diligently guided by our First Duke, created the honorable Order of the Firepath to recognize extraordinary martial achievements and outstanding gallantry."

Syreen had never heard of such an order until a few days before. Still, the time to learn more about its history was yet to come.

The herald continued. "Members of the Order of the Firepath are mighty warriors, and they are also skilled in leadership. As such, they have been recognized as Peers of our Realm. Due to the long period of peace and safety we were blessed to enjoy, there has not been a single new member for many generations, so that we cannot call them forward."

He nodded toward the duke and received a nod in return.

The herald thumped the floor with the rod. "The Duke now calls Fleet Commander in Charge Syreen Starborn to come before this Court and Company."

Her orderly stepped forward. "Your Grace, now before you comes Fleet Commander Syreen Starborn, Navigator of the people known to us as Forgotten People, former Lieutenant in the Duchy's First Skirmisher Wing, to receive your blessings."

He stepped back and nudged her forward to the second marking.

The duke rose. "Fleet Commander Syreen Starborn, are you ready to receive the accolade of Knighthood in the Order of the Firepath?"

"Your Grace, I am ready."

"This greatly pleases Us. Bring forth the chain."

The master of ceremonies appeared from behind a curtain and handed a chain of golden badges to the duke.

The duke presented the chain to the audience. "This is the original chain of Marvin Baker the Unrelenting, the very first knight of the order. Let it now pass to a knight once again."

However, he gave it back to the master of ceremonies and signaled her to kneel, which she quickly did.

"Fleet Commander Syreen Starborn, you have been deemed fit for this high estate by all people We talked to, and you have indicated your willingness to accept this honor from Our hands. Do you now swear by all that you hold sacred, true, and holy that you will honor and defend the Realm of the Duchy?"

"I will."

"That you will honor, defend, and protect all those weaker than yourself?"

"I will."

"That you will be courteous and honor your peers?"

"I will."

"That you will conduct yourself in all matters as befits a peer, drawing your sword only for just cause? That you will enshrine in your heart the noble ideals of chivalry to the benefit of your own good name and the greater glory of the Duchy?"

"I will—as far as my duties as enforcer of my people allow."

The duke nodded—during their previous consultations, she had pointed out her primary obligation, so her reservation was no surprise.

"Bring forth the sword of state."

He took a brightly polished blade from the hands of another herald. "Then having sworn these solemn oaths, know now that We, Hagthorn the Sixteenth, by right of arms, Duke of this Realm, do dub you with Our sword, Redoubtable, and by all that you hold sacred, true, and holy ... Once for Honor ... Twice for Duty ... Thrice for Chivalry ..."

She felt the tap of the blade on both her shoulders and on her head.

"Arise, Lady Syreen!"

He then exchanged the sword with the chain and placed it around her neck. "Accept from Our hands this chain, passed from knight to knight, which symbolizes the bond between our shields, linked to protect our Realm and all that peacefully dwell within."

"Thank you, Your Grace."

This should have been the end of the formal ceremony. The audience had the same expectation, as their roaring applause told.

But the duke didn't return to his seat. When the cheer of the crowd had finally faded, he signaled to his master of ceremony again.

"Lady Syreen, you asked Us to formally relieve you from your duties as Fleet Commander, so that you can follow your call to the greater good for us all. We knew that it would be hard, if not impossible, to find one among Our subjects to follow in your footsteps with equal dedication and skill." He paused. "However, now that you brought us peace, we no longer need the greatest warriors. Now we need organizers, instructors, loyal and experienced senior officers to rebuild our forces. We asked around and found one willing to accept this responsibility. Come forward, Admiral Connolly."

The officer appearing on the dais had gray hair and wrinkled features but saluted to the duke and to her briskly.

"Your Grace, I'm honored to be allowed to offer you my services again."

The duke took the admiral's hand and shook it. "William, I'm really sorry that I had to disturb your well-deserved retirement."

"Your Grace, we were all shocked when we heard about the attack on our orbital — and we all knew it wouldn't be easy to climb out of that pit. Luckily, Fleet was able to return the light to us." The admiral turned to Syreen and shook her hand, too. "My Lady, I am in no position to appropriately honor what you did for us. You achieved the impossible. You made us proud."

She bowed. "Admiral Connolly, I feel honored by your words. As I understand, you will assume the command from me. I do not remember the procedures, so I will do it my way today. Fleet currently consists of one frigate with a very experienced and reliable crew of six, fifteen former AP cruisers, yet to be formally taken over from their skeleton crews, and one dreadnaught which is already in the process of refitting to replace our orbital station. In addition, we are working with a lot of volunteers that formally don't belong to Fleet yet. As far as I've learned, reactivation and recruiting of Fleet staff may soon commence. This is what I'm placing in your lap."

The admiral glanced at his ruler. "Your Grace, you didn't tell me — that means Fleet is stronger in material than before the invasion?"

The duke grinned. "You may consider selling some units to replace them with smaller ships."

Syreen nodded. "Plus, Crown Commodore Reed offered some of his experienced staff to act as instructors for the next quartercycles."

Admiral Connolly showed a wide smile. "You make it easy for an old man. I'm so grateful. Now I'm truly confident we can get this done. My Lady, Fleet Commander, I'm ready to accept this responsibility."

Syreen saluted. "Admiral, I herewith transfer Fleet command to you."

Connolly saluted back. "Fleet Commander, I herewith accept command."

She saluted again. "Admiral, Fleet Commander in Charge, please accept my retirement from active duty now."

"Fleet Commander Syreen, I herewith accept deactivation of your commission. You are relieved from your duties toward Fleet at half pay."

"I'm Lieutenant now."

"No, you are not." The admiral waved at the duke. "Before you were knighted, His Grace promoted you to full Fleet Commander. Five silver stars."

She stared at her ruler, who grinned at her. "Only appropriate for what you did, isn't it? You shouldn't leave us broke, as I'm sure you want to have a little farewell party with some friends. Moreover, I wanted to be sure that you still outrank all the new staff we'll be hiring and training."

CHAPTER THIRTY-TWO

Fleet Commander Syreen was retired and dismissed. But Lady Syreen wasn't. The protocol still required her appearance at a press conference before she was supposed to attend a formal dinner with the duke.

Soon she found herself sitting in quite a comfortable chair on another dais — which created an illusion of audience — facing a friendly middle-aged man in formal suit and bowtie.

"Good afternoon, gals and lads, to your Deeper Insight Show. I'm your host Keith Gunnarsson, and my special guest today is the most charming Lady Syreen Starborn, Knight of the Order of the Firepath, retired Duchy Fleet Commander, Navigator of the Forgotten People, triple star angel of the merchant guild, and most of all, the hero who defeated the Association and gave us freedom again. Lady Syreen, how do you feel today?"

Syreen was glad he had settled for a short form of address, although she wasn't quite at terms with the *Lady* yet. Was she supposed to curtsy now?

Not now, I'm sitting. She gave her host her most friendly smile. *Showtime.* "Good afternoon, Keith. Good afternoon, my friends. To be honest, I feel a bit exhausted. The last few ten-cycles were very busy — there was so much to do to get us back to normal. But I'm also feeling relieved. The most urgent issues are resolved. Tonight, I may relax, and that makes me feel good."

"How does your retirement feel? What does it mean to you?"

"It means relief. You know, Keith, I've been Fleet for all my life. I don't know anything other than being a space jockey, and I'm happy with that. But the last kilocycles were difficult. I had too many burdens to bear. The role of Fleet Commander in Charge meant I had an obligation to my people—to you all—which I knew I couldn't fulfill before I had solved all the other problems. I couldn't just return here with guns blazing and shoot a few more AP ships. I had to make sure they wouldn't return—I had to make sure they wouldn't start throwing moon-sized rocks at my home world. My retirement means that I succeeded. I'm no longer needed in this role, because you're safe from this threat."

She sensed that Keith needed a moment to digest the *moon-sized rocks*. But he was a pro, he caught himself quickly. "How did you do it, after all? Why did you do it? Wasn't that close to madness—no offense meant?"

"No offense taken, Keith. Yes, it was madness from the beginning. Three outdated destroyers plus eight wings of skirmishers against an armada led by five dreadnaughts was at best hopeless. But Fleet never gives up."

"Yes, but still—one skirmisher against an entire fleet?"

"Impossible odds, yes. Unless you change the rules. That's what I did. I only survived the initial wave because I didn't fly by the Books. No one expected a skirmisher to attack a dreadnaught head-on. No one expected the importunate pilot to board the dreadnaught. And no one expected a solitary intruder to blow up that dreadnaught—by putting all safeties to extended maintenance, so that the reactor would overheat."

"But you were still aboard!"

"No. I left just in time in the borrowed corvette *Raydancer*. The dreadnaught's end covered my escape."

"Sorry, Lady Syreen, I have to ask that question—you indeed left the battlefield although you could have reentered battle?"

"Yes, I did, and yes, you have to ask that question. And yes again, I could have fought on here. It was a very hard decision to leave you all behind, under the enemy's heel, and leave the scene unfinished. But it was the only way. I needed every-thing—allies, support, intel, a new strategy. But most of all, I needed that single object of desire that the enemy was after—the *relic*."

"What *relic?*"

"They didn't know what it was either. They only had a clue that they could find a certain *relic* here in the Duchy—an item that would gain them access to ultimate power. They weren't told what it would look like, so they had little chance to find it from the start. And then it escaped from right under their nose."

Keith smiled. "So it was aboard *Raydancer* with you?"

Syreen nodded. "Admiral Ravenport arrived at the same conclusion, right and wrong together."

Now her host frowned. "I don't understand."

"They were looking for the key to a living ship. The key to a living ship is a living key, the only way to control a living ship—you need a pilot, a Navigator of the Forgotten People. But that pilot escaped. You know her."

"You?"

"Me, myself, and I, yes, a Navigator of the Forgotten Peo-ple."

"How did you learn about that?"

"Well—the first step was learning about the relic. I checked the dreadnaught admiral's orders before I blew up his ship."

"You—you checked his orders?" Keith stared at her.

"Yes. The second step was to learn more about that relic. I found a researcher following a seemingly related trace. To-gether, we found the living ship. But only when it opened to my touch and welcomed me as his pilot did I learn about my true ancestry."

"Wow." The interviewer seemed to check his knee. "About that corvette—you said you *borrowed* it. Is that term correct?"

"Yes. I did not initially capture it—which I could have done, but then I'd have had to change its call sign to Duchy, which wouldn't have helped my escape. So I convinced the AP to issue an order to take that ship and leave. That's why I call it borrowed, not stolen. Later, I captured it—from myself—and made it a Duchy Fleet vessel."

"Why would the AP have issued such an order?"

"Well—you could say I used a clever stratagem. The details are classified, though."

"Okay. Lady Syreen, what happened to *Raydancer*?"

"The corvette was severely damaged in the battle of Klondike. *Assiduous* harbored it in his hangar before it was put on display on the palace apron."

"*Assiduous?*"

"My ship, and my partner."

"A partner?"

"We're a team." *And I won't tell you all the spicy details.* She placed her arms on the armrests and waited.

Her host folded his hands. "Lady Syreen. You are the Duchy's first knight for more than a megacycle. What does this knighthood mean to you?"

"Aside from the nice decoration?" She gazed down at the heavy golden chain across her chest. "Well, of course it's a recognition of my achievements, and it's a great honor. But any award would have told the same. This knighthood is different. It's not easily granted. It means someone understood why I did what I did—that I did it for the Duchy people, not for my career. The most important aspect, though, is another."

Keith leaned forward.

She focused on him. "The most important aspect to me is the obligation I accepted with the title, and I'm not talking about good conduct. You've heard the words of my oath. I will honor and defend the Realm of the Duchy. I will honor, defend, and protect all those weaker than myself. I will draw my sword only for just cause. I will take the noble ideals of chivalry to my heart. And, despite the wording, I will do that not just to the greater glory of the Duchy, but to the benefit and safety of all mankind, as befits an enforcer of the edicts."

"Which means?"

"Fleet won't give up—only on a larger scale."

"Oh." He swallowed visibly. "You mean—uh."

"I mean that I'm a born-and-bred warrior, created to navigate my living ship, my warrior partner. That's my purpose, and our joint purpose is to enforce the edicts. We weren't created for courier or escort services. That's my flavor of knighthood."

Keith focused on her face. "I'm not sure if you're so brave or if it's something else—you were a skirmisher pilot . . ."

"And a kind of adrenaline junkie? Yes, during my first real battle I didn't think of much else but the next kill. That was the drill—that's the only way to make such a small bird useful in battle. Go in for the kill, shoot as many targets as possible before they get you. My wingmates did that, they scored, and they died with smiles on their faces. But the only reason I didn't die was that I didn't forget about my survival. I enjoyed the same stimulation, felt the same buzz, but I dodged hostile shots."

She kept his gaze captured with her own. "It's different with my partner. We're one mind and one ass. We're in a kind of trance, too—but we keep each other in check." She sat up straight. "You wouldn't want to oppose a living ship with a skilled pilot, like the Association did. Check the battle reports, if you like. And I assure you—I'm still learning and improving."

When Keith nodded, she reclined in her chair and smiled.

He glanced at his knee again. "Where do you find the

power for all this? How can an ordinary—or even extraordinary—human bear all this? Is that why you call yourself *Star-born?*"

Syreen shook her head. "I'm no human. I'm a Navigator of the Forgotten People, and while my people have similar features as humans, we're not related. When I feel worn out and desperate, I find relief in listening to my ancestors, to the songs the stars sing to me." She leaned forward and put one hand on his knee. "Keith, I *am* star-born. Listen."

She opened her mind. *Will I be able to let them all hear?*

Syreen felt a gentle nudge. *Yes, of course. Compared to mending hyperthreads, this is nothing.* She smiled at her host and leaned back. "Listen."

"Navigator Syreen, are you okay?"

That voice sounds familiar — oh, yes, Keith. The press conference.

She opened her eyes again, this time gazing down. "Yes, I think so." With her voice, memory of the latest events returned, and also her eyesight.

"You appeared—absent, in a way." He squatted down before her. "This extraordinary, almost magical moment must have affected you more than us."

She smiled and took his hands. "Did you hear her song?"

"I did. I felt enchanted—until I saw you, unconscious in your seat. I thought you might need help."

"No, not really. Just a moment to recover."

"Oh, I can understand that. We all needed a moment after that—I don't want to call it interruption. You asked me to listen, and then there was this marvelous melody. For a moment, I felt one with the world. So beautiful! Did you feel it, too?"

"Of course, Keith. It's my mother we heard."

"Your *mother?*"

"The Duchess, our central star, Keith. That's my mother, and what you heard, what I relayed to you, is her song. I can hear her all the time." She sensed his disbelief. "That was no interruption, Keith. When I asked you to listen, I meant this song. It didn't happen by chance, but because I caused it to happen, and I can do it again. Now."

Syreen reached out again. This time, she restricted her relay to the studio. While they listened to the Duchy's song, she smiled and nodded at her host. She could see him accepting her statement.

When she let the song fade, there was a glimpse of joy on his face. It gave way for a frown, his gaze passing through her, his attention focused elsewhere.

"What? Yes—yes—okay—are you serious? Say that again." He listened to another distant voice, probably via an ear implant, and then turned to her. "Did you know that this song—the first one—could be heard all around the planet and on all the ships in orbit?"

"Of course, Keith. That's how I envisaged it." She spread her arms. "I wanted to share our song with you."

"But that wasn't what you did."

"No?"

"No." Keith showed her a very happy smile. He radiated— admiration? "No. You made an entire planet fall in love with you."

CHAPTER THIRTY-THREE

Syreen tried hard to enjoy the formal dinner with the duke. She struggled a bit with her table manners until she remembered what her teacher had told her — *watch and copy*.

On the bright side, the food was really good, and the for-wine excellent. The service staff was helpful, attentive and friendly yet discreet.

The shallow chatter around her was harder to bear. Some people were talking as if their life depended on noise. Sadly, they had nothing meaningful to say. Her recent *epiphany* seemed to justify an extreme level of annoyance for them. Worst of all, she was expected to answer — kindly, as befitted a peer. She hadn't expected her oath to stab her in the back so soon.

After each course, the seating was rearranged, so she had to answer the same mindless questions all over again.

After dessert, the seats moved a last time, and she came to face the duke.

"My Grace." She insinuated a bow.

"My Lady." He bowed as far down as the table allowed. "We're infinitely blessed by Your divine presence and humbled by your modesty." He sat up straight again and smiled. "Forgive me — I couldn't resist. We have come to know each other during the last weeks and I'm aware you do not desire worship. However, your ancestry reaches much farther back than mine, and your message today made clear that you are of a nobler flavor of blood — figuratively spoken, of course. So allow me a bold suggestion. Let's put that Grace and Lady aside. I'm Hagthorn, the thorn in my enemies' side for some, the old hag for some others. Good friends call me Spike— that's an old play with words."

"Spike." She grinned. "What a wicked name for such a kind and gentle man."

"Says a truly enchanting siren. I assure you I can do *wicked* if need be."

"Touché." Syreen sensed expectation. *Oh.* "I would appreciate calling you a friend, Spike."

"So would I." He took a deep breath. "Syreen, my friend, may I ask you a delicate question now?"

"Delicate in what way? Aw, no matter. Shoot away."

"Thank you. Tell me one thing. What do you think, what made the stars create their own offspring right now, in our times? Just to stir up things?"

She shook her head. "No. No, surely not." *But this is the key question, isn't it?* "There must be a reason, and I must find it before it finds us." *And I know where to start looking. Peysoon will like that.*

She pushed her chair back. "I will leave you now."

PART THREE—EXPEDITION

Chapter Thirty-Four

An AP shuttle took Syreen up to orbit. She had volunteered for the co-pilot's seat, as the passenger seats had already been booked.

"I'd never imagined I'd fly shuttles again." The gray-haired pilot caressed the flightstick with wrinkled hands. "But I'm glad I can help, and somehow it feels like yesterday, aye?"

Syreen smiled.

"Y'know, gal, I've probably forgotten way more than you'll ever learn, aye? You'll work on our new, shiny orbital?"

"I'm returning to my own ship."

"Oh—you command one of our new tin cans? Big step up for a rookie, ain't it?"

Her smile widened. She still wore Duchy colors, but now without insignia—many new hires came without or with improvised rank insignia. So how would he know?

"Ah, don't think I won't notice your amusement, gal. During my first career, I mentored officers far senior than you. I could help you, too, if you need a senior noncom for your cruiser."

From her own first career, she knew very well how valuable senior non-commissioned officers could be. She thought of her foster-father.

"Which one is it? I can take you there once we've dropped off passengers at the orbital."

She pointed at a symbol on his nav display. "This one. My ship, *Assiduous*."

He turned his head to stare at her. "You're the Navigator, then? My apologies, My Lady. I didn't recognize you."

"No worries, Poppy." That's what she'd called her foster-father. She clapped his shoulder. "We're just two seasoned space-jockeys reminiscing old times, ain't we?"

He examined her face for a while. Finally, he mirrored her smile. "Aye, gal, we are. You'd do well as officer, y'know?"

"I did, Poppy. I had good teachers, good men like you. That's why I survived." She made a serious face. "Do us a favor, Poppy. Leave the shuttle jobs to others. Sign up as a teacher. Fleet needs people like you."

He made a face. "I tried. Too old, they said."

"Give me your tac."

He fetched his device and gave it to her.

She allowed it to scan her face. "Copy. Navigator Syreen sends her regards. I recommend the owner of this tac for the fast track instructor team. His records may be old, but his mind is fresh and witty. Consider him as first shirt for the *Liberty*. Stop recording." Syreen handed his tac back. "I'm sure admiralty will call you soon."

"But — the *Liberty?* Our new flagship? Why?"

"You offered your help to someone you regarded a young cruiser skipper. That's the kind of help we need — that's the kind of help the new skipper will need, coming fresh from the academy and still on probation. And if you have some old mates you can recommend — speak up. We spent many nights discussing flag and skipper positions, but we're short of good noncoms."

He nodded slowly. "Aye. I see what you mean. Yes, I'll ask some old friends."

And you didn't even flinch upon the first shirt, the senior enlisted advisor. You're the right one.

Syreen felt tempted to assume control for the final approach to *Assiduous,* but that would have looked as if she didn't trust Poppy.

He didn't fail her. He didn't hesitate to approach and penetrate *Assiduous's* crotch-like hangar door and set the shuttle down with almost no tremble.

She patted his shoulder again. "Perfect job, Poppy. Would you like a quick tour before you depart?"

He hesitated.

Syreen rose. "This is a once-in-a-lifetime opportunity, but that doesn't count, I know. So let me put it like this — I would really like to hear your opinion and your sound advice."

Poppy chuckled and left his seat, too, and then saluted. "Master Sergeant Harry McNish at your service, My Lady."

She returned a very crisp salute. "Glad to have you aboard, Master Sergeant."

"Thank you — I'm fine with Poppy, gal." He winked.

"Okay. Come on in, then, Poppy. Meet my partner *Assiduous.*"

Together, they left the shuttle.

It feels good to be back.

— Welcome back. You brought another new crew member along? —

Oh, no. Poppy deserves a tour around, but then he'll leave us. Wait, what do you mean, another new crew member?

— They're waiting for you in the mess. —

Who? Aw, they'll have to wait.

"So this is your formidable living ship?" Poppy asked, peering beyond Syreen's ex-AP shuttle into the dimly lit hangar.

"Welcome aboard." Assiduous's voice boomed through the huge hall. *"Let me show you more."*

Light flooded the hangar.

Poppy gazed around and then pointed at the rows of oval objects along the hangar walls. "What's that — eggs or bombs?"

"Both." Syreen waved him closer. "Either one could hatch

a new living ship — or turn a star into a supernova."

This statement earned her an aghast stare. "A supernova?"

"Yes. Or, put differently, we command the means to kill my kin — the stars. It's distressing to know they gave me such means themselves."

The sergeant nodded. "I'd call it scary. Or haunting. Such power, such responsibility shouldn't be burdened on a single person."

"My Navigator's never alone with this burden."

"Oh, sorry, Mr. Assiduous." He looked around, trying to find out where to talk to.

Syreen grinned. "He's all around us, Poppy. That takes some time to get used to."

"Oh."

"Come on, I'll give you the fifty credits tour."

CHAPTER THIRTY-FIVE

Syreen watched Poppy's shuttle slip through the hangar door. *He'll do fine.*

— This is a fine man indeed. I almost regret he's not coming with us. But he'll surely help the local people. —

I think so, too. Now, you told me of new crew members in the mess.

She turned around and left the hangar. A short walk took her to the large multi-purpose social room that everyone just called the mess.

She wasn't sure who to expect. Curiosity was killing her, but she resisted the temptation to sense forward.

When she entered, she found many familiar faces turning toward her — many more than expected, but a few others were missing.

Fifteen scantily-clad girls flocked around two men and one of her own kin.

— Our pregnant passengers decided to stay behind, to be with the fathers, as they said. —

Peysoon rose and bowed. "Welcome back, Navigator." He gestured toward the two men. "These nice people arrived two tencycles ago. We had a nice talk." He was interrupted by several girls dashing past him and assaulting Syreen with wide open arms.

Any plans about an orderly greeting disintegrated in a huge, convoluted group hug. Somehow even the two men managed to be part of it.

"Drake!" She held him tight before the old researcher could

be swept away.

"My Lady." He grinned. "Prettier than ever."

Pretty? Me?

But these words from a man leaning the other way warmed and soothed her mind.

His praise deserves a clear sign of gratitude. She stole his breath with a long, deep kiss.

Gay or not, he answered in kind, and with enthusiasm.

The spectators cheered.

When she sensed a hint of arousal, she considered releasing him from her hug—but he wouldn't. She considered it again when Charlene began to unbutton her uniform pants and Vivien tugged at the right boot.

Aw, this feels too good to miss.

Gentle fingers felt their way from the small of her back upward. There had to be some kind of blade or scissors involved, as she sensed a fresh draft at her back.

The same gentle fingers—they had to belong to Lucy—began to explore her hardened nipples from behind.

Another fresh breeze caressed her crotch, and then a firm boner poked her groin and made her raise one leg. Her labia opened. *I never needed much time to get wet.*

Another female hand guided the firm cock until it slipped inside. Drake moaned. The rest of her uniform somehow disappeared.

Together, they began a slow, three-legged dance. He moved cautiously to not lose contact.

This won't do. I need support to recline.

—Here.—

A rounded edge touched her butt cheeks. She opened her arms and leaned back, took her other foot up in the air, formed a V with her legs, smiled at Drake. "Do me hard."

Returning her smile, he continued with three more slow strokes. Then he grabbed her upper legs and accelerated.

He didn't take his focus off her bouncing boobs. Sweat was

running down his face. He was panting heavily.

I'm ready for the kill. Score!

Together with her, Drake came with a wheeze, pumping a few more times, then pausing and checking her.

She felt an aftershock of contractions, then a sudden emptiness — he had pulled out.

He was still smiling. "You're a force of nature in every way imaginable, not to be rejected for any reason whatsoever. But you already know that, don't you?"

Syreen touched his cheek to brush away a single tear. "Today, I was. But I didn't make demands."

"Oh, you did. Not today, but when you made us hear, when you made an entire world fall in love with you." Drake took a deep breath. "To be honest, I just wanted a hug and a kiss, but these ladies —" He waved at the girls — "obviously had other plans for us."

The Navigator turned to Vivien and Charlene, both all smiles. "So you came back. You didn't find a place to stay for good here?"

Charlene spoke up first. "We did. You know we went through hell on Gattaca. We had lost all hope, and then an angel came to lead us to heaven. Together with this angel, we faced dangers beyond comprehension, only to come out stronger than before. Moreover, we learned that we're even stronger together. You know I'm telling the truth, Syreen. You need us. And we need you, because this universe isn't ready to fully accept women yet."

— *She's right. We need them.* —

Hush, pal. She's not finished yet.

"Anyway — when you let us hear that song, the way it resonated in me, I knew we were bonded. The song told me we must follow the same path. And I'm glad, because I won't find a place where I feel safer or more comfortable than here, with *Assiduous* and you."

Vivien nodded. "That true for all of us — except for the few who found a father for their children within the Crown fleet. And Jona, Gwen, and Chiara, perhaps. They're following their partners."

Peysoon stepped forward. "They've gone with *Bumblebee*. I heard they officially hired on as junior sailors with Fleet. A minor favor Duchy admiralty was quite willing to grant the spouses of three of Fleet's highest-decorated officers. Their mission is to take Lord Hakon and Jacomo around so they can found a new guild tribunal and establish diplomatic relationships with some of the places you visited. Whether you planned it or not, the Duchy has become a place of political importance. Did you know that there's comm drone traffic twice daily now? *Assiduous* is tracking incoming communications—requests for consultations are coming from everywhere."

Drake pointed at the floor. "This is a nodix of power now. With the Association paralyzed, Fleet's fifteen destroyers together with the eleven Crown destroyers and the stingships are the strongest military force in this sector. The duke's willingness to deploy most of them on escort missions further amplified the Duchy's influence."

Syreen shook her head. "That was meant to provide the green crews with some practical experience."

"Maybe." Drake grinned. "But it demonstrates a willingness to accept responsibility for the safety of space travel to the other star nations. Merchants arriving here say it's the star angel's doing, and it makes them feel confident about a brighter future. Did you know? About a quarter of the haulers arriving here have mixed crews. I've heard of a few female junior pilots. Still learning the ropes, but hey!"

The Navigator shrugged. "I didn't tell them."

"I once heard an allegory," a gentle voice from the back chimed in. The girls moved to the sides to grant Syreen a view of Casey.

The waitress from Appalahoo sat on a table and wiggled her toes. "If you throw a stone into a lake, it causes waves that travel far. The larger the stone, the bigger the waves. I'd say you dropped a truly big rock."

Casey's words reminded Syreen of the lake on Klondike where she had left *Raydancer* and her team behind while she had traveled to Nysa and back.

"You don't have to do it all by yourself." Casey stood up. "Sometimes you're just the catalyst. And now, I'll fetch you a forwine, okay?"

Chapter Thirty-Six

With a smile, Syreen tested her labia before slipping into her pilot's chair. They all had shared a merry dinner with a lot of forwine, kisses, and a few girls having fun with each other. Thoughts of the latter sufficed to make her crotch slippery before she impaled herself on her ship's big cock. This sensation made it in turn easier to bear the little pricks in thighs and neck which were necessary to fully connect with *Assiduous*.

Ready to go, pal?

— Ready when you are. —

Okay. Next stop Kendar. Let's find one of your kin.

"Duchy port authority, this is Syreen. We're about to depart."

"*Bon voyage, Navigator.*"

She sighed, then took *Assiduous* on an outbound course.

— You are sad. Why? —

I'm leaving the one place I ever called home. It no longer feels like home, though. I did my duty, and now I'm free to go. But I'm not feeling relieved, I'm feeling forlorn.

— How can I compensate for this? —

I have no clue. I'm feeling comfortable inside you, but — I can't name it.

— Could you sing it? —

She held her breath and closed her eyes.

One day I might.

Next, she entered hyperspace.

When Syreen emerged from deep integration, she felt a sudden dizziness.

Strange.

She focused inside. *No, I'm okay.*

Not okay was Kendar's song, or, better put, Kendar's lament.

The star was grieving—about a lost child who never returned, and about a dying friend. *Dying?*

"Peysoon, to the bridge—now!"

Pal, tell me—how can we recharge a friend? How do you bottle sunlight?

— Pardon? —

The living ship—the dying ship—needs power. How much energy can you put in the shuttle?

— It's already charged to the max, but that's no more than a spark to a ship. —

Yes. We need more.

Where did *Assiduous* store his power? Everywhere—a fully charged living ship was beaming with power from every cell. If she wanted to take energy along, she needed to take a part of him along—or not?

— I can't disassemble myself. That's not how a living ship works. —

I wouldn't want you to. Just provide a kind of battery—like a jug of forwine.

— That's not how it works. You seem to assume that I own a kind of power core that could be extracted. But my body as a whole holds my energy. —

So I'd need another entity that holds its own energy. Like—like a child? Pal, can you charge one of our eggs?

—What? You want to hatch it? —

Not if I don't have to. Could it hold some energy without being hatched?

— I will try that. —

Thanks. If it works, put it on a skid and into the shuttle.

Peysoon appeared at the door. "Any trouble?"

"Come close and take my hand. We must link and sing a song."

"What kind of song?"

"We need to soothe your mother."

"Oh."

CHAPTER THIRTY-SEVEN

Syreen smiled at Peysoon. "Better."

He let her hand go. "It's still odd. A star feeling worried. A star cheering. A big fiery ball as parent. Sounds mad."

"It wasn't easy for me to get used to that idea, I can tell you."

"But you can hear them all the time."

"If I want to, yes. That may have helped. Are you sure you can't? Did you try to listen?"

"Not really. I — I wouldn't know how it works."

"Just open your mind, like you would if you tried to find other people like me. You'll feel my presence, you try to listen past me. Just be patient once you try." She sat up. "Right now, I wanted to ask you if you'd accompany me dirtside. You know the place."

He swallowed hard. "Of course. You can imagine I'm not enthusiastic to return there, but you're right — I know the place, and I know where to find the ship."

"Thank you."

"You're welcome — oh, did you already register our arrival?"

"No. I'm waiting for the port authority call."

Peysoon grinned. "Port authority? Why should they bother to maintain a permanent presence? They know the ore hauler schedules, and there's always a girl waiting."

"Ah, right — you mentioned something like that. Okay, I'll call." How long until someone would answer? "Kendar port authority, this is the living ship *Assiduous,* Navigator Syreen speaking. I need to check with one of my people here."

"Navigator, this is Kendar Orbital, Dock Master Rutter. Kendar is privately owned. We do not grant access to strangers. You may recharge and then leave."

Wow, that was quick. "Negative, Dock Master. I need to visit the planet. The Association's Admiralty granted me free travel and I plan to apply that grant here."

The next answer took a moment longer. *"Navigator, this is Governor Wilson. Kendar Mining is a private business. We will not grant access to strangers, that's my final decision. Your agreements with the Navy won't help you here. Nysa is far away."*

"Governor, I must insist. If necessary, I have to force access."

"You can't do that! Our Navy will come and get you!"

"As you just mentioned, Governor—Nysa is far away and won't help you here. Moreover, your lack of willingness to cooperate on such a marginal topic triggers my curiosity. You might be trying to cover illegal activities. I should collect evidence."

"You—you can't do that. This station is armed!"

Syreen shook her head, although he couldn't see that. "Governor, the moment you shoot at an Enforcer, your station becomes a legitimate military target, and you would gain nothing. We defeated dreadnaughts."

"Dreadnaughts—wait—the Klondike battle?"

"Yes. That's us."

"Well, then—do what you have to."

"Thank you, Governor. We won't bother you any longer than necessary."

She smiled at Peysoon. "That went easier than I thought."

"Wilson—the same spineless weasel as ever. He'll stab you in the back anytime if you don't watch out."

"Ah, but we won't let him, right?"

"Right."

Their trip dirtside was an easy ride. Syreen enjoyed

piloting the *modified* AP shuttle the old-fashioned way. She wasn't consciously aware of the kind of modifications *Assiduous* had applied, but the small spacecraft felt swifter than before, more responsive to her commands.

Peysoon pointed at a landing pad. "That one. This entrance is closest to the cavern access we need."

"Fine." She placed their shuttle down in the center, aft pointing at the heavy steel doors, and rose from her seat. "Built like a fortress — defense against pirates?"

"No. Those doors are meant to keep people in. Locked and guarded."

"I begin to understand your desire to leave this homely place." She winked at him, passed through the passenger compartment to the cargo bay, and activated the skid.

He operated the cargo door. "What's that? A welcome gift?"

"You could say so. We'll need it once we're there. Please, can you operate the skid?"

"Sure." He took the remote and wrapped it around his wrist. "I spent quite a lot of my time operating ore skids."

"I'm sorry —"

"But it's not ore. Don't worry, I can handle inanimate objects without drowning in dark memories. This is not a token of grief."

"Okay then." Syreen reached out and sensed five guards inside watching Peysoon and her approach the doors. *Open up.*

While they watched the heavy doors moving, Peysoon grinned at her. "Taking a shortcut?"

"Yeah, I did. I didn't come here to waste our time arguing with bullies. We're going in quick, before they can organize significant resistance."

"Suits me."

Peysoon took the lead, followed by the skid. Syreen trailed them, watching and sensing for any signs of opposition.

They passed a few mining workers—poor souls with broken minds and sore backs. Not even her nude shape stirred any attention in them. She felt sorry for them, but this kind of abuse wasn't her jurisdiction.

Soon they reached deserted corridors that underscored the appropriateness of calling planets *dirtside*. Peysoon had brought lights that mercilessly tore the dark veil from dust and dirt, crawly critters, and rough surfaces.

Syreen found out she wouldn't have needed them. When she opened her senses, she could easily tell open spaces from dense matter, could point out caverns running parallel to theirs, and could tell of the presence of other lifeforms, including a very familiar one lingering on the brink of existence. Exactly where Peysoon was leading them.

CHAPTER THIRTY-EIGHT

Her first living ship had been dark and wrinkled on the outside when she found it, but it had been ready to go. Syreen wasn't prepared for the worrisome shape she found at the end of this natural cavern.

"We can only hope it's still functional." Peysoon stepped to her side.

"He's alive." She reached for a wart next to the central hangar door—nothing like the huge portal *Assiduous* had presented, but rather like a maintenance hatch to an emitter duct.

She had to wait several centicycles before she sensed a dim flicker.

"I got that far before." Peysoon waved around. "It appeared bigger back then, but I think it's because I yet had to grow up. Oh, this time it's opening."

Syreen went on her knees and began to crawl through the door as soon as it was wide enough.

"It didn't do that back then." Peysoon's voice was muffled.

"You didn't have the key." Syreen found the pilot chair right before her, close to the door. The ship seemed to contain no more than this one room. "Bring the skid."

She climbed into the chair. The central dildo was limp, but still large enough that she had to feel herself up first.

The moment it slipped inside her, the ship made contact.

— *Who are you?* —

I am Syreen, Navigator of the People, coming to collect you.

— *You came too late. I'm no longer strong enough to leave.* —

You will be. I brought power. Take it.

169

But the ship was too weak. She had to do it herself.

Give me a tiny thread, good. Reach out for the skid. Connect. Now drink.

Peysoon leaned over her chair with a sad face. "We're too late, aren't we?"

"Be patient."

With the first trickle of power, the ship understood what she had offered. A stronger thread grew toward the egg and sucked up more energy.

Here you go.

— This is Assiduous's *offspring. I thought he was lost. —*

He's in orbit.

— Who is his pilot? —

I am.

— And who will be mine? —

I will, for a while. As far as I know, I'm the only living Navigator.

— You are the last one? —

You could say, I am the first. I am Syreen Starborn, daughter of the Duchess.

— This is unheard of. —

She felt the stick in her crotch grow. *You're recovering fast. Will you be able to leave with this charge?*

— It will suffice to reach Kendar. There I can recharge and re-grow. When should we leave? —

Ready when you are. Would you offer a chair to my companion?

— That livestock? —

Peysoon is of the People, too. You met him before — you told him to find a key, and here we are.

— Oh, that one. I wasn't sure whether he understood. I've been too weak for much too long a time. —

The ship grew a new chair. *"Welcome, Peysoon of the People. I am* Audacious. *Thank you for sending me a Navigator."*

"You're welcome. Sorry it took so long. The ways of humanity are not as straightforward as those of the People."

"I understand." *— Navigator, I'm sufficiently recharged and* *ready to go. –*

"Okay, so let's not waste any more time down here. Peysoon, we're leaving."

He quickly took his seat. "Leaving from here? How?"

"The cavern behind is wide enough. I assume that's how *Audacious* arrived here."

"Correct."

Syreen pushed the ship back cautiously. Some rubble scratched their skin, and then they were free. She sensed the twisted open cavern spaces leading outward and memorized a flight path.

– I can assist you in navigating the tight passages. –

I know you can, but I'm fine, thank you. Judging by your name, I may assume you're not timid?

– Timid? Of course not! –

Good. Brace yourself.

She knew where to go, she knew what the still weak *Audacious* was able to do in terms of speed and precision, of course with her guidance. She entered deep integration and accelerated audaciously.

– Hey! –

Audacious's protest came late. The next moment they were airborne and approaching open space. *Sorry, mate. You better get used to the way I'm flying.*

– That was reckless. –

I can assure you it wasn't. I'm a Navigator, I don't break my ship.

– You are still a hatchling. Assiduous *didn't teach you well. –*

He did, but now I'm teaching him. By the way, here we are.

They had reached orbit. As planned, *Assiduous* was right behind them, so that they could slip into his hangar without further maneuvers.

– You didn't prepare a rendezvous maneuver. –

I did, you just didn't notice.

She sat up, then climbed out of the chair. "Okay, we're

back. *Assiduous,* my regards to Governor Wilson. We won't bother him any further. Let's head for the exit, oh, and please ask the others to join us in the hangar, so that *Audacious* can participate."

— Sure. Welcome, brother. —

— Your pilot is mad. —

— My Navigator is skilled. —

Syreen recognized the signs of rivalry. She didn't care.

She waved Peysoon forward and exited after him.

Audacious claimed a large part of *Assiduous's* hangar — the living ship had been tight inside, almost cramped, but was still a mature living ship with all the necessary organs.

— Would you mind if I fetch our shuttle by remote? —

Oh, sure, go ahead.

One after another, her crew arrived.

Drake approached her. "Another living ship? I wouldn't have expected to find one on an inhabited planet."

"Me neither." Syreen waved at the newcomer. "Meet *Audacious. Audacious,* this is Drake. He found the library that held *Assiduous's* hideout, and he ultimately led me there."

"You did most of it," Drake objected.

"*Tell me.*" Audacious sounded harsh. "*How did you find him?*"

So Drake told his story of his research around the ancient library again. *Audacious* asked him a lot of details about museum exhibits and their locations while cutting Drake short about his travels.

"Do you want to hear the rest of the story?" Syreen asked.

"*Not now. I didn't expect that. We are late, perhaps too late.*"

"Too late for what?"

"*To prevent the destruction of our space-time structure, that is, to contain the Void.*"

"What void? I don't understand what you mean."

"*The Void is capable of consuming hyperspace. Once the hyperplane is gone, stars die and collapse into singularities — ultimately into one singularity. Only the Void remains."*

Syreen shook her head. "Sounds like we'd better put an end to such a nasty creature's existence."

"The Void cannot be ended, only contained."

"That sounds like stalling, not like a final solution."

"Yes. That's what I said."

"Well—what do we need to contain that Void?"

"Living ships, as many as we can get, with their pilots."

"New pilots."

"Yes."

Peysoon frowned and showed his palms.

When she gazed at Drake, the researcher shrugged.

"That won't be easy. We can't exactly print pilots, and everything else would take time. We're empty-handed, so to speak."

"No, we're not." Charlene waved at Drake. "He mentioned a shipwreck—perhaps it looks like a wreck for us, but could be reanimated, too? And if *Assiduous's* position was mentioned in another ship's library, perhaps we could find further clues?"

"Worth a try." Vivien nudged Peysoon. "We could try making pilots, chap. Clearly beats waiting for doomsday."

He shrugged. "It doesn't work that way."

"No." Syreen pointed at *Audacious*. "As he said, we're already late. We need grown-up pilots now."

"How?" Vivien still eyed the former master. "Clone them?"

*Clone them . . ."*Vivien, you're brilliant."

CHAPTER THIRTY-NINE

Syreen was lounging in a comfy chair in the mess, listening to the song of the nameless star they had selected to recharge *Audacious* and contemplating Vivien's idea.

She herself had been born by a star as a fully developed human child, not as a fetus. Could she ask the stars for a similar act of creation? Could she even ask for a grown-up person, and would that be advisable at all?

Drake entered the mess, thus interrupting her musings. He smiled upon her appearance — all nude, legs and arms spread invitingly wide — but didn't comment on it.

"Where are we going next?" he asked instead.

"I have no clue." She wiggled the toes of her right foot. "I honestly don't know where to start yet. I know how to fight something, but how to fight *nothing?*"

The researcher shook his head. "Our new friend seems to be quite tight-lipped about that topic. Or poorly briefed himself. Well." He took a deep breath. "If there's one thing my research taught me, it's patience. Just keep collecting pieces until you see the whole picture."

"If there's one thing your research taught me, it's that you need to put the right people together to achieve results."

Drake grinned at her. "Indeed. So, if we don't have all the right people together, we should find more."

"Back to question one — where to start?"

"Yes — but we've just established that there's no fixed path yet. Any cue is a good cue."

"Okay. You have one?"

Drake shrugged. "We know that early settlements are somehow connected to your people. Are there any other nations like the Duchy and Danos?"

"Maybe. Such information wasn't taught in Fleet academy. *Assiduous*, do you know any such nations?"

"How would I?"

"You incorporated *Raydancer's* library. Any matches of current star nations to your own data?"

"The stars are all where they should be."

Syreen rolled her eyes and smirked at Drake. "Okay. Let me rephrase my question. How many colonized star systems from your own library belong to single-star nations today?"

"Seven. That's the Duchy, Danos, Rathole —"

"Such a system exists?" Drake interrupted.

"You'd be surprised what I came across — Matin, Salamanca, Harmony, and Nizwa. The latter two were in Bumblebee's *log, too."*

"Harmony and Nizwa." She stared at her toes. "I have unfinished business there. And now I have good reason to return there."

Drake followed her gaze. "Which one first?"

"Oh, no, we won't start there. I'd say we start at Salamanca, the name has a nice ring. For Harmony, I'll need at least a platoon of marines anyway. But first, I must decide what to do with *Audacious*."

When her mind focused on the other living ship, she sensed a kind of echo. She grabbed it and pulled, like she would have pulled a strand from the nearest star.

— *Navigator?* —

Yes, it's me.

— *You are not seated.* —

I'm not even aboard. I'm sitting in Assiduous's *mess.*

— *For all I know, that's impossible.* —

Not for me. I don't need a seat to talk with Assiduous, *so why would I need a seat to contact you?*

— But you are several light seconds away, and there's no message delay. —

The limits of light speed do not apply to us. In any case, I know now that we can fly together. Although I think we'll have to take you piggyback through hyperspace.

— So you will take me along? I won't have to wait for another megacycle for a new pilot? —

I will have to solve your pilot problem, but until then, you will join us, yes.

— These are miraculous times indeed. —

Syreen smelled forwine and looked up.

Drake had made room for Peysoon who carried two mugs in his left hand and one in his right. The former master grinned at her inviting display and turned to the researcher. "Forwine for you?"

"Yes, thanks." Drake nodded at Peysoon and then winked at her. "I'll leave you two alone."

After he had walked away, Peysoon held out the second mug to Syreen. "For you, too?"

"Sure, thanks."

"You're welcome. You reached a decision where we're going next?"

"Yes—how did you know?"

"I didn't. You could say I sensed a feeling of determination. Whether it was you, or *Assiduous,* or both of you, I can't tell. But it seems like I'm somehow getting in tune with . . ." He shrugged. "Don't know with what."

"It's Salamanca." She saw a glimpse of puzzlement in him. "Our destination. We might find more clues there."

"Salamanca—oh yes, quite far out, one of the early settlements. I discarded that world in my initial assessment, but . . . well, you might have better ways to detect something."

She smiled and sat up. "What else do you know of that place?"

"Dull. Mining, Agriculture, small industry, mainly feudal system. Little to no trade activity, but they're guild members. No orbital station, just a small shuttle port. A dozen ground-based fighters to keep pirates at bay. They're part of the message drone system, although on a monthly schedule only, and their system is said to have a still active navigation beacon."

"That's extraordinary. What's their stance on visitors?"

"I didn't care to investigate that, as you can imagine. The dossier called them old-fashioned."

"Okay." She took a sip from her mug. "I'll consider an appropriate approach."

"Whatever that means." Peysoon shrugged.

CHAPTER FORTY

Syreen rose from deep integration. "Well, folks, welcome to Salamanca."

The system indeed had a still active beacon. There was no space traffic in the system, except for *Assiduous*. As they didn't cause any entry shock, didn't show a lot of emissions, and had entered the system at a respectful distance to the main planet, it could take some time before the local authorities would recognize their presence.

She hadn't come to sneak up on them, so she activated a transponder code.

"Salamanca port authorities for Enforcer *Assiduous*, Navigator Syreen calling. Would you kindly grant us permission to enter orbit?"

The answer came with a significant delay, more than the distance could explain. *"Enforcer* Assiduous *for Salamanca port authorities, this is Space Marshal Rutherford speaking. Please state the purpose of your visit."*

"Marshal Rutherford, Salamanca is one of the oldest human settlements in this sector. Lady Syreen Starborn, Knight of the Duchy's Order of the Firepath, would like to research whether you have any records about her people's origin."

This time, the answer came quick. *"Navigator Syreen, a knight of the Duchy will always be welcome on Salamanca. Please excuse my curiosity, but the identical names strike me."*

"Marshal Rutherford, I am the same person. In my role as Navigator of this ship I'm asking permission for myself in my role as Duchy knight."

"You're flying alone, My Lady?"

"Not quite. I currently host twenty-four guests aboard and my second ship tagging along."

"Twenty-four guests and no crew? Pardon me for being so inquisitive, My Lady, but curiosity is killing me. Unlike the Duchy, we rarely ever see visitors here."

"The Duchy had a few undesired visitors lately, but we rectified that — which is the cause I was knighted for."

"We received news of the invasion, as well as of the edict against Associated Planets. I'm infinitely glad to hear that the time of distress for your people is over. And now I'm even more eager to hear about the solution. Where did the Duchy find a fleet large enough, and the experienced leader to successfully deploy it?"

"Marshal, I should ask you for a little more patience, so that the retired Duchy Fleet Commander can tell you the whole story face-to-face. And if you can offer us a space large enough to set down, we'll gladly show you that fleet."

"Oooh, My Lady, we'll find such a place for sure. Would you consider to enlighten our entire House of Lords?"

"Whatever suits you best, Marshal. Oh, by the way, we've brought sixteen tons of rare-earth and heavy metals which we'd like to trade in for an equal amount of basic organic substances."

"I fear we can't afford your metals, but of course we can share our food with you, My Lady."

"Marshal Rutherford, I meant it as I said it. Sixteen tons of raw metal against sixteen tons of raw organics — organic waste, toxic substances, whatever you'd like to get rid of. I need to feed my ships."

"Your ships?"

"Sorry — I forgot to mention. My ships, *Assiduous* and *Audacious*, are living ships."

Syreen gently set *Assiduous* down on the paved parade ground and let the still smaller *Audacious* follow with minimal delay. Then she allowed herself to relax and have a look around through *Assiduous's* sensors.

Thousands of people were lining the borders of the parade ground and watching the spectacle—judging by their apparel, soldiers in the front ranks, commoners behind them. The word obviously had gotten around. Long rows of tall trees around the ground reminded her of Appalahoo. According to her records, Salamanca didn't have large sauroid predators, though.

After her statement about living ships, Marshal Rutherford had fallen silent. Salamanca had sent a set of coordinates as if it would tell all—in a way, it did.

The doors to underground hangars yawned behind the people at *Assiduous'* left side. The fighters that Peysoon had mentioned were weaving an intriguing pattern of green-and-red smoke in the air above them.

The crowd on the opposite side parted to give way to a formation of forty-nine soldiers in dress whites, marching in step in four columns of twelve men and women, led by one officer with peaked cap and saber.

Syreen could sense the puzzlement in their commanding officer. *"Assiduous,* illuminate our door."

"I can do a bit more than that."

Through their connection, she felt flashing lights running down their right leg, guiding the way to their crotch.

"Good idea, mate."

She slipped out of her chair and into her dress uniform. The beret came last. When she straightened herself and pulled the jacket straight, a whistle came from the door.

Peysoon was waiting for her in plain AP dress whites—no rank insignia, no decorations. He made a deep bow. "My Lady, you know I appreciate your usual natural appearance, but you look truly impressive this way."

She curtsied. "Thank you. Will you accompany me to meet our welcoming committee?"

"Of course."

When they reached the brightly lit main hangar, Syreen smiled. Her girls had formed two lines toward the door, standing straight in green jackets, tight green pants and shining black boots.

Charlene whistled, making them salute, and turned to Syreen. "Navigator, we're ready to receive guests. We were advised that the local customs might require decent manners, so we opted for formal clothing today. We won't embarrass you."

Syreen grinned and nodded. "You won't ever, but thank you all."

She spotted Drake and Crow in the back and waved at them. "Come, don't hide."

The two men lined up behind Peysoon and herself. She closed her eyes and checked the situation outside. The last soldiers were just reaching their positions.

She gave them another centicycle.

Finally, she nodded at Charlene. "Showtime. *Assiduous,* flash lights and then open the door."

The lights were just a courtesy to the officer outside, so that he could call his men and women to attention.

Once the main door had opened, she walked forward to the ledge, turned to the officer and saluted. "Navigator Syreen Starborn requests permission to come ashore, sir."

If the formal address had taken him by surprise, he was quick to gather his wits. He returned the salute. "Permission granted, My Lady. Welcome to Salamanca. I am Captain Harker, at your service."

So she exited her ship and walked up to him. "Thank you, Captain. Are there procedures to observe with regard to our visit?"

"I was specifically instructed that there are no procedures involved other than welcoming you and guiding you and your company of choice to the House of Lords. Any of your guests who don't want to join us are invited to enjoy our capital's hospitality to their own liking."

"That is very kind, thank you." She turned around. "You heard our host? It's your call."

No surprise, the three men were joining her.

Charlene guided the girls straight across the ground in something like a dance formation, too cheerful to be taken as mockery, but still impressively in sync.

It wasn't just Captain Harker who momentarily forgot his professional attitude when his gaze followed the happy parade—all his men and women stared after them.

Syreen clapped Harker's shoulder, thus pulling him out of his reverie. "My entertainment team. But don't take them lightly—they're seasoned veterans, having gone through battle with me."

Chapter Forty-One

While following their welcome committee toward a large building not far from the parade ground, Syreen opened her mind to the emotions around her, to both spectators and escort.

Predominant were curiosity and excitement, not surprisingly.

She found a lot of awe with a hint of fear and attributed it to the ship she had landed in their midst—undeniably a demonstration of power, even if unintended.

Diligence was strongest in Harker and Crow, and mirrored in the soldiers around.

One source radiated impatience—Peysoon, of course.

Harker left his column and joined her. "Do you do a lot of walking on your homeworld?"

"Not really. I'm a spacer. I was born and raised on an orbital station and spent almost all of my life in space. I've done most of my surface walking on remote worlds like Klondike, Appalahoo and Gattacca."

"I've heard of Appalahoo—a vacation spot with fierce wildlife, right? Not the first choice for a casual stroll, certainly not unarmed."

She nodded. "Truly fierce wildlife."

"Sauroids, I heard. Did you see one?"

"I met and fought several of them—with hands and claws."

"No!" He glanced at her. "But you weren't injured."

"Some scratches, nothing serious. But one of their top

predators lost his head after he tried to mess with me. I'm not someone to mess with."

"Of that I've heard—some pirates had to learn that the hard way, didn't they? And recently, Associated Planets."

"Indeed. You're quite well informed." She pointed forward. "Like the House, I assume?"

"My Lady, we don't have many visitors, but we're watching what happens around us, and the news about a triple star angel and about some real space battles was the most prominent stuff in megacycles. You may well assume that every lord has heard about you. What the news doesn't tell is why these events happened."

"I'm happy to offer some background. How large will the audience be? Will you attend, too?"

"The House of Lords has twenty-five seats, including the speaker. The Advisor's Council encompasses twelve more seats—you already spoke with the Space Marshal. Beyond that, there are some seats on the floor for petitioners and other guests, more than sufficient for you and your company. Finally, there's a gallery for the general audience with about two hundred seats for public sessions—but today's not public."

"Oh—well, why don't you join my team?"

"I, My Lady?"

"Yes—as my advisor on Salamanca customs and etiquette. That shouldn't cause a conflict of interest, so I'm sure your superiors will understand my need for a little support." She suppressed a grin when she sensed his excitement. "Would you mind relaying my request for aid to your superiors?"

Harker led Syreen and her entourage in through a wide and heavy two-winged wooden door.

The house was surely designed to be intimidating to the ordinary petitioner or guest, with the seats of the lords rising high above the floor in a semicircle and the advisors' seats in another semicircle below, but the effect was lost on Syreen.

Instead, she felt slightly offended — the choice of place seemed to indicate that the Salamancans felt superior.

Or had the assembled lords simply not considered this potential impression on their guest? Because using their most prominent place came naturally to them? Syreen opened her mind to their emotions while following Harker to a small dais on the floor.

She sensed a mix of admiration, curiosity and respect, and when she glanced around, friendly faces were gazing down on her.

One man in the lower semicircle rose. When he started to speak, she recognized him as Space Marshal Rutherford.

"Ladies and gentlemen, please welcome Lady Syreen Starborn, Knight of the Duchy's Order of the Firepath and her company with me."

There was a little shuffling when the lords and advisors rose from their seats.

Syreen curtsied.

Rutherford went on, "Lady Syreen, welcome to Salamanca and to the House of Lords. May I introduce to you the Lord Premier Venessa Blue Lake, Speaker of the House?"

Syreen straightened herself, and all hosts but one woman sat down.

Harker leaned over to her and whispered, "In case you might wonder, the rank and title of lord isn't limited to male persons on Salamanca."

She quickly nodded before directing her attention at Lord Venessa.

"Lady Syreen, in the name of our people, feel welcome and at home on Salamanca. Welcome to your company, too." She nodded at the four men. "May I express our hope that the most honorable Knight of the Firepath and her skilled

Navigator and star angel find some time to join us for dinner, so that the retired Duchy Fleet Commander will share her story with us?"

Syreen smiled and agreed with another brief curtsy.

The Lord Premier went on, "But first—and I must apologize for my curiosity—please enlighten us—why would you expect our records to give you more insight on the Duchy people's origin than the Duchy's records?"

The Navigator raised an eyebrow. "Oh. Pardon me, but I might have failed to mention a minor detail. While, in a wider sense, all Duchy people are Lady Syreen's people, we're not of the same origin. Don't let my human looks fool you. *My people,* the Navigator's people, are the creators of my living ships, until recently the so-called *Forgotten People.*"

The following silence was like turning deaf. Syreen felt as if she could *hear* the turmoil of emotions in her audience.

It didn't seem to be right to use her mind control to soothe them. There had to be another way. *Of course.*

She opened her mind further and reached for Salamanca's star. *Sing to me.*

Next, she took Peysoon's hand. *Sing to us.*

CHAPTER FORTY-TWO

"That was beautiful," Lord Premier Venessa said awhile after Syreen had ended her mental transmission. "But what was it?"

"Your home star," Syreen said. "One of the quirks of being a Navigator — I can hear the songs of the stars, and with some effort, we can relay their songs to you." Only then did she let Peysoon's hand go.

"So." The premier glanced left and right at her peers. "We're facing a true member of the Forgotten People, or Ancient Guides, as they're called in some of our records. We are so much honored by your visit, Navigator. Of course, you shall have unrestricted access to our records, and we will ask our historians to aid you every way they can."

"This is most generous of you, Lord Premier." Syreen curtsied. "In return, my ships and I will try to answer your questions, and your historians' questions as well."

"We'll be infinitely grateful for your precious time and any fragment of wisdom you're willing to share with us."

Syreen chuckled. "Now, please, let's not get stuck with these polite formalities. Yes, our time is precious, our mission is urgent, but we're not counting tencycles. Our experience is at least as precious, so it's necessary to share and spread it in case we fail."

"Fail? What do you mean?"

"Our mission is dangerous, success or survival are not granted. We're facing a serious threat, and in this case, *We* means all of us, my people, your people, other people we might not yet have learned about, the entire galaxy. Why else would the stars bother to create offspring?"

Most of the lords and advisors showed a puzzled face, some appeared startled.

"What does that mean, the stars create offspring?" Space Marshal Rutherford asked.

"That's what *Starborn* stands for. Syreen Starborn, born into a human-shaped body by the Duchy's central star. My parent is a huge fiery stellar object, and please don't ask me how that works. And if you feel shocked, imagine what I had to feel when I learned about it."

"How can you cope with it?" the marshal went on.

"By trying to act normal, by pushing all that supernatural stuff aside. Like, didn't someone mention dinner?"

Syreen placed her silver spoon down on the now emptied china plate, took her glass of forwine, and leaned back in the comfy chair. For a moment, she enjoyed the dessert's lingering aftertaste and ignored the noises and emotions of the people around her.

The hall seemed to be large enough to harbor a frigate, she noted with amusement, but the delicate glasswork covering parts of the walls and of the pale-yellow marble columns might suffer from its maneuvers.

Space Marshal Rutherford, sitting to her left at the long dining table, raised his own glass toward her, and they clinked.

"Duke's health," she said and sipped.

"Duke's health." The marshal sipped and smiled. "Do your people have your own toast?"

"I don't know. Should I ever meet one of my ancestors, I'll ask."

"Oh. Sorry, I didn't want to—"

She waved aside. "No worries. That distant past doesn't

cause me sadness. Not knowing if and where my kin might suffer today troubles me."

"Oh."

"That's why I came here. To find clues where my people might have lived in the past and might again live today."

"You really think there are more of your people?"

"Yes. One of us might be a curious twist of fate. Two are a pattern. I just don't see the whole picture yet."

Rutherford smiled. "If you see it that way — yes, you might have a point. In that case, why don't you give us some insight into your story so that we get an idea what to look for?"

"Sure." Syreen rose and glanced around the dining hall. "Do you have a dais or something?"

"If you like, you can step on the table. But it'd be as okay if you stay where you are. Mike and cam can read you fine anywhere."

"Okay." She nodded. "Ready when you are."

Someone seemed to have picked up the cue already — the chatter quickly faded, and she could sense the people's curiosity directed at her.

"Okay, folks. You already heard a lot about me, so some of what I'm telling you now isn't new, but my story will put it into context. My story begins with a flashing red light over my bedroom door — the general combat alarm for all Duchy pilots . . ."

CHAPTER FORTY-THREE

Syreen's throat felt sore. She'd just finished a comprehensive summary of her story that still had taken more than a cycle, and the audience had remained perfectly silent. No whispers, no coughs, no more than a quiet shuffle here and there—no one had interrupted her report.

Rutherford handed her a glass. She nodded gratefully and downed its contents. Then she opened her senses and gazed around.

Most people were still stirred up by her story. Most of the others were already directing their attention at their Lord Premier. Lord Venessa belonged to the first and larger group of people, though.

"Oookay, folks," Syreen said aloud. "Why don't we take a break now to let that story sink in, take a walk, enjoy some fresh air, and rejoin here in a halfcycle to answer your questions—which you surely will have by then?"

A tiny mental nudge made the Lord Premier nod and thus dismiss the audience. Syreen sensed relief in her as well as in many other people, including the almost-invisible, almost omnipresent waiters taking care of empty glasses and everything, who were given a chance for a break and then to catch up with their duties, too.

However, instead of taking a walk herself, Lord Venessa approached Syreen. "Lady Syreen, just a word, please."

"Sure."

"Your marvelous story triggered an idea—if you're looking for truly old settlements, you might consider Epirus. It once was our home world before the early settlers found Salamanca. Most decided to move on, some stayed behind. It's an independent mining world today, and not easy to deal and trade with—but surely less troublesome than Kendar."

"Thank you. That sounds promising indeed."

"I'm glad if I could help your cause. I will provide you with a letter of recommendation. It might alleviate their pathological mistrust of strangers."

Pathological mistrust? How promising.

Syreen smiled. "Thank you again, Lord Venessa. Once I arrive there, I will proceed with caution and diplomacy." *I sense you're worried.* "I'll try to not make things more difficult for you."

The Lord Premier shook her head. "Don't worry about us. You probably have enough on your plate already." She waited until another waiter had left with his full tray. "In private, if I may be so bold . . . how do you get along with this collection of truly handsome men? Do you enjoy their, hum, *presence?*"

Nicely put. "I didn't mention that, but my historian and his bodyguard aren't interested in women. About my kin—as I said, we didn't have the best start together. I'm trying to look forward, but I feel better when he's not too close."

"You don't feel lonely sometimes?"

"Never. There's always my partner—my ship."

"No, I mean . . ."

"Oh, that. Well, maybe I'll find me a handsome Salamancan once our formal event ends."

Syreen could sense amusement and a bit of arousal in her host. *So she's adventurous, too?*

The Lord Premier pointed toward the door. "Perhaps we should enjoy a bit of fresh air, too. Let the people do their work here."

Chapter Forty-Four

Syreen adjusted herself in her seat.

— I can change the seat. —

Oh, I'm fine, partner. I just need to convince myself of it. The seats in that hall weren't half as comfy, and the last session was long.

— Okay. —

She closed her eyes and relaxed. For a while, she was happy just enjoying *Assiduous's* reassuring presence with Salamanca's song in the back of her mind. However, there was more to sense.

People around were radiating excitement and happiness, curiosity and impatience.

There were their passengers. Their girls were excitedly exchanging the happy endeavors from their city visit. Drake and Peysoon were curious about her findings and plans.

There was a crowd of locals assembled around the parade ground, excited and happy to be allowed to watch a genuine living ship with their own eyes, and at the same time curious about the upcoming departure. Some were a bit impatient.

We can do something about that.

"Salamanca port authorities, Space Marshal Rutherford, this is Syreen. We're ready for departure. Thank you for your hospitality."

"Navigator Syreen, you're cleared to go. Air and space are free. Farewell, have a good journey, and may the stars always sing happy songs for you."

His last line made her feel warmth. He had listened well.

Her next announcement was for her passengers only.

"Folks, we're leaving. Ready for takeoff in five."

Am I stalling? No. It's sensible to check the flight path myself.

— Although we could fly circles around any potential obstacle. —

You're so right, pal. However, such a stunt might scare our new friends. There's no need to show off now.

— My Navigator is wise. —

Owing to my skirmisher pilot training. If you want to become a Duchy Fleet officer, you must learn to behave. She grinned. *Or you learn how to properly explain actions that are otherwise considered reckless.*

The sky above was clear, though, leaving no opportunity for such reckless behavior.

A thought made *Assiduous* rise a few legs above the ground. The excited feelings that she sensed outside grew.

Time's up. Let's go.

The living ship tilted upward and sailed away gracefully. Only after they had reached the vacuum of open space and rejoined with *Audacious* did Syreen allow for high acceleration.

"Okay, folks. We're doing just a little skip to Epirus. It's a mining world that'd been colonized even before Salamanca, as the Lord Premier told me. She also told me that Epirus might be less hospitable, so you'd better not expect much. By the way, we'll arrive there within the halfcycle."

Sadly, the tedious sessions with the Salamancan librarians hadn't yielded any further results. Epirus remained the only lead she had gained.

"Epirus, eh?" That was Drake's voice, picked up in the mess. "You seem to have a fancy for exotic routes and planets."

She grinned. "Well, I've found many good friends that way."

Her answer caused happy laughter in the mess.

Not only had she found her partner on a most remote, even uncharted planet, and thus made Drake and Crow her friends. On her *exotic* routes, she had found so many friends among the merchants she had escorted. On Gattaca she had picked up her girls, and during that journey had made friendship with Mo, Yusef, and Haiki. On Appalahoo she had collected Casey.

Who might I find on Epirus?

That's wrong.
— *What's wrong?* —
Syreen slowed them down but didn't leave hyperspace yet.
There's something wrong with the fabric around Epirus. It's weak.

She felt a shudder and emerged from her deep integration with the ship. "Girls, I might need you. Come to the bridge, please."

There was another disturbing fact. *I can't hear her song. Epirus is quiet.*

— *Her surface temperature doesn't match our library data.* —
Yes. She's dim also. Alarmingly so.

Vivien and Charlene were the first to arrive on their bridge. "We're here. What's up?"

"I need to do some urgent repairs here. Epirus is in trouble."

"Oh." Vivien approached the pilot seat, leaned down, and offered her neck. "Take what you need."

That wasn't what Syreen had had in mind, but Vivien's advice was sensible, so she bit and drank. Charlene followed.

When the next girl approached her chair, Syreen raised a hand. "Not yet, Lucy. But stay close, please. I don't know yet what to make of this."

She focused on *Assiduous* again. *Let's mend some space, partner.*

As she had practiced in the chasm, she reached out to the neighboring stars and plucked strands from them to create a delicate woven pattern. The stars answered with cheerful chords in their songs.

Syreen touched Epirus to attach the web but found no hold. Epirus felt cold and slick. But she also sensed a whimper, so she tried again — to no avail.

Let's try something else.

She already had a woven structure. By plucking *here* and *there,* she formed a kind of hyperstructural bag, which she then wrapped around Epirus.

This is tedious — and exhausting.

But she wasn't ready to give up yet.

Peysoon, please join me.

To her surprise, her next-of-kin was already present on the bridge. He only had to reach out one hand to touch hers.

On Kendar and Salamanca, his support had greatly enhanced her way of communicating with stars. It seemed worth a try.

Let's sing together.

At first, she sensed an echo, then resonance, then a variation.

And finally, a light, fine tune evolved.

Peysoon and Syreen picked up the cue and adapted their own song, and Epirus replied, where its song even found a dim resonance on the planet itself.

Yes!

But Syreen felt so tired . . .

Casey's worried face covered Syreen's entire field of vision. "Are you okay?"

The Navigator took a deep breath. "Yes, I think so. Partner?"

"We left the hyperplane and are currently sailing the Epirus system on a tangential trajectory."

She smiled at Casey. "I think we did it. Epirus is singing again."

"But?"

"I might have overstrained myself. It was an effort. Some-thing seemed to block my access to the star."

"How can that be?"

"I have no idea."

— *We might.* Audacious, *what's your take?* —

— *What we found here might be a sign of the Void.* —

But how?

— *Epirus was seriously weakened, that much we can tell. How that could happen, I cannot envision.* —

Casey frowned. "Hey, Syreen, are you with us?"

Syreen focused on her. "Sorry, I was checking with our ships."

"Oh, okay." The former barmaid rose and made a step back. "I'm still not used to that. Anything we should know?"

"Not now." She noticed that she still held Peysoon's hand, turned to him, and let go. "Thank you."

"Glad I could help." He smirked. "Somehow I sense what you're doing, but it still feels like a miracle to me."

"Consider how that seems for us." Casey waved her arms. "We're living and traveling in a miraculous ship, and we only understand half of what's happening."

She faced Syreen and smiled. "I'm not complaining. I'm just part of the enchantment."

The Navigator nodded. "Okay. Well—let me tend to some mundane tasks now. I think it's sensible to call the local au-thorities now."

"Of course."

Both Casey and Peysoon withdrew from her chair. Only now did she see Lucy and Ashley in the background together with Vivien and Charlene, all showing signs of fatigue—had she needed all four?

— *We might need more livestock in the future.* —

Yes. Now let me make that call.

She checked their trajectory again. They were still ap-proaching the solitary planet.

"Epirus port authorities for Enforcer *Assiduous,* Navigator Syreen calling. Would you kindly grant us permission to enter orbit?"

There was the usual message delay.

"Navigator, this is Epirus. You may recharge and travel on. We don't trade with strangers."

Nicer than expected. She chuckled. "Epirus port authorities for Enforcer *Assiduous,* Navigator Syreen calling again. I didn't come for trading, but for investigating my own people's past. I've learned that you're one of the oldest settlements around. I'm carrying a letter of recommendation from Salamanca."

"Salamanca, huh? You can take your letter and wipe your ass with it. And I tell you – " The grumpy voice was cut off.

Another voice continued. *"Navigator Syreen, this is Epirus Port Commander Cromwell. Please ignore the previous communication. On behalf of the Epirus government, please accept our heartfelt welcome. You may proceed to orbit at your own discretion. As you might know, we cannot offer you the convenience of an orbital station."*

"Commander Cromwell, thank you for your warm welcome. We'll arrive in orbit soon."

The message delay shrank with every call. Obviously this wasn't lost to the local authorities.

"Navigator Syreen, according to my readings, you're approaching too fast to make orbit. Or am I mistaken?"

"Commander Cromwell, your readings are fine. We're already decelerating and will make orbit in sixteen centicycles."

"Sixteen? Which class of ship is this, star angel? You're no longer flying that frigate?"

"This, Commander, is a *living ship.* The frigate was useful, but *Assiduous* is much swifter and faster."

"What is a living ship? Sorry, but we're kind of off the grid here. We don't get all the news."

"Off the grid? You mean, no message drones?"

"Not for the last twenty winters or so. What we know about the first triple star angel we learned from the few traders that still dare to travel here. Heavy strain on the emitters despite their best efforts to fine-adjust their jumps, is what they said."

Syreen recalled her approach. In hyperflight, the damage to the structure of space had hardly been noticeable, but in hindsight, she could recognize it. Or, better put, she could recognize how it had been before her recent repair. There were other recent memories coming along — for later.

"I've got good news for you, Commander. On my way here, I found out what made sailing your space so hard, and I could do something about it. Once I leave you, I will spread that news, and I will ask merchants to visit you."

"Really? Please, you should tell us all. May I be so bold as to invite you — and whoever you'd like to bring along — for dinner? I fear Epirus might fail with regard to the more exquisite dainties, but I can assure you our forwine is warming and our stew is spicy."

"I'll gladly join you and whoever you'd like to bring along, Commander, and I'm looking forward to exchanging spicy and heartwarming stories — about living ships, hyperspace, and old lore returning to life."

"Oh, angel, I'm so looking forward to meet you."

"If you don't mind, Commander, I'd like to collect one guest from your countryside."

"I'm not sure what you mean by countryside. I don't think we've got any place that would deserve to be called such. But, yeah, go ahead, go wherever you like."

CHAPTER FORTY-FIVE

Syreen glanced through the shuttle window. Edgy rocks, some of them larger than a frigate, formed a bizarre landscape. Their black surfaces seemed to swallow Epirus's light, and so did the dust on the leveled plains around them.

Swirling dust also filled the air above the ground. This planet made the term *dirtside* sound like an embellishment, and she could well understand why the settlers had decided to move on to Salamanca—most of them. She couldn't quite understand why anyone would wish to stay.

"We should take breathers and use the airlock." She nodded at Peysoon. "Otherwise we'll have all that dust in here."

"I totally agree." He shook his head. "What a lovely place."

"Yup. Let's go."

Once they had left the shuttle, Peysoon pointed forward. "I saw a building that way."

"You're right. But our subject's that way." Syreen waved tailward.

"Okay." He moved ahead.

She followed suit, wondering where her feelings would lead her. The gloomy landscape offered no clue, nobody had bothered to put up signposts, and the dust around unveiled no tracks. When she looked back, she saw their own footprints already disappearing.

"Where now?" Peysoon asked when they reached one of the big rocks. "Left or right?"

"Through." She shook her head. "Just kidding. She seems to be inside that rock. Let's turn right, toward the building, and look for an opening."

"Okay."

They had circled about a quarter of the rock when Peysoon stopped and pointed at a crack. "Here. Narrow enough to protect against some of the wind, wide and high enough to slip through."

Syreen smiled under her breather. "Feels right, but I wouldn't have spotted that."

"Well, I've had plenty of time to learn about cracks."

She had to chuckle about the double meaning. "In that case, lead the way, please."

They moved with caution.

Peysoon touched the surface. "Someone evened the worst edges. This isn't caused by natural erosion. By the way, do you need light?"

"No." Only now did she consciously notice the almost complete absence of light inside the crack. "Do you?"

"No. I wouldn't call it vision, but somehow I know where the openings are. Must be another trait of our people." He leaned forward. "Soft. Here's a kind of curtain." He passed through. "And a second."

He waited for Syreen to pass the first curtain, then he pulled the second one aside. "Wow."

Syreen peeked over his shoulder. A dim lavender glow filled the cavern. She recognized that it was caused by fine particles of dust, illuminated by bright lavender crystals in the rocky walls.

A solitary black-haired woman, almost as tall as Syreen, close to the back of the cavern turned around and stared at them. Her deep-blue eyes seemed to glow from inside. "Leave me alone!"

Syreen sensed surprise and fear. She placed one hand on Peysoon's shoulder and pulled him back. "Hello. I'm Syreen."

"Get out of here! Leave me!" The lank, pale woman waved her arms. "You're not safe here! Please, I don't want to hurt you."

The Navigator began to understand. "No, you won't hurt us, and we won't hurt you. You're safe with us."

"You don't know nothing! I'm a freak!"

Syreen stood up straight but left her arms hanging down her side. Very slowly she said, "You are no freak."

"I . . ."

"I know you. You are no freak. You are perfect the way you are — perfect as your mother created you."

"I — what do you know about my mother?"

The fear was gone. Now she was pure curiosity.

"Your mother was very sick. She overstrained herself by delivering you and couldn't recover on her own. We helped her, and now we're here to help you. First of all, to help you understand who you are, why you're different from the people around you, and why that's okay."

"You . . ."

"Please. I'm Syreen. This is Peysoon. What's your name?"

"Kaaly."

"Nice. Hello, Kaaly. Is there a place where we can sit and talk?"

Kaaly nodded and waved toward an alcove. "Please don't step on the mushrooms."

Only now did Syreen examine her footing. The cavern floor was mostly covered with long rows of half-dome shapes. She evaded them while following Kaaly's directions, with Peysoon in tow.

The alcove held two opposing benches and one table between them, cut from the rock, evened out and polished. Kaaly took one bench, Syreen sat down on the other. Peysoon smiled and leaned on the corner of the alcove.

Their host waited.

The Navigator nodded. "I can sense your emotions. You can sense mine, right?"

Kaaly nodded.

"Then you know I'm being honest with you. When you called yourself a freak, I told you that you're not. You know I'm telling you the truth. I want you to focus on me now as I'm telling you another truth. Okay?"

Kaaly nodded firmly, her eyes wide open.

"Okay. Kaaly, you are like me, and I am no human."

"No human? But — you said you met my mother?"

"That's what I said, yes. Kaaly, I *met* my mother about one winter ago. And now I will help you meet your mother, so to speak."

"What? How?" She almost jumped from her seat.

"We will sing, and you will listen. Peysoon, would you, please?"

He stepped close and took her hand. She opened her mind and reached out to Epirus. The star's song was still very weak, but resonated her call. *Sing to your daughter.*

She watched realization dawn in her new cousin's eyes, and with the dawn came the dew — a tear formed in Kaaly's eye.

Syreen let Peysoon's hand go and took Kaaly's. "Now you know. You are Epirus's daughter, Kaaly Starborn."

"But . . . but why? How?"

"I can't tell you how it works. But why? Because the stars need pilots. Pilots to fly to the stars, to fly a living ship."

"Fly to the stars? Me?" This time, Kaaly jumped up all the way and wrapped her arms around Syreen's neck. "Please yes, take me with you!"

Like a broken pipe. Kaaly's tears were running down Syreen's neck, under her collar, and further down her back.

Peysoon raised one eyebrow but remained silent.

"Don't worry. We won't leave you behind."

Kaaly snuffled. "You . . . you don't know Marcus. He's my master. He won't let me go. I . . . I am his best gardener, he says."

She loosened her grip and waved outside. "The mushrooms have a very rough skin. You can't harvest them without painful abrasions. But I'm healing faster, so I can harvest more."

"He's got no say in this."

There was a brief rush of air, and then a deep male voice boomed, "Who's got no say in what?"

Syreen frowned. She strongly disliked the emotions she sensed in that man. *Peysoon, do as you deem appropriate.*

The former AP master faced the new arrival. "And who are you?"

"This is my farm. I'm Marcus Korran, and whatever happens here is my call. Who are you, and what are you doing here?"

"My name is Peysoon. We're guests of Epirus Port Commander Cromwell. We're here to pick up one of our own."

"No, you won't." Korran reached for his belt. "You've got no jurisdiction here."

Syreen sensed Peysoon's mental command not to draw the weapon.

"You have no jurisdiction over our kin," he added. "Kaaly will come with us."

"Your kin? What nonsense is that?"

Syreen couldn't see it, but sensed Peysoon showing his fangs. Moreover, she could sense the sudden horror in Korran and the amusement in Peysoon.

Forget about us, was his next mental command.

"I think we should leave now," he said.

"I agree." Syreen took Kaaly's hand and gave it a gentle pull. "Come. Is there anything you want to take with you?"

"No. There isn't much to own on Epirus, and gardeners aren't supposed to have anything of it."

"Okay. Then come."

Chapter Forty-Six

"Epirus Port Authority, this is Navigator Syreen. Again thank you for your hospitality. I'm sure your situation will soon improve."

"Navigator, this is Cromwell, Epirus PA. Have a good journey, and our regards to Matin. Thank you for all you've done for us — the astronomers say Epirus is growing stronger by the cycle."

"Goodbye, Cromwell."

Assiduous dashed forward.

Syreen winked at Kaaly in her guest seat before entering hyperflight.

"Okay, folks. We're on our way to Matin. According to the records, it's an agricultural world. You may expect a lot of green, and the locals are known to be decent and kind. Once we're there, we'll have a little break. I need to get some help for Epirus organized, and I need time to introduce Kaaly to our team. So you better check if you can find your pants somewhere."

"Are we . . ." Kaaly began.

"In hyperspace? Yes. You can feel it?"

"It feels different. But no more — I think I'm too weak." She hesitated. "You know that we have to *feed* from time to time, do you?"

Syreen produced her canines for a moment. "Yesss."

"How do you deal with your . . . hunger?"

"I can control it. Can you?"

Kaaly nodded. "It's not easy, but I can — to a certain extent. Once I know I'm due, I have some time to choose my prey. If

I hesitate too long, it gets harder."

"How's it now?"

"Just beginning."

"So, if you'd feed now, you could control it well?"

"Sure . . . I mean, I just don't have to do it yet."

Syreen shook her head and made *Assiduous* leave hyperspace. They arrived at the outskirts of a lonesome star who nevertheless welcomed them with her song.

"We'd better do something about it now — Girls, I need two of you on the bridge."

Kaaly stared at her. "Your crew? You'd sacrifice them for me?"

"No. We won't sacrifice anyone. We're not draining them. They'll donate some of their power, and then they'll regenerate."

"I don't know if I can do that."

"If necessary, I will order you to stop. But don't worry, as long as you're not desperate, you're in charge."

Another tear formed in Kaaly's eye. "There's so much I didn't know."

"Hush. Don't blame yourself for things you couldn't know better."

"But I've killed."

"I did, too, when I started. Despicable people. I killed rapists."

Kaaly remained silent, but her tears seemed to stop.

When Heather and Jona entered, Kaaly's cheeks were already dried.

CHAPTER FORTY-SEVEN

"Matin Port Authority, this is the living ship *Assiduous*, Navigator Syreen calling."

While she waited for their answer, she called *Audacious* on a tight beam. "How are the two of you getting along?"

"My pilot is learning astonishingly fast. Kaaly is a prodigy."

"Why, thank you, old fossil. You're quite vital for your age."

"And she is way too cheeky for her age."

"Hush, dragonbone. Don't give away any bedroom secrets – uh, I mean, command bridge secrets."

"We will soon be able to operate independently, should the need arise. I would currently advise against hyperjumps or open combat, though."

"Hyperjumps sounds like fun – wait, open combat?"

"I will tell you more of the recent events once we're arrived. You need to know my story, and I guess our local hosts will be interested, too."

"Oh, absolutely. We both want to learn more, right, partner?"

"We have to. For the oncoming battles, we have to be prepared."

"Battles?"

"Keep calm. Wait for my story, and you will understand. The upcoming fights will be won by songs."

She felt *Assiduous*'s amusement.

– *They're getting along well indeed.* –

Yes, better than we could hope for. And here comes Matin.

"Lady Syreen, please feel welcome in the Matin system. I am Harbor Director Jacques Marlon. As there is little traffic here, you are free to approach Matin Orbital at your own discretion. We will

have two docks ready for you, right next to Veronica's Smile. *According to Captain Palmer's story, you might remember him?"*

"Indeed. What a nice surprise to encounter him here. Please relay my greetings."

We have a destination.

Assiduous dashed toward the small orbital station. After a brief delay, *Audacious* followed just as fast.

"We'll have everything prepared for your arrival until you're here — wait . . . no, probably not."

Syreen grinned. *No, surely not.*

CHAPTER FORTY-EIGHT

Syreen approached the small welcome committee with Peysoon, Kaaly, Drake, and Crow in tow. Four men were waiting for them—a gray-haired man in a black tuxedo, a lanky youngling in a white robe, a bald man in overalls, and a familiar, beaming face in a merchant captain's attire, spreading his arms.

The merchant's smile seemed to be almost too wide for the station corridor. "Syreen!"

She smiled at the other men and accepted the hug. "Terry!"

Captain Palmer held her away at arm's length. "Glad to see you in one piece. There were scary news stories all over the network."

He nodded toward the gray-haired man. "May I introduce? Envoy Julien Dupres, Matin representative for interstellar trade. At his side, Junior Guild Secretary Lou Salle. And last but not least, Harbor Director Jacques Marlon."

Palmer turned back to her. "Gentlemen, the triple Star Angel, Fleet Commander, Navigator Syreen of the Forgotten People."

"*Retired* Fleet Commander," Drake added into their hosts' embarrassed silence with a smirk. "Also known as Lady Syreen Starborn, Knight of the Order of the Firepath."

Should I curtsy or salute now? Syreen did neither. She bowed briefly and pointed at her company in sequence. "Dragutin Petran, researcher and historian, called Drake. Crow, his bodyguard. Navigator Kaaly of the Forgotten People. Peysoon of the Forgotten People."

Palmer found his voice again first. "Another Navigator? You never run out of miracles, gal!"

"Wait until she starts telling you her story," Drake said.

A loud "Ho-hum" made them turn to the envoy. "Please, Ladies and Gentlemen. Let's not get ahead of ourselves. There will be plenty of time to share these most interesting stories, and we'll all feel way more comfortable doing so in our VIP lounge, where we can enjoy refreshments and canapés."

Dupres pointed down the hallway. "This way, please. Be welcome on our little station."

She smiled and nodded.

Together, they walked toward the lounge in silence.

Syreen sensed how suspense was killing their hosts and reached out gently to ease their excitement. Kaaly relaxed and took Peysoon's offered hand.

I must remember that she's not used to so many people and their emotions.

The plush chairs and couches in the small lounge looked comfortable, and Syreen quickly found out that they felt even more comfy than their appearance promised. *I'll probably need assistance to get out of here.* She felt a tingle of amusement.

The soft crimson-and-silver curtains along the walls were a welcome contrast to the cold and blank station corridors.

The few waiters quickly left once everyone was provided with hot and cold drinks and little bits of food.

Syreen enjoyed the warmth of the mug in her hands.

Dupres sat up straight in his seat and held up his own mug. "Ladies and gentlemen, once again, welcome to Matin. Cheers or —" He turned to Syreen. "Duke's health."

She quickly overcame her surprise — of course, why shouldn't he know her familiar toast? "Duke's health."

The first sip was almost too hot. She blew over it and inhaled the intense aroma. Fruit, spice, herbs, and minerals. Next, she took a sip and enjoyed the taste unfolding in her mouth.

"An excellent forwine."

The envoy bowed forward. "Thank you. Our vintners try to get as close to the original wine as they can. Now, may I be so bold as to ask for the concerns that caused your visit?"

"Sure." She waved at Kaaly and Peysoon. "There may be more of my kin who don't know of their own ancestry. We need to find them and let them know, as we will need their help."

Dupres frowned. "And you expect to find one of your kin here on Matin?"

"Not necessarily. But I might find further clues on the Forgotten People, records, old lore, artifacts. The records on Salamanca, for example, guided me to Epirus, where I found Kaaly."

"Epirus? I thought you couldn't go there."

Captain Palmer chuckled. "I heard about that, too. Hard sailing—but that doesn't apply to a Navigator who crossed the chasm, right?"

"Right. By the way, I could do something about the hard sailing. Epirus is safe to go to now, and it would surely welcome some honest merchants."

The merchant captain raised his eyebrows. "I'm not sure what you're suggesting here."

"Life on Epirus is hard," Kaaly chimed in. "It's even harder if you have to rely on local produce alone. It's a gloomy place now, deprived of flavors, tastes, colors, and happiness."

"They don't need luxury items. Just basic produce of all kinds. The guild surely knows about their routine needs from the past." Syreen glanced at the young secretary.

Salle nodded. "Of course. I will prepare a list of the most urgent goods."

Dupres spread his arms. "If you'll allow, Matin will provide the first shipment for free."

The Navigator focused on the merchant.

Palmer shrugged. "Sure. I will deliver that first shipment. For free, of course."

"Thank you, Terry."

He shrugged again and smiled. "You know, Syreen—you can't deny such a minor favor to someone who can repair space and make it safe to sail again."

"Thank you anyway, Terry. I will provide you with the necessary navigation library updates and a seven-sigma solution for the trip."

"Oh, please give me a sealed copy of that solution. My pilot is quite proud of his navigation skills, and rightly so—I'd like to give him a go first."

"Sure."

The guild secretary leaned forward. "Is that why your ship is in such a good shape, Captain Palmer?"

"One of the reasons, yes. Good jumps, good routes. The other reason is that this Navigator"—he waved at Syreen—"taught us to be proud of our work."

"And now you're looking for another such Navigator here on Matin?" the envoy asked. "But how could one of your kin have arrived here?"

"No, I'm not looking for another Navigator here. If there were any of my kin, I'd already know. Matin would have told me."

"Matin?"

"She can hear the stars sing," Drake said toward the envoy. "And the stars know where their kin are."

Dupres glanced from the harbor director to Kaaly and again at Syreen. "Our records, then. Well, I don't know if there's anything useful in there, but if so, our librarians will find it for you. What I can tell you right away is an important facet of our history."

"You've got my full attention, Envoy Dupres."

"Thank you. Bear with me—I'll have to reach back far into the past."

Syreen smirked. "The farther, the better."

"Of course. Well, you might have heard about the missionary wars, about twenty megacycles ago, during the first wave of space exploration. Religious zealots tried to impose their rules on others, and where they didn't get their way, they did the ugliest things."

"They violated the second edict, I know."

"Several times, yes. Back then, different factions of zealots pursued different goals, but most of them agreed to eradicate any resistance by *heretics*—a term they applied to infidels as well as to rational believers. Moreover, their demands were quite, ah, unacceptable. Not just worshipping—one could have lived with that—but also sacrificing their people to the zealots for gory rituals, accepting permanent surveillance, and corporeal punishments even for minor failures." He glanced around his audience. "You see, not something you could shrug away easily. You had to fight and suffer, or surrender and suffer. Those were perilous times."

He nodded at Drake. "Anyway, Matin was one of the centers of resistance, so we do have records of that time. And one of our primary adversaries was a nation calling themselves *Harmony*—an infamous distortion of facts, as they were all but harmonic. You know such a place—Captain Palmer told us about them, and that made us remember and research. It's the very same world."

"So they are—or were—accessories to the violations."

"No. According to the records, they belonged to the main culprits. However, they somehow managed to slip past retaliation. Our records aren't clear on that. They were allowed to return to their planet and abandon their fleet, then await their sentence."

"Which never came," Drake said gloomily.

"Which never came," Dupres agreed. "After their defeat, they must've kept a very low profile during those wild times. The wars went on for at least another gencycle with some more attempted kinetic strikes—and a few successes. That must have messed up many priorities."

"But their sentence is still due." Syreen bit her lip. "I wonder where that might be recorded."

"Nysa, I'd guess." The envoy frowned. "Probably lost in some ancient archives that no one bothered to incorporate into their main body of data."

Peysoon stared at Dupres. "Why Nysa?"

"Well, back then star nations allied against the zealots. They called themselves the Associated Planets. Nysa had three habitable planets and a good industrial base, so they could afford to build huge dreadnaughts—that's the kind of ship you need to counter kinetic strikes, you know? Aw, of course you do, sorry. Anyway, as Nysa was the Association's military backbone, they became their administrative center, too. It was convenient to have jurisdiction over the zealots in one place, so they got that, too. Later, after the guild wars, Nysa also got the guild commissariat, as they already were a major trade node. But you're surely aware of that."

Syreen glanced at Peysoon. "Seems we'll return to Nysa earlier than expected."

She focused on the envoy. "I don't know what Terry—Captain Palmer—told you, but how they're treating women there is unbearable. That I haven't done anything about it yet is due to the lack of legal justification. But if I find proof of a yet unatoned violation of the second edict, I can act—and I will."

She saw and sensed sudden fear in Dupres, and then Drake's touch at her shoulder.

"Calm," he said. "Save your anger for them."

"Sorry," she whispered.

Dupres stared at her for a while. Finally he nodded and

relaxed. "I see."

"Sorry."

"It's okay. I know you're not angry at me. But if that spark of fury I just witnessed reflects only a fraction of the evil you found there, I feel truly sorry for their women. I will talk to our government. We might have a historic obligation."

"For what?" Peysoon asked.

"To provide you with the means for retaliation. You will need ground forces."

Syreen smiled. "Yes, I will. And I'll collect some more favors on my way to Harmony. There are some volunteers on Nysa, and some more on Nizwa. However, there's one condition."

"Which condition?" the envoy asked.

"Women only. Their women won't trust any males." She pouted. "What I need is a division of female marines with cat-o-nine-tails."

Dupres's eyes widened. He slowly nodded. "I will make your needs clear to our leaders. We will need transportation, though."

Syreen glanced at Peysoon. "I will try to borrow some dreadnaughts from the AP."

CHAPTER FORTY-NINE

The two living ships were the first to emerge from hyperspace. *Assiduous* quickly discovered the emissions of two small vessels guarding the primary entry points.

Syreen activated her radio. "Nizwa authorities, this is the living ship *Assiduous*, Navigator Syreen speaking. I'm accompanied by the living ship *Audacious,* and together, we're the vanguard of an expedition force heading for Harmony. Be prepared for the arrival of a fleet of three dreadnaughts, nine battle cruisers and twelve smaller units. Send my regards to Harbor Master Juanita and Guild Secretary Orville."

She didn't immediately get a reply. *Assiduous* picked up communication from one of the small vessels toward Nizwa.

Meanwhile, she listened to their star's melancholic song.

We're here.

Nizwa cheered.

— Here's our welcome. —

"Navigator Syreen, we're glad for your return. I'm Assistant Harbor Master Pablo. Docking bays Alpha one and two are free for you. Juanita asks to be excused — she's already busy with preparations."

Nizwa sang of more arrivals.

On time.

"Thank you, Pablo. Here's my fleet."

Twenty-four AP warships dropped from hyperspace in almost perfect formation — such that only the living ships could detect the deviations. The entry shock was almost negligible — indication of a well-tuned seven-sigma jump, even

215

though the AP instruments would probably only record it as six-sigma.

"Admiral Derfflinger, welcome, and my congratulations to your pilots for this excellent performance."

"Navigator Syreen, thank you for your praise. I will pass it on. We have a bet running among our pilots for the best navigating. I fear I have to reward them all."

The admiral's message was followed by the simultaneous unfolding of collectors by all twenty-four warships.

Peysoon stepped close to her seat and pointed at the three-dimensional display. "They're learning fast."

"They're eager to adapt. I'd say they like to be the good guys for a change."

"And the good gals."

They smiled at each other. Peysoon couldn't hide a little frown, though.

"I know," she said. "We'll need to get this over with soon. And we need to find more ships and pilots. I have a good feeling about that, though."

"Okay, okay. But that inevitable social event comes first, right?"

She sensed his amusement. "Right."

That *inevitable social event* took place in one of Nizwa Orbital's larger conference rooms. Aside from Kaaly, Peysoon, Drake, and herself, all twenty-four AP Navy commandants had arrived with Admiral Derfflinger, Lieutenant Samantha Rigg, AP Marines Colonel Barbara Whitfield, AP Marines Master Sergeant Rosner, Matin Marines Brigadier General Corinne Renard, and Matin Marines Sergeant-Major Elodie Pichon.

Their hosts were thus outnumbered and outranked. Harbor Master Juanita and Guild Secretary Orville had introduced the young Nizwa Lieutenant Colonel Mariella—who seemed to feel still uncomfortable with her very recent promotion—and a seasoned Sergeant Kaitlin.

"I'm sorry." Juanita frowned. "I promised you a legal foundation for your intervention, but I didn't find any yet. I can understand that you're no longer willing to wait. As you can see, we're prepared to do what's necessary anyway."

"No worries. We have a legal basis now. The folks on Matin had some records from the missionary wars, and Admiral Derfflinger could dig up the proof. It's almost twenty megacycles old and the sentence has yet to be implemented. So we have every right to go there and do whatever needs to be done."

"What does that mean?"

"I'm an Enforcer of the People, and their ancestors violated the second edict. When I visited them, I personally witnessed them still following their vicious ways. Their lack of repentance deserves no mercy. I could even justify eliminating their planet, but you know I don't want to do that."

"But you couldn't eliminate a planet." Juanita shook her head.

"Yes, I could." Syreen glanced around. "Just to make that clear to everyone—this was no empty threat. *Assiduous* and I, we command the means to wipe an entire planet from existence. The same applies to Kaaly and *Audacious*. I've asked for your help, for your forces so that we don't have to do that." She smiled and added a soothing mental push. "And because we want to make their women's lives better, not relieve them in a terminal way."

Kaaly waved. "What about the males?"

"Any resistance is fair game. We won't accept blackmail of any kind. If necessary, we will break their will." *That's among us, but you know how.* "I don't expect a fair fight. You shouldn't, either. This will be dirty. I'm prepared to match them, and I know there might be victims we can't save. We might suffer casualties, too—but not because we let them trick us." Syreen nodded at Admiral Derfflinger. "Once we appear on their sensors, we're committed. We will not withdraw."

She spotted a frown. "A question, Lieutenant Colonel Mariella?"

"I'm not sure what to make of that. It seems to limit our strategic options."

Derfflinger raised a hand. "Let me rephrase that, as we had the same question on Nysa. It is okay to fall back and regroup, if necessary. But we will not leave the Harmony system until our job is done, because that might subject their women to retaliation beyond our imagination. And the same more or less applies to our strategic advance on the planet. We can't just stop."

The Nizwa officer nodded. "How will we deal with substantial opposition then?"

The admiral pointed at her commandants. "That's what we've brought our Navy for. We provide the targets, they take them out. And yes, we have to expect collateral damage."

Colonel Whitfield grinned. "Not to forget the firepower provided by our assault shuttles. Oh, by the way, we've got forty shuttles with pilots for your teams. Each can carry up to sixteen marines in full battle rattle."

Now it was Mariella's turn to grin. "What's full battle rattle for you?"

"Padded suits, rifles, ammo, some heavy ordnance — you get the picture. Are you bringing anything special?"

"Yes, we are. Small as our forces are, we're still using heavy armor suits. My government provided me with three companies. That's a total of four hundred and eighty suits."

Her announcement caused a whistle from the Matin Sergeant-Major. "Now *that's* firepower."

Sergeant Kaitlin nodded. "Yes, and they can take some beating, too."

Lieutenant Colonel Mariella spread her arms. "I don't want

to start our planning session here and now, but you should know that we're prepared to distribute two of our three companies among your troops as support. First Company is specifically equipped for heavily armed fortifications, so I'd prefer to keep them together."

"That's a good prospect," Whitfield said. "But let's not get ahead of ourselves. We're only just getting to know each other."

Juanita approached Syreen and handed her a mug of fresh forwine. She pointed at Peysoon, who was chatting with Kaaly and Mariella. "Your mate is a handsome guy."

Syreen frowned. "He's not my mate." *He's the guy who had me tortured, but should I tell her, here and now? Just when I'm trying to form an alliance?*

Juanita fell silent.

Syreen could feel her embarrassment.

Colonel Whitfield stepped closer, Commodore Hardincourt and Lieutenant Colonel Mariella in tow.

Whitfield nodded. "Navigator?"

"Yes, Colonel?"

"I can see that you're pressed for time, but our joint forces could profit from an opportunity to train together. In fact, that might help us avoid severe misunderstandings. Do you see any chance to squeeze a few tencycles out of your tight schedule?"

Syreen could sense her sincere worries. Her request was sensible anyway, and Syreen chided herself for not having considered the need for joint maneuvers. "Your observation is correct. I feel pressed for time, yes. The situation's getting worse every day—but it's done so for generations, so I cannot pretend I have a fixed schedule. Let's make a deal—for our mission planning tomorrow, I'll bring a training location, and the two of you bring a draft training schedule. Okay?"

She didn't need her special senses to see the problem with

her proposal. "Hey, I only asked for a first draft, basically about the number of tencycles you'll need. Get together for a halfcycle and throw it together. You'll have plenty of time to iron out the wrinkles once we're on our way."

Her raised mug dismissed them. Before Hardincourt could leave, too, she addressed him. "Commodore?"

"Yes, Navigator?"

"When and where did your pilots learn that outstanding precision? How did you motivate them?"

He grinned. "Let me put it like this. Firstly, when we staffed our expedition fleet, we were looking for certain talents. Secondly, when you provided us with solutions to call our people back—you remember? Our navigators and pilots asked how can it be that we're doing jumps without the slightest feel of nausea? Well, what I did—I told my navigator to calculate another solution for the very same trip, and to refine it until he was happy with it. He failed. Then we put our heads together and did it again—by the book, and with attention on every detail. We fiddled with the trims over and over again, and bang! suddenly there it was. A perfect six-sigma solution." Hardincourt winked. "Our instruments can't tell, but it might have been almost one sigma level better. In any case, once my navigator saw that he could do it—and how easy it is—he was very motivated to try it again. Word spread, and meanwhile, there's an ongoing competition among AP navigators to find the best solution for well-known routes."

He waved at Derfflinger and held his own mug forward. After they had clinked and sipped, he went on, "New management approves, and our government doesn't complain."

"What *new management?*"

"Well, there are procedures to follow and sentences to be nailed down, but our new Navy admiralty clearly favors your sensible proposals—okay, demands—and is trying to make things work. Guild representatives within and outside the AP indicated their approval, thus showing us that we're taking the right way to raise the embargo."

"And you're facing no resistance?"

"Oh, there are a few boneheads, and there are quite a few crews who miss the old inspections—for one, because those are forbidden now, and for two, because there are no merchants to be inspected—but we'll get that sorted out." He took another sip. "Good forwine. Well, yes, I think there's a change for the better. We just mustn't let it slide."

"Well, I won't." She emptied her mug and sighed. "I haven't even really started yet."

PART FOUR—EXERCISE

CHAPTER FIFTY

"Here we are." Syreen sat up and stretched her limbs. "Our playground."

She routinely checked their surroundings. The AP fleet had arrived at the regular entry point, from where they could routinely decelerate toward the planet.

Kaaly and *Audacious* were already dashing forward.

"Where's this *here?*" Heather asked from behind.

Syreen smiled. "You're still here on the bridge?"

"One of us always is, just in case you need our support."

"Oh, nice, thank you." One thought activated her radio. "This place is called Backyard. It was an early settlement during the first expansion—at least that's what Matin's old records say. The soil looks fertile, but the ecosystem lacks a lot of nutrients that people would need to survive here. So they left this place fairly quickly. It's no holiday spot, but perfect for our purpose. We might even find some abandoned buildings."

She switched the radio off again and focused on Backyard's song. The song of tiny objects pussyfooting through hyperspace had already faded, now there was—Syreen jumped on her feet.

Assiduous! Audacious! *Contact!*

— A welcome surprise. —

Kaaly called next. *What is it? Shall we have a look?*

Backyard tells me of another living ship on the planet. Yes, try to find it and pick it up.

Will do.

"What happened?" Heather asked.

"There's another living ship on this planet."

"One more? That's, what, the fifth we know of, counting in the two Drake told us about?"

Syreen gave her a scrutinizing glance. "You remember?"

"Sure." Heather shrugged. "You know, I'm kind of out of a job here. Not much entertaining to do with two gay guys and one monk. Too much leisure time. Don't get me wrong, I'm not at all mad at you. Chose my original job 'cause I thought I didn't have much choice. Well, all the stories Drake's telling made me curious what else there is to learn. Once I started, there was no way to stop."

"I should feel guilty. There's so much you could do, but you're stuck here with me."

"No!" Heather firmly shook her head. "No. We're not *stuck*. We all know you'd let us go anytime, anyplace. We chose to stay, because this galaxy needs you, and you need us. We're part of something great. And in the meantime, *Assiduous* is a very patient teacher. We're aboard the best university in the known universe, at least as long as it's about hard science."

"You're studying science, then."

"You bet. I didn't want to get into Gwen's way, but occasionally, I watched what Haiki was doing to fix *Bumblebee*." She took a deep breath. "I don't want to sound like I'm boasting, but I've learned how a frigate works. Give me parts and tools, and I'll build you one."

Syreen shook her head in disbelief—not about Heather's claims, but about her change. "Sorry. I didn't expect that."

"Of course not. But you're the cause anyway. A catalyst for change. Big change."

"Okay." There was an idea—oh yes. "Can you pilot a shuttle?"

"What? No."

"Time to learn, don't you think? Come along, I'll show you how."

Chapter Fifty-One

Syreen frowned about the ship's sorry look. However, she had seen worse. It was resting on a sandy beach where Kaaly had put it down after retrieving it from a deep cavern.

Kaaly waved at the wrinkled body. "His name is *Incredulous*. He's too tired to take to space, he says."

"Well, we're here for some tencycles anyway. Let's go inside and have a chat."

She passed through the entrance together with Kaaly.

– *Welcome back, Kaaly. You brought a guest?* –

This is Syreen, Assiduous's *Navigator.*

– *Welcome Syreen. So you're a Navigator, too.* –

Hello, Incredulous. *Yes, I am, and I'm sure I'll soon find you a pilot, too.*

– *I doubt this will happen soon. There are too many stars, too many planets to search.* –

We found you.

– *Yes. That's a miracle that puzzles me.* –

There's no miracle involved. Backyard told me that you're here.

– *That cannot be.* –

Syreen closed her eyes and opened her mind. *Backyard, sing to us.*

Kaaly took her hand and joined her mentally, too.

– *That cannot be. And yet, it* is. –

Syreen smiled. *We're a new breed of Navigators. We're starborn. You'll soon find out what that means.*

– *I wonder what course of events caused this.* –

Audacious said we're supposed to fight the Void.

– WHAT? –

Syreen's concentration broke. She lost her contact to Back-yard.

"Ugh." Kaaly held her head. "That hurt."

– My sincere apologies, Kaaly. Syreen, did you just mention the Void? –

"I did." She paused. "*Assiduous* and I will fight. That's what I was born for. You're welcome to join our cause or go your own way, once we've found you a pilot."

– I admire your determination, but it's futile. There is no way to fight the Void. –

"I will prove you wrong."

– I will witness you fail. –

Syreen smiled. "Deal."

Syreen's crew was waiting for her in the lounge.

"And?" Drake asked.

"And what?"

"You've got another new member for your fleet, eager to support you. Doesn't that make you happy?"

She frowned. "He's not exactly eager to support me. I'd rather call him the sceptic."

"Sceptic. Hum."

"His name is *Incredulous,* and he makes that name come alive."

"So – he won't come along?" Drake looked truly worried.

"He said he'll witness me fail." She winked and grinned. "I'll show him."

There was a roar of laughter echoing from everywhere around. Even the floor seemed to be trembling, and people were grabbing for a firm hold.

Her eyes widened.

"What was that?" Drake uttered aghast.

"*Assiduous* laughing."

CHAPTER FIFTY-TWO

Navigating the chasm is easier. Syreen pouted. However, while she was no longer Fleet Commander in Charge for the Duchy, she was still in charge of commanding the expedition fleet bound for Harmony.

And fleet commanders were supposed to deal with complaints from their subordinates.

The different space marine units weren't getting along well. They had different approaches, different strategies, different ideas, different ways to do things, different gear, different skills, different training, different cultures, and worst of all, different rule books. So every once in a while, or almost all the time, things done by the book by one unit were violating the rules of another unit. Who was to judge? Their supreme commander.

Without explicitly saying so, the AP marines expected a ruling in their favor. They were providing the largest force, they were used to having things their way, and the AP had been the leaders of the original forces, back then.

The Matin and the Nizwa leaders expected to be regarded as equal partners—they claimed to provide a larger share of warriors *per capita*.

Some decisions were easy. Syreen asked them whether they regarded their own rules as helpful. If not, she would order them to disregard the unhelpful rulings.

Some quarrels could be tackled with logic. She let her ships dissect the problem, strip it to the core, and work out the most constructive answer.

Some issues were entangled in personal sensitivities. There was no logical, fact-based approach. Instead, she had to consider things like balance of power, pride and prejudice, egos in need of a pat. In these cases, there could only be one answer — fostering harmony.

This time, Colonel Whitfield and Lieutenant Colonel Mariella were standing before her in *Assiduous's* newly established conference room.

"What is it?" she asked, swallowing the *this time.*

The two officers looked at each other. Mariella nodded.

Whitfield waved toward the entrance. "General Renard. We were trying to work something out together, but she insists on having the final say because she outranks us."

Syreen frowned. "I thought we had already resolved that ranking topic."

Whitfield nodded. "We had — or so we thought. Everything worked fine until about two cycles ago. We were wrapping up the latest exercise results. We're not happy with our joint performance yet, so we voted to extend our stay and add a few more exercises, but she insisted on sticking to the schedule."

"I've seen the results. You managed to overcome your initial, uh, difficulties, and make the units collaborate. That's what we came here for."

"Yes, but the exercise results . . ." Whitfield paused when Syreen raised a hand.

The Navigator smiled. "The exercise results are just that — exercise results. Based on unchallenged assumptions founded on megacycles-old intelligence reports, only marginally enriched with current insights. We won't gain anything substantial from more exercises." She focused on Whitfield. "You're right with regard to one issue — General Renard doesn't have the final say. *I* have the final say, and I say we will go. I'll tell you why."

The officers weren't happy, but more curious than angry. *Good.*

"Firstly, I'm pressed for time. *Audacious* keeps telling me that I can't afford to waste time on trivialities. We agree that Harmony is no triviality, but it's not our primary target either. Secondly, the women on Harmony are suffering every day. How can we justify postponing their relief? Thirdly, I don't want to give Harmony more time for preparations. Although we didn't advertise our mission, it can't be kept secret. Eventually, they will learn about us and add things up. Message drone traffic is low hereabouts, but there is a regular schedule, and their next drone is due in four tencycles. You know what that means?"

Both officers were gazing at her, their minds racing.

Syreen didn't try to intrude any further. "You have four cycles to wrap up and get aboard. Questions once we're under way. Stragglers will be left behind. Understood?"

They still weren't answering.

"You got your orders." And, louder, "Go!"

Now both made a dash for the door. Syreen chuckled inwardly.

— You will really leave stragglers behind? —

If there are any, I'll tell Kaaly to pick them up. But their ships will be gone and they'll have a lot to explain once we've delivered them.

— Four cycles, then. I'll tell our team. —

Thanks.

She registered with content that he called them *team,* and no longer *livestock* or *passengers.*

CHAPTER FIFTY-THREE

Syreen rearranged her seating position. Having *Assiduous* inside her again felt good after all the hassle.

"Okay, folks. Listen. Fleet, you've got your calculations. We'll meet again at Harmony. Kaaly and I will clear the way, if necessary. Kaaly, ready when you are."

"Oh, I'm ready. Just wiggling my toes."

"I mean, ready to kick some male asses."

"Oh that, yes. Audacious *and I are ready to kick some asses all the way back to Backyard."*

Syreen smiled. "I like your spirit."

"You'll like my kicks even better."

Their synchronized thoughts made *Assiduous* and *Audacious* dash forward, with *Incredulous* riding on *Assiduous's* body.

Moments later, they entered hyperflight.

Syreen could sense their newest member's surprise.

Welcome to hyperflight.

— This is new. I must reevaluate my data. Old truths can no longer be considered axiomatic. —

— Never with her. — Assiduous seemed to grow inside her.

Calm, boys. We're almost there.

Harmony sang of a clear space. So she didn't expect trouble, and once they emerged, there wasn't any. Just that single planet circling its sun. Not even merchant haulers were present.

Showtime.

"Harmony port authority. This is Syreen, Navigator of the

Enforcer *Assiduous,* accompanied by the Enforcer *Audacious.* Please acknowledge."

"*Assiduous, this is Harmony port authority. Please state your business here and explain why you didn't use one of the standard jump points.*"

"Harmony port authority, we didn't arrive by hyperjump, so we bypassed the jump point. Our mission is to reestablish fundamental rules of civilized behavior and enforce compliance with the edicts. I'll have to talk to your government."

"What edicts? Government? Are you crazy?"

— There's a significant increase in encrypted message traffic, some to newly activating nodes. Power plants are starting up all around the globe. —

So they triggered the alarm. Well, let's see what they've got.

She opened a private line to Kaaly. "Might be they're up to trouble. Watch out for nasty surprises."

"Sure. We're prepared."

"Okay." Syreen didn't share Kaaly's confidence, but what else could she say? According to megacycles-old records, Harmony had abandoned their fleet, but what did that mean? Abandoned where? Back then, they had commanded the means to violate the second edict.

Whatever they could muster, it would probably take them a little more time. Moreover, Harmony—the star—should know about anything truly nasty.

Let's sing a song.

Syreen focused on the bass harmonics. There was something disturbing in Harmony's song, like an overlay with a different rhythm. *What's that?*

Assiduous provided her with a clue, and she didn't like it.

Nasty indeed!

"Kaaly?"

"Yep. Got your back."

"They've got something truly nasty. Ask *Audacious* about

solar rays."

There was a brief pause. *"Oh heck. Really?"*

"I guess we just found out how they could disappear from everyone's radar back then. If there was any force to deliver their sentence, it was probably wiped out."

"Not a good prospect for our fleet, huh?"

"Not at all. What bothers me is that they seem to be thinking they can pull this stunt through against three Enforcers."

"What would they know about enforcers? There weren't any during the missionary wars, Audacious *tells me."*

"They knew about the edicts. They should've heard about their origin."

"Yes, but did they make the connection?"

"After they heard what we did to the Association? They can't be *that* dense."

"Okay. I didn't expect you to bring such dangerous opponents to our mission."

"Me neither. This is a surprise for me, too."

"So what are we gonna do?"

"You will stay clear and hide behind the planet, and you'll take *Incredulous* with you. I will engage this weapon and disarm it."

"I could help."

"Have you already found out how to dodge a shot coming at light speed?"

"What? No — nobody can do that."

"I can. You already heard my story. You'll soon be able to do the same, but we won't start your lessons with a solar ray."

Which could funnel a large share of a star's power into a single, needle-like ray, strong enough to wipe out dreadnaughts and probably even a living ship. Syreen was primarily worried about the former but couldn't ignore the latter, either.

— It would surely be a major obstacle for our primary mission. — Okay, Joker. Let's go.

— What is our plan? —

Go and see.

There were five spheres floating in the cromosphere, each one able to withstand the heat — several thousand degrees — and still maneuver. Together, they could create some kind of force field and focus this heat on any target in the system.

Syreen wondered where that kind of sophisticated technology came from.

— It isn't sophisticated. It's robust. Hyperjump emitters are sophisticated. We are even more sophisticated. —

So we just fry their wiring? No. Too robust. Concussion pulses won't do any good either, huh?

— These machines are built to operate in extreme heat, extreme radiation, extreme magnetic fields and extreme gravity. We can surely cause some damage, but it will take time. —

While they try to shoot us. Not good. A torpedo would do quick work with them.

— Yes. I have three torpedoes prepared. Should I make two more? —

No. I don't want to hurt Harmony. We will have to do this the hard way.

— What's on your mind — oh no. —

Yes. We will hack them and instruct them to submit to gravity. Sturdy they may be, but they won't survive the heat and pressure at the core.

— Yuck. —

Yes. Sorry, mate. I know that's not tasty, but the alternative would be to bring the core's heat up. A supernova would do the job, too — but Harmony and their people would be dead.

— I agree with the rationale. I just don't have to like it. Let's get it over with. —

Yes.

They quickly closed the distance to the central star, carefully avoiding the solar ray's assumed field of fire.

Assiduous felt his way through the unknown device's brain.

Did you intercept any specific communication toward those spheres?

— *Just their wake-up call. I sense something stirring there.* —

Yes — she swayed their hip — *whoah!*

A powerful beam of light with the diameter of a battle-cruiser had barely missed them.

So they can shoot sideways. Well, it was just a guess.

She sensed *Assiduous's* question on whether to abort their daring approach — and how he discarded it before she even had time to think an answer. Next, she pulled them into a sharp turn, out of the trajectory of another beam.

Trouble, mate?

— *Yes. It's easy to hack one or two, but I must hack all five together, or they resume normal operation as soon as I focus on another. A very robust high-availability-pattern.* —

Need help?

— *No, just a little patience.* —

Take your time.

Syreen rolled, and a third beam missed.

She considered whether to place them between the star and the planet — would that weapon risk hitting the planet if she dodged?

That was the wrong question though. Would she risk the planet being hit if she had to dodge anyway?

Surely not. Whoopee. Another one.

— *Done.* —

Syreen remained alert but found no need to dodge again for several centicycles.

— *They're brain-dead now. Their consumption by Harmony's core is just a matter of time.* —

You're great.

— *I know. And I've got the greatest Navigator ever.* —

CHAPTER FIFTY-FOUR

Syreen's grim face made Peysoon approach her cautiously.
"I won't bite you."

"Okay." He relaxed. "You're worried?"

"I'm mightily pissed. That device fired four shots at an enforcer. Four! And the command came from this orbital. I should just wipe them from space."

"Just do it."

She took a deep breath. "I have personal reasons to dislike this kind of behavior. And I think I already made my point."

"Indeed. They —"

She raised a hand. "Hi, Kaaly."

"Did these sorry spores of a dried mushroom shoot at you?"

"These what? Yes, they did. Four times."

"And you haven't sucked them dry yet? Let's teach them!"

"Calm down, Kaaly. Let them stew for a while. They'll get their lesson soon enough."

"They don't look like stewing here. They're launching small spacecraft dirtside. Audacious *and I spotted six assault shuttles and twelve stingships."*

"Really? What do they expect to gain against a living ship? Aw, no matter. You can fry and eat any attacker at your own discretion. No prisoners."

"Eat attackers? You mean, take their blood?"

"You can do that, too. What I meant — *Incredulous* needs nutrients, organics and minerals."

"What — oh. Yes, Audacious *just explained it to me."*

"There's one bright side to all of this." She smiled at

Peysoon. "They have no clue what we're really after, and we won't tell them until we've got them pinned down good and proper."

"The women."

"The women, exactly. Oh, and here's their call."

A thought let a chair for her guest grow out of the floor. Peysoon nodded and sat down.

"*Assiduous, this is Harmony port authority. Our government advises you and your company to leave this system right now. You're no longer welcome here. We're commanding the necessary measures to implement our decision.*"

She showed Peysoon her predator smile. "Harmony, this is Syreen, Enforcer *Assiduous* speaking. We intercepted your instructions to the solar ray gun and evaded its first four shots. You are thus found guilty of four unprovoked attacks on an Enforcer of the People. I herewith place your world under edict. Previous sentences may be overruled. Your government and military, as well as any irregular forces, will be held responsible and will contribute to reparations. Traffic between surface and orbit is suspended, effective immediately. I will announce further measures in due course."

"*Hey!*"

Kaaly's outcry followed the lighting of a minor grazing shot at *Audacious's* body. Next, a spark from the ship's warts grilled the insolent attacker's wiring. More shots toward the now dancing living ship were answered by further sparks, until all twelve stingships were incapacitated.

Incredulous separated from *Audacious* and approached the nearest stingship.

Syreen felt a little remorse. That pilot might have had the best intentions to protect his homeworld, and she didn't know how he had treated women. Now he'd become reduced to basic nutrients.

There weren't even calls for help or mercy on the radio—there was no radio left intact on these ships.

Not nice. But merciful for the watchers.

"Assiduous, *what the heck is happening there?*" The port authority voice cracked.

"Harmony, our patience is exhausted. This stingship, and consecutively all others, will contribute to reparations with all their nutrients and minerals. The same could happen to your shuttles or even your orbital, should you decide to annoy me any further."

She cut the line and gazed at Peysoon. "I know. I said I'd dislike that. I might have to consider a different approach."

"What's on your mind?"

"Large-scale mind control. I'd like that even less, but it might work. The two of us together . . ."

He nodded. "Yes, it might work. However, we're talking about a different jump here. Letting an entire world share our reception of a star's song, making them voluntarily fall in love with you is easy — seven sigma, so to speak. Forcing these zealots to act against their firmest convictions, against deeply seared activity patterns, against megacycles-old self-delusions, is more like riding a wharf scooter in a storm, or like trying a one-sigma jump with worn emitters. Believe me, I've got some experience in mind control."

"So that's no solution."

"No. You can make them stop pulling a trigger, you can make them shut up, such things are easy. But any long-term commands will wear off."

"I thought you did that with some of your skippers and admirals."

"It works nicely to reinforce legit orders that are in line with the victim's values and beliefs. It works badly with people of conscience, so to speak. You know how I overcame this problem."

"Do I?"

"Searchers. Chimeras with ultimately broken minds. No values, no beliefs to be fought. Just obedience, and with their own power of mind control. They can renew fading orders."

Syreen frowned. Her memories of previous encounters weren't pleasant.

"Sorry." Peysoon placed a hand on her arm. "Back then, it looked like a good idea. From where I am now, it's condemnable — disharmonic."

"At least I can understand now why you did it. Doesn't make it better, but there's a logical reason."

"Thank you. Screw that logic."

"Yes." His hand on her arm felt good. She closed her eyes and enjoyed that last thought.

Chapter Fifty-Five—Kaaly

Kaaly considered her options. Watching *Incredulous's* gruesome feeding wasn't nice. Guarding him was no longer necessary—after Syreen's last announcement, the assault shuttles' pilots had decided to not annoy her any further and turned back to the ground. So what was she supposed to do?

Aside from having Syreen's back, of course. But floating in space as an easy target didn't do *Audacious* and her any good.

Better to be unpredictable, huh? Let's cover the whole planet and have a look at its night side.

— That wasn't part of the plan. —

Hey, I'm supposed to look for nasty surprises — and to kick ass. For either, it's a good idea to check someone's rear.

— You don't have Syreen's experience. —

True, but for one, I've got many winters' experience of avoiding trouble with males. For two, Syreen is just a thought away. For three, I've got you.

— I can't argue with the latter. —

See? Okay, let's go.

She gently steered into a high orbit. No one addressed them directly, although there was some message traffic regarding their movements.

Their sensors didn't recognize anything odd. But if the Harmony people had any other hidden nasties, they surely weren't putting them on display. If she wanted to find anything, she had to dig it up by nonconventional means.

Syreen had spoken of the star's song. What would it tell her?

Kaaly had no experience in communication with stars. Her area of expertise was listening to people — to recognize if they were up to mischief toward her, or to evade them whenever she felt that strange lust for blood.

She closed her eyes and focused inward. There was no star singing in her mind. Instead, there was a score of emotions radiating from the planet's surface. Confusion, curiosity, alertness, wariness clearly directed at them, at the strange ships commanded by an insolent *woman!* Determination, anger, and malice were trailing these emotions.

There was fear. Fear, pain, despair, shame — and a spark of hope. Female emotions, she could tell.

A strange sensation touched her mind. Hunger and lust, coupled with grim satisfaction. A single source, powerful, young but focused, and somehow familiar, like a relative — like a girl of the People!

And that girl was in trouble. Kaaly could clearly tell from both the girl's emotions and of the male anger directed at that girl.

She couldn't tell what exactly had caused the current trouble, but she knew there wasn't any time to waste. The males radiated confidence and excitement. The girl's emotions told of bitterness.

This will not be your Last Stand.

She sent a notice to Syreen. *Need to pick up a cousin.*

Next, she directed *Audacious* into a racy dive downward.

You know best what you can do, pal. We want to be quick.

— Acknowledged. —

The ship shot forward, ignoring air drag, storm, and heat. With all her senses opened outward, Kaaly noticed a sudden increase in message traffic as well as a wave of fear in the males that were approaching her new cousin.

Yes, you should fear. And, directed forward, *Cousin, I'm coming to your aid.*

Puzzlement. *Who's that?*

I'm Kaaly. Audacious *and I, we will pick you up.*

Alertness. *Who's* Audacious?

My ship. We're dropping right toward you. See the great ball of fire above you?

Yes. Sorry, but I must focus on those guys with their nasty neurowhips. They're close.

Command them to stop with your mind. You can do that.

Really?

Kaaly sensed the echo of her cousin's mental command. The males' minds went blank and disappeared.

— We're almost there. —

Audacious had to go slow for the last leg in order not to burn their target.

Kaaly felt a tickle. *What's that?*

— We're taking fire from rifles and railguns. Those can't hurt us, but would be dangerous to anyone outside. —

They're shooting us? That's unacceptable.

Audacious highlighted a bulky shape on wheels for her, hidden among tall organic structures on a nearby hill. His library identified them as *trees* for her.

— A shot from that heavy gun might cause minor damage. —

No, it won't.

Kaaly focused on the gun and triggered Audacious's concussion pulser. The gun and a large area around it disappeared in a huge cloud of dust and debris.

Oops.

There was a painful cry on her mind. Her cousin had been hit.

No!

Audacious had arrived. She jumped out of her seat and dashed toward the exit.

Her ship cleared a straight path past its innards for her. Within millicycles, she was outside.

Audacious was hovering over small wooden buildings hunkered along both sides of a dirt road. Eight motionless male bodies in brown overalls were sprawled along the road. Nothing stirred inside the houses, although Kaaly sensed the presence of a few more people.

Five men had cornered their naked target at the dead end of a narrow side alley. One of them held an elastic rod with a sparkling tip against her thigh. The short, black-haired girl was writhing in pain.

Kaaly despised what she had to do next. For most of her life, she had fought her urge for blood. This time, it was a necessity.

Drop those rods and freeze.

She squeezed through between the men and leaned over the girl. *Easy. Ignore the pain, it will fade.*

The girl relaxed and looked up with gray eyes.

Kaaly reached out a hand. "I'm Kaaly. Come."

"Nuuya." She glanced at the men. "I—I couldn't stop them."

"You've exhausted your powers. You need to recharge. I'll show you how it's done."

Kaaly approached the closest male—the one who had hit Nuuya with his rod—and pushed his chin up to expose his throat. Next she dug her fangs in his veins.

The other four men had to watch her sucking their mate dry.

Nuuya observed with horror and excitement—and with growing fangs.

The men were radiating utter terror—they obviously had realized their fate.

When Kaaly was finished, she let the man drop down. She licked a drip of blood from her lips and pointed at the next man. "Your turn."

– *Local reinforcements are approaching.* Assiduous *would like to know what's going on.* –

We've found a pilot for Incredulous *and some guests.*

She walked back on the main road. *Come out.*

Her mental command gave the local women no choice but to obey and step out on the street. Some cried out and clutched their frocks when they saw the lifeless men.

"Staying here on the scene will do you no good. You will come along with Nuuya and me."

One older women gathered enough of her wits to face her and speak up. "Are you the one fulfilling the prophecy? Are you the Angel of Liberation?"

"I have no clue what you're talking about, lady, but if you want to meet the star angel who came for your liberation, you better come with us." She pointed at *Audacious's* door. "Get aboard there, and hurry."

"The angel has come?" The woman had tears in her eyes when she turned to the others. "The angel has come!"

Kaaly decided that it wouldn't do them any good to have a ball on this road, and that another shortcut would be okay. *Get aboard.*

Meanwhile, Nuuya had finished the last man, and was beaming with new power.

She grinned with her stained fangs. "I reckon I'd better get in there, too, right?"

"Right." Kaaly ushered her flock forward, then squeezed past them and took an elevator to the bridge. Surprised calls followed her.

She quickly mounted her seat. *Ouch, I'm not wet.*

– *Trouble is close.* –

Let's go. She pulled *Audacious* up and thereby barely evaded a shot. A concussion pulse turned the motorized artillery into dust.

– *There are more.* –

I see. Too many, too close. We might be hurt.

– *No, you won't.* – That was *Incredulous's* message. The living ship dropped from the sky and dealt out EMP strikes all around them. – *Get out of there.* –

They quickly gained distance.

— Assiduous *is calling us.* —

"Hi Kaaly. Syreen here. Let's assemble and talk."

"Be with you in two. I've brought some women who'd like to talk with you."

"Tell them to wait. We have important things to talk about."

CHAPTER FIFTY-SIX

Syreen watched her two cousins. They were much like her, and yet different. Nuuya was about a span shorter, meager, and shy, and could almost make one forget that she was present at all. Her gray eyes didn't make her stand out, either. Kaaly was still two fingers shorter than Syreen herself, but radiating confidence and happiness with her sparkling blue eyes. Like Syreen, both had the pale complexion of a person rarely exposed to starlight, both had the same short black hair, and both hadn't much of a chest.

Syreen had politely asked all others to leave *Assiduous's* bridge, especially Peysoon. "It's too early for her to meet a male of the People," she had said, and Peysoon had agreed. Moreover, she had asked *Assiduous* to turn away the chair containing his huge tool.

She examined Nuuya's gray eyes—what horrors were hidden deep inside there?

Syreen approached her and hugged their new relative. "Welcome aboard, Nuuya. Welcome to the family. I am Syreen, and this is my living ship *Assiduous*."

Nuuya frowned. "What is all this about?"

"Do you remember your mother?"

"I had no mother. Probably killed at birth. Nobody knows. It didn't matter for our master, though. He likes pretty little things." Nuuya glanced at Kaaly. "As long as they keep their mouth shut and their legs wide open."

Syreen held her. "You're not born from a human mother. Meet your true origin."

She sang to Harmony, and then opened her mind.

Nuuya trembled, tried to escape the hug, then relaxed and stared forward open-mouthed.

Kaaly smiled. "Yes, I know. I felt the same initially."

"But . . . but—"

Syreen placed a finger over her lip. "Hush. You've got a million questions and don't know where to start. I don't know all your questions, but I do know where to start, to put things into perspective. Have a seat."

Nuuya watched the three seats growing from the floor, her gray eyes wide, then sat down without hesitation. Kaaly followed.

Syreen took the last chair. "Thank you, *Assiduous*. This is convenient, isn't it? *Assiduous*, my partner, is a living ship, just like Kaaly's *Audacious* and your *Incredulous*. Living ships were built by our People many megacycles ago, and they can only be piloted by female Navigators of the People. As you might have guessed by now, we're no humans, although we look like them. We weren't born by human mothers, we were created by the stars—and don't ask me how that works, because I don't know either."

"What's a Navigator?"

Syreen smiled. "A person who can fly a living ship through hyperspace."

"What's hyperspace?"

"Uh—that's the region between the stars where you can fly faster than light, so that you can travel from star to star."

Nuuya swallowed. "You mean, so that I can leave Harmony?"

"Yes." Syreen nodded. "Yes, you can leave. With your new partner *Incredulous,* you can go anywhere you like. Or you could help Kaaly and me." She sensed confusion and doubt. "You don't have to decide now. Should I continue with my introduction?"

Nuuya nodded. "Please."

"Okay. Our ships have been waiting for megacycles for a Navigator to wake them up. Our ancestors put them away in a safe place—or what they deemed to be safe—until they might be needed again eventually. That time has now come." She waved at Kaaly. "You might have noticed that we're all about the same age. As far as I know, I might have been the first of us. In any case, I was the first to find a living ship. It took some rather unlikely twists of events to get me there, but I won't go into detail now."

"How?" Nuuya asked. "How did you find me?"

Kaaly leaned forward. "Your mother told me after we arrived here. To tell the truth, we didn't come because of you. We came here to fix a terrible wrong here."

"You mean—there's—it's not—uh. Wait." Nuuya shook her head. "They tell us it's the natural way of life, how the Maker wants it to be. The males rule and sire, the females serve and deliver."

"That's not the natural order of things." Syreen frowned. "However, that's the way many males want it to be, and they've been facing too little opposition. Kaaly and I both had to learn that the hard way, although in different ways." She made a grim face. "I taught those males some hard lessons. You'll hear that story someday, too. What matters now is that for you, the rules have changed, and for the women in this system, the rules will change soon, too."

"You can't save them all. Not even if I knew how to help the two of you."

"We will have some help. I've recruited an army of female soldiers to set things straight here. Their fleet will arrive soon."

"They will be shot. We're not taught much, but the Maker's fiery eye will scorch any intruder, as the catechism says."

"But we intruders weren't scorched."

"No—that's what puzzles me no end."

"Because *Assiduous* and I scorched the Maker's fiery eye. It is no more."

Nuuya shook her head. "You're stronger than the Maker?"

Syreen considered her answer for a moment. "*Assiduous* and I together are, yes. *Audacious* and Kaaly would be, too. *Incredulous* and you can become so strong with some experience."

Their new cousin sat up straight. Syreen could sense her determination. "Teach me. Teach me how to become like you. What do I need to know to help others? What do I need to do to shed the anger and hate that try to overwhelm me whenever I think of my torturers? How can I be better than them, and worthy to command the powers of a god?"

CHAPTER FIFTY-SEVEN

"Let's focus on the current situation now," Syreen said. "Our fleet will arrive soon, and there are still a lot of mistreated women dirtside."

"You have no idea." Kaaly waved at Nuuya. "When I rescued her, they were using some kind of shock rods on her."

"Those are called *instructors*." Nuuya shuddered. "Whenever a woman forgets her proper place in the Maker's world, she receives an *instruction*. Few women ever need a second instruction."

"But you know about them," Kaaly said.

"Every woman knows. They make sure you get to witness an *instruction* at least once a year from the moment you can walk."

"How does that add up? If women don't get more than one . . ."

"You understood me wrong," Nuuya interrupted. "I said few women ever *need* a second instruction. That doesn't mean they won't get another. Instructive for the audience, you know? I've had a few myself."

"Oh dear!" Kaaly shook her head.

Syreen clenched her fists, gritted her teeth and felt her canines growing. After a brief gaze at Nuuya's face, she fought her anger down. "We're here to put an end to this."

"How can you be so calm?" Kaaly asked.

Nuuya sighed. "There's one thing you learn from those instructions—how to control your rage. Just a glimpse of defiance spotted in your eyes, and you're due. Trying to hide it doesn't work. You must truly get rid of it. You can't pretend to be docile, you must take it to your heart."

"Why did I find you fighting, then?"

Nuuya took a deep breath. "I wanted to survive. After your arrival was on the news, the men were talking about making an example—to crush any new hopes. Do you know what happens to women who fail to learn from those instructions?"

"I thought that wasn't possible."

"Oh, it was. Every now and then, a woman tortured badly enough would crack. Some would kill themselves, most became ghosts—mute, with broken gaze and will—but a few would fly into a frenzy. These poor souls got the wheel and then the stakes."

"The what?" Kaaly closed her eyes and took several deep breaths. "No, I probably don't want to know."

"No, you don't." Nuuya focused on Syreen. "You're the one in charge, right? What are your plans, and where do I fit in?"

Syreen nodded. "I'm in charge. My plans regarding Harmony are to crush any opposition and put my units in charge, while trying to keep the goal of relieving all these sorry women secret as long as possible. Then we will set up courts and reestablish justice." She saw understanding and agreement in Nuuya's eyes. "My plans regarding you—well, I didn't expect to find one of our kin here. But *Incredulous* needs a pilot, and that'll be you. While our forces clean up that mess, you can get acquainted." She imagined them joining and made a face. "I don't know if that works."

"Why?"

"Our ships are male."

"Uh—okay, well, but they're just ships." Nuuya glanced at Kaaly.

Kaaly shook her head. "The connection between a pilot and her ship is way more intimate than you might expect. It was a huge surprise for me, too."

"It's one of the reasons why living ships can only be piloted by females of the People." Syreen sighed. "I'm not sure if we can demand that of you."

Nuuya closed her eyes. "You're not talking straight. So I will. From my words—and from the fact you're both naked—I conclude that this *intimate connection* includes penetration. That doesn't matter. I *will* do whatever is necessary to assume my rightful place in this rotten universe so to aid you in setting things straight. As you might already have guessed, my pussy was never a private part anyway."

"You seem to take that easy," Kaaly observed.

"No." Nuuya opened her eyes and faced Kaaly. "Not easy. But here on Harmony, you learn to adapt to necessities. Your own will comes last. This universe isn't forgiving."

"No, it isn't." Syreen rose. "And here on Harmony, I won't be forgiving, either. If I had any such inclinations, they're gone after those shots at us."

Nuuya looked up. "So, where and when do we start?"

"Here, within the quartercycle. I have two more topics. First, I have three males in my crew. Do you have any issues with that?"

"No. I assume you wouldn't tolerate them aboard if they were like ours."

"Of course."

"Okay—what's the second topic?"

"You brought some guests who want to talk with me. Do you have any idea what they want?"

"They're women from my village. We couldn't leave them behind. They want to talk with the angel."

"The *angel?*"

"There's just one story secretly passed on from woman to woman through the megacycles—the story of an angel who will come and relieve those who have proven worthy, those who were obedient and devout."

"They assume you are that angel," Kaaly chimed in. "In a way, you are."

Syreen nodded. *"In a way,* I am. Okay, let's meet them. Kaaly, you go first."

CHAPTER FIFTY-EIGHT

Syreen let her gaze pass across the silently assembled women in their plain frocks. She could sense their fear, their hope, their excitement, their pain, and it was almost too hard to bear.

Harmony's happy song soothed and calmed her.

Okay, if it helps me, it might help you, too. She opened her mind and relayed the star's newfound joy to her audience.

Many of the women went to their knees. Almost all had tears in their eyes. They began to sing along, and it sounded beautiful.

Kaaly and Nuuya leaned onto one of her arms each. A gentle mental nudge made them copy her, made them listen on their own and radiate the tune themselves. Their threefold effort amplified secondary harmonics and thus added depth and complexity to the song. She noticed Peysoon gently aligning with them mentally and physically and agreed — true harmony could only unfold where a whole species cooperated.

Stand tall.

Her two fellow pilots let her go and stood straight.

The local women slowly rose, too.

Their joint song slowly faded.

Syreen nodded. "Good. Welcome, free women of Harmony, aboard the Enforcer *Assiduous,* my partner and a living ship of the Forgotten People. I am Syreen Starborn of the Duchy. We have come to change things for the better for your world." She allowed a moment for her words to sink in. "You already met two of my kin, Kaaly Starborn of Epirus and

Nuuya Starborn of Harmony."

She pointed at her fellow pilot. *"Starborn of Harmony* is meant in the literal sense. Nuuya wasn't born from a woman's womb. She was created by your central star — the one you seem to call the Maker's Eye. Please refrain from pestering her with questions — she only just learned about her true ancestry herself."

The women didn't look eager to speak up anyway, so she went on, "About the topic of angels — this is complicated. As Kaaly told you, I'm called a *star angel.* It's a title awarded by interstellar merchants to people they deem extraordinarily helpful — no, indeed supernaturally helpful. I can't argue with that because I do command abilities that must appear supernatural to humans like them and you — while they in fact are quite natural for my people."

She sensed a glimpse of understanding in some women. Others were still stuck in their awe.

"By another definition, angels are celestial beings who act as intermediaries between immortals and humans, as messengers, protectors, or guides. I cannot judge the *celestial being* part, but indeed, as we're created by stars, this definition isn't entirely wrong. I totally agree with the rest, though. Yes, I *am* a messenger sent by the stars to relay their songs to you, to sing of harmony and compassion. Yes, I *am* a protector sent to protect the fabric of existence and all that dwell within — including you. Yes, I'm here to guide you to make this world a better place — and to make that clear, it doesn't mean that I'll make your decisions for you. You've been ordered around long enough. I won't give orders, I will offer advice. No more and no less."

Time to get them involved. "Now that I told you who I am — are you ready to be guided?"

They remained silent.

After a little while, Nuuya stepped forward. "You know

255

me. I'm from your village. We shared much pain and little joy. I know how it is — was — to live on Harmony. Until a few cycles ago I was one of you, perhaps one who suffered more, because I wasn't willing to accept my place in this rotten world. I didn't learn well — how to keep my mouth shut, how to hide my defiance, how to avoid trouble — only well enough to survive. And suddenly I'm told I'm someone else. This isn't easy for me, and so I know it's not easy for you. But like me, you already took the first step. You dared to leave without permission. You can't go back to your previous life — and why would you want to? A bright future is out there for you to take. Now do the next step, acknowledge the change. Acknowledge that you are *someone* now." She focused on one older woman, held out her arms, and smiled at her. "Come forward, Eileen. Tell me what you're going to do."

Eileen hesitated, but then made a first step, and a second, and then she took Nuuya's hands.

Nuuya nodded and waited.

Eileen licked her lips. "I — I will speak with you. I will tell you how life is on Harmony. I will listen to your advice. I — I don't know if I can brave the *instructor*."

Nuuya gently squeezed her hands. "And if we take their instructors away?"

Eileen stared at her. "Then — then I'm willing to fight."

Nuuya gazed around. "Here is one *unbroken*. How about you all?"

One after another, the women spoke a quiet "Yes" or "Me, too."

Syreen felt a spark of confidence in them and gave them a little encouraging nudge.

Nuuya glanced at her and then faced the women again. "Let us start a movement for Harmony here and now. Let's call it the *Unbroken Choir*."

She let Eileen's hands go and took a step back. "Here's

what you can do. Soon, a fleet of soldiers will arrive—all female, and all appalled by what they had heard about your suffering. You will tell them what you know. And each time we relieve other women, you will sing our song to them, so that the *Unbroken Choir* will grow. Syreen, our mission, please."

"Thank you, Nuuya. A part of our mission is to reestablish harmony on Harmony. We will exact justice. This is not about revenge, although our strict justice may feel so to some or most of the culprits. That's why we're here. But, as much as your past troubles me, you are not the core of our mission." She waved around. "My living ship *Assiduous* is called an *Enforcer*. It was created megacycles ago for one purpose only—to protect and enforce the edicts. Edict number one is about keeping space and time intact. Edict Number Two is about keeping planets habitable. Edict Number Three is about keeping sentient life intact. In a wider sense, all edicts are about protecting harmony—and only there can you fit in. The core of our mission, though, is to protect not just this star and its planet, but *all* stars and planets from annihilation. And that's the reason why we cannot stay for long. That's the reason why we brought you the help Nuuya mentioned."

CHAPTER FIFTY-NINE

Syreen set down her forwine mug when Lieutenant Rigg entered *Assiduous's* mess and smiled.

"One for you, too, Samantha?"

"No booze on duty. But I'd gladly have one of that juice." She watched another mug grow out of the table. "Thank you, *Assiduous*."

"Good or bad news?" Syreen examined her visitor's face. The AP officer didn't appear overly worried.

"Can there be good news on a world like this?" The lieutenant waved her own remark aside. "The campaign's going according to our plans. You saw the kind of opposition they can muster during your first cycles—small spacecraft and some ground forces. They must've relied on their doomsday device—good that you could eliminate that threat—as their economy couldn't afford to maintain large ships or major forces anyway. We had no trouble crushing their armed resistance and arresting their leaders."

"But we had casualties."

"Yes, of course. You simply can't evade every unlucky ricochet all the time. But it's just that—accidents. No major losses due to misjudgment or such. Even in the few cases where they placed a trap for us, we suffered mostly scratches and bruises. These Nizwa battle suits can really take some— and once the smoke and debris settles and they emerge undamaged, the enemies just pee their pants. Must've been a shock for them." Rigg shrugged. "Happened quite frequently—initially, we usually came upon them before word had reached those bastards. Recently, the sight of a heavy suit alone makes them drop their guns and rub their faces in the dirt."

She took her mug. "The best news is that they still haven't realized it's about their women. Of course we're collecting their instructors — nasty little things, by the way — and telling them to kowtow. They can't fail to notice our gender, though. So I guess they're just cautious in general."

"And their women?"

"Oh, they're joining the *choir* by the score." Rigg sipped. "Ah, great. Knowing their story, you would expect flocks of sheep everywhere. That's how they played along for generations. But our shrinks say evolution worked out differently here. The males punished everyone — the submissive and the defiant together. The submissive were broken and eventually driven to suicide. The defiant were killed. Those with the willpower for defiance and the cunning to play submissive survived. Mostly wolves, you could say."

"What are wolves?" Syreen asked. *Should I be worried?*

Rigg didn't know, but some of this type of woman had volunteered to join their mission. Kaaly and Nuuya had taken most of them aboard *Audacious* and *Incredulous*. Had they invited trouble aboard?

Rigg shook her head. "Ah, I forgot. Predators, preying on herbivores. Hunting in packs."

"Oh, okay — like stingships going after a cruiser." *Or like certain sauroids.*

"Rather like going after a merchant. But that's the picture, yes. We were a bit worried that the pendulum might swing back toward retaliation, but their leaders are talking about a certain angelic message about fostering harmony. You must've impressed them. Some even asked if they could come along with you."

"Good." Syreen emptied her forwine. "In that case, I can leave you alone for a while. My fellow pilots need exercise."

CHAPTER SIXTY

Syreen adjusted herself in her seat, enjoying *Assiduous's* warm hug. *That went better than expected.*

— Where are we going next? —

Chengdu, close to the rift. We need to do some exercises.

Harmony sang them goodbye. Syreen sensed her own reply echo in Peysoon, Kaaly, and Nuuya.

"Girls, stick close to me. We'll do some hyperflight maneuvers. Kaaly, *Audacious,* you might want to copy them next. Nuuya, *Incredulous,* just try to get the feel. You should get acquainted first."

"Acquainted my ass. We're already fucking, what else could there be?"

Syreen grinned. "Did you try a deep integration already?"

"No, what's that — ugh, really?"

Incredulous *must've told her.* "Be patient, Nuuya. You may look forward to a steep learning curve, but we will still do this step by step."

Where I'll still skip the lesson about conventional hyperjumps, but well, they'll figure it out.

She checked the ships' positions — in tight formation — and their mental connection, then entered hyperspace for a short flight.

The star catalogue identified the star just as an unnamed pivot system. A barren, airless rock was barely large enough to count as planet.

They weren't alone, though. *Break up.*

The two haulers near the primary jump point hadn't

noticed their arrival yet—couldn't have noticed, as they had arrived without jump shock and at about seventy light seconds distance.

In exchange, she could easily read their emissions, even if those that reached her were a centicycle old. Hot reactors and hot guns told her that they were up to no good.

"Armed merchants, this is Navigator Syreen aboard the living ship *Assiduous*. For carrying hot guns, you're charged with piracy. You will surrender and discharge your guns immediately upon receipt of my message or be eliminated."

Audacious and *Incredulous* were on divergent trajectories, forming a quickly growing triangle with *Assiduous*.

Who taught you that? she said to herself, but approvingly.

"Gals, keep an eye on our surroundings. I'll pay them a visit now."

She activated the internal line. "Folks, seems we've caught two pirates with hot guns. We'll make a short break. Peysoon, would you join me for boarding?"

"Sure." His voice came from the lounge. "Meet me at the shuttle."

"I'm coming," Heather added.

Syreen paused, but only for a moment. *Of course she's coming. She's the shuttle pilot now.*

They met at the shuttle.

Peysoon frowned. "Are you sure those pirates won't try something nasty while we're approaching?"

Syreen smiled. "They might—if we let them."

"But we won't?"

"No." She turned to Heather. "Take us there. We will sing a little song."

Understanding dawned in Peysoon, and a big smile grew on his face. "We won't let them."

They boarded the shuttle right behind Heather, found a seat each, and tuned in to the unnamed star's song.

While Heather was busy piloting their shuttle out of *Assiduous's* hangar, Syreen began to overlay the melody with a theme of compliance and surrender, directed at the two pirate ships. Peysoon followed her tune and supported it.

CHAPTER SIXTY-ONE

After they stepped out of the shuttle and into *Assiduous's* hangar, Syreen frowned and turned to Peysoon. "That went smoothly."

"But you don't like it?"

"Not at all. I despise pirates, and I eliminate their threat wherever I encounter them, but that doesn't mean I have to like it. A man spaced without suit is an ugly sight. Moreover, we didn't find the originally registered crew, and that means no good for them."

Peysoon shook his head. "You can't worry about everyone."

She sighed. "I'll get over it. I always get over it."

"You sure?"

"That's how it works. I'm a soldier. I'm trained to kill and get over it." She waved forward and walked toward an elevator. "Remember who we are. We consume people for their power. There's no point in pretending. We are made for killing."

Peysoon followed her. "I thought we shouldn't."

"True." She stepped into the circle and invited him close. "A contradiction, isn't it? As an enforcer, I might have to eliminate entire populations, but at the same time, I'm supposed to protect them."

"How can you tell when to do what?"

They quickly rose toward the opening in the ceiling.

"It's all about harmony. All I'm doing is fostering harmony. Making people tune in. And, if everything fails,

263

removing discord."

"So you might have taught those pirates to tune in?"

The force field lifted them through the opening and stopped.

"Indeed." Syreen walked on. "Had I found them truly repenting, they'd be prisoners now. But their minds tasted rotten. There was only hate, greed, and mischief."

"Yes, I sensed that, too."

"See? Discord beyond repair. We could have forced them to change — and broken their minds in the process."

"Yeah, maybe."

Syreen entered *Assiduous's* bridge and approached her pilot chair. She turned around, focused on Peysoon, and began to shed her clothes.

He just stood and watched.

Only when she had settled into her chair did he take his own seat.

She refrained from listening to his emotions. It didn't feel right at that moment.

Instead, she focused on her ship and partner. *It's time to teach them rookies a lesson.*

— What's on your mind? —

Remember the chasm?

— Oh. —

"Fleet, prepare for maneuver in ten. Mission is to cross the *rift* — a region with serious damage to hyperstructure. We will do another hyperflight in linked formation and pass through the weakest area."

"This is not advisable," Incredulous argued. *"Even a living ship cannot pass seriously damaged hyperstructure."*

"Your objection is wise, but you are lacking crucial intel. Just take care of Nuuya, and we'll be fine."

She issued a call to her girls. It should be Lucy's shift.

"Gather at least four of your supporters on the bridge. They'll assist you in assisting me." Kaaly and Nuuya would have to rely on their Harmony volunteers.

"Sounds like you've planned some fun for us," Kaaly said. *"Are we sailing into a trap or straight into a pirate's lair?"*

"Better. Just wait and see."

A thought made her ship start moving. Kaaly and Nuuya, *Audacious* and *Incredulous,* followed almost without delay and dropped into a perfect triangle formation even before she could instruct them to.

They're adapting fast.

— They've developed a fine sense for harmony. —

Okay. Let's get them there.

The entire formation dashed away.

She quickly sank into deep integration and made them enter hyperflight.

The other two ships needed no guidance. Kaaly and even Nuuya were taking to the miracles of faster-than-light travel like freshmen to forwine.

What a beautiful sight, Nuuya thought aloud. *I could stay in hyperspace forever, if it wouldn't be so strenuous for my ship.*

— It isn't strenuous at all, — Incredulous objected. *— I stand corrected. With a skilled pilot, it's easy-going. —*

Skilled pilot, me? This is just my second flight.

— Hush, my little one. You're a prodigy. —

Oh, folks, Kaaly chimed in. *Can you see that mess ahead? Looks like someone ripped space into shreds. There's not a single thread left to travel on. We need to make a detour.*

— This damage is disturbing, — Incredulous added. *— I strongly advise to avoid that region. —*

Gals, we have a mission, Syreen reminded them. *We're sailing right ahead. But watch this.*

She plucked a strand from the next star ahead and enjoyed the sudden cheer in its song.

These stars are dying. They need our help.

With five more strands from five more stars, she started to weave a fine pattern. Their cheers joined into a choir.

— I'm witnessing the impossible. —

— It's a miracle. —

— This is my Navigator! Watch her magic. —

— You're proud of her. — Audacious noted approvingly.

— He's got every right to be proud. Again, I have to reevaluate. My fact base is outdated, old rules no longer apply, — Incredulous admitted.

Syreen finished her weaving and guided her fleet across the new structure. During their flight, she drank from two of her girls.

Where her repairs ended, they reached another damaged area.

Your turn, Kaaly. Did you see how I did it? But just do two or three.

I'll try.

— Don't try, just do, — Audacious thought. *— I will support you. —*

Syreen resisted the temptation to help Kaaly. She just watched.

Indeed, her fellow pilot succeeded in plucking a thread from another star on the second attempt. From there on, she managed to pull two more threads and weave them together with only a few minor problems.

Great, Syreen praised. *Nuuya, ready for your turn?*

Weaving? Really? I thought I left that behind on Harmony. But her protest came with a mental chuckle. *Let me try that path.*

She reached out for a different, yet untouched star. *It looks as if our recent repairs are spreading out. Can that be?*

There's an aftereffect, Syreen agreed. *We're providing the repaired framework and triggering the meshwork growth.*

Okay. Nuuya pulled and held a thread, felt for another star, pulled again, and linked both threads. *We need a weaver's shuttle, then.*

With growing amazement, Syreen watched Nuuya inventing a new and significantly more effective technique for hyperspace repair, adding parallel threads and then criss-crossing them with her ship—in fact, with all three ships in formation—and pulling threads along.

The stars never told me, Syreen noted.

What do stars know of weaving, Nuuya returned with amusement. *You need a housekeeper to show you. Now, let's finish these repairs and close that rift.*

Syreen was about to object regarding the power needed when she noticed that Nuuya didn't feel exhausted or over-spent at all.

Let Kaaly and me practice that method first, each on her own. That will help us understand what you're doing.

Sure, Nuuya agreed. *Go ahead.*

So you relieved me from growing mushrooms to make me learn weaving — as pilot of a ship that requires flying in the nude? Kaaly complained. *Oh my.*

But she was joking, too. She started weaving and soon didn't want to stop.

Leave a little rift to me, Syreen demanded jokingly, and tried the new method herself. Soon the other pilots joined, and together they wove another large stretch of space.

Okay, let's have a break, she thought. *I might need a bite now.*

Sure, Nuuya replied. *We can continue as soon as you find us a new rift.*

Only then did she realize that they hadn't just crossed the rift, but had followed its entire length.

CHAPTER SIXTY-TWO

Syreen guided her little fleet out of hyperspace and sailed system-inward.

"Nizwa authorities, this is the living ship *Assiduous*, Navigator Syreen speaking. I'm accompanied by the living ships *Audacious* and *Incredulous,* and I'm bringing good news. Send my regards to Harbor Master Juanita and Guild Secretary Orville."

She sat up and climbed out of her seat. She noticed Peysoon sitting in his chair. "You were here all the time?"

"Yes. I know I can never fly such a ship, but I can listen to the stars' songs, and I felt like I might eventually be able to support your weaving if I continue to watch and learn."

"You don't have access to *Assiduous's* senses."

"No, but I do have access to your senses if you open yourself, and you were quite open during the exercise run."

Syreen couldn't quite suppress a shiver when she remembered what he had done to her before — when she hadn't properly shielded herself.

Peysoon showed his palms. "Hey, don't worry. I know what's at stake. I won't take advantage of you."

"Oh — okay. Old memories, y'know?"

He frowned. "Yes. I know."

"*Navigator Syreen, this is Assistant Harbor Master Pablo. Welcome back to Nizwa, and I've announced your arrival to Juanita and Orville. They won't go anywhere until you're here. We've prepared docking bays alpha one and two and beta five, and Juanita sends her apologies that we weren't prepared for your third ship.*"

She raised one finger toward Peysoon.

"Thank you, Pablo. I don't want to let them wait, and don't worry about the docking bays."

Over and Out. Assiduous, *get us to the docking bay.*

"I'm still marveling about how quickly these two gals picked up my lessons. They've learned deep integration, hyperflight and hyperweaving within, what? Less than a tencycle in total? Skills I needed kilocycles to develop. Honestly, I'm feeling a bit frustrated."

"You shouldn't." Peysoon rose from his seat. "Your observations are right, they're following a route that you explored, and they're looking like fast learners. But that's not the entire truth."

He stepped forward and picked her uniform jacket from the floor. "Here. You'll need that. See, they're not just learning. They're copying you—anything you know, you learned, you explored, they just can read it from your mind and integrate it with their own experience."

She took the offered jacket. "Thank you." Then she smiled. "I didn't consider that, but of course, if they can just copy my memories, they're much faster."

"Not only your memories, but also the mental framework about how you apply your knowledge. In deep integration, you are one—three ships, three pilots, one mind." He fetched her pants. "I'm just listening, and I have to admit that I'm scared."

She slipped into the jacket and took the pants from his hand. "Scared? Of me?"

"Yes. When you're flying in hyperspace, when you're weaving, you're very focused, very dedicated. That's part of your lessons, of what you give to the others. But *how* you got there is part of your lessons, too, and I'm catching a glimpse here and there. About a huge sauroid, for example, and how you took him down with a well-orchestrated team. Oh yes,

I'm scared of you. Everyone should be scared. Even this *Void* should be scared, because you can't be stopped."

CHAPTER SIXTY-THREE

Syreen entered the large conference room with Peysoon, Drake, and Crow in tow. Harbor Master Juanita and Guild Secretary Orville were chatting with Kaaly and Nuuya. One steward carried a tray with four steaming mugs.

Juanita turned to them. "Four hot forwine for you?"

They all nodded and took the offered mugs.

"You're okay with the docking bay?" the harbor master asked.

"Oh, sure. Everything's nice and tidy, and after our long flight, the short walk offered an opportunity to stretch our legs." Syreen waved at the two Navigators. "Did they tell you the good news already?"

"Oh, no. They insisted it's your story. We couldn't squeeze the tiniest bit of information out of them. We can only guess that your mission on Harmony might have been successful by the fact that you're here and not there."

Syreen smiled. "Indeed. Yes, our mission was a success, and Nizwa's contribution played a significant role in it. In many cases, the sight of a heavy armor suit alone crushed every notion of resistance, making our victory rather gentle."

Juanita raised her mug. "May we have a toast to that?"

"Sure."

"Okay. To our victory."

"To our victory." The toast was repeated around the room.

Syreen emptied her mug and handed it to the steward. "Thank you. Well, our arrival didn't go as smoothly as our later conquest. Harmony commanded a weapon our ships identified as a *solar ray* — a truly nasty doomsday device, and the explanation of why fleets couldn't pacify Harmony in the past. We had to eliminate that weapon first, and discourage a few brave soldiers later, before we could approach the surface. From there on, the mission went well."

She waved at Kaaly. "My fellow pilot found another Navigator among Harmony's population. She came in time to stop some ugly violent actions and pick up her cousin. That way, we could provide a pilot to the living ship that we found on Backyard. His name is *Incredulous,* and he partnered with Nuuya. They're a good team already, and that's why we can tell you other good news."

Syreen turned to Orville. "I'm herewith formally notifying the guild of the reestablishment of safe travel across the region formerly known as the *rift.* My ship has already prepared the respective updates for the star charts and transmitted them to your guild data base on Nizwa."

"You've found new safe passages across the rift?"

"No, Mr. Secretary. I just said that there is no rift anymore. Together, Kaaly, Nuuya, and I, with our ships, we *repaired* this entire area of hyperspace. Everyone can do six-sigma jumps everywhere."

"That — that's priceless."

"Yes, and that's why I must ask you to publish my charts without fee."

Whatever Orville might have imagined, his sudden sour face made the others laugh out loud.

Chapter Sixty-Four

Unperturbed by the cheerful atmosphere in the conference room, Syreen leaned back against the wall and closed her eyes. *We did well, but will that suffice?*

She sensed Drake's reassuring presence approaching her. He remained silent, just stayed close for a while. His presence seemed to keep others from disturbing her reverie.

Can I really pull that stunt? Can I even fight an entity that's said to be untouchable? Not even considering victory . . .

But is that the question? I'm a born-and-bred warrior – I've been a fighter for all of my life. I'm the one to fight on when all others have failed, I was all that was left of Fleet, and did I despair? No.

I accepted the obligation coming with knighthood, to defend the weak, proudly so.

But now that I believe I know what I'm facing, how can I stand?

I simply don't know where to find that power again.

She sensed a tickle on her cheek — a tear.

She also sensed a warm touch on her shoulder, and then another, and then she felt herself pulled into a gentle hug.

Two female minds started singing in her mind, a male mind joined, and then Nizwa chimed in.

I'm not alone.

We're not alone echoed in her mind.

After another while, she felt comforted enough to open her eyes, and found her chin resting on Peysoon's shoulder, herself wrapped in his arms.

When she raised her head, he let her go.

"Thank you."

"I just . . ." His voice faltered.

"Thank you," she repeated, and touched his arm. "I needed that."

"Yes, but . . ."

"Hush. No buts." She took a deep breath. "My brother-in-arms."

He slowly nodded. "Okay."

Syreen gazed past him. Their hosts were silently watching them from the far side of the room.

"I'm sorry," she began.

"No, don't," the harbor master firmly disagreed. "Don't feel sorry for taking your time."

"But I'm—"

"You're welcome here. You feel so safe here that you can let go. We feel honored. Don't worry."

Orville nodded. "Don't worry. We must be grateful that you're sharing such a wonderful song with us."

Syreen glanced at Peysoon.

He shrugged.

Kaaly smiled mischievously. "Maybe we overdid it a bit."

Nuuya spread her arms. "It didn't feel right to hold back."

"Yes, but what was it? It almost felt like it was inside my mind," Juanita asked.

"It was," Nuuya said. "It couldn't work any other way, because you heard Nizwa's song—your star's."

"We can hear the stars sing," Kaaly added. "They are our parents. That's why we're called *Starborn*."

Nuuya linked arms with her. "That's why we can repair hyperspace."

Orville took a deep breath and glanced at Juanita. "Well, that's something to digest. What are your plans now, Navigators?"

Kaaly and Nuuya turned to Syreen.

Syreen smiled. "We'll do some more exercises in

hyperspace repair. Specifically, I plan to mend the route from Kyris to Moscow."

The guild secretary frowned. "Moscow? Where's that?"

"Behind the chasm."

The harbor master raised her eyebrows. "You don't go for small achievements, do you?"

"I can assure you, compared to what we eventually have to do, this is a minor feat." Syreen glanced at Drake. "Along the chasm, there are inhabited planets with fading stars, where the fabric of space is too weak for an evacuation. We might be able to save some of them."

"If their populations are still alive," Peysoon chimed in. "If it's only a bit like Epirus, their agriculture might have failed them already, and they might have starved to death."

Orville briefly closed his eyes. "If what you say is true — and I have no reason to doubt your assessment — they might be in dire need of food." He gazed at Juanita. "What can we do?"

The harbor master stared at the floor. "Nizwa is a small nation. We're not rich, and our military contribution already cost us a small fortune. But without the rift, we'll surely see trade soar, don't you agree? We might be able to dig up some basic provisions."

"Indeed." The Secretary turned to Syreen. "This is something the guild was never made for — raising donations. But what we were made for is organizing transportation, finding routes, and exploring new markets. That's what we'll do."

"I doubt others will be eager to join," Juanita said.

"I'd like to correct one thing," Drake chimed in. "About raising donations — if I remember right, there was a precedent after the guild wars. Back then, there was a woman from a rich family — I think her name was Francine — who bought a small hauler, hired a crew and an escort, and traveled to places which had seen heavy combat to provide them with essentials—emergency rations, medical provisions, basic communications equipment."

Orville nodded. "Of course, now that you mention it. She was the first star angel in our records."

"Exactly." The historian glanced at Syreen. "Today, the first *triple* star angel in your records will ask the guild for aid. You will, won't you?"

She looked at him in surprise. "Well yes."

Turning to Orville, she went on, "I'd be glad to accept any help for those victims that the guild can offer."

"Uh—well—uh, I think, well yes . . ."

Juanita poked him with her elbow. "Come on. You won't do this all on your own. I'm sure other secretaries will help us, and I'll find us some volunteers for the administrative part."

She turned to Syreen. "We will need some time to get this project running, with drone traffic delay and all. But we'll start spreading the word now."

"Thank you. Our repairs will take some time anyway. But your offer alone is a big relief."

Orville nodded. "You said you will create a route from Kyris. That's where the first relief fleet shall gather, half a kil-ocycle from now. Okay?"

"Okay. When you prepare the drone message, include the Crown units. They will provide escort services." She gazed at her company. "We will depart as planned, four cycles from now."

Part Five—Evaluation

CHAPTER SIXTY-FIVE

Syreen found nine merchants and two passenger liners docked at Kyris Orbital and, to her joy, one Crown destroyer — plus one AP-built light cruiser emitting a Duchy call sign.

The latter beat all the others to call her.

"Unknown ships from Duchy cruiser Raydancer, *please state your origin and intentions."*

She smiled.

Before she could reply, a second message followed.

"Enforcer Assiduous *from* Raydancer, *please ignore previous communication. This is Lieutenant Harvest speaking. Navigator Syreen, on behalf of Duchy Fleet, welcome to the Kyris system. We would be honored if you could join us for a mug of forwine eventually."*

"Raydancer from *Assiduous,* this is Syreen speaking. I'll gladly follow your invitation later. Bear with me, I need to speak with the authorities first." She paused. "Kyris port authority, this is Navigator Syreen. I'm accompanied by two more living ships, piloted by two more Navigators of my people. I'd like to ask for one docking bay."

"Navigator, this is Kyris port authority, Trevor speaking. You're welcome to use docking bays beta three to five, all free of charge. Moreover, I'm ordered to tell you that your permanent invitation to planetary Kyris has been extended to all of your kin with all living ships."

"Thank you, Trevor. This time, I want to meet people on Kyris Orbital." *And the invitation wasn't extended to all of my crew. I'm sure my girls would like to check the local venues.*

"If you'd like me to schedule any appointments for you, just tell me."

"Indeed, Trevor, I'd like to talk to the harbor director. Should Guild Secretary Jacomo happen to be back at Kyris, I'd like him to join that meeting. And maybe you could include the Crown skipper."

"Sounds like something's brewing. Would it be convenient for you to meet at the guild hall? Our director is currently there, talking with Secretary Jacomo."

"Perfect, Trevor. I'll bring my fellow Navigators along."

And cut.

She steered toward the orbital station. *Ladies, you'll be docking, too. You'll join me for a meeting with the authorities.*

What, no welcome party? Kaaly giggled. *Any dress code to observe?*

None that I'd know of. But people judge others by the way they dress. That's why I'll be wearing a uniform. Assiduous will tell your ships how it looks, in case you'd like to copy me.

That will be wise, Nuuya thought. *After all, we didn't come here to stir a riot.*

No? Kaaly sounded disbelieving.

No. I had riot enough on Harmony.

I had enough of dull on Epirus. I'd like to have a little riot for a change.

Ladies, please. Syreen grinned. *Join my crew later — they'll guide you to the party spots with or without riot.*

Deal.

Deal.

CHAPTER SIXTY-SIX

Syreen led her fellow pilots to the guild hall. Kaaly and Nuuya marveled at the colorful guard uniforms as well as at the marble-and-gold hall decorations.

Classy. Now I know why you proposed uniforms. Nuuya plucked some imaginary fuzz from the sleeve of her white jacket. *Makes us look like we belong here.*

Makes us look like we've got something to say. Kaaly chuckled.

"Follow me this way," Syreen said and led them to a small conference room with the familiar plush chairs in ebony and burgundy.

Two men were waiting for them. The guild secretary in his formal robe bowed. "My Ladies, nice to meet you. Lady Syreen, I'm delighted to see you again so soon. May I introduce to you our new harbor director, Jon Steed."

The stringy young man at his side bowed, too. "My Ladies, I'm honored." He focused on Syreen. "We didn't meet last time—you were in a hurry back then."

"Yes—she caused quite a stir," Jacomo agreed.

Syreen shrugged. "It wasn't the time for ordinary meetings. That's why I had to leave."

"Do you still hear Kyris's song?" the harbor master asked.

Syreen nodded. "Always. She's here with us all the time."

Jacomo glanced at her company.

She sensed his curiosity. "May I introduce Kaaly, Navigator of the living ship *Audacious,* and Nuuya, Navigator of the living ship *Incredulous.*"

Jacomo and Jon bowed again.

The guild secretary then waved at the round conference table. "Please have a seat. May I offer refreshments?"

"Hot forwine for me, thank you," Syreen said and chose a seat. Kaaly and Nuuya joined her left and right and ordered the same.

Jacomo grinned and unveiled a tray with five steaming mugs. "Seems I've won the bet."

Jon shrugged and sat down, facing the Navigators. "You know your people, Jacomo."

The secretary placed the mugs around the table and took another free chair. Then he raised his mug. "Duke's health!"

"Duke's health," Syreen answered. *Old story here.*

Okay. "Duke's health," Nuuya and Kaaly echoed.

Jon followed suit, and then they enjoyed the hot drink in small sips.

Syreen felt strong, happy emotions approaching, placed her mug down, and rose again.

The door opened, and a man in a Crown captain's uniform entered. "Hello Syreen. I was told I'd find you here."

"Welcome, Jaime. May I introduce you?" She turned around. "Captain Jaime Jones, Crown fleet. Jaime, you probably already met Guild Secretary Jacomo and Harbor Director Jon Steed. These are Kaaly and Nuuya, Navigators like me."

The captain bowed. "I thought there could be no one like you."

Kaaly chuckled. "You've got a point, Jaime. We're all different, but we have a few things in common. First and foremost, we're flying living ships."

"We're flying hyperspace," Nuuya added.

"Please, Captain, have a seat," Jacomo chimed in. "Would you like to have a forwine, too?"

"Yes, thank you." The Crown officer sat down and waited for Jacomo to serve another mug. "Thanks."

Jacomo nodded and reassumed his own seat. "Navigator,

you asked for this meeting."

Syreen had returned to her seat, too. "Yes. We're bringing good news. You might have heard about the rift—a region difficult to navigate—between Chengdu and Nizwa."

"Mostly impassable, our records say." Jacomo nodded. "And pirate-infested, too—until a certain star angel did something about it."

"Right." Syreen smiled and pointed left and right. "Well, the three of us could do a bit more about it. I've already formally notified the guild on Nizwa of the reestablishment of safe travel across the region formerly known as the rift, together with the respective star chart updates. You will now receive your own copy." *Assiduous, relay the data.*

The guild secretary returned her smile. "But that's not what you came here for."

"No. There are three announcements I want to make."

"I'm listening."

"You may start recording."

"Oh." Jacomo raised his eyebrows and did as suggested. With a hand wave he motioned her to continue.

"First announcement. My Navigators and I, we will start repairing the *chasm*."

The three men leaned forward, their faces showing disbelief.

She went on. "We plan to open a safe route between Kyris and Moscow soon—and safe means, suitable for seven-sigma jumps."

Jacomo, Jon, and Jaime froze.

"We suggest that the guild starts preparations to establish a regular drone traffic across the route that we will chart."

She waited for Jacomo to nod.

"Second announcement. We plan to reconnect inhabited worlds, worlds that are in severe distress due to their fading stars. We suggest that the guild starts preparations to establish relationships."

She took a deep breath and reached out with her mind to soothe the still stunned men.

"Third announcement. On Nizwa, the first triple star angel in history formally asked the guild for assistance in raising donations and organizing transport of essential goods to these worlds — following the example of the first star angel."

Jacomo gasped.

She leaned forward. "I'm looking forward to many volunteers. The first relief fleet will gather half a kilocycle from now — here on Kyris, at the entrance to the new route."

She gestured at Jacomo to end the recording.

While the secretary and the director tried to wrap their minds around her last announcement, she turned to the Crown skipper. "Jaime, spread the news among our fleet. You'll be going home, and I want to ask you to escort the first relief fleet."

He almost jumped out of his seat, went to attention, and saluted. "Yes, Sir!"

Syreen rose without hurry and returned the salute. "Thank you, Captain. Moreover, you will surely assist Kyris in maintaining order during the assembly."

"Of course." He relaxed. "Does that mean you no longer need us for escort services on this side?"

"To be honest, I'm not sure. Once the embargo is lifted, I expect the AP to step in. Perhaps some systems will reevaluate their obligation toward safe trade and commission their own escorts — now that they've seen Crown fumigators in action, they might develop similar designs or simply ask for your construction plans."

"Once we return home, I will ask our government for support of your cause. Perhaps we may do escort services along the new route."

"That would be highly appreciated, Jaime."

The skipper briefly closed his eyes. "Do you know what a big issue the chasm is on our side? We've seen worlds disconnecting from trade and travel—their last drone messages were desperate. Many politicians say something must be done—but no one knows what could be done."

He gazed at his mug. "Now, suddenly there are things that can be done. Donations, relief fleets, escort services. I hope I'm not wrong but I think you will see more help."

Kaaly glanced at Syreen, then at the secretary. "She didn't mention it yet, and this isn't for the official records, but these repairs are not our real mission."

"Not?" Jacomo glanced back and forth between the two women. "But . . ."

"These repairs are exercise," Kaaly explained. "We need to practice before we go to war."

"War? What war?" The harbor director sat up straight.

"Look," Kaaly said. "Syreen surely explained before that poor jumps cause damage to hyperspace. That's why you should always aspire to the best possible solution. I must admit that I don't know anything about hyperjumps. My tutor"—she waved at Syreen—"skipped that lesson and taught me hyperflight instead."

She shook her head. "I tried to learn everything. I watched attentively, both her and my ship. I examined the environment that should become mine. I looked very closely and I tried to understand what they were showing me. Hyperspace isn't as fragile as you might think. It's not easily destroyed. Yes, poor hyperjumps do real damage, to an extent that some routes are not safe for travel—but not to disconnect and ultimately kill stars."

"What are you trying to tell us?" Jacomo asked.

Syreen only listened.

"I'm trying to tell you that there's something else eating away hyperstructure. It's like—uh—you're cutting your skin, and don't clean it, and then fungus gets hold of the sore spot and spreads. You get the picture?"

Jacomo and Jon nodded.

"Good. The same must have happened at the rift, and I assume I'll find the same signs at the chasm."

"A hyperfungus?" Jon asked.

"Ah, no—the analogy ends there. It's not a fungus, not anything tangible, just the opposite. Not an entity, an un-tity, so to speak. We call it the *Void,* and we must fight it." She blinked. "You don't think the stars would bother to create Navigators just to maintain your routes and meddle with your petty quarrels, do you?"

"Uh—I..."

A tiny light flashing on the table surface in front of Jacomo caught their attention.

The secretary tapped the table. "A message. The most honorable Minister of Foreign Affairs, Her Royal Highness Antaria Vod Merodion of Kyris, would dare to ask the most honorable Lady Syreen Starborn, Knight of the Order of the Firepath, triple star angel of the merchant guild, Navigator of the Forgotten People, and her new sister Navigators, for a private come-together any time it would please her. Her Royal Highness suggests Meadow-in-the-Lakes as preferable location."

He looked up. "A reply would be highly appreciated."

"A meeting on the surface?" The harbor director shook his head. "That's unheard of."

"Yes." Jacomo patted his shoulder. "When the Navigator is around, all kinds of *unheard-of things* are happening. You'd better get used to it."

Syreen rose and motioned her *sisters* to follow. "Gentlemen, we're leaving now. When a good friend calls, I won't hesitate to follow. You may announce our arrival within the cycle."

CHAPTER SIXTY-SEVEN

Syreen directed *Assiduous* into a gentle descent. *We don't want to announce our very first visit dirtside Kyris with a storm, do we?*

— *As you wish.* —

She grinned, not sure whether her mate really grasped the peculiarity of their situation.

— *I am aware of the local reservations toward planetary visitors.* —

Okay, mate.

She never had considered calling her fellow navigators *sisters,* but the term felt appropriate. At the very least, they were *sisters-in-arms.* Otherwise, in what way were stars related?

Kaaly and Nuuya were the only passengers aboard. All her crew — Drake, Crow, the girls, even Peysoon — were roaming Kyris Orbital for their own different reasons.

She could sense her *sisters'* intense curiosity. Was it just about the planet — for Nuuya, her first foreign planet ever?

She felt a bit curious herself. So far, the only planet that had made her feel comfortable was Nysa, but her memories of her first visit there still gave her the creeps. What would Kyris be like?

Assiduous's senses told her of norm-like gravity — a good fifth more than usual on ships and stations, as spacers would always like to reduce the burden of weight, and as such close to the conditions mankind were made for. The same applied to the atmospheric mix and pressure. Winds were mostly gentle, precipitation low, and clouds rare where they were heading.

The surface looked bumpy — oh yes, *mountains*. She had heard of that kind of landscape. The Duchy had mountains, too, sometimes visible from orbit if one bothered looking.

Give us a visual.

They were heading toward a kind of spacious bowl with tall rocky walls engulfing about three quarters of a clear lake. A lush-green island with trees and grass rose from the lake's center like a nipple. A dozen foamy veils of water fell down the walls into the lake, and another, much larger waterfall emerged from the lake through the bowl's opening.

I sense harmony.

— I agree. This place sings its own song. —

You're talking of songs, mate?

— I'm capable of adapting to my Navigator. —

Syreen sensed his amusement.

— The vegetation would suffer from my weight. —

I agree.

— I can set down on the water surface. —

Good idea.

Assiduous's door opened. Syreen made a step forward and paused.

Snowy mountain crests, misty waterfalls, the tops of tall trees, green grass, and a solitary, tall woman at the shore were mirrored in the lake surface.

Of course, the wide expanse of water between the hangar door and the shoreline was due to the ship's leg-shaped extensions.

— You can step out. The elevator field works fine. —

She noticed the shimmering ring over the water.

Oh. I was marveling at the view.

— Okay. —

Syreen stepped forward, followed by Kaaly and Nuuya. Together they were carried to the shore.

It was their host's turn to marvel as they were gliding toward her.

The aristocrat was barely covered by a thin, short dress that left little to imagination, and Syreen instantly felt overdressed in her plain white uniform.

"Welcome, Syreen," she said and spread her arms for a hug.

"Thank you, Antaria," the Navigator replied, accepted and returned the hug, and then waved at her company. "Kaaly Starborn of Epirus and Nuuya Starborn of Harmony, my fellow Navigators."

They exchanged more hugs.

"Thank you for coming so fast," Antaria said and waved toward a small hut between the trees. "Come along."

Syreen walked at her side. "My friend called, so I came."

Antaria laughed happily. "You'd be quite busy if you answered every friend's call so promptly."

"Not at all." Syreen shook her head. "You are the first and only one who ever called me friend."

The local woman almost stumbled in her step. "The only? But why?"

"I don't know. I always had wingmates, teammates, crewmates, supporters, and allies, even sisters-in-arms—all kind of nice people, but no one ever came up with friendship."

"But that's . . . uh, wow, I wasn't aware . . ."

"Which makes our relationship truly unique, doesn't it?" Syreen took Antaria's hand. "But let's not make a fuss about it. Just take it as it is. That's what friendship should be, right?"

The hand felt warm, and for a moment a bit shaky, but then her friend returned the grip. "Yes, right."

Quietly they continued toward the hut. When they came closer, Syreen could see more details—a wide porch, a table, chairs, small feathery creatures with wings . . . *Oh yes, birds.*

"All made from local wood," Antaria explained. "Except

for the windows, of course."

"It's beautiful. This is your place?"

"Sometimes. It's a retreat, a place to find peace, when you want to think things over—or talk with friends in private. Why don't you make yourself comfortable on the porch? I'll fetch us some fresh juice."

When the three Navigators sat down, the birds flew up. Syreen reached out with her mind and soothed them. Soon the little creatures rested on their shoulders or legs.

That was how Antaria found them when she returned from the hut with a tray loaded with a jug and four cups.

She placed the tray down and poured the cups. "I shouldn't be surprised. You have a thing with animals, don't you? I've heard a story about a place called Appalahoo."

"You could say so, yes. It didn't go as well as with these little birds here, back then."

"Were they too shy?"

"No. Too aggressive."

"Oh. But you're unhurt."

"I'm healed. My adversary's head now decorates the local shop."

Kaaly giggled, Nuuya frowned.

"Would you like to tell us your story?" Antaria sat down, too. "If you can spare the time, that is."

"I didn't come here to hurry," Syreen agreed. "Well. Back then, I had just discovered my living ship, and he needed time to heal and grow. So I traveled with merchants . . ."

CHAPTER SIXTY-EIGHT

"I think you know the rest of the story." Syreen emptied her cup and held it out when Antaria lifted the jug to pour another. "In the end, I rejoined with *Assiduous*, defeated an AP fleet, and returned to Kyris to pick up Jacomo's good advice and his message vault."

"That's a very condensed summary of the events I heard of," Antaria said with a smile, "but that part of your story seems to be documented quite well by your historian. Dragutin, right?"

"Yes. We call him Drake." Syreen placed her cup down. "Why don't you tell us your story now? Is there anything I can do for you?"

Antaria made a stern face and sat up straight. "Yes. I wanted to ask for your sound advice. But let me explain a few things first." She made a wide gesture. "Kyris is a peaceful place. Not as quiet as this island, but by far not as busy as our station. Our villages are lively, but not hectic. We like it that way, so we keep strangers from coming here. We don't want large flocks of tourists roaming our retreats, or merchants pressing our producers, or, let's say, people with sneakier intentions sneaking around. We already have enough own sneaky people—you already met some."

Syreen nodded.

"Yes. We send those ones to space where they can vent their energy to some extent. Actually, we don't want troublesome activities up there either, so we let them keep each other in check. Most of the time, that works fine. Sometimes we have to intervene, sometimes our intervention comes late, and sometimes we're beaten to it. You know what I mean."

Syreen nodded again.

"Well. All that's working fine for the males. But what can we do with our restless women? We can't send them to space, where they fall prey to the bad guys. We can't make them ship cats, but there aren't many other jobs — until recently someone changed the rules. And that's what I wanted to ask you about. Is it safe to let our young women go?"

"Oops." Syreen hadn't expected that question. "How can I explain?" She glanced at Nuuya. "I'd say no. It's never really *safe* out there. There are pirates, there are inspectors overstepping their rules, and there are bad places. Perhaps not as bad as Harmony was, but places where sneaky people gather. Space stations with dubious reputations, where space-faring women are regarded as of dubious reputation, too — basically, any woman traveling with merchants must be a ship cat, that was the rule."

She raised one hand before Antaria could interrupt her. "That's what your women still must be prepared for. There is no guarantee that they'll remain unhurt. They have to understand that. But things are changing. Talk with merchants traveling through Kyris if they're willing to hire female crew for real jobs. Some already do. Talk with Jacomo whether the guild would want to make rules of conduct that merchants would sign up to — voluntarily. Crews might protect their crewmates from mischief with or without such rules of conduct. Or, your women might join another nation's navy — ask the Duchy ambassador for vacant spaces. The Duchy has never had issues with female navy."

Antaria gave a wide smile. "See? I knew you'd come up with sound advice. I will do as you suggested and ask around. I will tell our candidates about the risk involved, and if they're willing to take it, they may go. And your last suggestion leads me right to the other question I wanted to ask—would you suggest Kyris should have our own navy?"

Syreen leaned back to ponder that question.

Kaaly chimed in. "Definitely yes, depending on what you're willing to afford. You should have your own harbor patrol to deter pirates and to sort out the traffic that will inevitably increase with the route across the chasm that we're about to reopen. You can sell escort services. And your women will be much safer as crew on your own ships."

"Yes." Nuuya focused on their host. "Teach your women to fight. In this universe, they need to stand their ground."

Antaria's eyes were glittering. "Oh, we know how to stand our ground. We're just good at hiding that fact to strangers."

"In that case, I'd suggest you talk with Captain Jaime Jones and Ambassador Hakon about that topic, too."

"Indeed." The aristocrat glanced skyward. "I might ask Captain Jones whether Crown would sell us a few of these fine little warships—at least he could relay my question. Those seem to be way more efficient than the units built on this side of the chasm."

"They are," Syreen agreed. "Definitely best for your purpose—escort services and harbor patrol."

"I will ask them for trainers, too," Antaria mused, still glancing at the sky. Then she focused on Syreen again. "I'm sorry. I'm selfish, only following up on my own topics, while you must be troubled with issues of the most severe nature."

The Navigator shook her head. "We didn't visit you to burden you with our worries."

"You came as a friend, to help a friend. That's what friends do. Let me do what friends do, too. Let me help you. Tell me."

So Syreen told her what she knew.

CHAPTER SIXTY-NINE

Syreen sighed. "I'm not sure if we've got what it takes to defeat the *Void*."

Antaria placed her palms together and breathed inside. Then she took her hands down. "I didn't think trouble could be that deep. Anyway—did you tap all sources you can get at already?"

"I don't know any sources."

"You do. What about those traces that led Drake to Kyris? What about the guild rolls? What about that guild monument? What do your parents tell you?" Antaria glanced around. "We don't know much about the Forgotten People, except that they were people, not stars. What caused them to change that? How could they? Back then, when you came here first, on a tactical retreat from the AP, you decided to start investigating before returning home to defeat them. In my humble opinion, you need to do the same now. Start investigating before you try to defeat this strange Void. Some more exercises might do no harm, but consider what you want to unveil to your enemy now before you're prepared to commit to a full fight."

"Your advice is sound," Nuuya said. "Once we start the real fight, it might be unwise to withdraw."

"We need to strike fast, and strike hard," Kaaly said. "But indeed, we should know where and how to strike."

Nuuya gazed from Antaria to Syreen. "I don't know any of the places you mentioned, My Lady, but in hyperflight, it won't cost us much time to go there, I'd guess."

"I'd skip those traces Drake mentioned," Syreen said. "For

one, he already checked them. For two, they were just fragments of ships. However, Jacomo might be willing to show me the guild rolls. We'll see what they tell us."

"That'd be a quick win," Kaaly said. "What kind of guild monument was that?"

"As far as I learned, it was there long before the guild was founded." Syreen glanced at Antaria. "It's built on a barren planet that was chosen to found the guild. I don't know whether its origin has ever been investigated, but it seems to be the origin of our edicts. Now that you mentioned it, I'm a bit curious about it. Yes, we should definitely go there."

Their host smiled and nodded. "I wish you good luck in finding more wisdom there. There's another thing I'd like to ask you now."

"Go ahead."

"I don't know much about hyperspace. But I know that even our tiny snippet of space with its few thousand inhabited planets on both sides of the chasm contains some billions of stars. And even if some hundred thousand ships are traveling this vast, empty region, aren't they still like a few drops of water in this lake that surrounds us? Aren't they but a glowworm's glimmering against the stars' bright shine? And even if their jumps are reckless and violent, how can such tiny, random actions cause so much damage?"

Syreen briefly closed her eyes. "This is a good question. It isn't easy to explain." *And she won't be satisfied with Kaaly's fungus explanation.*

"Try complicated then."

Syreen gazed at her for a moment. Then they both had to laugh, and the other two Navigators joined in.

"Let me start with your comparisons. All registered ships together, commercial, military, and private, are still less than one droplet in this lake." She waved toward *Assiduous*. "Other than that really huge droplet there."

Kaaly giggled.

"And if there was a ship powerful enough to force its way through hyperspace unhurt with a one-sigma jump, the damage it would inflict still couldn't cause anything like the rift or the chasm. However, you would be able to notice that jump across hundreds of lightyears. No, let me put that differently — *Assiduous* and I would be able to notice that jump across hundreds of lightyears." Her gaze wandered from Kaaly to Antaria. "And, what's more important, we would still be able to notice that jump a kilocycle later."

Antaria sat up straight. "Oh." Next, she leaned forward. "I think I see where you're going. Go on."

"It's somewhat like throwing a stone into our lake. The waves will travel a long way. And while the stone is truly small, our lake's surface — in this analogy — is very easy to stir."

"Many waves, running forward for a long time," Antaria observed. "Add more sources, and their amplitudes will add up — until the delicate structure cracks."

"Exactly." Syreen nodded. "Now comes the complication."

Antaria smiled. "The cracks will affect following waves, will split them and thus amplify the damage."

"You already know that?"

The aristocrat shrugged. "I don't. But the way you illustrated it, it seemed logical. The formula set to describe that effect must be a nightmare, though. It will take weeks to write a first draft."

"But why would anyone write such a draft?" Nuuya asked.

"Because that's how science works." Antaria wrinkled her nose. "That's the stinky part of it."

"So you're into science, too?" Nuuya asked on.

"Of course. You don't become Minister of Foreign Affairs if you don't know your ropes. I hold doctor's degrees in astrophysics, political science, and political economics, and one professorship at Kyris's Space Academy."

CHAPTER SEVENTY

Once they exited hyperspace, Syreen relaxed. "Here we are," she said aloud, although there was no one else on *Assiduous's* bridge.

Her ship didn't reply.

"We'd better find some intel here," she went on. "I need results."

Their research in Jacomo's guild rolls had yielded nothing new, only confirmed the location of the barren planet that they were currently approaching.

"Okay. Let's go down."

— *You seem to get the hang of talking with yourself.* —

"Indeed. You might have noticed that I'm somewhat nervous."

— *How could I not notice? We're linked, physically and mentally. We share our conditions. You agitate me, I calm you down.* —

"You're not excited?"

— *I sense your excitement. I'm patient. Patience comes with age, you know?* —

"You fossil."

— *Hatchling.* —

Syreen sensed his amusement, but their short banter had mellowed her nervousness.

She focused on leading her little flotilla dirtside.

Inside and outside line.

"Okay, folks. We've arrived at Guild Prime—that's how the negotiators labeled this world. Gravity is zero point eighty-nine standard. Gas is mostly nitrogen, at low density, so you'll need breathers. Temperature at destination is low but not freezing, so I recommend warm clothing, but you won't need protective suits. There is no wildlife, so no danger to expect. Ask your local tour guide for more details."

Surprised calls from her passengers made her smile.

Guild Prime's planetary rotation ensured that the surface received sufficient heat from its star all over. It also caused significant gas movement near the terminator.

The terminator had passed their destination about a cycle ago and wouldn't approach again for three more cycles, so they had a smooth ride down.

"Meet me at the monument."

Syreen gazed at the triangular surface before her. Its bottom extended at least a thousand legs on both sides. As all the monument's edges had the same length, its apex rose over fourteen-hundred legs into the sky.

Most of the surface sparkled in the star's light, with the exception of the huge plates covering the pyramid's bottom all around.

While sensing Peysoon and Drake just behind her, she waited until her sisters had joined her. Their ships were parked at a respectful distance of about the length of one edge, so their walk had taken a good halfcycle.

"Impressive," Drake said. "Is that truly one crystal? It must be the largest diamond in the entire universe."

Peysoon nodded. "I can't see any cracks. It doesn't look like it's made of tiles."

"It doesn't look like it's hollow, either."

"Yeah, right. That's what *Assiduous's* sensors said, too. Just one big crystal." Syreen tried to peek inside, but only saw more sparkling. "Almost impossible to occur in nature, almost impossible to be made."

"That's what I thought of living ships, too. Almost

impossible." Drake turned to her. "As impossible as being star-born."

The Navigator sighed. "Thanks for reminding me. Yes, I know. I have to accept its existence as a fact."

Her sisters stepped to her right side.

Kaaly pointed forward. "Okay, now where's the entrance?"

Syreen shook her head. "I don't think there's supposed to be an entrance."

"What are we doing here, then?"

"Checking the inscriptions." Syreen pointed at the plate before them, rising ten legs up. "Perhaps they'll tell us more."

"To me that looks like gibberish. I don't even know the symbols."

"Me neither," Syreen admitted. "Drake?"

"Not any symbol set I ever heard of."

— I can read it. — Assiduous's mental voice radiated surprise.

"What does it say?"

— The grammar is twisted, but it reads like this. Edict Number One. The deliberate damage of the fabric of space, especially actions that could create a rift, or the destruction of living stars, is proscribed. Edict Number Two. The deliberate destruction, sterilization or rendering uninhabitable of worlds, especially, but not limited to, kinetic strikes, large-scale application of nuclear or biological weapons, and systematic destruction of geological stability, is proscribed. Edict Number Three. The deliberate interference with the genetic code of intelligent beings is proscribed. —

"Sounds very familiar to me." Syreen walked left toward the next plate. It showed something like vertical scratches. "And this one?"

— Oh. This is worse. —

"Just read it out."

— Edict Number One. Space fabric damage deliberate proscription. Rift creation specialization. Living star destruction proscription. Edict Number Two. —

"Okay, okay. The same edicts, only different symbols and different grammar?"

— *Yes.* —

"Let's check the next ones."

"Boooring," Kaaly complained, but followed.

"I have to be sure." Syreen led them all around the structure. After one cycle, they returned to the place where they had started.

"Okay, and what does that tell us?" Nuuya asked. "We found just one readable plate in Common, but they all say very much the same."

"It means that the creators were quite serious about these edicts," Peysoon said. "But indeed, without any context, this doesn't help us any further."

"There is context," Drake objected. "First, the monument itself. Somebody made sure that it stands out. Second, the planet. Wiped blank. That's a statement in itself, and combined with the second edict, it's a warning."

"You don't think it's just what the edict warns about?" Nuuya asked.

"No. Any planet falling victim to such destruction would still give some clue about what it was — ruins, remnants of life, if only lichens or such, mountains and rivers, vulcanism, whatever. This planet was wiped perfectly blank. I'd say that's what happens to violators."

"Yes," Syreen agreed. "We command the means to do so."

"Really?" Kaaly gulped. "Blank like this?"

"Ask *Audacious*."

Kaaly seemed to gaze inward for a moment, then she stared at Syreen. "Oh."

"The question remains," Nuuya said. "What can we learn here beyond what we already know."

"Whatever it is, it's not on these plates." Kaaly stepped up to the monument and placed her hand on the crystalline surface between the plates, looking back at her companions.

"And there's nothing else, or is there?"

She frowned and turned to the monument again. "It feels warm and alive. How can crystalline carbon feel like that?"

"Open your mind," Peysoon said. "Syreen, why don't you sing us a song?"

Syreen refrained from smacking her head. *Yes, obviously.*

Then she started singing to the central star, and it tuned in, like all the stars she had met before.

The overall song was not like the songs she had sung before, though. There was another tune underlying the main theme, and when she focused her mind on it, its source felt much closer.

Kaaly slowly began dancing in time, her hand still on the monument.

– WHO ARE YOU? –

Syreen Starborn of the Duchy, Navigator of the living ship Assiduous. *Who are you?*

– WHO ARE YOU? –

The question seemed to be directed elsewhere.

Kaaly Starborn of Epirus, Navigator of the living ship Audacious.

Nuuya Starborn of Harmony, Navigator of the living ship Incredulous.

Peysoon Starborn of Kendar.

– WHO IS THE DEAF ONE? –

Syreen grinned. *Dragutin Petran, historian, human. Our guide and assistant. Who are you?*

– THE NAVIGATORS MAY ENTER. –

Enter where? she was about to say, but then the *one-piece* surface unfolded like a curtain and unveiled a brightly-lit tunnel.

"Ladies, we've got an invitation. Sorry, guys."

She waved forward, and Kaaly went first. Nuuya followed Syreen. Unsurprisingly, they had to walk some distance, as the tunnel led toward the center.

They arrived at a small cavern. Aside from a crystalline pedestal in its center, it was undecorated.

Kaaly ambled along the walls, Nuuya stopped at the cavern entrance.

Syreen slowly approached the pedestal. "Somewhat disappointing. No diamond dildo?"

She glanced at the fine facets around the erect shape's surface that rose up to her hip. "Or at least not my size."

Kaaly finished her round, linked arms with Nuuya, and stepped forward. "Did we come here to fuck or to learn?"

"To learn." Syreen closed her eyes. "I only thought . . ."

"What?" Kaaly pulled Nuuya close.

The Navigator raised her index finger before them.

We came to learn.

– And learn you shall. Sit down and open your mind. –

Three chairs rose from the floor. Syreen opened her eyes, pointed at two with her arms, and took the third.

I'm ready.

Me too.

Me too.

– So learn. –

CHAPTER SEVENTY-ONE

Syreen dropped into a chair in *Assiduous's* lounge. Kaaly and Nuuya did the same.

"As if we hadn't been sitting around long enough," Kaaly commented sourly.

"Got a sore ass?" Nuuya asked and shuffled in her chair. "Boy, what a ride."

Assiduous conjured up three steaming mugs of forwine, each close to a Navigator.

They enjoyed their drink in silence.

Syreen was aware of the presence of many curious people sitting or standing around them in the lounge, and she was glad they were granting her a moment of contemplation.

There's enough to contemplate for a lifetime or two. I don't even know where to start.

"Can't we just go and kick some *Void's* ass?" Kaaly pouted.

"It's got no ass," Nuuya said.

"Really? I mean just figuratively."

"There's nothing figurative about the *Void*. That much I understood." Nuuya leaned forward to sit on the edge of her chair. "No kicking."

Drake dared to speak up. "So you were successful?"

"So to speak," Nuuya agreed. "It was overwhelming. We've got a flood of answers, now we just need the questions. Like, how long were we in there?"

"Two tencycles," Drake said. "After you entered the monument, we had to return to the ship, before the terminator storms came. *Assiduous* then said we just had to wait."

"Two tencycles," Kaaly echoed. "No wonder I'm feeling hungry. *Assiduous*, why don't you serve us a hotpot, please?"

"Did you get anything tangible yet?" Peysoon asked.

Bowls with steaming contents and spoons rose out of the table.

Nuuya nodded. "Yes, we did. We had a little time on our march back. Like, who built this monument? Our people did, before they decided to leave their physical existence behind."

Peysoon gasped. "What does that mean?"

"They decided to integrate their minds with the stars." Nuuya waved her arm. "To strengthen them."

"Against reckless jumpers?"

"Against an enemy—capable of ripping space. The *Void*. Oh, and that way, they would hide from it."

"And give up their mobility." Peysoon shook his head. "Well, they must've had their reasons. They must've reckoned that they can't win a fight with their living ships."

He gazed at Nuuya. "But they seem to have changed their minds because they created you. Why?"

"Isn't that obvious? Because we are a new breed of Navigators. We can do hyperflight, and we can repair hyperspace. Our ancestors couldn't do that, and they needed a lot of time to come up with their invention."

Kaaly chuckled. "Basically, they bought themselves some time to think. But now we're supposed to fight—somehow."

"They didn't tell you how?"

"Nah." Kaaly spread her arms. "We're supposed to find out ourselves. They gave us the tools, we'll invent the method."

"Trial and error, then," Peysoon said.

"Yes, with a very narrow margin for error," Nuuya said. "Not a bright prospect."

Syreen put her spoon down. *"If you can't win, change the rules.* That's the story of my life. My odds of winning my first battle were much worse, but I won, nonetheless. From there on, beating impossible odds became a kind of pastime — and our odds now don't look so bad to me."

"Why would you think so?" Nuuya asked.

"For one, just what you already said — we can fly hyperspace on sight. We won't jump blindly into a trap. For two, again your point — we can repair hyperspace. For three . . . yes." Syreen paused. "Three we are. Three *different* Navigators, yet in tune. We'll see how that helps, but I'm sure it will. For four, we have you, Peysoon, and that's another novelty."

"Our people had no males?" he asked.

"Oh, they did, but without mental abilities. Didn't you notice? When you join our song, it's like a booster. You're amplifying our powers." She tapped the table. "For five, our ships, our partners. Deep integration isn't new, but the way we integrate is. The Navigators of old were dependent on physical contact. We're not. *Assiduous* and I, we're permanently linked. I don't know if you noticed, gals, but while we were inside the monument, he was with us. Right, pal?"

"I shared the data feed, correct."

Kaaly looked up in surprise. *"Audacious,* you too?"

— I'm with you. —

Nuuya looked glassy-eyed for a moment. Then she nodded. *"Incredulous* was there with us, too, although our ships weren't invited."

"We were *invited,"* Assiduous disagreed. *"The imprint allowed us in."*

"What imprint?" Drake asked.

"The core of the monument contains two imprints — one of the first Navigator, and one of the first living ship, Mischievous. *An imprint is a kind of copy of the original mind, with full memory and personality and limited processing capacity."*

"A kind of backup?"

"Indeed. This is how a living ship can survive long periods of inactivity — like the three of us did. In any case, Mischievous's

imprint invited us in when it noticed our bond."

Syreen gazed at Peysoon. "So, the seven of us together should be able to do something."

"But what?" Drake asked. "Did you learn more about what this Void is?"

"Nah," Nuuya replied. "But we learned a lot about what it is *not.*"

She raised her left hand and began to count fingers. "One. It's not a sentient being. It's an un-being. Two. It's not even an entity. It's an un-tity. Three. It's not the ultimate incarnation of evil. Evil requires a purpose, a goal, and the *Void* pursues no goals. Four. We can't even say that the *Void* is an *It,* or a *Them.*"

Kaaly sighed. "It's frustrating. How do you fight something that just isn't?"

"Perhaps you need to un-fight it?" Drake mused. "It sounds like it's the essence of un-existence—perhaps you have to force existence upon it?"

The others exchanged thoughtful glances.

Part Six—Escalation

Chapter Seventy-Two

Syreen found ninety-four merchants and three AP troop carriers orbiting Kyris, plus sixteen more haulers docked at Kyris Orbital. Three Crown destroyers seemed to be herding the school.

"So many!"

She scanned their call signs and noticed some familiar ship names. "If I start calling acquaintances, we'll still be here next kilocycle."

One thought activated the line. "Kyris port authority, this is Syreen. We're just passing through on our way to the chasm."

"Navigator, this is Kyris port authority, Trevor speaking. Before you move on, please contact Captain Lewis on the carrier Iron Hill. *He's been waiting for your arrival."*

"Thank you, Trevor, I will call him right away."

What could an AP troop carrier captain want?

"Iron Hill, this is Navigator Syreen. I learned you've got a message for me."

"Navigator Syreen. This is Iron Hill, *Ensign Riota speaking. I'm forwarding you to Captain Lewis immediately. Please stand by."*

A moment later she heard another voice. *"Navigator Syreen, this is Captain Lewis. Welcome."*

"I heard you've got a message for me."

He laughed. *"Not exactly a message. You're planning to repair the chasm. We brought help."*

"I don't think you can help me where I'm going, thank you."

He laughed even more. *"Yusef said you'd say that. Don't you want to hear first what kind of help I'm talking about?"*

"Yusef? Now you've got my undivided attention."

"Yusef said you would need a larger crew where you're going. Chiara and he have been rallying volunteers for your cause, and we're delivering them. Iron Hill *carries four hundred volunteers from Harmony,* Ruby Harbor *carries four hundred volunteers from Salamanca and Epirus, and* Emerald River *carries another four hundred volunteers from Danos and the Duchy."*

– This might help indeed. –

Hush, partner. Let me talk. "Captain Lewis, that's indeed something. I just don't know how to care for them."

"Yusef mentioned something like that, too. We're carrying provisions for a kilocycle each."

"How could all that happen?"

"Hey, Navigator, the first triple star angel in history asked for help. People were asking how they could contribute. So . . . well, now we're here. One carrier, one living ship. Right?"

"Right. Okay, *Incredulous* will meet *Iron Hill, Audacious* will meet *Ruby Harbor,* and *Assiduous* will meet *Emerald River.* Would you call your fellow skippers?"

"Of course, Navigator."

"Oh—and please tell our future crew that we're happy to welcome them aboard. We'll be there in a halfcycle."

"Sure. On behalf of my fellow skippers, we'd like to invite you and your fellow Navigators aboard to make our passengers welcome personally. If you like."

Oh.

"That's an outstanding idea, Captain Lewis. We will do as you propose. And you and your fellow skippers—and any crew you'd like to take along—are welcome to be our guests aboard our living ships while we're loading your provisions."

"That's an offer I cannot decline. Thank you, Navigator. We will meet your ships soon, then."

"You're welcome, Captain."

Yes. And we'll spend some more time talking.

— The additional crew will help you recharge with less need to consume anyone. —

Sure, pal. We'll need more room for them.

— We already envisaged that. —

We?

— We ships. While you were talking with the Captain, we started growing more quarters and more storage. That's no big deal, those will fit well inside our current bodies. Perhaps not as spacious as people are used to. —

I have no clue what they're used to. Just make sure the lounge is spacious enough.

— Of course. Don't worry about space. We even have running tracks in our hangars. —

Oh my.

CHAPTER SEVENTY-THREE

Syreen took a deep breath. *Finally. Ready to go.*
Their guests had left, not without regrets—but they had other duties as AP officers and AP crews.

The *additional crew* had settled in after a warm welcome by their seasoned members. It had been a big relief when Heather had asked if she should do the welcome speech and tell the newbies what they had volunteered for—Syreen wouldn't have known how to explain what she and her sisters needed. They just had to be there and smile, as Heather had put it in the clearest manner.

Jacomo had sent her a score of message drones to send back once the route was safe for passage, so that they wouldn't have to return themselves.

Okay. Inside line, all ships.

"This is Navigator Syreen. You're used to such a call before departure, to prepare for the jump. I was pleased to hear that you had a smooth journey with smooth six-sigma jumps to reach Kyris. What we're doing now will be different, we're doing hyperflights, not hyperjumps. You hardly notice a smooth jump, but you won't notice a hyperflight at all, so actually, you don't need to prepare yourself. Just get comfortable, get to know each other, familiarize yourself with your ship's layout, and don't hesitate to ask if you miss something." She paused and listened to their excited chatter in *Assiduous's* lounge—surely no different than the other ships. "We'll soon start the first repairs. We'll go slow there, get you used to the routine, and then we'll do more. Okay, we'll enter hyperspace in five. Have a good journey."

Goodbye, Kyris. We'll make your friends sing again.

Soon after leaving Kyris—and yet at a distance that would otherwise have cost quite a sequence of jumps—they reached the outskirts of the chasm.

Time for weaving, gals.

"Four supporters to the bridge, please."

A moment later, Jona arrived with three newbies in tow. "Watch me," she said. "And don't feel fear—I've done this before."

Ready, Kaaly signaled.

Ready, Nuuya agreed. *You do the warp, I do the weft.*

Huh?

Nuuya sent a mental chuckle. *I'll do the crisscrossing.*

Oh, okay. Syreen reached out for the first star and noticed Kaaly doing the same.

Let's have a break. Syreen felt her sisters' agreement and exited hyperflight close to a red giant.

A neck was leaning over her. She gladly accepted the offer to recharge.

Vivien took the donator in her arms. "Okay, Mim, that's it for now. Get yourself some food and then take a nap."

Mim showed a weak smile. "Glad I could help."

"You did," Syreen said. "Together, we just rebuilt about a third of the route across the chasm."

"With only eight donations?" Vivien asked. "That way, we'll hardly ever need the other four hundred donators—oh, wait, we'll do more repairs than just one track, right? There are many disconnected star systems, aren't there?"

"Indeed." Syreen slowly rose from her seat. "We'll reconnect all we can find. That's where the relief fleet will be going."

"Shouldn't we already have passed some, then?"

Syreen frowned. *Partner?*

— *Our libraries don't list inhabited worlds along this leg. It's striking indeed, now that Vivien brought up the question. As if this region of space never contained inhabitable worlds.* —

Strange. She smiled at Vivien. "You asked a very good question, Vivien. The answer is no, there are no inhabited worlds in this region, and that's peculiar."

"Oh, okay. I was just curious."

"Never stop asking. We're not omniscient. You're a valuable part of the team."

Vivien smiled back. "Thank you."

When Syreen entered *Assiduous's* enlarged lounge, she had to pause. *Wow.* There were so many tables, and all seemed to be occupied — then she spotted Crow waving from a table to the right. She walked his way and saw Drake, Peysoon, and Casey sitting with him. On her way she passed other tables with many volunteers, female and male, their chatter falling silent when she walked by.

"We kept one chair free for you," Drake said. "Casey said you might be a bit overwhelmed with the new layout."

Syreen sat down and smiled at Casey. "Thank you."

"Busier than Appalahoo during the season," Casey said. "Of course, this mission is way more rewarding."

"And no less exciting." Syreen gazed around. "Although it might not seem that way yet."

"We haven't started fighting yet, right?" Drake asked.

"Looks like that, doesn't it?" Syreen shook her head. "No, it doesn't feel like battle, agreed. But even if it feels more like laying a new cruiser's keel, we're already in the heart of the fight."

"How's that?" Peysoon asked.

"We're reclaiming territory that our opponent already deemed his. It's a quite powerful counterstrike, and even if I don't know how an un-sentient untity could *take notice* of what we're doing, we should eventually expect some kind of reaction — where I have no clue how it could look like."

"So we're at war," Drake concluded.

"Yes."

"That doesn't seem to unsettle you."

"No." A steaming bowl appeared before Syreen. "Thanks, partner." She picked up a spoon. "I'm a soldier, born to fight. War is my natural habitat. And now I'd like to enjoy this pot."

CHAPTER SEVENTY-FOUR

Syreen checked her readings. Like in the previous five systems, the planet had once been habitable and inhabited until its star had begun to fade. Like in the previous five systems, the star had cheered upon their touch and begun to heat up. Like in the previous five systems, the radio frequencies remained silent.

Unlike in the previous five systems, this planet still emanated unmodulated electromagnetic waves. *Someone seems to be using electricity.*

— Someone or something. —

Hope dies last. Let's call them, in case someone's listening.

"Perignac port authority, this is Enforcer *Assiduous*, Navigator Syreen speaking. Is there anyone able to answer our call?"

ACK. The short reply was strong, followed by silence.

Ouch.

"Okay, folks, we're going down. You've got our back."

"We've got your back," Kaaly replied. *"Audacious and I are keeping an eye outward."*

"Incredulous *and I are staying close in orbit,"* Nuuya added. *"Good luck dirtside."*

"Thanks."

She let *Assiduous* slowly descend toward the surface, roughly to where the reply had come from.

— Electromagnetic activity is increasing, but still on a very low level. —

Living conditions?

– *Very low pressure. Air too thin to breathe.* –
Nice.

A huge rectangular flat surface at the bottom of a deep canyon drew her attention. *That might be a landing field.*

– *It can serve that purpose.* –

And there seem to be doors in the canyon wall.

She placed *Assiduous* down gently, his *legs* and hangar door facing the canyon wall with the door-like shapes.

"Peysoon, would you join me at the hangar door in ten? Formal attire, please."

"*Sure.*"

Nine centicycles later, they were both standing at the hangar door in plain white uniforms with breathers in their hands.

"No more signals?" Peysoon asked.

"Silence so far. Let's see what we find." Syreen pointed forward, and the hangar doors parted to let them pass. They quickly fitted their breathers.

Nothing stirred when they crossed the landing field.

The gates were large enough to let a shuttle pass through, but there was also a small door at one side, labeled *Airlock* in Common. They walked up to it.

Peysoon pointed at a wheel for manual operation, mounted on a man-sized hatch. Syreen nodded, and he turned it.

It moved easily, and the hatch slid sideways to unveil a small chamber, dimly lit by some kind of crystal.

They stepped inside. Peysoon turned the inside wheel to close the outer hatch.

A hissing sound indicated a change of pressure. Soon their breathers switched off. Peysoon then operated a similar wheel on the inner hatch.

The huge cavern before them was almost dark. About twenty legs deeper inside, three bald humans in white floor-length robes held up poles with blue-glowing crystals.

"Welcome to Perignac, Navigator Syreen," the middle one said in a female voice and bowed. "Your presence is a miracle to us. Hyperspace hasn't been passable for generations."

Syreen pointed at her side. "This is Peysoon. And you are?"

The local speaker hesitated. "I—I am Rita, outworld provost."

She pointed right, then left. "These are the acolytes Timo and Tori."

"So you received our call, right?"

"The—the tabernaculum announced an arrival. While we were preparing ourselves, it replayed a message. Please tell us, who is this enforcer *Assiduous?*"

"*Assiduous* is my living ship. Together, we were able to pass hyperspace where no conventional ship can pass, and together with my sisters and their ships, we were able to repair it."

"I can hear your voice loud and clear, but your words make no sense."

Syreen sighed and briefly glanced at Peysoon. "You're right. You might lack crucial background information. First, have you ever heard of the Forgotten People?"

"That's just superstition."

"They are my ancestors, and I feel quite real. The same applies to the ship I arrived in. Or do you think I'm a product of your imagination, and your tabernaculum's replay just a glitch?"

"No." Rita took a deep breath. "If I can still trust my senses, your presence is a fact. But I have no way to prove or disprove your claim of ancestry."

"You don't, but I have. Listen to Perignac."

Boost me.

She opened her mind and sang. The star replied, and Peysoon helped her to share their message.

They sang of their people, their ancestry, their loneliness, their joy of being reunited.

Syreen saw that joy mirrored in their hosts' faces.

Long after the song had faded, they were still too excited to speak.

The Navigator waited patiently.

Finally, Rita found her wits. "Navigator, we're infinitely grateful for this revelation. But what does that mean for us?"

Syreen nodded. "The structure of space and hyperspace around Perignac and the neighboring stars is stable now. Your star will regain her power and shed her warmth on your world within a kilocycle."

"Truly?" Rita's rod trembled. "We're so tight on power, that would be a big relief."

"You're probably tight on everything, aren't you?" Syreen didn't wait for Rita's nod. "Stable hyperspace means the route from Kyris is open for conventional merchant ships. The merchant guild has already gathered a relief fleet there—they're just waiting for the message drone."

Rita sighed. "We can't afford anything."

"You don't have to. It's a relief fleet—many worlds have donated supplies to help you. For free."

"Why would anyone do that?"

Peysoon pointed at Syreen. "Because the first triple star angel in history asked them."

Tears filled Rita's eyes. "A star angel?"

Timo and Tori dropped on their knees and lowered their heads. "Praise to the heavens above. Praise!" Their voices broke. With their bodies shaking uncontrollably, their wail filled the cavern.

What's happening? Peysoon shook his head. *I mean, they're excited, but . . .*

They must've placed all their hope for survival on that—um, partially superstitious—belief in a star angel coming to their rescue. Now they're seeing their impossible dream come true.

What can we do?

Hold her tight. Syreen pointed at Tori. *Let her feel the reality of your presence. I'll hug Timo. Soothe her, comfort her. Subtly.*

Syreen felt a gentle touch at her right shoulder. When she looked up, she saw Rita's wet eyes and cheeks.

"I'd like to invite you and your partner to our city, to show you how we managed to survive—powered by our hope."

The Navigator shook her head, let Timo go, and rose. "How can that work?"

"I will show you our treadmills, our geothermal factories, our nurseries. It works—barely. It works because we're limiting our population to what the community can feed, and that's not many."

"How many?"

"Currently twenty-thousand."

"Of how many?"

"Before the separation? Around two billion." Rita shrugged. "At first, our ancestors thought it was a temporary problem. They built and sent out spaceships. When those failed to jump away, they recognized the true dimension of our problem. Then our star began to fade." She took a deep breath. "Killing anyone was out of the question, but aside from a strict birth control, they asked for volunteers. Many old people decided to go, so that the few children could live. It was a steep decline."

"Without fights?"

"Almost. There were desperate people who couldn't adjust. They were allowed to leave. Of course, their ships couldn't jump. They had to do it the conventional way."

"What does that mean?"

"Hibernation and sub-light travel."

Syreen frowned. She couldn't imagine how such a journey had to feel.

"Those staying behind placed their hope into other worlds. They said, the stars will send us their angels one day. At first, it was a joke, then a saying, and eventually it became the heart of our faith. And here you are."

Syreen gazed forward. "They couldn't have known how true that was."

"What was true?"

"That the stars sent their angels. Peysoon, my sisters, and I, we weren't born from a living mother. We are starborn — created by those fiery celestial bodies that our ancestors merged with so many megacycles ago. It's the truth." The Navigator focused on Rita's eyes. "You heard her song."

The local provost took several deep breaths, and then stepped back.

Syreen noticed her intent to kneel quickly enough. "Stop."

Rita stopped.

"Look into my eyes." Syreen waited for her to comply. "These are the eyes of a mortal. My duties are different from yours, but I can already tell that you serve your duties as diligently as I serve mine. So we can meet as equals. Don't get fancy ideas just because I can do things you can't. I'm sure I couldn't do what you and your people did here. And don't think I was lucky where you weren't — it was a hard and painful path I had to go to arrive where I am now, and today is *your* lucky day."

She sensed the emotions racing and decided to give Rita a subtle soothing mental nudge.

Soon the woman regained her composure. "Now. Navigator, Star Angel, Bringer of Good News, I already bade you welcome. Please, follow me to meet our Mayor, and let our people see our first visitors in generations. And then we will celebrate."

"We will do so." Syreen linked arms with Timo and her. "However, bear with us if we don't stay long. There are more worlds to reconnect, more people to save."

Rita's arm twitched. "Oh. Of course. How many?"

"Honestly, I don't know. I can't tell whether we're in time or too late until we arrive and someone answers our hail."

"How can you bear that?"

"I don't know. I'm a soldier, I will always carry on. That's what I do."

CHAPTER SEVENTY-FIVE

Syreen felt dizzy. She found herself lying on a soft, flat surface. When she tried to move her head, she felt like dropping.

"Syreen?"

She opened her eyes. When the blurry sight cleared, when she managed to focus, she recognized Nuuya's familiar face leaning over her. "What happened?"

"You were unconscious," Nuuya stated the obvious. "Two local women — Rita and Tori — brought you back aboard."

"And . . ."

"Two men brought Peysoon. They're all worried, but Casey and Drake are taking care of them."

Syreen refrained from shaking her head. "I'm not sure . . ."

"Rita said when you walked out onto the stage, you dropped like a stone. *Assiduous* said their emotions must have overwhelmed you."

"Ugh." She tried to remember. "Yes, I agreed with Rita that I should talk to their people. I felt their expectation, and then Rita announced a visitor, and I walked out — and then, nothing."

"Perhaps you should have shielded your mind."

"Sure I should." Syreen managed a weak smile. "Easy to say in hindsight."

"You should rest now."

"Yes and no. I should talk with Rita now. I assume Peysoon is okay?"

"Crow is with him. Yes, he's okay — knocked out like you, but otherwise unharmed."

"So he didn't shield himself either."

"Seems so." Nuuya nodded. "I'll get Rita."

I really passed out?

— Yes. I could feel it. I was worried. I called Incredulous *first. Then I sent Drake and Crow to see after you. They met the locals when they were bringing you back. —*

Oh. That could have gone very wrong.

— Unlikely. I knew that you hadn't sensed hostility. So I told Drake to expect to find an accident. —

Phew.

Rita entered the room with a worried face. "You're okay?"

Syreen managed to sit up and smile. "I'm okay. Your feelings must've been overwhelming."

"That's what *Assiduous* said. He's your ship?"

"Yes. That sounds strange, doesn't it?"

Rita shrugged. "Initially, yes. Compared to singing stars and starborn angels, no. Even compared to faster-than-light travel and ripped hyperspace, no."

"You're taking that easily."

"I've had a little time to contemplate the recent events. We had generations to learn about being cool. Excitement costs power. Power is scarce, so you'd better be cool and pragmatic."

Syreen sighed. "Indeed. Okay, I think I owe your people another visit and an explanation."

"No, you don't." Rita firmly shook her head. "Firstly, you're on a mission, and you already spent enough time here. Secondly, Nuuya stepped in for you. She's a nice star angel too, even if not registered with the guild. Thirdly, Charlene joined her and gave witness to your impressive feats. We've heard what we needed to hear. Now it's time for you to move on and save more worlds. Maybe you'll return to Perignac one day."

"Maybe."

CHAPTER SEVENTY-SIX

Syreen pulled a strand from another star and attached it to the growing web. An instant later, Kaaly attached another strand from the opposite side. Nuuya's strand dashed back and forth and imposed more structure on the growing mesh.

— I've studied data on historic fabric weaving. While the analogy is amusing, it certainly lacks depth. —

Depth?

— Textile fabric is three-dimensional, with a two-dimensional web plus thickness. Hyperspace is four-dimensional, and so are our results. —

Ah. Syreen chuckled, but then focused her mind again to pull the next strand.

Strange, Nuuya signaled. *See there.* Her mental focus showed them a stretch of fabric where the meshwork wasn't growing further. Just the opposite—some freshly woven strands seemed to wither away.

Like someone's taking a bite, Kaaly commented. *Or — a certain no-one.*

Let's fix that. Syreen assigned them a few stars and pulled *Assiduous* around, toward the new damage.

Kaaly and *Audacious* dashed forward. *On it.*

Incredulous stayed behind.

"Oh, okay." Syreen reassigned Nuuya's stars and followed Kaaly.

The two Navigators quickly pulled strands across the new damage, only to see some of them wither away immediately. Only when they wove a tight net did the fabric stay in place and intact. However, this tight weaving required a significant effort. Soon Syreen felt weakness.

I need a break and fresh blood.

Me too, Kaaly replied. *However, if we let go now, our work will crumble. Moreover, I feel like I need to suck them dry.*

That shouldn't happen.

No. It would be a disaster for my crew's spirit. But I'm so weak already . . .

Hold out, I'm coming. Nuuya sounded fresh and powerful, like she just had fed. Which she probably had done. She took over and quickly fastened a few more strong strands. *Now take your break. Quick.*

Call reinforcements to your bridge, Syreen advised Kaaly. *Only return when you're on full power. I'll help Nuuya first.*

She dropped out of hyperspace and deep integration.

"Spares to the bridge. And anyone who's ready." Then she pulled her first girl close and sank her fangs inside. She had to struggle to let go soon enough.

With four donations, she felt strong enough to rejoin.

Syreen instantly saw that Nuuya was in trouble. The withering seemed to be most intense around *Incredulous.* Her sister fought bravely to pull new strands, but the number of nearby stars was limited, and those stars' power seemed to be fading as well.

I'm coming.

She began to pull more strands from distant stars and braided them into stronger connections to support the damaged weave. More braids supported these initial links. It was tiring work.

Move aside. Kaaly dashed into their middle with a harpoon-shaped power rod and hauled it deep into the wasteland. *Now let's get our defenses up. Take turns feeding. Nuuya first.*

They started weaving again, this time using braided strands.

Once Nuuya returned, Kaaly focused on warp braids, and Nuuya added weft braids.

Syreen dropped out briefly, then contributed with renewed power.

This seems to hold. Nuuya pulled a few more strands in place.

They watched the mesh grow and brittle structures renew.

Syreen checked the edges. *Yes. This works.*

Let's give our ships a break to recharge. Nuuya indicated a strong star at some distance. *That one looks good.*

"So, what was that?" Syreen asked aloud. The Navigators were meeting in *Assiduous's* lounge at the newly labeled *Skippers' Table.* Peysoon, Heather, and Drake were with them, and were listening attentively.

"That was the first counterattack," Nuuya said. "I don't know how it's done, but this non-sentient non-being seems to be capable of targeted actions against us and our efforts."

Kaaly shook her head. "Most of all because this strike was aimed at fresh and strong hyperstructure, not at worn-out, pierced, and jump-stressed old hyperstructure."

"Yes, almost as if drawn to it," Nuuya said. "I checked *Incredulous's* recordings."

"You have recordings?" Kaaly asked.

"You don't? Anyway. The recordings show that the initial *bite*—let's just call it so for now—targeted not a particularly weak spot of our new fabric, but a particularly crucial and only slightly weaker spot for its structure." Nuuya flexed her fingers. "However, once that attack had begun, our rebuild efforts were hampered, unlike before. There is a measurable difference between a damaged hyperspace region without the *Void* and a damaged hyperspace region with the *Void.* I'd like to investigate further on that topic."

"What did you make of Kaaly's counterattack?" Syreen

asked. "That harpoon strike was brilliant."

Kaaly beamed.

Nuuya frowned. "Indeed. It directed the *Void's* attention away from us, so to speak, as it offered an exposed crucial node. That worked well, even though it was a rather expensive move. Kaaly, you might want to refine that method to get more yield with less effort."

"But—"

"Hush," Syreen said. "Sorry to interrupt you, Kaaly, but power consumption is something we must observe. Firstly, because our resources aren't endless. Secondly, because re-charging—feeding—costs precious time. Time we might not have in the middle of battle."

Kaaly shrugged and nodded. "Of course you're right."

"Hey, don't let that stop you from doing what's necessary," Syreen went on. "We encounter a new problem, we come up with a solution, that solution works, all fine. But after the fight comes the debrief where we check that solution and discuss whether there are other possible approaches, less costly solutions, better strategies, better tactics, better preparations. For example, we need more supporters on the bridge and more supporters on regular standby."

Nuuya nodded. "We should make our repairs more robust. Braided strands do help. We shouldn't rebuild crucial spots. We need a different weave that supports itself."

"We need a better power flow," Kaaly agreed. "It doesn't help if we deplenish the neighborhood. Our repairs must be self-sufficient."

"We should have a regular feeding drill during our repairs." Syreen glanced at her crew. "It's not good if two of us have to drop out at the same time. We should take turns, even if we don't expect trouble."

"Anything else we didn't think about yet?" Nuuya gazed around the table.

"Yes," Peysoon said. "Where can I help?"

"We have to think about that," Syreen said. "Can you see what we're seeing?"

"If I focus on your thoughts, I get a glimpse of it. But I'm primarily a passenger here."

Nuuya shook her head. "We'll have to change that. You must join us."

Chapter Seventy-Seven

When *Assiduous* dropped from hyperflight, Syreen took a deep breath of relief. *Done.*

"Moscow harbor authority, this is the living ship *Assiduous*. I'm Navigator Syreen. I am accompanied by the living ships *Audacious* and *Incredulous*. Port of departure was Kyris. Please forward my regards to Guild Secretary Ivanow. I would like to meet him at the soonest."

The answer came with little delay.

"Navigator Syreen, this is Moscow harbor authority, Lieutenant Arjunow speaking. Welcome back to Moscow, Star Angel. You're cleared for a high velocity approach to Moscow Orbital Three, docking bays Alpha One, Alpha Three, Alpha Five. The secretary will be ready upon your arrival."

She raised her eyebrows.

"Lieutenant Arjunow, thank you for your friendly welcome. We will arrive for docking in twenty-five centicycles."

She turned to Peysoon. "Last time they detached an escort for me. There's way less fuzz this time."

"Casey told me the story of your visit here. You've impressed many people on this side of the chasm."

"Not as much as we'll do today."

Peysoon smiled. "Of course not."

"Will you join us?"

"Sure. Plain whites?"

"Exactly. Oh, I think I'll wear the chain."

"Then I'll rehearse your introduction."

When they stepped inside the dock, Kaaly and Nuuya

were already waiting for them—together with a nineteen-men-strong honor guard.

A guard with captain's stripes stepped forward and saluted. "Navigator Syreen?"

Syreen and Peysoon returned the salute. When Peysoon took down his hand, he said, "Captain, this is the most honorable Lady Syreen Starborn, Knight of the Order of the Firepath, retired Duchy Fleet Commander, Navigator of the Forgotten People, triple star angel of the merchant guild."

The captain smiled. "And conqueror of the chasm. Welcome back. I'm Captain Petry. Please follow me. The secretary awaits you."

Syreen went first. She sensed Kaaly, Nuuya, and Peysoon marveling at the shiny uniforms, at the red-and-silver guild guards, at the red-and-silver pillars at the entrance to the guild hall, at the almost-black doors that stood wide open, at the solitary man in the silver-lined red robe in its center.

The man bowed. "Navigator Syreen, welcome back. Navigator Kaaly, Navigator Nuuya, Coordinator Peysoon, welcome to the guild at Moscow. Please follow me inside."

Coordinator, huh? Peysoon asked. *Appropriate, ain't it?*

Indeed.

The secretary led them into the same small conference room she knew from her last visit. This time, no guards followed them inside.

"Please have a seat. Forwine for all? Yes, fine."

They sat down and waited for the drinks.

After a toast and a sip, the secretary just gazed at her and waited.

The Navigator nodded. "We were successful. After returning across the chasm, we established the edict, overcame some resistance, and brought the Association back on track. The edict soon will no longer be necessary."

"That's good to hear. So you came to return the Crown and Finney ships?"

"No. They will return on their own soon. I had another reason to return. Please record three announcements."

"Oh." The secretary held back his comments and tapped the table. "Go ahead."

She nodded. "First announcement. Together, my Navigators and I have started repairing the chasm. Effective immediately, a safe route between Moscow and Kyris has been reopened. The Kyris guild has already deployed drones for regular message traffic."

Of which we carried some. She didn't voice that.

"The first drones will soon arrive here. My ship will provide you with the respective navigation data for safe seven-sigma jumps. This data is to be distributed free of charge."

Ivanow only nodded. He knew when not to negotiate.

"Second announcement. On our way from Kyris to Moscow, we were able to save and reconnect thirteen guild worlds with surviving populations. My ship will provide you with a list. These worlds will rejoin the guild network as soon as possible."

She marveled at the secretary's calmness.

"Third announcement. On Nizwa, the first triple star angel in history formally asked the guild for assistance in raising donations and organizing transport of essential goods to these worlds—following the example of the first star angel. I herewith repeat my request on this side of the chasm, more so as my Navigators and I will try to reconnect as many guild worlds as possible."

Only now did a first tear run down Ivanow's cheek. "You think that you can save them?"

"I think that we can save some. We can open hyperspace for safe travel. We cannot feed the people, so that's what I'm asking the guild for."

"For provisions?"

"For raising donations and organizing transport. The guild

will spread the word, and the guild will tell volunteering merchants where to go. That's my plea."

Peysoon raised one hand. "Should any government feel inclined to contribute, the guild will help to coordinate their destinations, too. Right?"

"Thank you. Yes, that would be helpful." Syreen focused on Ivanow again. "Mr. Secretary, during my last visit, Crown Guild Commissar Okamele expressed his worries about border worlds the guild had lost contact with. My take is that he would be glad to help those worlds if he only knew how. We do know, now. I can only say *please.*"

The secretary nodded. "If you put it like this, I know what to do. I will forward your plea to the local authorities and to all merchants present or arriving at Moscow. And, of course, I will send a fast courier with your announcements and your plea to Crown." He glanced down, and then focused on the Navigator again, this time with a smile. "For the records, would you agree that broken hyperstructure and fading stars are directly related to the first and second edict?"

"Yes, of course."

"Would you agree that your countermeasures are also significantly related to these edicts?"

"Yes." *What is he up to?*

"In this case, I will rate this message as codex priority. This will not only facilitate the fastest possible delivery, but will also surely trigger the commissar's undivided attention."

Syreen returned his smile. "And it will doubtlessly put all related expenses on his purse, not yours, right?"

The secretary showed a mischievous smirk. "You cheated on me last time. You were pretending you were a soldier, not a merchant. Remember? But you know our ways very well."

"I'm a Navigator. I know all the ways."

They glanced at each other.

Then they both broke out in laughter.

CHAPTER SEVENTY-EIGHT

I don't like what I see. Syreen checked their surroundings again. This was the worst area in hyperspace they had ventured into so far — and yet, even here, stars were still alive, and their planets still habitable.

We could try a different area first, Nuuya commented.

We can do this, Kaaly disagreed. *Come on.*

I don't think there are easy regions anymore, Syreen thought. *Nuuya, your turn.*

Okay.

Incredulous advanced. Nuuya started pulling braided strands and linking them. Syreen and *Assiduous* followed and added a sturdy mesh inside Nuuya's framework.

Soon, some filaments near the edge started to fray out. Kaaly and *Audacious* dashed forward and reinforced the meshwork.

Syreen directed Nuuya toward a pair of yellow stars.

Good choice, her sister agreed. *That dual star offers some powerful support.*

Their new method caused a more robust basic structure, which they then could fill with Nuuya's warp-and-weft fabric. Either could be done by one Navigator alone, which allowed them to drop out in turns for their feeding, at least as long as they weren't attacked.

Here it comes, Peysoon warned.

Not at the edge they just had fixed, but at a different place, the fabric dissolved.

Kaaly shot a small dart at the *Void*. Nuuya prepared some

sturdy braids. Syreen pulled a few strands across the opening to darn it. While Nuuya reinforced the repaired area, Kaaly shot more tiny structures at the emptiness.

Their patchwork seemed to hold — for a while. Then the seams began to ripple.

Oh crap.

This is not good, Kaaly sent.

Focus on the backbone, Nuuya sent. *We can't risk losing the main power stream.*

There are three main attack routes, Peysoon sent. *Once they join, we're cut off.*

If they join. Syreen focused on the first route. *Nuuya, the second route. Focus on the primary structure. Kaaly, recharge.*

This won't solve the problem, Nuuya objected.

No, Syreen agreed. *This is about damage control, regroup, recharge.*

Okay. For now.

Syreen plucked and braided strings, mended broken seams, spliced strands, wove patches, darned holes. The repairs seemed endless.

I'm back, Kaaly reported. *Nuuya, you're next.*

Kaaly took over at the second route.

Syreen checked her work. *This might hold for a while. Peysoon, keep a watch on it.*

Then she turned to the third route. The damage was severe and spreading. Again, she started with the most urgent fixes — protecting crucial joints so that the damage couldn't rip them apart.

But she felt growing exhaustion. *I can't hold out much longer.*

Be thrifty, Peysoon suggested. *Focus on the vital points.*

That's what I'm doing.

Back in line. Get your drink, Nuuya sent.

CHAPTER SEVENTY-NINE—KAALY

This is a strange kind of fight. I'm used to brawls, I can take some, and I can deal out. I know how to break a nose, how to kick balls, how to take someone's breath.

To be fair, there was never much fighting on Epirus. Once or twice a winter, we were allowed to gather for some festival, where I had the chance to meet other people. There were a few nice people—women—and a lot of not so nice people, that is, almost all of the men. I had quickly learned that the best way to get rid of them was to discourage them. Strike hard, strike early. Never let them gather their wits. That'd been working fine for me.

It's different this time. We're taking some, we're dealing out, but we never kick balls. The *Void* can't be discouraged. And how can an un-sentient untity be prevented from gathering their wits?

That's why this battle isn't working well for me.

Okay, throwing structure at chaos seems to cause some effect, and constructing defenses works even better—but neither lasts.

All our bravery and determination won't help us if we exhaust ourselves by creating sandcastles.

What do we have to change?

CHAPTER EIGHTY—NUUYA

We cannot hide anywhere. Unless we could run fast and run far, we're acting in plain sight—where I still don't understand how *sight* works with an un-sentient untity.

I've learned to keep a low profile, to pretend I'm not even there, or if I'm there, to act so inconspicuous as if I wasn't. But I've also learned how to survive once I'm spotted—act devotional, act submissive, never argue, never look up.

I've also learned to never apologize, never admit an error, to never offer an opening for accusations. That's helpful now, because I'm sure the *Void* won't accept apologies.

And perhaps that's part of the solution. We must not leave it an opening. It will find and attack any flaw in our hyperstructure.

Only I thought our beautiful structure with braided strands and woven fabric already was flawless. Obviously it isn't, and just as obviously, we're not able to tell the difference.

There must be a solution. After all, old hyperstructure isn't easily affected. How can we make new hyperstructure as robust as the old one?

It must be the way we're doing it. We're just offering structure, and then the stars make the fine mesh grow. That's not enough. We must create the final mesh.

But how?

CHAPTER EIGHTY-ONE—PEYSOON

I can only watch while the girls are doing the impossible. I can't see the other two, but I sense their minds—they're as much burdened as my pilot. I feel their exhaustion as much as their admirable determination.

I feel their growing frustration. Through Syreen's senses, I can see what they're doing, how they're creating marvelous filigree hyperstructures. I can see the strands, the weaves, the growing mesh, and I can also see the withering where the enemy attacks our work.

Most of all, I feel Syreen's worries. She already knows—the way the battle is going, we're on a losing streak. We can't afford this war of attrition. We're slowly depleting our resources, while our enemy doesn't need any.

I'm still not sure what to make of this enemy. I once commanded a fleet. I learned how to fight space battles, I knew how to fight on the ground.

I knew how to fight ugly older men and how to evade their attention. I knew not to be there when they were looking for entertainment. I guess that's something I have in common with the girls, one way or another.

Both Kaaly and Nuuya had to evade men with dubious intentions on their home worlds as well. It was different for Syreen—she had to evade AP inspection teams with dubious intentions during her travels with merchants.

We all know how to escape attention. We should operate less conspicuously, below the enemy's scan sensitivity, so to speak—but how to do that against an enemy that doesn't even exist?

CHAPTER EIGHTY-TWO—SYREEN

I mustn't waste time. I'm drinking my girls' blood in quick succession, sending them my gratitude mentally, with hardly enough time to register their names.

They can feel my worries. Even though they can't see the fight, they know that it's not going well.

They don't know why.

I don't know why, either. But I should know. That's my job. I've appointed myself leader of this small fleet. I was taught to be a navy pilot. I'm the seasoned soldier who has fought numerous battles.

We should have everything. We're diligent, brave, discerning, well-orchestrated, observant, powerful, and yet, not really effective.

Our refined structural approach is working well—until the enemy takes notice, or however his counterattack is triggered. We seem to attract more attention than the damaged hyperspace everywhere else, as the damage we're taking is a lot more severe. Somehow, we should attract less attention instead.

There's not much time to contemplate. I feel satiated, at least with regard to blood, so I must return to battle.

OW. That's Nuuya. What happened?

She's close to the frayed edge of our structure—which has shrunk since I dropped out—and *Incredulous* has taken damage!

Retreat, Nuuya. Retreat and regroup. Kaaly, join us.

What's your plan? Kaaly asks.

We need to try something different, I tell them. *The stronger we're weaving, the more ferocious the Void's counterattacks are. Let's try subtle.*

Subtle? Nuuya asks.

Sneaky, Kaaly replies.

Exactly. Let the Void eat this — we'll start at another edge and build something new.

We don't strike back? There's clear disappointment in Kaaly's thought.

We do, but it won't feel like a strike.

Low profile, I like that, Nuuya replies. *It should be perfect.*

We're starting to weave a finer web. No more braided strands, just finest filament, almost undetectable . . .

— I can't fly there, — Assiduous protests.

Hush, partner. Let it grow.

I can't tell if the new fabric indeed remains undetected, but it remains unmolested while we're expanding it.

This work is less exhausting than the permanent fight. We can easily expand it further, and soon we've created more hyperstructure than before.

Aiee!

Pain shoots through my entire body — no, through our joint body. The painful cries of my sisters echo in my mind.

Hyperspace around us folds away, shrinks back from us. How is it possible that we're still flying in hyperspace? Just a tiny strand is holding us together, and I feel the whimper of the nearest star while it's holding us.

I'd reach out and sing a song to soothe its pain, but can we afford the time for singing now?

Realization strikes me like a hammer.

It's the wrong question. Can we afford any more time without singing?

Gals, sing with me.

Huh? That's Kaaly.

Peysoon is the first to intone a new song. At first, I don't recognize the tune. Then it becomes apparent—it's a song of unity and of growing together.

We join in, and the song grows stronger. The star cheers, and that tiny strand resonates. Our pain fades.

Kaaly is the first to cast out a delicate crystal ball. Resonating from our song, it unfolds to a beautiful carpet that quickly connects to our strand and expands.

Nuuya adds fine spherical shapes. I follow her example with little tesseracts that nicely fit into her gaps.

There's no room for much side thought. We're singing, and space around us is filled with harmonic structures—no, with the essence of harmony.

Peysoon's singing boosts our efforts. The decaying parts we had to give up begin to resonate and regrow.

There's no more need for feeding—we're singing without pause, thus flooding the chasm with structure and repairs. Stars are flashing and cheering with the touch of our meshwork.

CHAPTER EIGHTY-THREE

To Syreen, it felt like limping out of hyperspace. *Assiduous* didn't have much more to give, and the other two ships hadn't fared any better.

Crown's strong sun promised recharge and recovery.

But first, it was time for a call.

"Crown harbor authority, this is the living ship *Assiduous*, Navigator Syreen speaking. I'm accompanied by the living ships *Audacious* and *Incredulous,* and we're asking for permission to approach orbit."

She needed a little patience.

"*Assiduous, this is Crown port authority, Harbor Director Thorwaldsen. Guild Commissar Okamele has just been notified about your arrival.*"

She registered several priority messages to ships currently approaching Crown to alter their course and clear the way.

"*Assiduous, Audacious, Incredulous, you are cleared to approach Crown Orbital, Alpha docks, at your own discretion. May I express my worries about your ships' current condition? Did you run into trouble during your repairs? Can we do anything to assist you?*"

"Thank you for your offer, Director. Yes, we ran into some trouble, but could overcome it. Our ships and crew are in sorry condition indeed. We need nutrients and some time to recover."

"*Call me Niels, Navigator. On behalf of the Crown government, you and your crew are invited to whatever you need, in orbit or on our planet.*"

"Thank you, Niels. Our ships will need two tons of raw organic material—nothing fancy, even organic waste will do. Our crew would like to enjoy something just a bit more sophisticated, and I think most of them would like a stroll under an open sky."

"Navigator, what would you think of a fine luxury seaside resort with white beaches?"

"Me personally, not much, but I think my sisters and our crew would be delighted."

"Consider it settled, then. How many crew do you have?"

"About four hundred each."

"Twelve hundred . . . wow. Never mind, we'll make that work. Do you need shuttles? And may the commissar and I meet you once you're settled in?"

"We're happy to meet you. Don't worry about shuttles, as you said seaside. Our ships can set down on the water and drop off our crew. They will relax closer to your star, then."

"Again, consider it done."

"Thank you." *We can rest now, gals.*

PART SEVEN—EPILOGUE

CHAPTER EIGHTY-FOUR

Syreen heard the sound of sand grains moving under weight. The familiar mental auras of two men were getting closer to her deck chair.

She briefly considered sending for her uniform — she had left it in her suite after the first day and not touched it since — and decided against it. She felt good without and wouldn't want to change it.

"Lady Syreen?"

She opened her eyes and looked into the harbor master's face. "Hello, Niels."

His cheeks were slightly flushed, and his eyes were focusing not only on her face.

Guild Commissar Okamele was enjoying Thorwaldsen's embarrassment. As a former passenger on her ship, he was already used to open nudity. He also didn't hide his admiration for her female shape.

"Congratulations, Navigator," he said. "In the name of the guild, thank you for reopening a route across the chasm. My very personal thanks for your efforts to reconnect some inhabited worlds along the route. You surely remembered my serious worries about their well-being." He frowned. "Secretary Ivanow didn't mention your ships' poor condition, though. You must've taken a beating?"

"He couldn't mention that because he didn't know — the beating happened after our visit to Moscow. We left him to make more hyperspace repairs."

"Oh, right, he wrote something like that — we were

wondering what that was about."

Syreen glanced at the beach behind the two men—Peysoon and Kaaly were walking along the waterline holding hands and looking happy. She appreciated that. Peysoon could be a nice guy, but her relationship with him was too burdened with events from the past.

"There's a story behind the chasm. During my last stay, I told you about the damaged hyperstructure. What I couldn't tell you back then, because I didn't know yet, was the main cause that makes such damage spread, that makes hyper-structure deteriorate so quickly. My ancestors knew that cause—they called it the *Void,* and they feared it. They feared it so much that they decided to end their physical existence and become one with the stars."

Both men gasped.

She nodded. "After I left you, I learned about my origin. I wasn't born by a woman. I was *created* by the Duchy's central star. Thus I'm calling myself Syreen Starborn now. The same applies to my sisters and to Peysoon, and I'll tell you that story later."

She waved at empty deck chairs next to hers. "Why don't you take a seat? The staff will be glad to provide you with refreshments."

She waited until both men had followed her advice, then nodded. "Okay. We left Moscow to do more repairs, or better put, to fight that enemy. Initially, that worked well, but when we approached an area with more severe damage, we found out that our work wasn't lasting. The enemy fought back."

She spared both men the philosophical aspects of an enemy without self-awareness.

"We found a better method. Harmony and teamwork—the strength of my sisters, the orchestration of my brother, and the dedication of our crew were the foundation of a much more resilient construction. However, once we were committed, we couldn't stop. In this regard, the *Void* is like a disease—the moment you offer it an opening, it will spread again. The only solution is to finish the job, to complete the repairs."

Thorwaldsen shook his head. "What a story. And what does that mean, complete repairs?"

The Navigator smiled. "Why, we repaired the chasm. All of it."

CHAPTER EIGHTY-FIVE

Syreen enjoyed the cool breeze's gentle caress as much as Crown's warmth on her skin while she was listening to the sound of the breaking waves. The fruity aroma from the cocktail glass at her side mixed with the salty ocean smell.

Oh yes, living on a planet has its nice aspects. And calling this white sand dirtside *doesn't do it justice for sure.*

After another confirmation—*Yes, there is no chasm anymore*—the two shocked men had left to spread the news. They'd join her later for dinner again, and whatever the night had to offer, and she'd tell them about their achievements regarding the edict. They'd learn that the primary culprit, the mastermind behind all the evil that the Association had spread, was not only her prisoner but also their valued guest and an indispensable contributor to their victory.

They probably wouldn't need her to find out how many more inhabited worlds were reconnected and thus spared the cruel fate of slow starvation or worse.

They might be able to conclude themselves that her ships were no longer needed to carry the Crown fumigators and Finney stingships home—but she would fulfill the sad obligation to tell them about the loss of Captain Scabbia and her crew and ship.

Later.

What will I do next?

There's no edict to be enforced, no chasm to be repaired, no world to be saved anymore. Who needs a Navigator with her living ship?

I could pay my only friend a visit.

I could offer escort services. **Assiduous** *would surely appreciate the occasional pirate snack. Otherwise, we're independent — any uninhabited world with organic lifeforms can provide us with all necessary nutrients.*

However, our crew deserves entertainment, at least those who want to stay with us. So we need to dock now and then — free for all of us star angels now — and make use of local services, which could quickly deplete our scarce financial funds. And I won't employ our crew as entertainers of the exotic kind. So we need income.

I could offer highspeed courier services. "Your message or freight delivered anywhere within the tencycle." She giggled.

Who am I fooling? We weren't created for courier or escort services. We're warriors. We need to be vigilant. The Void can't be eliminated — after all, it is *elimination. There can be temporary defeat, but no final victory.*

I just need a hobby to spend my time and to earn some credits.

Drake would probably like to do field research with me. There's so much to learn about my people's history. Perhaps we can even find another living ship, or another Navigator — or another male Amplifier?

She felt a welcome tingle in her crotch. *Oh yes, that idea's a turn-on. And about offspring — what if we hatch one of* Assiduous's *eggs? How do you raise a baby ship?*

There was still this tingle. And there was a young waiter with a nice smile. She smiled back. *Perhaps it's time to tend to some basic desires. No more world saving.*

The End

ABOUT THE AUTHOR

I am Valerie J. Long, born in 1963. I live and work in Germany as an IT project manager. I like role playing games, and I like putting my ideas on paper. I like all kinds of Science Fiction and Fantasy, I like music, and I like making you chew your nails off.

www.ingramcontent.com/pod-product-compliance
Lightning Source LLC
Chambersburg PA
CBHW061318170626
46817CB00001B/222